LOGORRHEA

...

GOOD WORDS
MAKE GOOD STORIES

• • •

JOHN KLIMA, EDITOR

BANTAM BOOKS

LOGORRHEA
A Bantam Spectra Book / May 2007

Published by Bantam Dell
A Division of Random House, Inc.
New York, New York

Book design by Helene Berinsky

Bantam Books, the rooster colophon, Spectra, and the portrayal of a
boxed "s" are trademarks of Random House, Inc.

Library of Congress Cataloging-in-Publication Data
Logorrhea : good words make good stories / John Klima, editor.

p. cm.
ISBN 978-0-553-38433-8 (trade pbk.)
1. Short stories, American. 2. American fiction—21st century. I. Klima, John, 1971–
PS648.S5L64   2007
813'.010806—dc22   2007005885

Printed in the United States of America
Published simultaneously in Canada

www.bantamdell.com

BVG   10   9   8   7   6   5   4   3   2   1

CONTENTS

INTRODUCTION

"Autochthonous" means "originating where it is found," as in "the autochthonal fauna of Australia includes the kangaroo." To me, that's a step above writing the type of sentence everyone tried to get away with in grade school vocabulary: "This sentence has the word autochthonous in it."

Of course, some of you know where this sentence comes from and why the word "autochthonous" was held in high esteem by logophilists a few years ago. It's the same reason that "Ursprache," "pococurante," "prospicience," and "succedaneum" were important at one time: they are all words that have been spelled correctly to win the Scripps National Spelling Bee. The complete list of some seventy-five words has a nice mixture of words that I know and words that I don't.

Looking back over the years, there are many words that I could use in conversation. Maybe not just any conversation, but ones I *could* use. Words like "knack," which was the winning word in 1930. "Sanitarium" suggests that 1938 was a crazy year. And hardly anyone was awake enough to remember "narcolepsy" in 1976. All words I could potenially use in conversation, and there were many more throughout the years. But the last six or seven years? Heck, let's look at the last eleven:

* 1996—vivisepulture
* 1997—euonym
* 1998—chiaroscurist
* 1999—logorrhea
* 2000—demarche
* 2001—succedaneum
* 2002—prospicience
* 2003—pococurante
* 2004—autochthonous
* 2005—appoggiatura
* 2006—Ursprache

Before this anthology became a reality, there weren't any words in this list that I had encountered in my reading, much less ones I could use in a sentence. My interest in spelling bees was mild, at best. This was until I heard people raving about a documentary called *Spellbound* that came out a few years ago. (Filmed in 1999, *Spellbound* featured the winning word "logorrhea.")

It was amazing to see the effort the students and their parents put into preparing for the spelling bee. They displayed an intensity and a focus that was downright scary sometimes. Despite this intensity, the competitors all expressed happiness at just being a part of the bee.

But what about beyond the competition? Will the winning words of today become words that are commonplace in the future? Will autochthonous be a word that we hear on the news when people describe Earth? Or are the words merely a means to an end, a way to make the competition more difficult throughout the years?

That's for the authors in this book to decide. Each of them has taken on a spelling-bee-winning word and crafted a story around it. The stories you are about to read show how you can take a difficult word and make it something entertaining, something easy to understand.

LOGORRHEA

The Chiaroscurist

● ● ●

HAL DUNCAN

The First Day Of Creation

IN THE NOOK of the tavern, the old man's face—or part of it—catches the fireglow slanting through the frame of oak door left ajar as he leans forward across the table, elbows on the wood, a glinting silver mechanism in one hand going *clunk, chik* with the flicking of a thumb, while, with his other hand, he holds a cigarette up to his mouth to draw in a breath—*foosh*. He holds it for a perfect moment of satiation, head raised now so that his bliss-closed eyes come out from under the shadow of his hat's wide brim, as if basking in the warmth of sunlight blood red through their lids; and even beneath the bush of drooping grey moustache that his fingers seem half-buried in, there is a hint of smile on the lips pursed round the roll-up. *Let there be light,* I think, and then he leans back, disappearing into the leather shadow of the nook to blow out billows of blue-grey that curl and unfurl in the air like offerings of incense rising. An invocation in volutions, the breath of smoke immediately conjures up, in my mind's eye, an image that I seize—that old man's face half-lit as now in sharp chiaroscuro, shrouded in the swirling nebulae of chaos, of the first day of creation.

I must have him for my God.

—Maester, your stout.

The barkeep blocks my vision for a second as he lays the tumbler of black liquid on the table, and it brings me sharp out of the reverie.

—Grazzis, I say out of habit. Thank you. How much?

He waves a hand as I reach into my longcoat's inner pocket.

—Full board and beer, he says. It's all on the Monadery.... Fader Pitro's orders. He hopes—*we* hope—to make your stay here as pleasant as possible.

With a tilt of my glass to him I take a sip and smile at the busy tavern of sandminers and craftsmen, quarriers and traders, farmers in for a few quick jars before Evenfall; it's not the sort of place you'd find in the Merchant Quarters of Vrienze or Nephale where I so often have to smooth my way from one commission to the next with smiles as painted as the courtesans...but it's not so different from the harbour inns or carters' lodges that I spent much of my apprenticeship in with my own Maester. Fewer knife fights, I suspect, though.

—I'm sorry that we didn't have your room ready, he says.

—No problem, I say. A well-poured stout is all it takes to keep me happy.

—I've sent word to the Monadery that you've arrived.

—Maya grazzis. Thank you. Thank you.

The bells of the Monadery di Sanze Manitae toll Evenfall, audible even over the tavern din of lewd jokes and earnest discussions, which changes tone in response to the knell as arguments find quick, laughing resolutions; chairs scrape back, friends say good-byes, off home down the cobble-street slopes before darkness descends. The door opens and closes, opens and closes, until there are only a dozen or so customers left, drinkers more devoted, or perhaps who live in the safety of the lamplit squares and strazzas of the market area, close enough to scorn superstition for the short walk home. The atmosphere becomes more homey with just these groups of three or four here and there, without the escalating racket of voices raised over voices raised.

Relaxing with a second pint, I watch the swirling settle of foamy stout, the silken eddies of shades of brown separating gradually into tar-black body and a white head thick enough to sculpt; and my mind drifts back to my commission, the vague images and ideas for it that rise into momentary resolution only to sink back into the darkness. There are only so many scenes to choose from, of course—the conventional tableaux of Invocations and Pronunciations, the Exile From The Garden, Orphean's Journey, and so on—and I have hardly even discussed with my patrons the layout of the antesanctum to be painted, let alone laid eyes on it—but if I have one fault it is my enthusiasm over grand schemes. This will be my first work on such a scale—not just one little frescoed wall- or altarpiece, but a full antesanctum—and I feel . . . the anticipation of a young lad sitting in a brothel for the first time as his Maester, hand on his shoulder, says, *Tomorrow you will be a man, eh?*

● ● ●

A *tump* from the nook—feet dropping onto floor—turns my head and I see that the old man's face is visible again. Is he still sitting down? Then the door opens fully as he comes out into the tavern proper and I realize his height. He's gnomish, or *hobben,* as they call them in these parts, and I find myself caught in a fleeting sense of shock and shame, staring at him as if he has no business to be here and then looking away quickly because *I* have no business even thinking such thoughts; it's not so much disgust as it's the fear of disgust, the knee-jerk reaction of a tolerant and open-minded man, suddenly panicking at the challenge of reality. *Are you? Are you sure? Did the word* grotesque *not whisper through your head for a fraction of a second when you saw the stump of him?*

He asks the barkeep for another and the man pours him a draft of what looks like a wheat beer, golden but cloudy. I only realize I am staring when he notices and raises his glass to me. I salute him with my own, my momentary angst dissolved in the return of that aesthetic impulse. His stunted body is of as little interest now as when it was hidden in the shadows of the nook. His deep-lined face, as robust as it is wrecked, is all I see. The face of God.

He turns to go back to the nook and I wonder if it is his exile or simply his privacy; there are many taverns that would not serve his kind at all and I imagine that even if the hospitaliter himself is friend to all, some of his customers may be less inclusive.

—Sir, I say. A moment. A word.

—Yes? he says.

—I have a . . . request, I say.

The Measuring

—IT IS THE PERFECT blank page, is it not? says Fader Pitro.

In a way he is right; the antesanctum of the Monadery di Sanze Manitae, skinned in its fleshtone of plaster, with its floor of mottled concrete, is an almost empty space; only the unvarnished oak intricacies of the dais with its pulpit, altar, and chorum pews create any sort of complexity—that and the ribbing of columns and windows that break up the side walls into architectured rhythm. Then there are the doors of the entranceway behind me and the two doors at the back, to either side of the dais, leading into the forbidden sanctum. On the whole it is, to the layman, a plain and perfect ground waiting humbly for its frescoes, murals, or mosaics. But I am a chiaroscurist. Even the simplest of spaces may contain the subtlest tricks of light latent in the slant of sunbeams through windows sidling round from dusk till dawn.

—There's no such thing as a blank page, Fader, I say.

I work by eye and foot at first; before the measurements and calculations begin, I scout the vacant hall in an intuitive way, pacing its length and breadth, circling and crouching. I note the southwesterly aspect that will send a shaft of late-afternoon light through the circular window high above the entrance to the wall over the altar—slightly right of centre and down. I observe the rhomboid slices of long morning produced by the windows in the southeast wall, geometric projections on the facing plaster, the shadow of the Monadery Tower outside that will rupture this pattern between dawn and noon. As much as I appreciate the work of the masons who have built this spare but sublime little chapel for the brooders of the Manitaen Order, it is the architecture of light that I revere, as mutable as it is stable, cycling with the days and seasons, changing its very substance from granite grey to marble white with the gathering and scattering of cumuli and stratocirrus across the sky. The antesanctum—any building—is only a shell in which the light builds its own structures, not a blank page but a blueprint which a chiaroscurist like myself seeks to give form.

When I'm finally satisfied that I have the key points and the general flux of light fleshed out in my mind into a rough terrain of potential drama—highlights and low points—I turn back to the doorway and notice Fader Pitro still standing there, picking at a loose thread on the hem of his cassock's drooping sleeve.

—You don't have to stay, I say to the Fader. I'll be here for a while and I'm afraid it won't be very interesting to an observer.

He gathers his long hair into a ponytail and brings it over one shoulder, twirls a finger round a curly white lock; the Manitaens wear unusual tonsures I have noticed, shaved at the sides like a horse's mane. The Fader plays with his when he's thinking.

—I do have business to attend to, he says. Dukes and books, he sighs. But I'll send Brooder Matheus to keep you company, in case you need anything.

I tell him there's no need to bore the poor brooder with such duties, but he shushes me with a waggling finger.

—Brooder Matheus will find it a relief, I'm sure, he says. And it will stop him ruining any more vellum with his godless scrawl. A hand too used to the hawk's hood, he mutters, and none too delicate with its feather. Honestly . . .

He wanders off, muttering to himself about spoiled second sons and the quality of tutoring amongst nobility these days.

I pick my carpetbag up from the doorway where I left it on entering the antesanctum and open it on the altar to take out my instruments, the sextantine and the compass, chalks and slates, coalsticks and notepads, measuring tape and—most important of all—my photometer. It is the most expensive item I possess, a delicate precision instrument that I keep in its own wooden case, padded with cotton wool and fretted over on each trundling-cart journey from town to town, from commission to commission. When my Maester first gave it to me, indeed, I often irritated the poor carters with constant guidance over how to take the bumps in the road less jarringly or sat with the case in my lap for the whole journey, unsnicking the latch every ten miles or so to check that it was still intact.

I lay all these instruments on the altar like a surgeon's tools, and am unlatching the photometer's case when voice and footsteps echo behind me.

—How does it look?

Brooder Matheus, I assume; the same elven lad who came to fetch me from the tavern this morning to meet with Fader Pitro. He gestures to encompass the antesanctum, and nods at the photometer in my hand.

—Is that for measuring the light?

He seems genuinely interested, the look on his face that of a child who longs to play with an adult's toy but knows it would be wrong to ask; so I show him the way the hood widens and tightens to set the aperture, the glass bulb inside with its incredibly fragile vanes and tiny metal sails to catch the light as a windmill catches air, how one holds it up and looks through the eyepiece at the back to see the flickering rhythm, the earpiece for listening to the tone of whirr.

—Is there no needle, no gauge?

I shake my head.

—It takes a while but you learn to . . . *hear* the speed, to *see* the force of light, I say. Now, I'll have to ask you to be quiet for a bit, if you don't mind. I want to start my measurements.

—Of course, he says. Of course.

The Separation Of Light And Dark

I CLOSE THE SHUTTERS on the window a little more and come down from the stepladders to check the effect, step back up to adjust the mirrors and, satisfied finally, take my place at the easels. The tavern's attic is one of the most effective studio spaces I have ever had, with its four small windows—embedded two on either side of the sloping roof—solid fits for my rigging of adjustable reflectors and screens. Clamped into place on the window frame, I swivel and tilt them until the daylight that pierces the room does so exactly where and how I want it to. My Maester would have been horrified at this, working as he did in sun-drenched spaces of whitewashed walls and floors, seeking to suffuse his work with that airy quality so bold and innovative in his day, the thin washes of colour in his tempera frescoes painting religious mystery in pastel tones lit up by the white of plaster glowing like moonlight underneath. Gauche and opalescent, his works still shimmer like the air on a hot summer day. *God is light,* he used to say. *And that is what we paint, what we are paid to paint.* A traditionalist, he did not approve of the chiaroscurists' innovations.

—I am not sure I approve of this, grumps Iosef.

The old hobben sits on a child's schoolchair, elbow on the desk-arm, fist under his chin, brows furrowed in a glower that's more uncertain than unhappy. As a hobben, I know, his religion stands against the graven images that are my livelihood. Idolatry, he calls it, and if it were just the money involved—no matter what others might say about "gold-grubbing gnomes"—I do not think he would sit for me at all; but over these last few weeks of nights of drunken blather in the tavern's candle-lit warmth, we have come to respect each other's utterly opposed opinions, enjoying the sheer intransigence of each other's attitude. He was a rephai—before the pogrom that burnt him from his home and drove him through fields of horror to eventual sanctuary here under Fader Pitro's sackcloth wings—and the tradition of argument runs in his blood. For the hobben, God is not reached through images but through words, through the text and the exegesis of the text, debate, discussion. So he sits for me as a favour to a new friend, I like to think—but probably also as a favour to an old friend, Fader Pitro. And then also, there may be just a little of that secret thrill so many humble men have when you ask them to sit for you.

—Admit it, I say. You're flattered by the thought of being the face of God.

—I am *not,* he says. It's a blasphemy. Pride and arrogance, that's what it is, he says, to think that you can give a face to God.

He digs into a pocket for his tobacco and cigarette papers, starts to roll a cigarette. I study the changed position for a second, then lay down the coalstick with which I have been sketching on the right-hand easel, shuffle over to my left and pick up the chalk sitting on the left-hand easel's lower clamp. I have worked this way ever since I struck out on my own, leaving my Maester to his dreamy pastel tones; I use two easels, one with white paper clipped to it to sketch in charcoal-black, the other with the blue-black paper of a draughtsman, on which I sketch in chalk. If God is light, as my Maester insisted, well, the world we live in is filled with the shadows cast by His material creation, by these forms of flesh absorbing so much on the side that faces Him that on the other He is utterly absent. I find that to capture this effectively, to grasp the form of the subject, I have to sketch my studies in dual media, layering charcoal shadows on a ground of light, chalk highlights over midnight blue. In the actual work, of course, these dual perspectives should be fused.

.   .   .

—But what is so blasphemous, I say innocently, about letting our imagination give a human face to that which we don't understand?

He lights up his cigarette, puffs on it and coughs, then points at me with it as he lectures. If I were one of those artists who must have their subjects sit like silent statues while I sketch, I think Iosef would drive me mad. He cannot sit without talking, cannot talk without gesticulating—though he tried, bless him, stiff as a board the very first time he sat for me, like a youth being interviewed for membership in the highest merchant's guild, until I told him that he wasn't a king sitting for his portrait, that I *wanted* to see the varied attitudes and angles of his self; to just *relax,* man. So now he leans forward to make a point, sits back in satisfaction afterwards, crosses his arms or waves them in the air. He jabs the air with his roll-up.

—The Absolute doesn't have a face, he is saying now. God is infinite, transcendent, and you limit Him when you try to define *that which cannot be defined.*

I trace the jut of solemnity in his jaw, the old man's outrage in his bottom lip, almost petted as he blows smoke out and up.

—But I only try to define His face, I say. Where the presters and the rephais and the imams, why, you try to define His *mind.* Wisdom, justice, and mercy, no?

I switch back to the easel of white paper, carving a curve of black upon it with the coalstick, the furrow of a knitted brow.

—Is it not pride and arrogance, I say, to think that you can give a *mind* to God?

—You . . . , he says, shaking his head. Heresy like that will get you into trouble.

His voice goes quieter, softer.

—You should be careful, Maester.

The Protection Of The Innocents

—IOSEF, I THINK you should go inside.

Fader Pitro worries a rosary between his fingers as he gazes out over the Monadery's low, dry, stone wall, over the red-tiled roofs of the town, the jumble of houses that slope down the hill and scatter out into the patchwork farms of the surrounding countryside. He stands, unsteady in the middle of the rockery in the western corner of the gardens, screwing his eyes to watch the road from the north, from Nixemburg and Murchen. I know what he is looking at. A cloud of dust. The flash of armour. The flutter of a banner. There are peregrins coming.

I hold the door of the antesanctum open for the carter who brought the news along with my latest supply of paints and primers, feeling helpless as he carries each barrel past me, lays it down carefully in the centre of the concrete floor. Brooder Matheus, my unofficial apprentice these days, helps him, humping the crates of coalsticks and chalk that I will need before I even pick up palette and brush; I have the preliminary design now for the interior, but it will take me months just to transfer the sketches from paper to plaster; the scaffolding has not even been erected yet.

The carter lays another barrel on the ground, a blond rock of a man, unconcerned by our atmosphere of agitation. Brooder Matheus keeps glancing at Iosef and the Fader. Iosef has a look set on his face.

—The Fader is right, Iosef, I say. Now's not the time for stubbornness.

Iosef crouches down to clip a twig off a shrub with his secateurs. Ignoring me completely, he stomps over to a bench set against the wall, puts the secateurs down and picks up a fork and trowel. He puts them down again and turns to me.

—Am I to spend my life cowering in the shadows? he says angrily. Is that what I am? A half-thing of the darkness? Half the height so half the man? *Hide in the shadows, Iosef?*

He points past me.

—Maybe I can crawl under the altar and hide there, eh?

I think of the stories he has told me of his old town, of hobben boarded up inside their burning homes, the elders of his little community dragged out into the streets to have their beards hacked off with razors as trophies for the mob, gnomes who had harmed no one moaning out of broken, skinned jaws. Choking in a smoke-filled hiding-hole.

He strides past me, past the carter and into the antesanctum.

—Perhaps you should spend the night here as well, Maester, says Fader Pitro.

—No, I say. I'll be alright.

—And how she *squealed* for her mother!

I gaze at the flame of the candle, the flicker so vibrant, so alive, and without pattern. How can something so chaotic be so beautiful? The candle is low, most of its wax now dribbled and solidified as white trails layering the dark green glass of the bottle that serves as candlestick. A molten lump like some limestone grotto's creation, slick and glistening in the dark. A drip of wax splashes on the table and I dip a finger into it before it cools, smooth it over the fingertip with my thumb.

—Some more of this fine cat's piss here, man.

The peregrin officers fill the tavern, though there's only half a dozen of them; they fill it with their boorish brags, their swaggering contempt that shoves its way through crowds with elbows in the side or hands flat in the face, and with the ugly stares of men hungry for violence. Brooder Matheus and I sit at a corner table, safe with the carter across from us, as calm, he is, as if the peregrins were simply nuisance children running wild in the absence of authority. Everyone knows the reputation of the carter's guild, men who are trained to see a cargo safely through the wildest regions of the hinter, whatever bandits or demons might lie in their path. Everyone knows the legends.

—I hear . . . , says one of the peregrins, I hear there's a filthy hobben in this town.

The carter slugs his beer back and stands up. His voice when he speaks is quiet, loaded.

—Brooder. Maester, he says. Do you have a message for the Fader?

He has no reason to return to the Monadery, of course, but . . .

—If you're going that way, I say, I think we both might join you, eh, Brooder?

Brooder Matheus nods and downs the last of his beer for courage, coughs.

—You are mistaken, m'sire, says Fader Pitro.

His voice, outside, is loud and clear but there's a waver in it, audible fear. The peregrins are gathered outside the very doors of the antesanctum, the officers and their whole band. They announced themselves on the staggering march up from the tavern with a pounding drum of swords on shields, a chorus of ape-calls. There are curses and laughter now.

—Bring him out and we'll cut him down to size! shouts someone.

More laughter.

Brooder Matheus sits on a crate, looking nervous, and I wonder if there's anyone out there he would recognise, some second cousin twice removed perhaps. Elven nobility, I think. Iosef stands on the dais itself, a hand touching the altar. They would not kill him in a house of God, would they? I stand at the door, listening.

—There are no hobben here, says Fader Pitro, and I hear the sound of someone spitting in reply.

The carter moves me aside with one hand. The other holds

his spike, the seven-foot steel-bladed lance that can be used as sword or staff or spear. There is a story that the guild was formed from an order of knights sworn to protect the early peregrins on their way to the Holy Lands, before these sons of the grey erles twisted the pilgrimages into a crusade. Even if there is no truth to it, I have seen for myself the brutal skill with which a carter wields his spike. He takes the brass handle of one of the doors and swings it full open, suddenly, smoothly.

The hellish orange of torchlight pierces the antesanctum, picking out Brooder Matheus as he stands up from the crate, a palette knife, of all things, in his hand. Iosef at the altar. The peregrins cannot fail to see him there, surely. But they cannot fail to see the carter either, the way his eyes and spike capture the flame of their torches and reflect it back at them, so bright that the antesanctum behind must be darkness in comparison.

He simply stands there, silent, until they leave.

The Temptation Of The Faithful

—I HAVE TO GO, I say. Brooder Matheus will be waiting for me eager as a pup. I lay the first stroke today.

—Brooder Matheus can wait till you've had breakfast, says Rosah.

She kicks down the bedsheet and pulls herself up onto her elbow. I admire her as I pull on my linen trousers and shirt, all crisp and freshly laundered, perfumed by the petals left in the bottom of the basket by Maria, Hier Nerjea's wife, who rules the tavern's lodging rooms with the same ironclad sense of hospitality as her husband rules the public house below. Rosah is beautiful and she lies there on the bed, my angel whore, knowing it. Her skin is pale as porcelain, paler than it should be with such amber hair and eyes of flashing green; when I undressed her that first night I expected freckles, copper skin, the feel of powder on my fingers as I caressed her face, but there was only the silk of skin, as soft and clean as if it were just out of the bath and towelled dry. It is I who am usually masked in powder, charcoal and chalk-dust griming my face and fingers when I come back to the tavern late to take my supper and drink with her, and later as the night goes on, slip my arm around her waist and pull her, laughing with lust the both of us, up to my room. Rosah's beauty is unsoiled by rouge or eye shadow, her only concession to vanity the vermilion lipstick with which she paints my chest with a kiss each night over my heart. I feel my cock stirring as I look at her coquettish contrapposto pose, the locket that hangs between her breasts, the trim of her fuzz; I am remembering her salty taste. I leave the shirt untucked as cover, shaking my head.

—You will spoil me for other women, I say.

—Then you must marry me, she says. Take me away from all this and make an honest woman of me.

I sit on the bed to kiss her. It is a little joke that has developed between us these last few months, but like all such jokes it has just the tiniest sting of truth behind it. We are both sometimes, I think, a little sad, thinking it might be nice and knowing it will never happen.

—Me? I say. I am as much a whore as you. More so, mi caria, since I have slutted myself in more cities than you could probably imagine.

—Ah, but if you took me with you when you go, I could give you some competition, I am sure.

I laugh. I love Rosah, as a friend and as a sensual delight, as a favourite whore and as a trusted confidante; and her fondness for me runs deep enough for her to declare now and then, on some night when perhaps she feels a little lonely, *Tonight there is no money and no clock, mister painter, no limits, only you and I, and we will explore each other's body as if we had never even touched before.* We are both whores, yes, but I think we are both whores by vocation, willing to give more of ourselves in our work than most.

But neither of us will ever lose ourself in the other, I know. Even in the nights when we make love rather than merely fuck, we are never truly *lovers*.

—I have to go, I say.

—Artists, she says. You're no whore. You're more married than the Nerjeas.

—Tonight? I say and kiss her on the forehead.

—Eat something, she calls out the door after me as I go down the stairs. Maria! make him have some breakfast.

—Breakfast? I say.

I throw the apple across the antesanctum to Brooder Matheus, who catches it in one hand. I polish another on my shirt and take a crunching bite.

—Fader Pitro was asking how things were going again, he says. I told him you're two months behind and that yesterday you completely wiped the first four panels of the southeast wall.

He takes a bite out of the apple, a mischievous gleam in his eye.

—I am a bad influence on you, I say.

—It's the truth.

I am behind schedule admittedly, but what the brooder didn't tell the old monk is that the cleaning of the panels is the next stage of the process. I look around at the surfaces of the antesanctum—what you can see behind the scaffolding—ceiling and walls all but covered in the chalk and charcoal sketches copied from the papers that now carpet the concrete floor. The panels above the door and behind the altar alone have still to be filled; I have not made my final decision on the latter yet and the former, well, the idea I have in mind I would rather keep from the Fader's prying eyes right now.

As for the four panels that I "wiped" yesterday, though, the ones around the far-left window—Brooder Matheus may be amused at the thought of the Fader in a flap but yesterday it was himself looking on in horror as I went at them with my rags and fluids. I gave him a few minutes of panic before explaining that charcoal and chalk make a less than effective surface for my technique and, you see, I have the images that belong there imprinted in my mind now, so I only have to close my eyes to visualize them. The cleaning was only preparation for the real work to begin.

The outlines of the four panels bordering the window are the only charcoal marks left from the previous months of work on this area. Offset and defined by one line running out from each corner of the window, the panels should produce a sort of elliptical structure on the whole, moving the eye around from this one to the next. I decide to start with the panel on the lower left.

The brooder has already prepared the buckets of water and the basins we will need, so I crack open the barrel of plaster mix and set him to work while I wind the clockwork pick then start to vandalize the smooth pink skin of the first panel. The little steel point of it whirrs as it hammers, chipping away at the surface, roughing it up so that the plaster I apply will bond. There should be no danger of my work crumbling off the wall three years after completion in the middle of some funeral . . . as happened with di Vineggio's *Nocturna d'il Houri*.

I finish preparing the first panel and take the first two basins of plaster from Brooder Matheus, handing him the pick to wind. It is the same sculpting plaster in each bowl—thicker than normal plaster, softer than clay—but where one basin is white the other is tinted dark with the same black ink the monks use in their Vellumary. The two will mix a little as I apply them, but that is to be expected. I will be painting over them anyway; all I am doing now is building up the undercoat of light and shadow, the white that will shine through from beneath a cerulean sky, the darkness that will lurk behind a devil's eyes, building it up gradually, with a finger and thumb of slick plaster here or there, a thick wet lump smoothed into shape with a knife, another lump on top of it.

Slowly the form of a face starts to take solid shape, as if emerging from the very wall. After a while, I stand back to un-crick my shoulders.

—It catches the light, says Brooder Matheus. Where you've put the white plaster, it catches the light coming in the window. Just so, just . . .

—Just right? I say. That's the general idea.

The Seeding Of The Earth

—And, generally speaking, do you have an idea of when it will be finished?

It has taken me two years just to do the ceiling and the Fader manages to sound casual in his enquiry, but I can hear the note of worry in his voice. The costs are escalating now that the paint is flowing and the wagon rolling constantly between here and Murchen, bringing the pigments and media I require from the great Artist's Market of the Strazza d'il Tintorum, powders made from rock and plant, sulphuric yellow from the Salt Sea or green-gold sapphiron from the distant Aurient, porphyr made from molluscs' shells in the Phonaesthian city-states or the iri-descent verdan of Aegys's crushed scarab wings. Elysse, north and south, is full of natural hues, nut browns and ochres, um-bers and siennas, and I make full use of these, but the pigments most saturated with yellow, red, and blue must be imported from their more exotic origins, so these materials are expensive; and although the brooders' benefactor, the Duke Irae, is rich with the plunder of the Holy Lands even he may balk at paying such a ransom for escape from Hell.

So the Fader sees the antesanctum only a fraction complete, and thinking of how much money it has cost already and how far it has to go, has visions of catastrophe.

•   •   •

—It will probably be finished, I say, the day after you give your-self a heart attack, Fader . . . at this rate. Or if you want I could paint the rest all white and you could tell the Duke it symbolizes God's eternal radiance. That way it would be finished within the week.

He twirls a lock of hair between his fingers, brushes his lips with the end of it.

—It's not *my* heart giving out that I'm worried about, he says. The Duke has expressed his desire to have . . . given all the hon-our that he can to God while still on this earth.

I grab a bar of scaffolding, swing from my crouch up on the plank down to the platform beneath. Holding onto a ladder that rises up past me, I lean out into the fifteen feet of air that separates me from the Fader and Brooder Matheus standing behind him.

—Tell him he could die tomorrow, I say, so he should swear his sons to carry on his patronage. Or tell him that the Butcher of Instantinople shouldn't be such an old maid.

I wrap paint-rags round my hands and slide down the ladder.

—Tell him, I say, that God will not *let* him die until his pur-pose is fulfilled and he stands here, where you and I are standing, looking up into His face; that if he dies before the antesanctum is complete it will be the greatest sin he's ever committed.

Brooder Matheus points at my forehead and I touch the wet-ness, wipe the paint off with the back of my hand. Alizarin crim-son. Fader Pitro looks unusually stern, but he seems a little distracted, as if there's something less tangible than money and time worrying him. Brooder Matheus puts a hand on the Fader's arm.

—Tell him it will be worth it when the chapel is finished, he says. Look. Is it not true?

•   •   •

A mix of indigo and porphyr, the night sky painted on the ceiling of the antesanctum is not black but blue, the purplish hue so deep that in contrast with the crescent moon of Iosef's raptured face and the plumes and strands of clouds he breathes into existence, it recedes as into an eternal darkness; but it is a poor chiaroscurist who does not understand that there is colour even in the deepest shadows, so although I work in light and dark, there is no black upon my palette, no black in the night sky. I keep a watch on the Fader's tilted, swivelling chin of pointed beard as his eyes follow the path mapped out for them. On the barrel ceiling, the low relief of Iosef's face sits off-centre and down so as to catch the eye first by catching the diffuse sun coming in the windows of the southeast wall. The subtler forms of streams of smoke modelled around the image of the Creator lead Fader Pitro round and out; smoke becomes scatterling clouds in a night sky, spatterings of stars. At the edges of the ceiling, as if the viewer is looking up from the middle of a forest clearing, thick plaster foliage of branches and leaves is painted in the olive drab of night and edged in bone white. An owl rises from a branch but otherwise it is a quiet sky, the first few days of Creation. Mankind is yet to appear; the unborn animals are only suggestions in the insubstantial swirls, seeds waiting to be sung and sprung into existence under Orphean's feet.

—We can't all create a world in six days, I say.

Fader Pitro's eye travels the scene, his body turning, stepping back and round to the side every so often to accommodate his angle. I watch with pleasure as he is brought back to the face of Iosef, the beginning and the end.

—I'm just hoping that it's not six years, he says.

But he nods. He looks around at the sculptures pressing out from the walls all round, shapes emerging from the plaster as if they too are part of the moment above, emerging into existence from the clay of the earth beneath the sky, and he nods, mutters some vague encouragement and leaves.

—Iosef is ill, says Brooder Matheus after he has gone.

．　　．　　．

—Schitze! says Iosef. I'll be tending their garden and their grave-yard long after the Fader is fertilising my plants. Pitro's a worrier.

—I've noticed, I say. I sometimes think he only took his vows to give his fingers rosaries to play with.

But twice tonight Iosef has been racked by coughing fits that halted conversation as he creased with the effort of containing them, the table shuddering under the weight of his hand. He will not see a doctor and he will not give up his rituals of to-bacco, however much his lungs and throat protest with rasping hacks and muffled judders; that much became obvious when I joined him in his nook, taking the chair diagonally across from his customary cushion-raised booth seat, and tried to broach the subject—and the air turned blue with curses and with smoke blown in my face. I'm not sure which of them made my eyes sting more, the invective or the noxious weed, but I thought bet-ter of continuing the role of nag. It doesn't suit me anyway.

Of course, I can remind him of how others worry for his health. Absurdly, I say. But they do worry.

—Let's talk of something else, he says. Have you decided on the designs for the end walls yet?

He takes a drag on his roll-up and I wince as he explodes into another fit, spluttering into a white-knuckled fist. He thumps the table in frustration and I ignore it. The hobben have a phrase—*ch'yem*—which roughly translates as *May it be*. The will of God is inevitable, they mean, as I understand it. I think it is a phrase very close to Iosef's heart these days.

—The end walls? I say. I do have some ideas.

The Exile From The Garden

—And whatever will they say at the sight of a whore painted as blessed Queen Titania?

Rosah looks over her shoulder at me with an arched eyebrow;

she finds the whole idea both wicked and delicious, but rather than being in conflict over what I've asked of her she has thrown herself into it with delight. It is strange, but having heard her say her prayers at night—more open and relaxed with me as she has been in this last year or so—I have discovered a quite pious side to my Rosah, with the little saint statues on the shelf in her room, the single candle that always has a flower at its side, and her tiny bowl of honey and coins. I think that if I'd asked her to be my Titania two years ago she would have refused, saying it was sacrilege, and I would have . . . laughed probably, in shock. Now I'm not sure why she agreed at all; perhaps the deeper the belief in sin, the greater the thrill of courting it.

—They'll say you are the very image of her, says Brooder Matheus.

She blows a kiss at him and he mimes a catch, grinning, but blushing at his own boldness. At least it brings some colour to his cheeks; the two of us got roaring drunk in the tavern last night, after visiting Iosef up at the grounds house, and if I woke up with a hangover, the poor brooder, by the look of him, was at death's door. The original grey erle.

Matheus and I now pace about the studio, setting up the easels and the paper, arranging the mirrors and shades on the windows. Rosah sits on a bench before us, leaning over an open chest of props, holding necklaces of coloured glass jewels up to her throat, throwing feathered boas and fur stoles over her shoulders, trying on a stuffed snake, a tiara—and all the while glancing at herself in the mirror like a child playing dress-up. Every so often, these last few months in particular, I find myself glancing at her when she is not looking and I feel a joy I can hardly explain. It is in moments like this. I try to put my finger on it. She is not performing—no—she is not performing for *me,* or for the brooder, not seeking our attention, but simply, happily, lavishing it upon herself.

I think that is it. She is no longer *my* Rosah. Now she is simply Rosah.

When Brooder Matheus and I have everything set up to my satisfaction, she drops the centaurian's helmet that she's holding back into the box and stands, walks into the centre of the room.

—You're ready, yes? Where do you want me? How do you want me?

—In white silk, I say. Just a moment.

I dig the dress I want out of the box, not so much a dress as a drapery of veils and ribbons, and while I untangle it, tease out the folds and complexities, she slips off her shoes, hikes up her skirt to peel down her stockings.

—Brooder Matheus, she says, will you help me with this?

Her hands reaching behind, she turns her back to him and the brooder looks hesitant and shy for a second before taking those steps across the room. His fingers fumble with her buttons, but after the first couple, the rest come loose easily. I notice the delicate confidence with which he slips the straps off her shoulders, the way he can't help but smooth the palms of his hands over her skin. Last night, in drunken camaraderie, he confessed to me how unsuited he feels to his vows. He had little choice in the matter; as a second son, the law of primogeniture leaves him no estate, no path to follow but war or religion. And while he has no great urge to join with his noble elven brethren, to go and slaughter the demon races that now rule the Holy Lands, he said, chastity was never his strong point.

It's funny, I suppose; in all the years we've known each other now, watching him grow from adolescent to adult, I had always pegged him as, at heart, an innocent naïf. As it turns out, our naïve brooder lost his virginity two years before I did, and spent most of his youth from that point on tupping any girl who batted her eyelashes at him.

• • •

Rosah's dress slips off her shoulders and crumples on the ground at her feet. She steps out of it and takes the white silk costume from my hands, begins to wrap herself in it. It adorns without hiding, veils without disguising. Every curve of her, every sacred secret place of her is somehow more revealed with it on than in her nakedness, and I'm more sure than ever that this is the Titania of the Exile From The Garden that will go on the wall above the antesanctum's entrance. This is the faery queen, the virgin whore, the spirit of lush forests, of morning dew like the sweat on a lover's body, of oceans salty as blood and semen, who runs her fingers over the vine-wrapped trunks of trees, the green-veined cocks of men, through grass and hair, as the ruler of them all, the mother of all living things, mother of Orphean who died for our sins.

I dip into the box again and pull out the velvet robe, dark purple, long and soft as fur. Brooder Matheus reaches out a hand for it but his eyes are on Rosah, transfixed; it takes him a few seconds of grasping in the air to realize there's no point in me giving him the robe quite yet, and then he turns to me with a wry, sheepish smile on his face, red with a blush or with the flush of sexual tension. Finally he pulls the cassock over his head and stands there, cockish and puffed with an uncertain audacity. He runs his fingers through the dark red hair that silks over his shoulders, brushing it back, half nervousness, half pride. I hand him the robe and he pulls it on, leaves it hanging open. Slender and straight beside her curves, he is the dark to her light, the auburn to her titanium white. The Oberon to her Titania.

As they turn to each other, their hands, their bodies, beginning that exploration of the world outside innocence, discovered in an age long before our own, I walk to my easels and look from chalk to charcoal and back again, trying to decide which to begin with.

The Last Days

I AM ON THE LAST panel now. It has taken me four—no, nearly five—years to paint the antesanctum of the Monadery di Sanze Manitae and at last it is almost complete. I sketch directly onto the wall now, working as fast as I can and keeping a rag at hand to correct my errors and insincerities. Insincerities? In any painting such as this, in any work of a chiaroscurist such as myself, it is easy to become too bold in the drama, too theatrical, too focused on the power that light and dark have to evoke a profound sense of mystery. Subtlety is lost when the artist blusters his own ideas in forms too overblown, brushstrokes too broad. Of all the panels of the antesanctum, I cannot allow this one to lose its import in mere impact. I will not.

So I draw with chalk and coalstick onto the pink plaster, and again and again, I find myself cursing and taking the rag to the wall in bitter frustration because this structure is too crude, that contrast too bold. Too clichéd. Too unusual. Too trite. Too grandiose. It should be the simplest panel of them all, in some ways, for its subject is the most universal. It is one of the most traditional of scenes, though it is usually placed in some dark area, as a hidden mystery.

I am drawing the body of Iosef, which lies upon the altar now. I am drawing death.

I work nonstop for two days finding a form that does not really satisfy me but is, at least, not an insult to his memory, not the self-important sweeping statement of a young chiaroscurist more concerned with the glory of his work than with who and what it is meant to represent. Even as I begin the modelling work, layering on the black and white plasters, building up the relief sculpture of Iosef's ruined body, I do not know if I can do him justice. Will this reduce his life to no more than an empty symbol, only resonating for the viewer because it is so hollow without the totality of his life to fill it? How can I show in the cracks of his knuckles and the stumps of his fingers, the way those hands worked so delicately with the flowers and herbs of the Monadery garden, or rolled his cigarettes with such unconscious ease and precision that half the time his eyes would be on something else, on myself or Matheus, as he lectured us on our many follies? How can I show in the still barrel of his chest, the wheezing up-and-down of it as he lay in his sickbed for that last year and a half, fighting to keep the last breath in his body? How can I show that the smoke that ruined him was not just the smoke of his own creation but the smoke of his destruction, of the temple with his congregation gathered in it on their holy day to sing the word of God, and the mob outside with fire?

I only knew him for four years and there is so much that I did not know.

All I can show are these last days of him, of his remains.

The decay of the body is quick in the heat of summer. Skin of Payne's grey; it blotches phthalo blue and viridian in the shadows; it dulls with the yellow ochre, burnt umber, burnt sienna of rot. Maggots wriggle, iridescent and ivory white in the slick of him. The surface of the altar is stained with the blood pooled and coagulated in the lowest areas of his body in the early stages of decay, now transformed by the process into some thicker, darker fluid. I see haematic red in it, alizarin crimson. It glistens aemberic orange in the candlelight. Every colour in my palette is mixed in the putrefaction of the corpse and I paint them on the wall in layer upon layer. I mix paint with plaster and sculpt with my fingers until my nails are filthy and broken by the scratching.

Fader Pitro sits vigil over Iosef's body while I work, because this is the tradition of the hobben and there are no others in the town to perform the rites. I think that Iosef would have wanted the Fader at his side anyway, but this is cold comfort to the monk; he frets that he is failing, that he cannot do it *properly*, that it should be done *properly*. The brooders recite verses from the Old Book in Litan but they do not know the hobben words or the soaring wavering tunes this poetry should be sung to, so as I work, their choral chants echo in the antesanctum, giving the same sentiments in the words and song they know.

We have sent word to Matheus and Rosah but I do not think they will arrive before the burial.

I am laying a stone on his grave when I feel the hand on my shoulder. Rosah. Matheus stands behind her. I embrace my Titania, kiss her on the forehead. Matheus and I shake hands, both of us two-handed, clasping each other's grip firm and tight as if anchoring each other. We talk for a while, words that we forget as soon as they have been spoken. Sometimes there is laughter, sometimes tears. Matheus is still not sure of what he will do now he has left the Order, but the two of them seem, even in sorrow, to have found their true vocations in each other. Have I really finished now? they ask. Yes. And did I really paint the Death Of God as the very focus of the whole chapel, the work you see first as you enter through the doors? Yes. They will see how the structure of light and shadow in the antesanctum demanded it. When they see it they will understand, I hope.

After a while I leave them to have some time alone at the grave and return to the antesanctum.

The walls are filled with the townsfolk and the brooders, every character based on one local or another—the Nerjeas, Rosah and Matheus, even Fader Pitro as a saint in one high corner—but it is Iosef whose face holds you as you walk in, not in the moment of creation on the ceiling but on the wall behind the altar, on a dead body, lying on its back with its head turned towards you, the face staring out with hollow eyes, eaten away to bone here and there, a white skull cloaked in the shadows of flesh and night. I do not know if I am satisfied with it. I could not hope to paint, in his death, the whole reality of his life; all I can show are his remains, on the painted artifice of an altar on the wall behind the real thing as if it were a dark mirror still reflecting what is no longer there.

Maybe those few precious glimpses that I had, in the years of moments that I knew him . . . maybe these are enough to know the form of someone, even if the rest is darkness.

Lyceum

● ● ●

LIZ WILLIAMS

WHEN SAO ENTERED the Lyceum, he saw that the Duality members had already arrived and were conversing upon the steps. Their back-faces were turned towards him and he took the moment of respite to check that all was as it should be, that the welcoming committee had hung the correct banners from the pillars and that the air was scented with a dust pleasing to the Duality. There had been a regrettable incident during the last confluence, involving the Murn, and they did not want a similar unfortunateness occurring on the Duality's first visit to Karquom for many years. But all appeared correct. The mica-fronted columns of the Lyceum glittered in the desert light; the three-hundred-foot windows showed the panorama of the eastern mountains in their best aspect. Apart from a little turret, the last traces of the Uniqt city had been swallowed by the sandstorms during the previous season, something Sao regretted as a life-long archivist, but which caused him to feel a kernel of secret relief. The Uniqt were gone, and now Karquom belonged purely to the Lyceum.

Not many universities, especially human ones, had the luxury of an entire planet. At least they didn't have to fight for funding. And it had become a popular conference venue, as witnessed by the presence of the Duality now.

"Vice Chancellor?" Archivist Moynec sidled up. "Things seem to be going very well."

"So far." Sao had been accused of a predisposition towards gloom. He had retaliated by saying that he'd stop being a cynic when he stopped being proved right. "What about their welcoming banquet? Did you get those fruit?"

"Yes, yes, everything came exactly as it was ordered and we have followed the preparation instructions *most* carefully."

"I gather that's essential," Sao said. "Someone—I forget who, perhaps Therabin—once said that a predilection towards poisons was the mark that a race had reached its apogee of decadence."

"One could hardly characterise the Duality as decadent," Moynec reproached him. "After all, if not for their wisdom and generosity, very few of us would even be here."

"True. I suppose if one *has* to have an elder race, it might as well be this lot."

"Well, it could be worse," Moynec said, and there was a brief pause, as they both contemplated just how much worse. The Uniqt had demonstrated that. And look what had happened to them, whereas here were the Duality, chatting about whatever highly advanced aliens chatted about, over light wines and sugared fancies.

"Vice Chancellor, about this banquet . . ."

"Yes?"

"I'm concerned about the seating arrangements."

Sao silently called upon gods in which he had never believed. "You've had the instructions for the seating arrangements for months. What's the problem?"

"It's just that—seeing them here, you see, I've never actually *met* anyone from the Duality before, and it's rather brought it home to me. What they are."

Grant me patience. Moynec was proving even more incoherent than usual. Sao had noticed lapses in concentration on a number of occasions. Perhaps it was time the old boy retired. "And what is that?"

"Well—which one do they eat with? Which face?"

"The front one, of course, Moynec. Look at them. Which one are they drinking with?"

Moynec looked. "Ah. The front one."

"I must confess that I have very little notion of what constitutes ingestion etiquette among the Duality. Perhaps it's rude to eat with the mouth of your back-face. Perhaps it's just not done."

"They speak with their back mouths, though."

"Yes, but for pronouncements concerning the past, as that's what they see out of their back-faces. Maybe with the front . . ." Sao gave up. "I hate to admit to ignorance, Moynec"—*especially in front of you*—"but I really know very little about janus species."

"There aren't many of them. The Duality, and some rat-thing on Chorvus Eight."

There was no further time to discuss the issue. Sao had been observed. A member of the Duality was gliding towards them, using—Sao had a moment of panic before recalling the signifying robe-pattern—front-face. The Duality member's caster-feet made a displeasing squeak against the marble floor. Sao winced and hoped it wouldn't be noticed.

"Vice Chancellor! How delightful!" The Duality member's front face was male, signifying his primary gender, and to Sao's untutored gaze, fairly typical of his species: a broad forehead beneath a central ridge, large oceanic eyes with a slit pupil, and a nose and mouth that appeared classically human until the nose briefly flared to reveal the dust-gathering flanges within. Sao assumed that an early visit by the Duality was responsible for large chunks of classical human myth—they had certainly been around and spacefaring for the requisite twenty thousand years—but given the behaviour of early human deities, he had never felt it was politic to ask. Besides, humanity had done enough to change itself in the interim without getting snippy about visits from—after all—benign aliens.

"You may call me D-jiva," the Duality member was saying. Was there a brief echo from his hind-mouth? Sao could not tell, but it wasn't a pronouncement concerning the past, so probably not. "Such a pleasure to be here. One of my colleague's ancestors is alleged to have visited Karquom during the time of the Uniqt. An unhappy period."

"Indeed. Might one ask whether this was before the Uniqt slaughtered all other indigenous life on this planet, or afterwards?"

"Before." D-jiva's brow furrowed. "My colleague, A-vokt, tells me that his relative was attempting to bring resolution—to explain, in other words, that it was not in fact essential to prove one's worth to one's gods by rendering oneselves the only species in existence. Alas, the attempt failed."

"At least they didn't have spaceflight," Sao remarked.

"Quite so. I must say, the presence of your institution is a vast improvement."

"Culturally sanctioned genocide is not usually an evolutionary advantage," Sao said. "Even in academia."

"I gather there were only two of the Uniqt at the end," D-jiva acknowledged. "One can't help wondering if they had second thoughts."

"I can't help wondering what happened to the sole remaining one."

"Ah, well, that is supposed to be the last mystery of the Uniqt," D-jiva said.

"I should have said that it was hard to care," Moynec said, with a shudder.

"That, too. Now. Vice Chancellor, as designated confluence

spokesperson, I have already reviewed the banqueting arrangements and I must say, your institution has excelled itself."

"I certainly hope all will prove satisfactory," Sao said. He had entertained serious reservations about the wisdom of agreeing to a banquet in which everything—everything being, moreover, an alien substance—had originally been toxic. The reason for this was apparently not decadence at all; it was intended to bring home the essential impermanence of life—although, given how long the Duality lived, and what was now known about the continuation of existence, this seemed rather superfluous to Sao. Those reservations about health and safety were still present; he'd be glad when this whole thing was over.

"I must not take up more of your valuable time," D-jiva was saying. "I know you have other things to be concerned about besides our little poetry confluence. You have a lyceum to run, after all." With a fluid bow, he spun gently on his casters and wheeled back to the main grouping.

"What a pleasant fellow," Moynec said.

"Charming. But then, all of them are." Sao sighed. The encounter had brought the usual academic bickering and moaning, the atmosphere in which he spent his days, into sharp relief. What a pity reincarnation had been comprehensively disproved—although he doubted that he'd led a pure enough life to return as a member of the Duality.

An hour later, Sao was beginning to calm down. Everyone had survived the hors d'oeuvres, a collection of plant dishes from various jungles around various parts of the galaxy. Things that were blue and coiled, that wafted a sinister perfume across the banqueting hall. Things that were green and slimy, served beneath a dish in case their foul odor caused a miasma to build up within the confines of the Lyceum. Things that were small and black, like wizened brains: the seedpod of a rare sentient orchid. Sao remembered those negotiations; he had been rather shocked that someone might be prepared to sell off what were essentially their children, although he had been assured that they would grow more. It still seemed . . . *unnatural,* but then that was the essence of this banquet, in many respects. Perhaps the Duality, despite their philosophical ideals, were slipping past the peak of true civilization.

After this initial course, a pause was announced and a series of poetic readings were presented. Sao sat restlessly through this: his speciality was history, and poetry did not particularly interest him, particularly poetry with a lot of long, weighty silences to allow listeners to ponder on an especially abstruse semantic fragment. He was grateful when the entrees were brought in and the banquet recommenced.

Gratitude, however, lasted only so long. The first course of the entrees—some kind of flambéed whelk—passed without incident, but not so the second dish. This—Sao surreptitiously consulted his notes as a series of domed platters were carried in—was probably the most toxic of all the food: a form of moss from the swamps of a world called Destire, which released a vitriolic toxin when disturbed. The toxin dissipated within nine seconds, and there was then a window of about three seconds during which the moss was edible. Left to its own devices, it decomposed rapidly into a stinking mass. A light at the head of the table was to be lit, signalling the edibility of the moss after the required period.

Sao watched uneasily as the transparent domed coverings were lifted. The moss—an unobtrusive beige beneath the covering—began to glow as the toxin was released, a rather impressive neon green. The glow grew brighter, and brighter yet, until Sao nearly threw his Vice Chancellor's long sleeve across his eyes to protect them.

The light had come on—Sao blinked. But it wasn't the light at the head of the table, it was a ray, a brief flicker of neon blue, coming from the direction of the desert. He could see the little turret of the Uniqt outlined against the rocks: it had come from there—but surely, he had imagined it.

But the glow from the moss was not quite dazzling enough to stop him from seeing, with a dizzying sense of disbelief, D-jiva start to rise from his place, crying, "No! Wait!" as Duality member A-vokt leaned forward and spooned a glowing morsel of moss into his mouth. It didn't take long. A-vokt seemed to quiver, then grow still, and then pitched forward into the still-glowing plate.

At least the sudden demise of the Duality member stopped anyone else from eating the damned stuff. Sao was already on his feet and halfway down the dining table by the time A-vokt's shocked colleagues started to react. He was propelled more by horror and dismay than by forethought, so it was just as well that when he reached D-jiva's place, the Duality member's hand shot out and caught his arm in a grip like an iron clamp.

"Wait a moment," D-jiva said, in two mellifluous voices. "Empty the room. Then we can talk."

Morning. Vice Chancellor Sao still hadn't gone to bed, but the customarily grim results of a night without sleep were being postponed by adrenaline. Their eventuality might, however, be indicated by the fact that, when not being appalled, he was considering D-jiva's hind-face and reflecting that she was really quite attractive from this angle. The huge, calm, blue eyes, the delicately aquiline nose and curling mouth . . . he could not help but wonder what lay underneath the Duality member's flowing robes. He was too old for this kind of thing—never mind lèse-majesté, it practically verged on the blasphemous. In either case, it would not do. He had to concentrate on the matter at hand.

"Suicide," Moynec remarked, for what must have been the thousandth time. "It must have been suicide."

"Members of the Duality," D-jiva's female face replied, "are not prone to suicidal thoughts, let alone actions."

"The conference was dedicated to the frailty of existence,"

Sao said wearily. They had been over this several times; the conversation was developing the character of ritual. "Perhaps he felt an obligation to make a metaphorical point. This is an institution of learning, after all. Where better to illustrate a delicate ontological argument?"

D-jiva's hind-face smiled with an ancient benevolence. "We are not prone to such crude illustrations. Metaphorically, in the context of the poetry which we have experienced this evening, such an act might be considered the philosophical equivalent of a child's scribble."

Sao was too tired to be chastised, even by a member of an elder race. "You might be right. But who knows what really goes through people's heads?" *Especially those endowed with two faces.* He expected D-jiva to demur, but instead the Duality member was silent.

"D-jiva?" he said.

"Chancellor?" The huge blue eyes turned an oceanic gaze upon him and he saw that they were filled with an unfamiliar, a *human,* anxiety. "May I speak with you privately for a moment?"

Moynec, as Sao had expected, was only too pleased to be relieved of any semblance of responsibility and dispatched to his overdue rest. Once the old academic had tottered off, D-jiva turned to Sao.

"You must suspect that this was murder."

Sao rubbed his eyes. They had stopped focusing properly some time ago and everything seemed fuzzy. "Yes. Of course. But you didn't mention it, so I didn't mention it, and we've all been stepping around the subject. We don't have any kind of law enforcement here, D-jiva." Belatedly, he realized that he probably should not have called the Duality member by name, but D-jiva didn't seem to mind. "This is a lyceum, and nothing else. We have proctors."

"If you don't mind my asking," D-jiva said carefully, "do you often have trouble with students?"

"No. Well, occasionally. But not the kind of trouble that a normal planetside university—Belen, or Faunta, or Tsajarai, for instance—might experience. This is primarily a postgraduate institution, so the students who come here are older. Some of them are in their seventies. It's expensive—we have to make a living, we're not quite self-sufficient yet, things have to be shipped in—and let me be honest with you, this is not an egalitarian place. It's elitist. We are probably the best human university in the known universe. Groundbreaking research gets accomplished here. The Lyceum has solved the question of life after death. It has proved the existence of the human soul, it has made great strides in the question of whether the universe is teleologically oriented. That's not cheap. People have nervous breakdowns all the time. Occasionally, with the young and impressionable—people kill themselves. But not one another, and not guests. There's no crime here. Why would there be?"

"No plagiarism? No rivalry?"

"Departments aren't structured like that. They're largely individual affairs. We are talking about geniuses. Geniuses don't tend to work in teams, at least, not on the level of discovery."

D-jiva swivelled round to reveal his front face. To Sao's secret relief, it looked as weary as he himself felt.

"I accept that. I also accept that your proctors must handle this, and I understand that a forensic freeze has been placed upon the banqueting scene."

Sao was silent for a moment. "The proctors—all right. The proctors will do as I tell them, which is why we have placed the forensic freeze on the hall. I have made sure that word has not gotten off-world. The Duality are an elder race; I wanted to discuss with you what kind of legal issues might be paramount."

The discussion took a great deal of time, and afterwards Sao felt like a wet rag. Apart from dealing with D-jiva, he had to confer with the proctors and watch the security footage of the banquet. The whole thing seemed fairly straightforward, if baffling.

A-vokt had indeed leaned forward several seconds before he was supposed to and taken a mouthful of lethal moss. No one was standing near him; the nearest person, at least a foot and a half away, seemed lost in contemplation of his own dinner. Sao could not see what had prompted the Duality member to act as he had.

Once informed, the proctors swung into leisurely action. The banquet hall was thoroughly investigated. Sao asked two of the proctors to take a look at the Uniqt turret, but they reported that they had found nothing. The Duality members present were confined to their quarters, in the politest of ways, and questioned. When Sao examined the transcripts, however, he discovered that the answers received were oblique in the extreme.

"This doesn't make a whole lot of sense," he complained to D-jiva. "Here, when asked the routine question of where Duality member S-paith was during the time of the incident, S-paith questions the notion of existential presence within a limited time span rather than simply replying that she was sitting at dinner."

He thought D-jiva might have sighed. "I'm afraid the minds of the various members are on higher things."

Sao's eyebrows rose. "Higher things than the death of one of their colleagues?"

"You said it yourself. When the mystery of life after death is solved—as it was within the Duality several centuries ago—it's hard to take even a murder as seriously as it might have been once upon a time."

"I can't help feeling that this isn't really the point. Perhaps it's my old-fashioned human sensibilities."

"To be honest, Vice Chancellor, I tend to agree with you. A-vokt might indeed be in a better place, consorting with the group soul of the Duality. But I need A-vokt down here, in this life, to assist in a tricky diplomatic issue on Essack Four next month. We might be on what passes for leisure activities at present, but that does not mean serious business must be ignored.

Besides, there is a general feeling that this has *ruined* the poetry confluence."

"Lowered the tone?"

"Well, quite."

"So we are still required to investigate?"

"It might not stop at A-vokt," D-jiva pointed out. "Presumably you would rather not have members of the Lyceum slaughtered one by one, just in case someone has lost all sense of proportion."

But it seemed that the other members of the Duality did not feel the same way.

"A-vokt's death was most regrettable," one of the female front-faced members informed Sao. "But one cannot dwell on unpleasantness. A-vokt is even now partaking of the wisdom of the group soul after his sojourn in this incarnation."

"Yes, but—"

"And there is work to be done." With a firm smile, the female rose and glided before Sao to the door, which she held open for him. The rest of the Duality would, she said, be leaving in the morning.

Sao felt unable to give up. Requesting the proctors' records, he watched the banquet recording once again, and as he did so, the conversation with Moynec came to mind.

The hind-face of the Duality sees the past, only by a few seconds; the fore-face glimpses the future, and the two are merged into a kind of present. What if something had interfered with this process, so that A-vokt had seen the moss as it would be in a few seconds' time, safe? Remembering the light he had glimpsed, Sao left the study and went to the gallery of the banqueting hall. He was sure that the proctors had done their best, but he had to check for himself.

It was late and the Lyceum was quiet. The only sound was the soft rustle of Sao's robes, hissing against the stone floor as he walked. Beyond the columns, and the windows, the desert was still beneath the smallest of the moons: Sao felt as though both of them were looking back at him, the moon a hard chilly eye, the desert itself a presence.

Outside, the desert air bit at his skin and he clasped his robes closer. He hesitated for a moment, thinking: *This is unwise.* But he did not believe in ghosts or spirits: how could one, when one knew what happened after death? Then he hastened to the turret and up the crumbling steps to where he had seen the light, and crouched down to probe beneath the balustrade.

There was nothing there. He did not even know what he had expected to find: some kind of device. Perhaps it had been implanted in the stone itself, but even though Sao peered closely, he could not see any fissure or crack where the stone had been disturbed.

He straightened up and turned. Someone was standing behind him, a figure out of the desert shadow.

Sao's hand went to his heart, an instinctive, protective gesture. He had not thought to bring a weapon.

"I'm not going to hurt you," Moynec said and smiled a ghastly grin.

"Moynec?"

"Moynec is dead. I no longer need to disguise myself under false and human names. My true name is Eshara," Moynec said. "I am the last of the Uniqt."

"What?" Sao backed against the wall of the turret; it felt reassuringly solid.

"My mother came from the last of the line," Moynec said. "Uniqt females reproduce parthenogenetically. You do understand, don't you, that as the last male I had to take vengeance? For the last two decades, my private research has been the development of a temporal disrupter. Originally, I hoped to travel to the Duality, but this was naïve: they do not allow the lesser races into their territory. So I had to wait for them to come here."

Sao glanced around. Moynec stood in the doorway; there

was no way out except around him. He must keep Moynec engaged.

"One can understand," Sao said, "that you would wish for revenge."

"You do not know," Moynec said, very softly, "what it is like. You cannot. I am the last. This is my world. I am sorry, Vice Chancellor. I've enjoyed our conversations, even though your comprehension is sorely limited. But I must take my planet back."

There was no indication that he was about to move, to draw a weapon. But then Moynec was crumpling to the floor, falling without a sound, and a needle-weapon was clattering across the ruined stones.

D-jiva stood behind him, arm upraised.

"I saw the future," the Duality member said. "He was about to use the gun on you."

You know what comes next, and yet you still fear it. Sao, shaking, said, "Thank you." And called the proctors.

They found the temporal disrupter in Moynec's rooms: a small box, with a blue flashing light. Inside lay a tangle of wires which, when tested, proved meaningless.

"Unless they've missed something," Sao said to D-jiva, doubtfully.

The Duality member made a dismissive gesture. "They have not. This is not a real device. Just some wires stuffed into a box."

"They've done tests in the medical wing," Sao said. "He is not Uniqt, of course."

"No. Merely someone who has gone quietly mad," D-jiva said. "As had, it seems, A-vokt himself. While you were undergoing your own investigations yesterday, I took the most recent samples of A-vokt's poetry and did my best to analyse them. I am not the poet that A-vokt was, but I think it is there all the same. Guilt, and the wish for repentance. Futile, of course, since such an action would not have brought back the Uniqt. It appears that A-vokt discerned some romance in dying at the banqueting table on the world which his own ancestors failed to save."

And both he and Sao sat silently for a time after that, staring out at the burning glare of the desert, at emptiness, at that which is gone.

Vivisepulture

• • •

DAVID PRILL

"HEY, WHERE THE HECK is that music comin' from?"

This was Big Jim McDiffie at a Memorial Day backyard barbecue, circa 1974, back when you knew exactly where pretty much all music came from; that was the appeal—you can't hum along to the Unknown. Penny-loafer jingles, tinny children's songs from the ding-dong man's truck (according to moms everywhere, the music meant the truck had run out of ice cream), the mailman whistling an old Johnny Mercer standard, side A of the soundtrack of the suburbs.

And most importantly, Big Jim's school song:

> Wave the flag for Hillmont High School
> Her colors black and gold.
> Marching always on to victory,
> No matter who the foe.
> So, we'll forever praise and cheer you,
> Our Gobblers brave and true.
> Wave again the dear old banner,
> Hillmont High we're all for you.

Brought a tear to Big Jim's eye. Used to, anyway.

Big Jim had been a star athlete at Hillmont High, lettering in football, baseball, basketball, and cheerleader-chasing. He was the missile-firing quarterback in football, pitcher and cleanup hitter in baseball, and all-city forward in basketball. Until a back condition knocked him out of his roost. His spinal column was twisted like a snake on hot blacktop. The doctors said his athletic career was over and out. It was too frustrating to attend the games as a spectator, so began the isolation with occasional detours into alienation. Almost felt like he had already graduated, especially since he didn't spend much time in class anyway. He spent less time hanging out at the Red Barn with the gang, tough guys with french fries dangling from their mouths, more time wandering alone down the paneled-station-wagon-lined streets. His coaches had always admired him for his ability to see the whole playing field, to anticipate what was to come, to be one step ahead of the other players. Now Big Jim, as he wandered, was trying to see the whole field, the future, but he couldn't see much at all; the field was too big now, and there were too many unknowns.

Like the music, today.

Big Jim may not have been the smartest guy on the block—he once saw a sign in a yard that said *Free Wood Chips* and thought it was a political statement—but even he could conclude that the music didn't fit in here, in the suburbs of his mind. Anybody could hear that.

Where was that music coming from anyway?

Big Jim asked the question.

"I don't hear anything," said his mother. "Have another ear of corn."

"You don't hear that? Listen. It's music—beautiful, sad, hopeful music, woodwinds and quiet brass, the plucking of strings—you don't hear that? It's beautiful, wonder where it's coming from."

"You're hearing things," said his kid sister.

"I hear something," said his dad. "Not sure what. Doesn't sound like music to me. A factory, a plane, the wind, something faraway, not music, not music at all."

I'm hearing things, I'm wondering things, Big Jim thought.

The wind shifted, and the music flagged.

Later, after the coals became ash and the rest of the family settled in before the idiot box, Big Jim remained outside, as the early summer night crept over the bungalows, the Big Dipper slopping darkness into the northern sky. He listened, he couldn't catch anything.

I want to hear it again, Big Jim thought. *I want to hear that music. Why the heck do I want to hear that music?*

A while back a group of boys from prestigious west Hillmont formed a rock combo called Foxen. They played covers of popular songs. They were named after the leader of the group, Greg Fox, whose parents had given him a Sears Silvertone guitar and amp for his birthday and tolerated the din. Foxen practiced in the basement rec room of Greg's house, where they also threw bashes for their friends from school. They charged a buck to get in, which included free sodas. Big Jim wasn't allowed to attend the shows after he threw a punch and accidentally knocked over the Silvertone amp. Big Jim didn't mind—the music they played didn't stir up much inside him.

The doctor had prescribed heavy walking for Big Jim in order to strengthen his back muscles. He walked at night, roaming through industrial areas and along railroad tracks, on rainy cold nights and on T-shirt-and-sneakers nights. It was drudgery at first, but then he grew to like it, and even after his back had healed to the extent it ever would, he still tramped the streets.

• • •

Once while he was out wandering, a car passed by Big Jim, a '65 Polara, containing Macy and Greg Fox. Big Jim and Macy had dated up until his back malady knocked him out of the race, and even for a while afterwards until she seemed to grow weary of the constant walking, walking, walking; okay, like, you know, a girl shouldn't have to, like, soak her feet after a date, okay? Can't blame her, he told himself; they traveled in different circles nowadays.

The Polara slowed when it saw him. A Foxen cover of "Radar Love" blared out of the car speakers.

"Where are you going, guy?" Greg asked. Macy smiled self-consciously and maybe a little provocatively from the passenger side. What was that about? He didn't understand that. If she was done with him, she shouldn't act like she wasn't.

"Nowhere," Big Jim said, keeping his eyes away from them. "Just walkin'."

"You still owe me for bustin' that amp, man."

Big Jim didn't reply. The Polara filled with laughter and peeled off down the street, taking "Radar Love" with it, the bass line like footfalls along the avenue.

Big Jim never did dig that song, the Foxen version even less.

"Did Macy dump you?" his kid sister asked after he returned from his wandering.

"What's it to you, half-pint?"

"I saw her riding in a barracuda with a fox!"

"Polara."

"Well they were driving fast."

"Lookee you, there's plenty of fish in the sea. You should know all about that, shrimp."

"Well *I* never approved of her—I think you can do much better."

"Oh you think so, huh?"

"I do! I do!"

"Maybe I'm happy the way I am."

"You don't look happy."

"Listen, squirt, I . . . ah, what do you know. I'm goin' to bed."

It was a sleep-at-the-foot-end-of-the-bed night, windows up as high as they could be pushed, and after the rest of the house headed to slumbertown, the breeze rallied.

From the east.

Faint, hardly audible music found its way into an upstairs bedroom among the dusty trophies and sun-paled pennants.

Beautiful, sad, hopeful music. Now that he was alone with the music, now that it wasn't filtered through the family proper, Big Jim understood. He connected. The music spoke to parts of him that nothing had ever spoken to before, parts he barely knew existed within himself. It was sweet and melancholy and most highly personal, a whisper in the ear, a note furtively slipped under the door.

Big Jim went to the window.

He listened, straining against the screen, wanting to get closer to the sound.

Once again the wind shifted, and the music found another home.

When he slept . . .

Big Jim dreamt of the music. He dreamt of the woman who was making it, a beautiful angel-hair blonde, royal-wedding white dress, embraced by irises and daffodils and daisies, a genteel look on her face, hugging one of those big ol' violins, a cello, yeah, a cello, her soul was so beautiful—oh, so much better than Foxen, way better than Macy. Hillmont High could only wish to house so fine a specimen.

When he woke . . .

Big Jim wished he was still in dreams. He hustled to the

window and listened, but overnight a warm front had settled in, bringing along a day that promised to be still and humid and . . . quiet.

The hot spell hung tight all week. Big Jim serial-dreamed of the music, of Her, and he began to worry. What if after the front moved through, the breeze returned but the music did not? *I should have tried to find her that first night,* he thought. *I shouldn't have waited.*

Saturday was his dad's birthday, and he wanted to go to Uncle John's Pancake House, so that was the plan. Uncle John's was famous for their early-bird and night-owl pancake-and-egg special—you got three buttermilk pancakes or toast, and two country-fresh eggs as you like them, all for a buck and a half.

"Is your back hurting you today, Jim?" his mother asked. "You're so quiet. You've hardly touched your pancakes, three of them for a buck fifty and I'm not even including the country-fresh eggs."

"No, I'm okay, Ma. I'm just waitin'." He hummed the music of the late hours, and hoped like hell for a change in the weather.

Big Jim slunk back to the Red Barn during these still times and didn't know why. Maybe wanted to see if there was anything left of his old life. Maybe that's what he wanted to see. But there wasn't anybody there, there was no aroma of the french fryer in the air, in fact the Red Barn was closed for repairs.

The cold front swept through town late on Saturday night.

Tagging along on the winds was a lonesome melody.

Big Jim sat bolt upright in bed.

He busted out of the house and was on the front sidewalk while the melody was still hot in his head.

Now he wandered the streets with a purpose, drawn to the music, allowing himself to be reeled in, passing by the dark signposts of the suburbs, the Jolly Troll Smorgasbord, the fiberglass Jolly Troll perched on the boulder out front looking like a grim sentinel, the windmill at the putt-putt golf course a haunted, damned place.

He stopped and listened, then backtracked, keeping the music in front of him, trying not to get sidetracked. It seemed, slowly, and in very small degrees, that he didn't have to strain as much to hear it. Big Jim found his anxiety and anticipation growing as he homed in on his dream.

And then the wind suddenly died. And the music with it.

Big Jim lingered, and listened, and hoped.

But the wind didn't return, not that night. He didn't take it personally. It was just one of those things.

Better luck the next night—a strong, steady breeze, a bona fide wind, and Big Jim didn't waste any time. He reached the Menacing Troll while the first notes were still fresh in his head.

Now Big Jim was heading down the hill to Southtown Shopping Center, home of Red Owl supermarket, Dave's Shoe Repair, Jolly's toy store, Kresge's dime store, and other icons on the Hillmont scene. Southtown was a modest dream of early suburbia, surrounded by vacant lots. Santa's Workshop, which was hauled out to the middle of the parking lot in early December, spent the summer months lonely and abandoned-looking in the weeds behind Southtown. As a kid he wanted to peer into the dusty workshop windows, afraid of what might be lurking in there, afraid an inmate-eyed Saint Nick and his rabid reindeer would be peering back.

Used to be a bar on the nearby service road, but it had been shuttered long ago when a new elementary school had been built in the vicinity—a neighborhood dog visited the bar with some regularity, and the story goes that the patrons would give the pooch a beer or two and send him home in a cab.

The rest of the lot behind Southtown had been undisturbed as long as Big Jim could remember. But now a strange building had ended its peace, and it was that building, Big Jim realized, that was the source of his new soundtrack.

The building was white and classical and out of place. It looked like a temple, a museum, with columns and ornate decorative doo-dahs, an edifice that had been there for generations, not the usual go-go basement rec room architecture of the suburbs. It was like one of those buildings they showed in that humanities class he slept through last year, the type of building you'd see on a field trip to the planetarium downtown.

It's funny, Big Jim thought as he walked by Santa's Workshop and through the weedy lot, booting a discarded Fanta bottle, sending it clinking into the brush. *Even though I'm so close to the music, to the beautiful one, that it doesn't really sound any louder than it did from my bedroom window.*

Big Jim approached the building in a hurry, stumbling over the debris in the field as he closed in. A night critter scuttled into the heavier brush up against the hillside. The tall, grated windows were dark. An odd smell occurred to him as he went up the steps and passed between the columns leading to the heavy-duty ornate front door.

He knocked, twice, then leaned into the door, and as the music rose he stepped inside. . . .

"Boy, do you ever look crummy!" Kid Sister told Big Jim the next morning, invading his room without knocking. "Where did you go last night? I tried to stay awake, but I just couldn't!"

Big Jim rolled over and peered at her. "Stay far away from me, kid."

"What did you do? Did you commit a crime? I bet you did! You robbed Jolly's, I betcha. That's what I would rob if I was going to rob something. Can you imagine, yo-yos, hula hoops, ant farms and Frisbees, German microscopes and Japanese kites, whee!"

"Kid, I have to ask you something." Big Jim sat up.

"Ask *me*? What can this shrimp possibly tell you?"

"Yeah, look, serious stuff now, okay?"

"I'll be good."

"Promise me something, kid."

"A cross-my-heart promise?"

"Even bigger than that."

She came to the bed, wonder in her eyes.

He leaned in close to her. "Lock me in my room tonight."

Her eyes grew white.

"Don't let me go out, kid. Lock me in. Lock me in good."

"You're scaring me! Jeepers, quit kidding around!"

"I can't tell you about it now, kiddo. Someday I will, I vow to you. Trust me. Lock me in my room. No matter what I say, don't unlock that door!"

Her small narrow face hardened.

"Good girl."

Midmorning.

"Phone call, Jim," said his mom. In a hushed voice: "I think it's a girl."

Big Jim banished his first thought, then took the call.

"Hello?"

"So who are you seeing now?"

"Huh?"

"Margie and Pete said they saw you going into a building in back of Southtown late last night. Who is she?"

"Macy? Is that you?"

"Is it someone from school? Debbie Morning?"

"Macy, this isn't a good time."

"Oh yeah, you play the big mournful loner, but all the time you're wandering around from girl to girl—didn't the time we had together mean anything to you?"

"Huh?"

And so forth, and when Big Jim hung up the phone, his mother said, "Say, have you got a new girlfriend there, Jim? Good for you. I always thought you could do better than that Macy Allen, you should bring your new friend over to the house sometime, maybe for dinner, maybe tomorrow night, hmm?"

"Oh, yeah, sure, Ma."

Is it that obvious? Big Jim wondered, hightailing it out the front door. *Is her song in my eyes? Is her face reflected in mine?*

Down the sidewalk, the suburban totems returned to their daytime splendor.

Singing his own song.

Lock me in my room.

Please don't let me hear the music tonight.

"Kid, kid, are you there? Listen, I wasn't thinking straight when I told you to lock me in here. It was a joke. We kid around, don't we? So unlock the door now, okay? Don't you hear the music, can't you understand? Listen! Hear it! Are you there, kid? Are you with me, kid?"

Time passes, the room is torn up, souls are tormented, bed-sheets are rumpled terribly. Visions of long strings, a strange orchestra. This sweet love.

"I'll let you out on one condition."

"Anything."

"I'll let you out if you let me go with you."

"It's a deal," Big Jim said.

The doorknob rattled and turned.

Big Jim quickly pulled open the door, nabbed the kid by the arm and yanked her into the room, locking the door behind him, and made his getaway into the night before she could yell for Mom.

"I figured you'd be back."

"I tried to stay away. It's . . . her . . . it's . . . the music."

"It freaked me out too, first time I heard it. Got used to it after a while. Part of the job, you know."

"I could never get used to it."

"Same deal as last time, okay?"

"Right. Here's the money."

"I'm sorry to do it this way, it's just that I'm not supposed to do this, I'm taking some risk here."

"I understand."

"Fifteen minutes. I'll come get you."

"Thanks."

When the quarter hour expired, and they walked back to the entrance, Big Jim asked, "Have any of them ever, you know, left?"

"Not since I've been here."

"But it could happen."

"Sure. That's why we're here."

"It will happen."

"It might happen."

"If you believe?"

"You never know."

"You tricked me," said Kid Sister when he returned. She was sitting on his bed, arms crossed, looking older than he had remembered.

"I didn't mean it. Forgive me. I'm weak."

"That was very mean."

"I hurt my back. Things haven't been the same since."

"You've never been like this. You've never been anything like this."

"This is grown-up stuff—you wouldn't understand. You're just a little kid."

"Take me with you, I wanna understand."

"No, please don't ask me."

"Please."

"I can't."

"I'll tell Mom."

"Traitor."

"You called me a little kid."

"Forgive me."

"Think about taking me with. Think about it, just think about it for a minute, okay?"

"You never know what will happen, if you believe."

A car in the parking lot the next night.

"I can't let you in, not now."

"Why?"

In a whisper. "Family."

"Hers?"

"Tonight isn't good. I've helped you out, now you have to help me out. Go home."

"Can I talk to them?"

"You need to leave."

"I can come back later."

"I don't know how long they'll be here."

"I'll wait in the weeds, over there."

With a shrug. "Suit yourself."

Big Jim crouched in the weeds partway up the hillside until the visitors left the building. They were weeping. He felt an empathetic wave roll over him, but didn't truly understand the implications of their tears.

Big Jim's girl troubles continued, Macy making her presence felt again. Who is she? What does she have that I don't have? I just rode around with Greg Fox to make you jealous. I'm not doing anything tonight. Do you want to go to the drive-in?

Big Jim looked out the window. The tree branches were swaying with the wind, the young green leaves rippling.

I can't. Not tonight. Forgive me.

That night, Big Jim knew Macy was following him from the moment he hit the boulevard. He saw her lurking among a line of cedars across from their house. He didn't turn, didn't acknowledge her. He kept walking, no longer wandering, no more wondering, knowing exactly where he was headed. He took comfort in that. It was a good feeling. It made him feel right.

Now thoughts and memories about Macy came into his mind, fighting for attention with the music of his soul. He tried to conjure up the details of their relationship. Fuzzy blobs of yesterday. They hung out at the Red Barn, she and her #3 combo, he and his #5, good old number five, the chicken basket, onion rings, cole slaw, amen. They attended drive-in movies and pretended to be film buffs. Their favorite refreshment was the chili dog. Cruising down Penn Avenue, getting into an occasional drag race. Was there talk of marriage? Was there an open bottle?

When he reached the entrance, Big Jim turned to the darkness and said, "Macy, come here."

She had been hiding behind Santa's Workshop, and now hurried across the lot, coming up short at the Doric columns.

"What's that weird smell? What's that creepy sound? What is this place?"

"The music, it's the music, that's what you're hearing," Big Jim told her. "Isn't it the most beautiful music?"

"So this is where you meet your girlfriend?"

"Do you want to come in?"

"I'll give her a piece of my mind, you can count on that!"

When the door opened, the attendant looked at both of them and said, with a short laugh, "Table for two?"

The moon broke free of the clouds, injecting the land with white. The wind settled down; the wanderer had come home.

Beyond the entrance was a modest foyer, past that an arched doorway leading to a larger room with a vaulted ceiling. The lighting was subdued, deep red and gold.

"Well, this is different," said Macy. "I didn't even know this place was here. Didn't there used to be a bar somewhere back here?"

Into the main room, circular and smelling of flowers and fetidness, Macy hesitated. "What in the world . . ."

Big Jim wore a happy smile.

The attendant was smirking.

`Alcoves along the curving walls, interior circles with slabs, each with a well-dressed patron resting on it in a highly prone position.

Wires led up from the residents to a common destination in the ceiling: a harmonium-like device with an air-pressured bellows positioned among the ventilation screens. Occasionally the wires jiggled, causing tones of various octaves to emanate from the organ; taken together they formed a strange, dark symphony, a new American songbook.

"I . . . I don't understand," Macy said, stumbling numbly through the main room.

"Welcome to the Hillmont Leichenhaus," said the attendant in a tired monotone. "Our Leichenhaus was built by the Society for the Prevention of Premature Burial, Hillmont branch. Throughout history there have been cases of people thought dead, reviving after being placed in their final resting places; vivisepulture as the scholars call it, or in common language, being buried alive. The horrible deaths, the chewing of fingers, the crushing of skulls against the casket lid in a desperate bid to escape their early interment, have haunted the generations. It would be safe to say that in earlier years the subject was a matter of much consternation for proper society, including the composer Chopin, King Leopold I of Belgium, the poet Edmund Yates, Lady Burton, wife of explorer Sir Richard Burton—just to name a few. Often they stipulated in their wills that they were to be decapitated or worse after the death certificate was signed to avoid the horror of a premature burial.

"Was there a better way?

"Yes!

"The Leichenhaus, the House of Corpses, was originally conceived in Germany in the 1800s. The Leichenhaus was a transition place between life and death, a waiting room, if you will. You can't be too careful, why take chances, you may be next! You're asking yourself how it works. All our guests are carefully monitored in a very scientific manner. Sensitive wires are attached to various parts of the anatomy. Any movement by the waiting ones will result in the wire being pulled, creating a clear tonal chord up *there*."

"Now listen to this next part," said Big Jim. "It's swell!"

"I know you're asking yourself—but what are all these sounds I'm hearing now, this music? Does that mean all the residents here are not really dead, are in fact alive? To the uninitiated observer it may seem that way, but in fact as the human body rests in this twilight state, gases are eliminated, tissues are in transition, the body as a whole does not in fact truly ever rest.

As a trained Leichenhaus attendant, however, I can usually determine which sounds are from this natural regression, this settling if you will, and which sounds may indicate an individual has been given a premature verdict of death."

They reached the most precious of slabs.

She lay still, pale, perhaps slightly bloated, the flowers framing her entire body, the scent sweetly choking them.

"See," Big Jim said, "there isn't anything for you to be jealous about, Macy. Listen to the music . . . isn't it beautiful?"

Macy stepped backward, her eyes wide.

"You're crazy! You're crazy! She's dead, she's dead, they're all dead!" Macy screamed and ran for the entrance.

As she escaped back toward the known Hillmont, Big Jim and the attendant stood at the stately threshold of the Leichenhaus.

"She doesn't understand," said Big Jim.

"Most of them don't."

"They're not really dead, not for sure."

"They wouldn't be here if we were sure."

Macy disappeared over the hillside.

Big Jim thought of the flowers circling his beloved. *She loves me, she loves me not.*

"She followed you," Kid Sister informed him when he returned. "I used my spyglass on her and I saw her follow you."

"You saw who?"

"*Macy.*"

"Oh, okay, yeah, yeah, yeah."

"Well, what happened?"

"Well, what happened was that Macy and I came to an understanding, I think. I think if you ask her she would say the same thing. Understand?"

"Oh. You *are* the grown-up, I guess."

"Yeah, that follows."

Finally some stability came into Big Jim's life. He felt that he had finally made a clean break with his past. He had to—there was no way to straighten his spine, no way to turn back the hit parade. School was out.

But what of the future?

Perhaps it was meant to be. Perhaps that was why he had found her, made the connection, heard the music, got strung out on her. Maybe something stirring inside her, maybe this is what drew him to her instead of one of her compatriots in that twilight world. Maybe he would be there when she awoke.

In his dreams that night he dreamt that he roused his beloved with a kiss.

Then the music changed.

It happened two nights after Macy's visit to the Leichenhaus. Big Jim almost slept through it. He didn't spring to attention when he heard it, just slowly came to consciousness, climbing out of several heavy layers of grogginess.

Fully awake, he listened hard. A change, subtle yet distinct. Colder, more discordant. A factory, a plane, the wind, something faraway, maybe not music, maybe not music at all.

Big Jim got up and followed the well-worn path down to the Leichenhaus, realizing with some alarm that it was the path that led him to the Leichenhaus, not the music itself.

The attendant didn't answer his secret knock, so Big Jim let himself in and stepped into the main room. Darker here, shadows

laying over the scene. He breathed easy when he saw the familiar alcove still occupied. Thank goodness. The change in the
music must mean that time was running out for her. He had to
move fast.

He drew close, quickly leaned in and pressed his lips to hers,
the cold jumping across the void.

Big Jim pulled back. Something was wrong. The form on the
slab was larger, the hair darker, the corpus fresher.

"Her family came this afternoon," said the attendant, appear-
ing behind him.

Big Jim looked dumbly at the man, fingers on his lips.

"Sorry. They usually don't give us much warning."

"They came this afternoon?"

"They felt it was time to take the next step."

"She's gone."

"Yeah."

"Where did they take her?"

"Don't know. Not my business."

"You must have heard something."

"A hole in the ground with a headstone on top, that's all I can
tell you."

Big Jim scanned the big hall, running from alcove to alcove,
hoping there was a mistake, praying she had just been misplaced.

"Sorry, guy. I know it's a blow."

Big Jim blew out of there, his mind rocking in disbelief. He
had trouble finding his way back home, kept making the wrong
turns, confusion and despair, the twenty-minute trip taking two
hours.

Kid Sister fortunately was asleep on the sofa. He placed a
blanket over her and quietly went upstairs.

He shut the window to keep the new music at bay, opened it
again so he wouldn't miss anything, then lay in bed, wrapping
himself in the covers, fingering his still frigid lips, coldness
through and through him, through and through.

•   •   •

Much later, Big Jim is out wandering. Wandering without direction, hoping for elation, listening for her music, believing that wherever she may be, the music will find him.

Wandering through parks with stone markers and freshly turned earth. Hearing nothing, the silence of their situation, it would be easier to hear her in these places, a soloist among the congregations of the dead.

Big Jim wanders by the Hillmont High stadium one Friday night. Bright lights shine down on the field, green with white stripes. The stands are filled with people, many familiar faces, although less familiar than they used to be. How they cheer, how they breathe. The players dash around the turf, legs churning, sharp cracks sounding when they collide. They rise after having fallen, every single time.

The school band is playing a song.

The crowd is singing along.

Big Jim stops outside the tall fence beyond the end zone, fingers gripping the wire. *No alcoholic beverages allowed on the premises,* warns a sign.

Big Jim listens to the music.

> *Wave the flag for Hillmont High School*
> *Her colors black and gold.*
> *Marching always on to victory,*
> *No matter who the foe.*
> *So, we'll forever praise and cheer you,*
> *Our Gobblers brave and true.*
> *Wave again the dear old banner,*
> *Hillmont High we're all for you.*

By the time they recite the final line, the music and words sound like gibberish to Big Jim. A national anthem from a country whose name he can't pronounce. White noise. Big Jim turns and heads back into the darkness, to the burying places, crouching low among the mounds, the markers, his fingers chewed down to the knuckle, skull bashed against the bitter ground, listening for an old song, a song of life and death and eternal hope, the song of his soul, the heartbeat of his beloved.

E·C·Z·E·M·A

ec·ze·ma \ iġ-'zē-mə, 'eġ-zə-mə, 'ek-sə -mə \
noun

: an inflammatory condition of the skin characterized by
redness, itching, and oozing vesicular lesions which become scaly, crusted, or hardened

Eczema

● ● ●

CLARE DUDMAN

THE THREE CROWS were at Melissa's funeral. I was in the mood
for noticing everything. It seemed as if everything had become
louder, brighter, sharper—and yet I didn't feel I was really there
at all but looking at it, a spectator, uninvolved, too numb to
care. It was a small affair—just Laura and a few people from her
office and a couple of the long-standing neighbours—so the
crows stood out. They were silent, hooded as usual in their
black scarves and cloaks, their faces hidden in shadow, one of
them with a pair of black plastic-framed glasses protruding over
the opening for her eyes. "Crows" had been Melissa's name for
them. She had seen them move in a fortnight ago when everything had still been all right. She had called me to the window—
she had been in her favourite spot, perched on the arm of a
chair, a place where she had liked to think she was invisible
from the street, hooking back the net curtains just a little with a
finger. Melissa liked to think she knew everything—that no one
in that street was able to twitch an eyebrow without her taking

note. But in fact all she ever saw was the detail—the important things that should have concerned her the most, she missed.

"Robin!" she'd called. "New neighbours." Her voice had ended with a little surprised shriek. It had been the start. I realize that now. I think maybe I knew it then. It was that shriek rather than her words that made me rush in to see what was wrong. Her face had the pale radiance of the moon and she was rubbing a place in the small of her back.

"I think I must have strained something," she said. "Strange, maybe I moved too quickly." Then she'd smiled at the thought of that—that she would ever move her cumbersome frame any more quickly than was absolutely necessary—and twitched the curtain again. "Look, three of them, all of them covered up in black, just like crows."

They had no furniture, nothing at all. Melissa waited at her post all day for something to follow them into the house, but nothing did. Her pain got worse, although she didn't complain much. The crows' lack of belongings seemed to agitate her more. "They must have something! No one can move into an empty house without anything at all." Her hands twisted but the rest of her seemed more inert than ever. Eventually she summoned me to her side with an urgent bark of my name so that I could support her as she lumbered to the bathroom.

Once the crows had gone in they had not come out, not once, she reported as we moved carefully along the hall, much more concerned about this than the pain in her back.

"Maybe I should phone the doctor," I said.

"No"—she shook her head—"I think they'll be OK. They're probably settling in. Maybe their stuff arrived when I wasn't looking."

But we both knew this was unlikely. Melissa had been at that window every day for weeks.

• • •

"Was it the allergy?" Laura, the nearest thing to a friend Melissa had had at work, peered up at me through thick frameless spectacles. Melissa's attendance at the place had been too spasmodic to make many acquaintances. Laura's wineglass tipped as she spoke so that the contents speckled her clean white shirt. "I knew it was bad, but I didn't think it could . . ." Her voice trailed off. She noticed the wine and tried to brush it off but the drops were spreading and coalescing.

I nodded. It seemed the easiest thing to do. I wasn't quite sure what had killed my sister, but I knew it wasn't the allergy. She just seemed to give up in her sleep.

"Well, at least she went peacefully." Behind Laura something fluttered. The three crows. The tall one was shifting her large black cloak as if she were ruffling her feathers. The one with the glasses tipped her head abruptly and the light reflected from the sun whipped across the room, making everyone squint. The smallest one gave a loud yawn that was as deep and as raucous as a caw. Three crows, I told Melissa—because I was sure she was still listening to my thoughts—you were right, Sis. Laura gave up on her blouse, tipped her head in a nod and walked away so there was a clear space between the three black-gowned women and me. They were watching me, waiting, I thought, and I vacillated for a few seconds. I bent down to scratch my right calf, rubbing the material against my leg to calm the itch there. Another bite, I thought: Melissa had been plagued with them too. A present from the cat, I'd told her, but she'd shaken her head. I scratched again, lifted the hem of my trousers so I could dig in my nails, and then stopped. There was no familiar redness, no slight swelling from poison, and no pinprick of a sting, just a round patch of white flaky skin that was coming away with the touch of my fingers.

In front of me all three of the crows stepped backwards, then they whispered together. I didn't want to know what they were saying. I breathed in deeply then out again, fighting an urge to run. If I could escape into the open air then I could pretend none of this was happening. I could walk home and Melissa would be there, as she always was, looking out of the window, ready for me, smiling, telling me everything was all right that I'd just been having one of those dreams again. But I stood where I was. I decided I needed a drink. I could manage if I had a drink, just enough to take the edge off everything, to make it less sharp, bright, and real, to take me further away than I was already. I steadied myself against the wall and then lurched towards the bar, gulped at my drink and looked for the three crows. They had gone. It seemed to me that where they'd been, there was a space darker than everywhere else. I went over and stood there. It was cold and smelled of feathers.

"Where did they go?" I asked Laura.

"Who?" she said, smiling sweetly.

"The three women."

She frowned and shrugged.

"Like crows. In black, with gowns, all over them, like this . . ."

She shook her head. "Honestly, I didn't see anyone. I'm sorry."

Then Melissa laughed. I swear it. It was so loud that I looked around. Of course there was no one there, just a few of Melissa's old acquaintances staring at me.

Laura touched me lightly on the shoulder. "Are you all right?"

"Maybe I'll just get some air."

The street was in darkness when I got back—just the orange glow of streetlights illuminating a small patch of pavement around them. The one outside the crows' house was flickering—a faint crimson and then off again—as if it were a lighthouse warning about the end of the world. Or maybe it was warning about the crows. Their house was in blackness too, so I peered in as I passed, then jumped back. Just for an instant a face had peered back at me—white and oval with black holes for eyes. Melissa laughed again. Stupid boy. She was always saying that, even though we had long been adults. She had been bossing me around ever since we were children, even though she was a couple of years younger than me—though no one knew for sure how much younger. My origins were, as they say, shrouded in mystery. "You were found near an egg—Mother told me," Melissa announced one day in the middle of an argument when Mother had been long gone, and therefore no longer available to confirm or deny. "It was an old one, but very large, and you were lying beside it—whining as usual—with a shrivelled yellow thing attached to a cord going into your stomach."

I had touched my navel through my shirt—I had always been self-conscious of it—it was much larger and deeper than any other navel I had seen and looked as if a significant part of my stomach had been sucked inside.

"You were instead of me," she'd added cruelly. "I was what they really wanted—a child of their own. But they picked you up because they couldn't leave you there. You were squawking helplessly in the middle of a quarry and they were blasting out more rock all the time, so Father picked you up and hid you in his haversack, and told everyone later that you'd been born in their tent in the middle of their field trip—an unexpected by-product of a highly successful investigation."

"What had they been studying?" I asked numbly. Mother and Father were both geologists.

"Precambrian schists. They were hoping to find early evidence for life and got rather more than they bargained for."

"Did they think I was Precambrian then?"

Melissa had shrugged, suddenly and obviously bored. "Maybe. I dunno."

We spent the rest of our childhood waiting for our parents to return. They were always off on one field trip or another, until they went on one final field trip to Tierra del Fuego and were shunted from their canoe into icy weed-congested water by a large and very irate sea lion. Neither of them ever resurfaced. Their fate was reported in Santiago and there was a short note in the *Journal of the European Geologist*. We hardly missed them, but I would have liked to have asked them about the egg. By that time we were independent; a succession of child-minders and relatives usually failed to show up, so Melissa and I were left to our own devices. She became mother, but I failed to turn into father. I remained helpless little brother—she soon outgrew me—a condition she exploited to the full.

Even so, when I stepped into our empty house that night I wanted her back. Even Melissa's bossiness was better than loneliness. I called her as I always did, and for a part of a second expected a reply. She eventually spoke when I was lying on my bed scratching both my legs at once because the other one was itching now too.

"Always too sensitive for your own good," she said, tutting in the dark. "Stupid boy. Stop crying. You're wetting your pillow."

I was between work. But then, I was generally between work. The only jobs I seemed to keep were those that involved no contact at all with the human race. There was something about me that put people off. Melissa said it was because I had spooky eyes and I used them too much. They were a very pale green, and since my skin was fairly dark—a sort of burnt plum—I suppose they stood out, and I didn't seem to need to blink like most people.

"You stare," she said. "It's unnerving."

Eventually I was assessed by the school psychologist who put me down as "borderline?" I don't think she'd come across anything quite like me before. "Try to blink, Robin," she'd said, rather more kindly than my sister. "Then maybe you'll make some friends." I tried. It didn't work.

•   •   •

The next day was cold and damp and our neighbour Irene was at the door. "I've made out a list, Robin," she said, holding out a piece of paper decorated with pictures of hideous yellow flowers. "It's what you have to do when someone dies. Ken and I came up with it last night. It'll be easier if you get on with it right away." She glanced up at me once, then tipped her head away again. I tried to scratch the back of my knee without making it obvious. She'd known me since childhood but had never been able to look me in the eye. I took the paper and thanked her, then she scuttled away.

I sat down by the table gloomily. Most of the list seemed to involve me going to see people; there seemed to be little I could do online or even over the phone.

"Well, get on with it," Melissa said. Even as a spirit she was bossy.

"This is all your fault," I told her.

"Do you think I wanted to go?"

I shrugged.

"Well I didn't. I was relying on you going first and giving me a few years of peace."

I grinned. "Please stay," I said. But after that there was silence.

I am good at finding things out. It is the one thing I can do. Irene and Ken had provided telephone numbers but not addresses, so I worked systematically through the list, finding the addresses from my computer and then planning a route through town. When I had finished, before I could think too much about what I was doing, I grabbed my coat and dived out through the front door. My legs were still itching. The flaky white patches had spread over each leg up to the knee. I had thought about adding "doctor" to the list but in the end had written down "pharmacist" instead.

The day passed in a grey sort of haze; eyes stared briefly into mine and then dropped away. They didn't try to engage me in conversation, just gave me the information I required in clipped careful tones and then stood up so that I would stand too—and go. I looked forward to going back home where I could hide. The pharmacist took one look at the rash on my leg and refused to give me any medication. "I can't if I don't know what it is," he said. "You need to see the doctor."

"Just something for the itch," I pleaded. "It's driving me mad." It was too.

But he'd shaken his head. I hated him. Surely he could hear the desperation in my voice. "Please!" But the stubborn old head had shaken again. In the end I had bought some cream off the shelf of a supermarket, figuring it would be better than nothing.

It started to rain as soon as I stepped off the bus. It was as if the clouds were waiting for me to emerge so they could empty all they had on top of me. By the time I reached my front door I was saturated and shivering. Just as I reached into my pocket I remembered that I didn't have my key. Something inside me snapped. I swear I heard it. It was as clear as Melissa's sigh that came immediately afterwards: stupid, stupid boy. I sat on the doorstep, my head lowered in my hands so that no one could see my face. I was too old to be crying; too old to lock myself out; too old to be feeling quite so desperately alone. I should have other people in my life: a woman, maybe some children or at least work colleagues or a few friends I could rely on seeing in the pub. But I had no one. I had never had anyone except Melissa—Melissa who had scorned the colour of my eyes, but had put up with them, Melissa who had put up with me even though I stared at her, Melissa who had loved me in her own way.

I tried to think of what I could do, but everything I thought of seemed to involve talking to people, so I sat there awhile longer, scratching the length of my legs and then my arms, hoping that some other idea would come to me, but nothing did. The itching was spreading—up my legs and then slowly up to my waist. My forearms were also starting to itch and as soon as I had finished scratching one part another part immediately demanded attention.

"Robin?" It was a strange, rasping voice. I opened my eyes. Three pairs of feet in identical black lace-up shoes stood in a line in front of me. I looked up. The crows.

They didn't seem wet. In fact, as I looked I could see raindrops bouncing off them and then trickling down as if whatever they were wearing was made of something like polythene.

"Come," the shortest one said in a voice that seemed creakier than the others', and walked slowly down the path toward their own house. As soon as we opened the gate to the crows' house the rain stopped. I turned to go back to my own house but the tallest one took me by the arm and propelled me firmly forward. The shortest one led while the middle one took up the rear.

Inside the house only I dripped. The light came on automatically—a glow from some indiscernible place along the top of each wall.

"Come, sit." The small one gestured me forward.

"Where?" Each wall was lined with books, but apart from that the room seemed empty.

"Here," she said, and she sat. I waited for her to fall onto the ground but it didn't happen. The light was bad. There must have been a seat but I just couldn't see it. She settled back.

"Well?" The three crows looked at me expectantly. Then they faded away completely.

I was always inclined to faint at the slightest provocation—yet another thing that marked me out as different and strange—and I suppose I'd been through a lot. I woke feeling weak, and I noticed, as I moved my head gingerly from side to side, it was supported by a long sofa that had obviously caught me as I fell.

"What is this place?" I wanted to get up but my legs felt too heavy. So for a few minutes I lay quite rigid—my heart stampeding inside my chest—the only part of me that could move. All three crows hovered over me, twittering and cawing in some language that I couldn't understand. When at last I felt I could try to get up, the tallest one swooped forward and pushed me firmly down again.

"Wait." She sat down again by her two sisters opposite me. While they regarded me I scratched quietly, both arms then both legs and then a swipe across the base of my belly, and then my legs again. It did no good—scratching seemed to make the itching more demanding and more desperate. I dug my nails deeper and deeper, lifted my trousers and shirt to remove great sloughs that flaked into small white scabs. They littered the space around me like tree blossoms after a storm. I felt repulsive.

"How long have you been like this?" the one with glasses asked.

"Like what?" I snapped back. The itching did not improve my temper.

"Molting."

I looked up. "It's not molting," I said. "I've just got some sort of rash."

Even though I couldn't see her lips I am certain I could hear them smile. Her glasses shifted slightly. "Believe what you will, brother."

"I'm not your brother!" I stood up and glared at them all. The only sister I had ever had cackled softly in my ear. She was fading. I knew I was losing her.

"But we can help you, bro—" the tall one said, looking from one crow to the other. "Shall I?"

The other two shook their heads. "Let him go," said the short one. "He's not ready yet."

"I'll take him back," the tall one said, and led me out through the rain and to my doorstep. She paused by the door and stooped down, pressed the side of her head against the wood and poked something into the keyhole, listening and turning as though she were cracking a safe. Then she stepped back, nodding at me to try the door. Of course it opened. "Take this," she said, holding out a bottle. "One drop in the eye every night. It will help with the itching." The glass was garishly multicolored, with a matching stopper. I turned to thank her but she had gone. There was just the sound of the door shutting across the street and I realized that time had changed.

Time is always changing, I realize now. There is nothing constant or reliable about it at all. My few years of childhood, waiting for my parents to return, took as long as the decades that Melissa and I spent alone, and after she had died time changed again. It was erratic—long hours and then short days; times filled with activity that passed in an instant and then long evenings with no one to amuse but myself. For the first few days the neighbours visited briefly, then resorted to posting cards through my door and running away. I saw the crows only at a distance: a small black huddle getting on a bus, or the tall one on her own at the checkout of the supermarket. Even so I had the feeling they were watching me; as I passed their house I could feel their eyes and the faintest twitch of something moving where they had been.

I kept my head down and tried not to look at anyone. I suppose I should have been worrying about money, but Melissa and I had always kept our money at home, unimaginatively hidden under my mattress, and there seemed lots left for now. The itching was better. As long as I remembered to drop the crows' potion into my eyes every night. I still itched, and I was still losing my skin—all over my body except for my face—but it was not the frantic itching that it had been; and I could go for hours without scratching at all. This was a blessing, as I had to learn to shop—it was always something Melissa had insisted on doing by herself. I begged her spirit to come with me, but she faded before we reached the start of the store. So I shopped alone. I was like an explorer in a new exotic territory: everything confused me, every purchase required some decision—how much, what sort, what quality. I got a lot wrong—rice that congealed into a pudding when I wanted separate grains, cheese that was mild when I wanted strong and hard when I wanted soft, meat that was out of date by the time I came to cook it. I became slower, more careful, studying the labels, keeping my head down so that my eyes did not disturb anyone.

"Robin?"

I had been studying the coffee. I wanted it ground, not in beans, and not too dark. I looked up. It was Laura, Melissa's old colleague, her magnified eyes blinking behind her glasses. I smiled, remembered to blink, and then looked away again.

"Is it you?" She stepped closer, peering through her glasses to see me. "I thought so. How are things?"

When I didn't answer she crouched beside me and we looked at the shelves together. I had been there a full five minutes already, a long, slow five minutes, and was on the point of giving up. "What are you after? This is good," she added, not waiting for my answer. She pulled a packet from the shelf and put it in my basket, then stood up. "Why don't we try it out together?"

I blinked.

"Well what do you say?" she said briskly. "Dinner at your place, or are you too busy?"

I could tell by the way she wrinkled her nose that she could smell the milk souring in the fridge and the fruit rotting in the fruit bowl.

"Forgive me for being blunt, but it looks to me like you need help," Laura said, picking up potato peelings from the kitchen floor. She stopped and looked around her. "Look, maybe I can do something. I'll pop round every night after work. Would you like that? I can give you a to-do list, like Melissa did."

I opened my mouth. How did she know Melissa did that? They must have known each other more than I thought. "And in return you can do some jobs for me. Actually I could really do with an extra pair of hands at the moment. I'm redecorating."

We grew close. It was all her doing. Beneath her prim skirt and cardigans Laura was all woman and I, of course, was all man. She stroked and purred with expert precision until we were combining genetic material on a regular basis. Laura's eyesight was weak, I discovered, which was a godsend: she could see neither my disturbing eyes nor my skin and even missed the blossoming of fresh sloughs each morning on the white sheets.

As soon as Laura's decorating was finished she moved in with me. "Only sensible," she explained. "We can live on the rent of my flat." She had discovered the pile of cash underneath the mattress and it was getting no larger.

The crows did not approve. They were watching me quite openly now. Even Laura noticed them at their window or standing by their gate: motionless, silent, waiting for me to pass by.

"Why are they there?" she asked. "What are they doing? Is it some sort of sect?"

I didn't answer. There was no point. I didn't know. It was only when I reached the end of the phial of drops that I realized I would have to speak to them again. I put it off until the itching became unbearable and even Laura had started to notice my writhing.

The crows' door opened before I knocked. It was the tall one, who seemed to be younger than the rest. I tried to speak to her alone but she led me to the front room, where the two other crows were sitting.

"We can give you no more," the small one said, before I opened my mouth.

"But . . ."

"That's why you've come, is it not?"

"Yes, but why? I need some, please."

"We can ease it for only so long."

"Please, I can't stand it."

But they just shook their heads and looked at their hands.

Cruel. Mean. Unfeeling. I marched out of their house cursing them, and slammed their door. With my jaw clenched I marched to the doctor's office and stridently demanded immediate attention. There was, of course, an examination and a full barrage of tests.

"A type of eczema, that's all I can tell you. Until I get the results I can't be sure. In the meantime use this."

It was a cream that stung but did nothing to help the itching. By the following evening I was desperate. Laura looked on as I marched wildly around, scratching myself and demanding that she scratch me too.

"But your skin is coming away!"

"Carry on," I said through gritted teeth.

I had ants crawling over me with fast impatient feet. I scratched and the feet became faster. I scratched again and they stung with poisoned little needles. By now I was removing great welts of flesh with every scratch. Pain was beginning to replace the itchiness and I couldn't decide which I preferred.

"There's something underneath," Laura said. "I can feel it. You can only go so far and then there is something that doesn't come away like the rest. It's dark, purple, like new skin. Look."

I looked at my arm. She was right. It was strange I hadn't noticed it first. It was slightly shrivelled and looked wet, and it worried me. It was also worrying Laura. "What's happening?" she said. "I'm scared."

"I don't know."

"Maybe I should phone the hospital."

"No."

"But we have to do something."

"Leave me alone." I shook her off.

"What then?"

I didn't answer.

"Robin?"

"Stop nagging."

"I'm not. Please Robin, let me help. Let me phone someone."
Her voice was high, plaintive, and getting on my nerves.

"I'm going out," I said.

"Robin!"

She tried to grab my arm. It burnt where she touched.

"Leave me, for Chrissakes, leave me alone."

After I slammed the front door I paused—but there was only
one place to go.

The crows' house was in darkness and had an empty feel about
it—there was a complicated spider web stretching over half the
doorframe, and the wind had blown a dune of leaves and empty
candy wrappers against the door. Even though it had only been
a day since I'd last been to see them, it looked like no one had
been near the place for weeks. Time had changed again. I
knocked on the door miserably and without much hope—I felt
sure they must have moved or gone away—but it opened immediately. It was the tall crow, the one I thought of as younger than
the rest, but she looked different: her shoulders were hunched
like those of a vulture and even though she was still enveloped
from head to toe in thick black cloth I could tell she had lost
weight. Her gowns hung around her as if supported by a frame-
work of sticks.

She led me silently and slowly into the front room, where the
two other crows slumped in chairs.

"We can't give you any more," the one with glasses said quietly when I explained why I'd come. "It was the only bottle we had, and anyway it would be of no use. It's too late for that."

"What do you mean? How do you know?"

The older crow nodded to the tall one, who was still standing at the doorway. Taking her hood in both hands, the youngest crow threw back the hood and unclipped the cloth that was covering the rest of her face. She was maroon, bald, and had the same pale green eyes as me. We stared at each other for a full ten seconds without blinking. Then she undid something at her neck and the rest of the gown fell away. She was covered in a white sleeveless shift; her bare arms a mottled purple and red, with veins standing out in little tracks. She smiled and held out her arms. "Little brother," she said. "You see, we know exactly how you feel."

She beckoned me to her with the tips of her fingers, but I stood where I was and looked around me. The other two crows had thrown back their hoods as well. The small one's face was darker, with a drooping jowl, while the one with glasses had a face that was more square and pale, but we were all the same colour of plum and our eyes sparkled the same acid green.

"Who are you?" I said.

No one replied. When she saw that I was not going to go to her, the young one walked slowly to the wall and sat on nothing. I watched as a chair seemed to grow out from the wall to envelop her. I backed away. There was something wrong with me; I wasn't seeing straight. Walls do not make themselves into chairs. They don't flow and then solidify like jelly—and yet this one did. I touched something with the heel of my shoe and at once something enclosed me and pressed me down. I tried to get up but was pressed down more firmly. Another chair.

"Listen," said the short crow. "There is not much time."

.   .   .

They live in a land out of time, they told me, an island of sharp peaks separated from everywhere else not by sea but a greyness that is sometimes a little red like the sky. There are no other beings like them, and there have been exactly five thousand of them ever since the oldest one can remember, and that is a long time indeed. The deaths are infrequent but they do occur, and whether the death is caused by accident or disease, it is foretold seven months in advance by the arrival of an egg. The mother receives no clear warning of its arrival except for a little swelling in the abdomen the night before. The egg laying is painful and sudden and almost destroys the mother with the effort. From then on the egg is watched and the people watch themselves. Someone is about to die. They are wary of each other, especially kind to those who seem most vulnerable. It is a time of almost unbearable tension, and the first indication of fatal disease or injury is greeted with relief by almost everyone concerned. The dying one once identified is feted and then pampered. Prayers are said so that the sick one is assured of peace. This is what normally happens, but when Robin's egg was laid it was different. Robin's mother Elanoma had always been strange and willful. She had liked to go to the edge of the greyness where she could make out the voices from other worlds. She had been alone there when the egg had come. No one had heard her cry out at its painful passage from her body onto the ground, and then scream as the egg rolled off her world into the greyness beyond. Elanoma had watched as it had disappeared, gasped but then said nothing. She went back to the village and watched for someone to sicken but no one had. It was too much anxiety for someone to bear alone, but Elanoma told no one. She had become thin, ill-tempered, and then deranged, fit for nothing. From time to time she would wander around the settlement screaming and crying but no one knew what was wrong.

It was only when she fell one night that anyone suspected what had happened. The doctor examined her and it was clear that she had recently been delivered of an egg. They asked her what had happened to it, and when she didn't make sense, the island was meticulously searched. Meanwhile Elanoma sickened, and just before she died had an hour of serenity during which she was able to explain where her egg was gone. Of course someone had to go after it. With 4999 people instead of five thousand, life felt uneven and unbalanced. There were disturbances in the streets, fights among friends, and a strange persistent feeling of someone missing.

After a year of this, Elanoma's sisters decided that the only thing to do was to search for the egg again—or rather, what had been in the egg. They covered themselves and crept away in the night. It had been a long hard journey to the bottom of the chasm of greyness and then a run back up into the light of Robin's world. The run was crucial, and had taken them a long time to perfect: the speed, the number of paces, all was quite specific. But at last they had done it. They had entered Robin's world and smelt the air and knew they were only just in time. Robin was about to change and he would need help.

"It is what we all go through," the spectacled one said. "The change. It is the final phase, the final growth. Once adult, you have to become young again in order to grow old."

I shook my head in a futile effort to clear it. Nothing was making sense. I knew they were like me, that much was obvious, but the rest...

"Show him."

The young one got up and stepped forward. She took my arm and held it in her hand and then with the other hand caught hold of a piece of my skin and pulled sharply. The pain was only slightly worse than the stripping away of a well-adhered Band-Aid. She pulled again and again and then stepped back. I peered at my hand. All of the old skin had gone and what was left was smaller and pinker: the hand of a child.

"You have to become young again in order to grow old," the older one repeated. "It's what happens."

I examined my hand. It didn't seem like mine, but when I flexed my fingers they moved.

"You have to come with us. Quickly. We went through the change long ago. It makes us less adaptable and we cannot stay much longer in this world. Already we are becoming weak. We have to go while we still can, and you have to come with us."

"But I don't want to."

The crows looked at each other.

"Why?" said the old one sharply.

"Laura." I was finding it difficult to make sense.

"You have to leave her," the spectacled one snapped.

"I won't."

The three women spoke hurriedly together. Then the old one spoke again. "You have to come. You can't stay here and neither can we. This is not your land, not your time. You belong somewhere else, with us." She looked at me expectantly as if she thought I was going to change my mind, but I wasn't going to. Laura and I had plans.

"We have to take you back," the spectacled one said. "Without five thousand everything is wrong."

"I'm not coming."

They talked together again, their voices urgent, sharp, and agitated. Then the old one flopped back on her chair. "We have to go," she said. "Soon."

Now that the skin had come off my hand it was no longer itching. I started to pick at the skin on my other hand.

The spectacled one stood and examined her sister. Then she turned to look at me. "We will go now and you are coming too. No arguments. It is impossible for you to stay, whatever you think you want. Your world needs you and you need your world."

I sank back in my seat and it softened behind me. The old woman struggled from her chair and came towards me, her hand outstretched, her face set. I smiled. She was just an old woman. But then the two other women appeared beside her and together they seemed strong and determined. I shut my eyes.

"Come, child," the older one said. "Take my hand."

I knew where we were. Melissa had called it Robin's Nest; everyone else called it the Queenside Quarry. They had finished extracting years ago and had left everything as it was. The hole in the ground was enormous, big enough to comfortably hold a small village, and most days a mist collected in the bottom, making it seem even deeper than it was; a great hole without end. Whenever I had looked at it I had always felt something pulling at my insides, and now I knew why: beyond the greyness was the place that had been my home. The three crows stopped a couple of feet above where my parents had found my egg. There was a wide ledge leading down into the quarry at one side. It was like a roadway disappearing into the mist.

"Look," the spectacled one said.

There were footprints in the rock of the ledge. I'd heard about such things before—fossilized footprints of people who had lived long ago.

"We left them for ourselves," said the old one, and I wondered how long they had been in my world. "It is the only way back."

"It is important to match the pace," the spectacled one said. "One foot and then the other. Keep it fluent, fast."

"But I'm not going."

"You must. You must run with us, back into your own world."

"No," I said, and wrenched myself away. "This is my world now."

The spectacled one went to run after me but the older one stopped her.

"No," she said. "I'm too weak. If we don't go back now, we never shall. It will be better to be missing one rather than four."

"And maybe another egg will come," the young one said gently. The two older ones exchanged hopeful glances and then smiled at her.

"Perhaps."

"Yes, perhaps."

The young one ran to my side. She was gentler than the other two. She caught my hand in hers, and for a second it felt so comfortable there I didn't want to let her go, but I did.

"Watch carefully so you know what to do in case you change your mind."

Then the three of them left me; picked up their gowns to above their knees and ran, one after the other, their feet finding each footprint, faster and faster until, just before the mist, they disappeared. I followed slowly after them, down into the mist until I could see the bottom. It was empty. I tried calling out, but all I could think of calling was hello. I didn't even know their names.

By the time I reached home again the itching had eased. Skin was falling from me in great fleshy welts now and my arms and hands were the size of a child's. Laura inspected me silently, her lips pursed. "Does it hurt?" she asked at last.

I shook my head.

"Why don't you ask someone what's wrong?"

"I shall."

"When?"

But when I wouldn't say she banged down the dish she was drying and told me she'd had enough. She took her clothes into Melissa's old room and slept the night there. I could hear her sobbing in the early hours but I left her alone. I needed to think.

When I removed my pajamas in the morning a man-shaped piece of flesh came away too—every part of me: my legs, my chest, my face, and my hair, even my nails. Underneath the skin was like the skin on my hands had been yesterday—new, soft, and smooth. I touched myself in wonder, relieved that the itching had finally and completely gone. It took me a little more time to realize that the world around me was larger. I placed my new small foot in front of me and looked at it: I would need new shoes. Then, as I struggled to reach the handle of my wardrobe, I realized that I would probably need new clothes too. I grabbed at a shirt and pulled it down off its hanger towards me—it swamped me and the shirttails dragged on the floor. I shrugged it off, put on my dressing gown, opened the door and went into the kitchen to make myself some breakfast. Laura was in there already. When she saw me she opened her eyes wide and screamed.

"Laura?" I said and stopped. I had the high voice of a young child.

Laura stopped screaming and started breathing in small gasps. When I stepped forward she stepped backward, falling over a stool and then pressing herself against the housing of the sink.

"What are you?"

"Robin!" I squeaked.

"You can't be."

But I couldn't think of a way to prove it to her.

She swept wildly around the house looking for me, ignoring my assurances that I was in fact standing in front of her.

"What have you done with him?" she asked at last.

"Nothing, nothing, nothing. I'm here, woman, listen to me!"

She looked at me with her eyes narrowed.

"I'm Melissa's brother."

"How do I know that?"

"I pasted the Coeur de Lys wallpaper on upside down in your flat."

She sat down, finally convinced. Her hands were shaking. "What's happened?"

I could think of nothing else to tell her but the truth.

She looked at me with round eyes, panted slightly, and then burst into tears. Her glasses steamed up. I went over to her and patted her head with my child's hand but she brushed me away.

"Stop it, go away."

When I didn't go, she looked up. "I mean it," she said. "Go away."

So for a few hours I did. I found an old pair of shorts that were only a little too big, and borrowed a T-shirt and a pair of sandals from Laura's wardrobe. Then I walked up and down outside the house until I felt a strong sudden urge to investigate a small brook that ran alongside the edge of the park. When I returned to our house I was covered in mud—and Laura was packing.

"I don't understand what's happened—" She held up her hand when I started to explain. "And I don't want to understand. All I know is I can't live with a five-year-old stranger."

"But I'm your boyfriend!"

"Don't say that, it's sick."

"But I am!"

"Be quiet," she snapped. "I'm thinking."

I went to stand near her and realized with a start that they were my clothes she was packing. It was my house and she was throwing me out. I stepped backward. She looked so large. Her face was red, and she had taken her glasses off to polish them. Without them she looked different, slightly piglike. When she put them back on she looked at me with her nose wrinkled, glaring at me as if she didn't know me—and I realized then that we were strangers. She had never known me and I had never known her—and in fact I had never known anyone, not even Melissa. I was alone in this world and always would be. Something dropped away inside me and I remembered the young crow's hand. I wished I could feel it still. *Sister,* I thought, *my real sister.*

Laura sat still for a few moments staring at me, then suddenly got up, reached up to the hook on the wall for her keys, grabbed me by the arm, and marched me out to her car. "There's places for people like you," she said. "And they're nowhere near me."

After she had deposited me with a fat, kind woman at the social services department of the council she went on to the police station to report the fact that her boyfriend was missing. Of course I was never found—they were looking in the wrong place. Even though I protested in my highest, loudest voice that I was Robin Chandler, no one believed me.

So I had to go through childhood again. It was not pleasant the first time and it is even worse now. You have no voice and most of the time you are invisible. In the place where I live now there are ridiculous rules: I have to go to sleep while it is still light and when I ask for a little beer to help me sleep everyone laughs. I am expected to eat all the food—mainly slush—that is put in front of me and I am expected to listen quietly to every damn-fool thing everyone says to me. I am not allowed to tell them to go to hell and my access to anything of interest is curtailed. It took me less than a week to decide to run away but it is a month before I find the opportunity. Of course I know exactly where to go.

As I approach the quarry I find myself holding my breath: what if the footprints are gone? What if I can't find them? What if there are people around and I can't get near them? But the footprints are still there. I breathe in deeply and evenly. They are just like I remembered but filled in with a little water now because it has just been raining. The mist is higher up the side, it will only take a few paces before I am swallowed by it and that thought comforts me; maybe it will hasten my journey. I place one of my feet into the first footprint. Of course my foot is too small. I have to stretch my legs out as far as they will go in order to reach the next footprint with my other foot, and in doing so almost fall sideways. I give a little hop to steady myself, but then I have stepped out of the prints. I place my foot in the next footprint and almost fall again. They seem to be getting farther and farther apart. I stand and remember the youngest crow's words about the pace. Of course the footprints get farther and farther apart as the person that made them started to run. It is impossible.

As a child it is acceptable to cry. In fact it is expected.

"Hey!" There is a man in the distance with a dog.

I start to run, my feet hitting some footprints but missing the rest. The mist is closer now, swirling around, grey and then red. But my feet keep missing the footprints. Behind me the dog starts to bark, so I run a little faster. As if my life depends on it.

Semaphore

• • •

ALEX IRVINE

WHEN MY UNCLE MIKE died, at the ripe old age of ninety-seven, I had the belated realization that I had at some point come to believe him immortal. Of all the people I ever knew, Uncle Mike was the most able to laugh at death. I wonder if he lost his sense of humor and died of the loss.

Every boy at some point worships his father. Unlike them, I had twin idols: my brother Daniel and my uncle Mike. Because I worshipped the ground Uncle Mike walked on, I tried his gallows humor on for size; but because I acquired the habit during World War II, while the world stood around watching the extinction of our extended family and the rest of European Jewry, I found that my early efforts were a little tone-deaf. Like many eleven- or twelve-year-olds, I figured out how to be callous before I learned about reflection. This tendency, like a number of others more or less salutary, I absorbed from Daniel . . . but he has been gone long enough that I can no longer mourn him, and Uncle Mike's passing is fresh in my mind.

I'm an old man now, or at least the approach of my seventieth birthday makes me feel old, and like many old men I am trying to figure out why I was the kind of young man that I was. Trying to put in order my understanding of my previous self, as you put your worldly affairs in order when you realize that you're closer to death than birth. The answer has to do with Uncle Mike, but more importantly with my brother Daniel, who in February of 1942 shocked the entire family by not only entering the PS 319 spelling bee but winning it—and this as a fifteen-year-old eighth grader of no academic distinction whatsoever. Because he hadn't turned sixteen or started high school, he was going to be eligible for the national tournament if he got through the regional that spring. The mystification of the Rosenthal family of 327 South Fifth, Williamsburg, was complete. None of us even knew Daniel could spell. His grades had sure never given any sign, and I don't think I'd ever seen him read a book in his life. God is mysterious that way.

Daniel, I think, was just as surprised and discombobulated as the rest of us, and as it turned out, he had his own plan for avoiding the frightening possibility that he might be exposed as something other than a garden-variety South Williamsburg truant. He got someone to sign his papers—none of us ever figured out who—and he enlisted in the Army three days before regionals. His best friend, Howard Klinkowitz, who was a year older, joined with him. The Klinkowitzes had gotten out of Leipzig in 1936; Howard, who was born there, got the nickname Klinkojoke after telling Daniel that Witz meant joke in German, but the one time I called him that he hit me on the arm so hard I had a knot for a week. After basic, Daniel was assigned to the Signal Corps. Five months later, and a month after the remaining Rosenthal clan turned out to watch the battleship *Iowa* launch from the Navy Yard, he drowned when a U-boat sank his troop transport at the approach to the Straits of Gibraltar.

The word that won the spelling bee that summer was "sacrilegious."

God is mysterious that way.

I was four years younger than Daniel, and two years behind him in school. He was my only brother. The only way I can describe the effect of his death on my four sisters is by comparing it to what happens when you take a crayon and color something as rich and as deep as the paper will hold, then you take your fingernail and scratch away the thickness of the color. My sisters were thinned out somehow. They seemed less real. Same with my father, and all I can say about my mother is that she was always strong enough to keep herself together no matter what life threw at her. The Germans got him, she muttered under her breath. The Germans got him.

Me, I had never felt more real in my life. It sounds ghoulish now, but it didn't feel that way then. Something inside me was born, or came into itself, when Daniel died. And something else fell away, which in retrospect I can identify as belief. If before I had been religious in a diffuse, osmotic kind of way, after Daniel's death I balanced my psychological scales by telling God that if he was going to take my brother away from me, I was going to take myself away from him. Not that I could have articulated any of it at the time, and in the course of events I would partially reverse this decision, reopening a space in my mind for the idea of God without giving myself any responsibility for worship or real belief. Belief—real belief—came later, with the ability to reflect. Reflection: from the Latin for "bending back." I indulge in puns once in a while, now that I'm too old for anyone to complain about it, and I can say without the least irony that I bent over backwards to avoid reflection through the awful years of the war.

I told my sister Miriam once—she was closest to me in age, so became my sibling confidant after Daniel died—about how strangely alive I felt even though I spent most of my days with my mind split on parallel tracks of grief and anger. This would have been just before Halloween in 1942, while we were all still stumbling around in shock. Miriam looked at me and said, "It's a dybbuk. It's Daniel's dybbuk."

Which it wasn't, but that was the kind of superficial explanation we were all grasping for. Miriam perhaps more than most; a dreamy girl, she reeled away from the news of Daniel's death, beginning a long descent into loony mysticism which culminated in her turning into a kind of den mother for a group of beatnik poets and jazz musicians holed up on Minetta Lane in the Village, and then dying of drugs and cancer and heartbreak in 1960. The world was full of dybbuks to her, with all of these boys leaving New York, so many of them returning as names spoken in regretful voices, wails that riffled the laundry strung out the back windows of Williamsburg.

The conversation spooked me, even though I didn't believe in dybbuks. Or God, really. Especially once I started to dream about Daniel. *There's no such thing as dybbuks, you dumb shit,* he said.

Well, I thought to myself in the dream, *you would know.*

Yeah, he said. *I would.* Then he said, *Yoo-hoo will help.*
What?

I woke up. The hordes in the basement were already crashing around. Children hollered, adults hollered back. I think they were speaking Polish, but I heard words I recognized as Yiddish too. It was barely dawn. I cursed all immigrants, especially those that crammed into the basement below our garden-level apartment. It was a cave down there, and now it was a cave bursting with haunted-looking people who didn't speak English and served for my parents as object lessons in why my sisters and I should feel fortunate. Occasionally this worked for a minute, but not when it was the crack of dawn and I'd just been rousted from uneasy sleep. Bad enough that my brother was dead and Hitler was taking over the world; why should I have to be woken up by screaming foreigners?

Simplicity, like I said. In retrospect it seems glib to the point of sacrilege, but in the midst of heavy emotional aftershocks, you (by which I mean me) boil things down into primary colors and the most selfish emotions. So I got out of bed, even before my father and mother had stirred in the big front bedroom and long before any of my sisters had cracked an eye in the little back room next to the kitchen, where they were compensated for the cramped arrangement by at least having a view of the garden. I slept in the room between, on the couch. It was Daniel's bed; before he left, I had been relegated to a pile of blankets on the floor. I thought of him every morning when I woke up, because the broken-down couch cushions seemed molded to his long, rawboned frame; I began every day conscious of the ways in which he was larger than I was, and of the way in which I had begun to struggle with the size and shape of his absence.

Grasping at the fading memory of the dream, I thought: *Yoo-hoo?*

That afternoon—it was a Wednesday, I remember, I think

sometime in November—I scraped up a nickel and bought myself a Yoo-hoo. Daniel was right. It did help. I was cutting school that day, rationalizing the act as a small homage to my brother, and with my bottle of Yoo-hoo I walked brazenly up Keap within a block of PS 319 and jumped the turnstile onto the Fourteenth Street-Canarsie Line, headed for Manhattan. In the tunnel under the river, I became suddenly conscious of the water over my head, and I started to think of Daniel. *Full fathom five my brother lies, those are pearls that were his eyes* ... I started to cry, and just like that the Yoo-hoo wasn't helping anymore. I got up and shoved my way out of the car to stand on the coupling until the train clacked into Union Square and I'd gotten myself under control again.

Had Daniel died quickly? My imagination boomed with the impact of the torpedo, the rolling wall of fire engulfing the passages belowdecks. I saw pieces of steel curling and tumbling through the gradations of light below the surface, finally lost in the pelagic darkness—and wondered if pieces of my brother Daniel might have danced among those fragments of his ship, until they came to rest together on the seafloor. Epipelagic, mesopelagic, bathypelagic, abyssopelagic, hadopelagic. Already I was absorbing words, letting them pour into me as if Daniel's death had ruptured me and a sea of language was drawing me into its depths. Walking past the few lonely theatergoers, I knew what I would do.

Or had he survived the initial impact, and felt the ship tilt, spilling him out of his bunk onto the angled steel floor? When the lights went out, had he known how to get out? After fire, water—had Daniel spent his last moments clawing at the ceiling of the ship's hold, looking for the hatch he knew must be there while around him the transport groaned and boomed its way down? I closed my eyes, to feel the darkness of drowning. I imagined that Daniel had somehow survived until the ship had come to rest on the ocean floor, and that he had had time to write a letter in the blackness, with the water slowly leaking past the stressed rivets to rise icily over his feet. At last the room, filled with water, would have been completely silent, with the letter he had written drifting loosely away from his lifeless fingers, the slow action of the water loosing graphite from paper until his last thoughts were diffused into the cold and dark.

Dear Josh, Daniel is reading in my dream. The paper crinkles in his hands, and I don't look at his face. *Stop being such a shithead. I am dead. It doesn't matter how.*

Drip, drip, drip, of seawater from the paper. It crinkles anyway. I smell mud.

Danny, I start to say.

Cut it out, he says. *Listen. You want to do something? Fine. Quit with the torpedo and the ship and fire and smoke. How many times are you gonna play that little movie in your head? Enough already. So you got an imagination, that's great, but use it. Or don't, but anyway quit.*

What do you want me to do?

You're already doing it, he says. *I mean,* abyssopelagic?

And I woke to the uproar of the refugees in the basement. Refugee: from the French *réfugier,* to take shelter or protect, first used in reference to the Huguenots; all the way back to the Latin *refugium,* and all the way back before that to that long-lost moment when all of the little phonemes and graphemes came gasping and creeping up onto the beach of language, leaving behind them the undifferentiated ocean of sound. *This is what you did to me, Danny,* I thought.

At breakfast I started spelling words out loud. My sisters got into it. They collected newspapers and hit me with whatever they could find, and then it turned into a game they played among themselves. Each of them focused on words that began with the same letter as their first names: Miriam, Eva, Ruth, Deborah. After a month of this I was convinced that I knew every word in the language that began with those four letters. Mnemonic, elegiac, rotisserie, diverticulitis. Malevolent, esoterica, rubicon, demesne. And I think I knew every word in the language that began with a combination of those letters. Dermatology? Forget it. I give you dermanyssidae, which is a family of mites that infest birds and lizards and whatever else. I think my favorite of all of them was merdivorous, which means exactly what you think it might. Synonym coprophagous. A merdivorous grin.

My sisters knew what I was doing. So did my parents. None of them stopped me. I think they figured this was my way of working out Danny's death, and they liked the way I was serious about something. Before this I'd been flighty, accidentally good at school but never dedicated to it—nor to anything else, for that matter. Like a lot of children of immigrants, I reacted to their resolve and perseverance by becoming indifferent to everything except the Dodgers ... and, in my case, spelling.

So they quietly encouraged my newfound interest in spelling, recognizing it for the homage it was. Mom did have a tendency to stiffen and get quiet when I started spouting off Anglo-Saxon roots during one of my etymology binges. They sounded too much like German to her. She saw the effect the whole game had on my sisters, though, who started to seem more substantial again, their colors more vibrant, as they came home from the library with new words to challenge me. They asked doctors and lawyers, people whose lives revolved around jargon, for new ones. I soaked them all up, a glutton for words to fill the space left by Danny's loss.

At the same time, I was spooked by my own obsession. Miriam's dybbuk comment rang around in my head. If the dybbuk took over someone close to it to complete an unfinished task, didn't it make a certain kind of sense that Danny would come for me? Was that why I was dreaming of him?

I told you there's no such thing as dybbuks, he's saying to me in a dream. We're sitting next to each other, about to parachute out of a C-47 that's bucking and shuddering from flak. I think my dreaming mind has borrowed the scene from a movie, but the thought is stripped away like the streaming silk canopies opening below the plane and then ripped away out of sight.

Maybe you're just telling me that so I don't know you're one, I say.

It's his turn to jump. He cracks a smile at me over his shoulder. *You have weird hang-ups,* he says. Then he's gone.

Waking up, my first thought was that I'd never heard anyone say hang-up like that before.

It didn't stop there. Didn't stop anywhere, really, even though as the war dragged on and the news out of Europe mounted to a pitch of awful horror that penetrated even my self-obsession, I learned to stop talking about it all the time. The lesson came at the breakfast table late in 1943. The Fifth Army was in Italy, the U-boats that had murdered my brother were vanishing from the Atlantic, and Hitler was beginning to pay the price for his dream of conquering Russia. Guadalcanal and Midway had cut the Japanese down to size. The war was turning.

My father built pianos. Well, he did until Pearl Harbor. Then Steinway and Sons, like every other manufacturer in the country, tried to figure out some way to make itself useful to the war effort. After backing-and-forthing with the War Production Board, Steinway settled on parts for the CG-4A glider, which was basically a vehicle for controlled crash landings. It didn't have to fly; it just had to fall from a C-47 tow plane to earth without killing the pilot and wrecking whatever it was carrying.

It wasn't easy, that's for sure. There's a famous story about how Henry Ford tried to get into armaments production during the First World War, and found out that although he knew just about everything there was to know about making cars, that didn't mean he had the first clue about how to make boats. By World War II, Ford had the war-matériel game figured out— they turned out a pile of CG-4A's—but Steinway sure didn't. They cut and recut, jiggered processes around, held the Army's blueprints at various angles... and still the glider wings came out wrong.

Until one day my dad lost his temper on the factory floor. I imagine him there, surrounded by jigsaws and racks of tools, ankle-deep in sawdust and hemmed in by the suits demanding to know why the company who made the greatest pianos in the world couldn't make something as simple as a wing for a glider that was only designed to crash.

"You leave me alone for a day," my dad said—he said a lot of other things, but I'm giving you the story as I got it, in its bowd-lerized (from Thomas Bowdler, nineteenth-century English physi-cian who published a kids' version of Shakespeare without all of the dirty jokes and gore) version—"You leave me alone for a day, and I'll figure it out."

They did, and he did, and Steinway made glider wings. The company also turned a nice dime by painting a bunch of unsold uprights olive drab and selling those to the Army as "Victory Verticals," but my dad didn't have anything to do with that, ex-cept indirectly, and that part of the story comes later.

The reason I bring up his job is that he used to come home from work, and with help from my uncle Mike, read the letters we got from relatives in Europe. By 1943 we all knew what was going on. There had even been demonstrations in New York; that spring our whole family went and stood outside Madison Square Garden while inside various luminaries demanded that the government do something about what the newspapers were delicately calling the "plight of the European Jew." Not that any of us thought the demonstration would do any good. The way my mordant Uncle Mike put it, "We demonstrated in 1933, when the Nazis were just burning books, and look where that got us. Now they're burning us."

In 1933 I was two years old. For some reason Uncle Mike's comment got to me. I felt for weeks afterward that I was a creature of futility, doomed to merely witness.

Anyway, in 1943 some letters were still getting out. For some reason the Nazis were more likely to let letters through if they were written in German—for that matter, Jews who spoke German were marginally more likely to get on protection lists and survive in the camps—so our cousins in Poland and Czechoslovakia wrote us in German. They got letters—don't ask me how—to another cousin in Russia, or sometimes a former business associate who fled to Sweden, and the letters got passed on, eventually, to us. My parents got some of it because they spoke Yiddish, but my Yiddish vocabulary was restricted to insults and endearments, so I waited for Uncle Mike to pause and catch me up via extempore—and, I'm sure, idiosyncratic— translations. (Idiosyncratic, from the Greek *idios* and *synkrasis,* "one's own mixture." Extempore is even better: from the Latin that means "out of time." What did you do to me, Danny?)

What I tried to do was pick out words that were interesting, or that I didn't know, or that I knew something about but not enough. Reflexively I would try to spell them, or test them against my embryonic knowledge of etymology. This time what happened was a little different. The letter mentioned Auschwitz, and I thought Klinkojoke. My mouth opened and, louder than I meant to, I said to Uncle Mike, "In German Witz means joke."

Of course I shouldn't have said it. Not then and there. But it was one of those moments when you suddenly discover that you're attuned to something that you find irresistibly adult—the small, gruesome ironies of language—and Uncle Mike had the blackest sense of humor of anyone I've ever known. And that little coincidence in the Germanization of Oświęcim (not so unlike the Germanization of Kalienkowicze to Klinkowitz) was the kind of cruel witticism the Nazis would have appreciated, or for all I knew did appreciate. In the same vein as *Arbeit Macht Frei*. Or the "model ghetto" at Terezin. I meant it to be a sort of letter of introduction into the mysterious and seductive adult sphere of world-weariness and caustic humor.

Silence fell at the table. Uncle Mike put down his fork, and in a gesture for which I have always been grateful, tried to save me from my own idiot flippancy.

"That's America," he said with a chuckle. "Education, education, education."

"You ought to be ashamed of yourself," my mother said, with a coldness in her voice that I'd never heard before. "The Germans killed your brother. They're killing every Jew in Europe. And you joke about it. You spell." She twisted the last word, making it sound filthy somehow, as if spelling was something you did to little kids when nobody was looking.

"*Zol zein,*" Uncle Mike said quietly. "He's just a boy, Sarah." He folded the letter up and handed it back to my father. I learned to stop talking about spelling after that.

My sisters left me alone, too, so my spelling mania became a solitary preoccupation. I struck a balance in my head, learning to live with the sense of triviality that came from obsessing over words while my people were being erased from the earth.

Danny got it, at least.

You're on a roll, kiddo, he says to me that night. We're walking along a beach. This was fall of 1943, so I'm guessing the beach was somewhere in Italy, although it could have been Wake or Bougainville. I followed the war in Europe more closely, though, for obvious reasons, so I'm guessing it was Italy. Salerno, probably.

Sesquipedalian, he says to me. I spell it.

See? he says.

Screw you, I say. We walk along the beach a little farther. Artillery rumbles over the horizon. Soldiers climb out of the ground and run backwards into the ocean. A B-24 rises up in flaming pieces from the ocean and eats its own trail of smoke on its way back up into the sky.

Seriously, Danny says. *You're a hell of a lot better at this than I was.*

Sesquipedalian's easy, I say. *Spelled just like it sounds. Nothing tricky about it.*

Danny's laughing. I smell saltwater, and I notice his uniform is wet.

It was true, though. Compare sesquipedalian with the winning word in 1942, sacrilegious. I knew that one, too, but it has that tricky transposition of the I and the E. Like sacristy, not like sacred, which is what you would expect.

Winter came. The refugees in the basement stole our coal and erupted in furious arguments before sunrise. I learned words. My bar mitzvah came in January, and suddenly because I went to synagogue and read a blessing, I was supposed to follow the Commandments. I couldn't make anything make any sense because I was an obsessive with no possibility of putting my obsession to use. I was running out of eligibility, too. Age wasn't going to be a problem, at least not unless the war lasted a lot longer than people were saying it would; but I was due to finish eighth grade in June of 1944, and unless there was a regional that year, I would never get a chance to compete. This possibility ate at me, kept me up at night, had me devouring newspapers and radio broadcasts and movie newsreels for hints that the end was coming.

Do we need to apologize for the fact that as children we fail at things that no child should be expected to do? Perhaps in extraordinary times we do. Looking back—now that I've had fifty years to learn reflection—I can tell you that what I really wanted was my family safe. I wanted no more Judenfrei, no more letters that had to travel ten thousand miles to get from Poland to

Brooklyn, if they got there at all. No more lists of the dead, and rumors of the missing. No more pale sisters silent in their room. No more mother bursting out in rage-fueled accusations that I wasn't good enough, wasn't serious enough, wasn't Jewish enough.

And the spelling bee started to stand in for all of that for me. Maybe it's superficial, or cowardly, but I couldn't handle it. I think I came to feel that the only way for me to survive it was to strip myself of whatever parts of my identity left me vulnerable to the horror of it all, and substitute the endless gluttony for syllables that got me up in the morning and lulled me to sleep at night while the adults conferred in the kitchen over school, work, the war, the Shoah.

Which nobody was yet calling the Holocaust, at least not with a capital H. (Holocaust: from the Greek *holokaustos*, "burnt whole." Word used by Greek translators of the Torah for burnt offerings to God; there's irony for you.)

"He turns to words," I heard Uncle Mike say to my mother one night in the kitchen, when they thought I was asleep. "What could be more Jewish than that?"

God is mysterious that way.

I decided to fail the eighth grade. By the spring of 1944 it was clear that there would be no spelling bee that year, and although I was failing at so much else I would not fail the memory of my brother—even if not failing meant I had to fail.

So I quit doing homework, and started cutting school almost every day. It was late enough in the school year that I had to work pretty hard at being held back, since my grades from earlier in the year were pretty good, but I was counting on the establishment of a downward trend to make up for that.

The truant officer came to our house three times. My mother slapped my face. My father, skinny with sorrow and overtime, shook his head in weary disgust. On Passover, my sisters, taking a break from helping my mother cook for the seder, huddled like a flock of birds and sent Miriam over to make overtures. "We know what you're doing," she said. "Daniel wouldn't have wanted you to."

"Maybe I'll ask him," I said, cruelly, and she went back to her flock of four.

I do ask him, while we're walking through the pulverized rubble of some European city that night. Fires smolder in the ruins. Danny, me, and a couple of stray dogs. Aircraft engines thrum overhead, but the sky is a featureless black.

So am I wrong, Danny?

What do I know, he says. *I'm just a dybbuk.*

What you are is fish food, I say. In waking life, he is the only thing I can't be flip about. Here it's different.

Not even that anymore, he says.

What were you doing when it happened? I ask him.

He looks me in the eye. *It?*

When you got killed, I say. *When the torpedo hit.*

Signaling, he says, and pantomimes a semaphore. I don't catch the letters. *Telling the ship behind us that one of our engines was acting up and we could only make eight knots.*

He sees the question in my eyes and goes on. *Yeah,* he says. *I was on deck, astern over the engine room. The fish hit us square under my feet, bounced me into the drink. Then the water coming in through the hole sucked me right along with it.*

His retelling is pitiless, and makes me ashamed of the movies I played in my head. Still I want him to answer my first question, but I can't ask it again.

Never was a very good swimmer, Danny says. *But it doesn't matter.*

I can feel onrushing wakefulness, like the Dopplering sound of a train whistle. Then he's crying, my dead not-dybbuk fish-food maybe-ghost of a brother. *Yesterday Howard went home,* he says.

. . .

Morning brought news that it was true. Klinkojoke had died when the B-24 on which he was a nose gunner got shot up over Bad Voslau, Austria, and crashed in the English Channel on the way back. Deborah, Ruth, and Eva cried for a week (Eva from the great distance of Morningside Heights because she'd gotten a scholarship to go to Barnard and was living in a dormitory there). They'd loved Klinkojoke, and Miriam cried because they did. I was so scared because of what Danny had told me that I had to scare somebody else, so I told Miriam.

"Danny told me about it last night," I said. We were out in the backyard garden, which was one of the few good things about having a ground-floor apartment. The air was cool, and beyond the concrete patio the whole yard was turned up and cordoned off into a victory garden. "He also told me how he died."

She'd been suffering a recurrent sniffle over Klinkojoke, but it stopped and she got absolutely still. "That's not funny, Josh."

"Remember what I told you right after he died? It's been happening ever since."

Miriam got up from the bench where we were sitting and went back inside. We never talked about Danny again. I always felt that what happened to her after the war was my fault, and that if it hadn't started when Danny died, it started that April Sunday morning, just after Passover, on the patio next to the stakes and strings and shoots of the victory garden. But I don't know how I could have done it any different.

In June—the day after the Allies landed at Normandy—my parents were notified that I would be required to repeat the eighth grade unless I completed summer school. My father took me aside, and we both understood that he was doing me a favor by relieving my mother of the duty. "You're thirteen years old, Joshua," he said, "and for twelve of those years you've been the smart one of my boys. Now I want you to tell me, man to man. Are you doing this because you got the idea that you need to be more like your brother now that he's dead?"

This was the longest speech I'd ever heard my father give, and it took me a minute to recover my surly equanimity. "What if I am?" I asked him.

"Then I'll get you on at Steinway," he said without missing a beat. "If you're just going to clown around at school, you might as well get the hell out of it and make some use of yourself."

For as long as I've been alive since then, I've been trying to figure out if there was something I expected less than that. I thought about it.

"Can I work for the summer and then go back?"

My father laughed. "That's exactly what Mike said you would say. Okay. That's what we'll do."

And we did. I got on the train with my father every morning that summer, while the Allied pincer tightened on Germany and the Marines ground their way toward Japan. My job was to tape the keyboards and pedals of old unsalable Steinway uprights so they could be spray-painted Army green. Victory Verticals. I taped them, they went in for spraying, the paint dried, I peeled the tape. Then came the best part of my job, which was stenciling PROPERTY OF THE US ARMY on the back of every one. At the end of every day I rode the subway home with my dad; he complained about the lousy quality of the wood they were getting for the glider wings, and I picked white paint out from under my fingernails. I never did ask him how he got me the job. The wartime economy had the country as close to full employment as it ever got, but it's my guess that plenty of grown men—or women—would have taken the job I had as a thirteen-year-old kid. I imagine a conversation in which my father, covered with grease and sawdust from the factory floor, goes to Mr. Steinway and explains the situation, whereupon Mr. Steinway does a favor for the guy who finally got the wing design right. It's the only time in my life I indulged in a little nepotism (from the Latin *nepos*, "nephew"; originally the favors bestowed by a pope on his illegitimate children). Something about the daily physical work, the routine of getting up early and working had an effect on my dreams. I didn't talk to Danny all summer, even in July when Majdanek became the first concentration camp to be liberated and all of our worst suspicions began to be confirmed.

Maybe that was coincidence, but I don't think so, since Danny was there again as soon as I decided to go back to school in the fall.

It's raining like hell, and we're dangling our legs off one of the tracks of a burned-out Panzer tank. *You think it's going to be over this year?* I ask him.

How should I know? Danny says. *You going to pass your classes this year?*

The truth is, I don't know. I've got one extra year to play with age-wise, and by the time another year has gone by, I'm going to know every word in the English language. I'll be invincible. Is that worth deliberately failing another year of school? I'm inclined to think it might be.

I don't know, Danny says. *How much longer do you think you can ride this grieving-for-your-brother horse?*

Shithead, I say. *I'm not grieving for you anymore. You won't leave me alone long enough.*

What are you talking about? I left you alone all summer.

And now you're back.

You're not answering my question.

I still don't answer him. After a while he shakes his head. *Your heart won't heal,* he says.

*   *   *

It was such a strange thing for my wiseass brother to say that I walked around for days thinking about it. Then the days stretched into weeks, and I was treading water in school, unable to concentrate on anything—even learning new words—because something about Danny's words was like a fishhook in my brain. Ambivalence was everywhere: I was passing school but barely, the Reds turned Majdanek into a brand-new concentration camp for Polish resistance fighters, Miriam had come to life but only because she was dating a boy my parents didn't like. Her dreaminess had somehow hardened into rebellion while none of us were looking.

I went to school long enough to finish an algebra test and keep my head above water, then lit out and just walked around the neighborhood. I walked down across Broadway, underneath the elevated tracks. Briefly I thought about stealing a car even though I had no idea how—or that maybe I could just get on the train, switch to another train, get on a bus at Penn Station and disappear. Except I didn't have any money. It was January. I was about to turn fourteen. Winter rain was dripping through the elevated tracks.

Something made me turn and walk east on Broadway. A train thundered by overhead, and as I looked up through the slatted trackbed to follow its passage, I saw a sign. FUGACCI AND SONS, TAILORS. Each of the initial letters, even the A, was bigger than the others, and red while the others were black. An acrostic: FAST.

Then came one of those moments where everything that has been a mystery makes sense, and as it does you condemn yourself for an idiot because you didn't figure it out before. For so long I should have known, but at last I put it all together.

Yoo-hoo will help. You have weird hang-ups. Yesterday Howard went home.

Your heart won't heal.

YHWH.

All along, he'd been saying God. God. God. God.

Some kind of animal sound came out of me, drowned out by

the train passing overhead. "Ah, Danny," I sobbed. "Why didn't you just tell me?"

I felt something break, physically break, inside me, and I leaned against one of the I beams holding up the elevated tracks and wept for my brother. That was why I had dreamed, why he had spoken to me, why—God's will being God's will—he had died in the vortex of ocean water near the Straits of Gibraltar. There is no greater pain than complete acceptance of a truth you wish was a lie. I fought it, but that's not a fight you can win.

New Yorkers being New Yorkers, people left me alone, and I felt it all leaking away, the resentment and obsession and the paralyzing sense of impotent witness drowned beneath the iron and the rivets and the indifference of the train. It ended right there in the rain, this grief-stricken rebellion against my patrimony. Because that's what it was, what I can call it after fifty years of bending back.

I went back to school, but not that day. Instead I went home, and found my mother listening to Walter Winchell on the radio. Winchell was talking about the liberation of Auschwitz.

Seven months later, it was all over. My eligibility for the spelling bee ran out in June, with an invasion of Japan looming. Then came Hiroshima and Nagasaki, and ticker-tape parades, and the counting of the dead. My older sisters Ruth and Deborah went to college like they were supposed to, Ruth to Michigan and Deborah following Eva to Barnard. I never talked to Danny again. But when a kid named John McKinney from Des Moines, Iowa, won the spelling bee the next summer, that jubilant postwar summer of 1946, I felt like the winning word was a last word from my brother, and I made a little room for belief.

Semaphore.

God is mysterious that way.

The Smaragdine Knot

• • •

MARLY YOUMANS

Infinity, when all things it beheld
In Nothing, and of Nothing all did build,
Upon what Base was fixt the Lath, wherein
He turn'd this Globe, and riggalld it so trim?

...

Who Lac'de and Fillitted the earth so fine,
With Rivers like green Ribbons Smaragdine?
Who made the Sea's its Selvedge, and its locks
Like a Quilt Ball within a Silver Box?

—EDWARD TAYLOR,
from *God's Determinations*

I'M A CHILD of the Puritans, though my forebears would cast me from the golden rows of the Elect, as surely as the Angel barred Adam and Eve from the garden. But I take an interest in the "sad" colors, the hymnodies that scared the wolves, the hunkered children—as numb in their cloaks as stumps by a frozen church. Foremost of my kin who crossed a sea of mermaids to the New

108

World was a certain minister, scholar, and poet. Centuries after his death, the leather-bound book wherein he had buried his poems was unearthed in the Yale Library. Championed by the Anglophile banker-poet, T. S. Eliot, his sermons and poems are still read.

What hasn't been known is that he kept a history of his forays into other realms. He was an adept of Puritan meditation techniques meant to restore the bridge between mortals and God. A session began with an elaborate calling-up of tangible place—the drawing room of Hell with its gilt-framed mirrors, the sogged landscape of straw outside his door, a countinghouse where a clerk tallied the gold coins called *angels*. The more solid the imagining, the greater the chance that drops from the fount of God could fly past the stars until a seeker found himself in a waterfall of Spirit. Following prescribed steps, he might commune with men, God, or angels, his soul aroused, and be floated toward new resolution by streams of love and desire and that cataract, joy.

He used no magic; being in strong communion with the next world, what was shadow to other Puritan divines eventually became living presence to him. Neighbors spied lights streaking through the house, and one Goodman Brewster testified that he had glimpsed an angel, eyed like a peacock, at the minister's deathbed—the visitor stirring the fire on the hearth with bright hands.

The journal was inscribed with the title, *The Smaragdine Knot*. In childhood, I was enraptured by the mystical, fierce, and passionate accounts. A year back, I felt a blow to my sense of family because of this book.

"I'd like to borrow the *Knot*," I told my great-uncle Samuel, a long-retired professor of Renaissance history. He has been steward of the book so long that we've forgotten when it passed from great-great-great-great-aunt Tabitha.

"Gone," he groaned, slapping the arms of his chair with both hands.

"What do you mean—where?"

"I don't know, Simon. Your uncle Saffin borrowed it. Your niece Amy peeped into the thing and left it on the playroom floor. Ann had a go at it, leaving the book on the porch, to be plucked up by my brother."

"So what happened?"

Great-uncle Samuel shook his head. "Chauncy was feckless from the cradle. The mallow! The downright squash! Who knows? A major family treasure, and he 'can't recall.' You can shake the old dodderer and hear the seeds rattle. I'd like to boot him in the backside." He crooked a finger and scratched at the dottle in his pipe.

"You'll get burned."

"No chance." When Sam leaned to inspect his handiwork in the light from the window, his rumpled white hair blazed in an aureole. "I'm as tough as cuticle."

He rapped the pipe on the arm of his chair until crumbs sprang from the bowl. My aunts try to sweep Sam's messes and trim the whiskers fountaining from his ears. I say, "Don't bother—wait till he's dead," but they don't listen to nephews.

"What can we do?"

"Do? Just don't tell the Neddie club, or there'll be a hell's own tithe to pay."

"*Is* there such a thing?"

"Sure. Bunch of Neddie scholars." Decades ago Sam had decided that calling him *Neddie* would lift the curse of excess gravity from our ancestor.

"You could record the bits you remember."

"Wouldn't have Ned's way of lathing a phrase. 'Baroque wilderness': that's what the critics call his style."

"I'll bet you know some by heart—"

"Not a bad idea. But it'll crop up in some half-witted place. Ann will dredge it from a hamper, Saffin will find it wedged in a golf bag—or perhaps Chauncy will prove thief."

"Is that possible?"

"Hasn't got either the brains or the snap. I'd respect him more if he'd hightailed it to Timbuktu after flogging the book at the pawn shop."

"They wouldn't know what to make of it. Weird name, *smaragdine*."

Great-uncle Samuel was hacking at his pipe with a pickle fork, and I recalled that my aunt Bideth had been on a wild hunt for just such an essential item, the handle chased with flowers.

"From the Greek, a highly respectable polysyllabic. Smaragdines are in Burton, Scott, Thackeray—scads of others. Everybody likes an emerald. I'm fond of a seventeenth-century description: 'an excellent fresh green, far passing any leaf.'"

"So it's an *emerald* knot."

"That *fool*, Chauncy!" Sam jabbed vigorously with the pickle fork.

"Why? Why an emerald knot, I mean."

"Linked to God's promises and the tribe of Judah. And Bacon talks about the *Tabula Smaragdina,* the emerald tablet of Hermes Trismegistus. Alchemical revelation by a learned Rosy Crucian and all that."

"Yeats. Madame Blavatsky," I offered. The names marked the outer limits of my feeble knowledge about the Rosy Cross, acquired in college.

Samuel shot me a glance I took to be cautiously approving. "At least I have one relation who hasn't been claimed by the powers of ignorance."

I nodded; then, recalling that he detested nodders above all species of the male kind, massaged the nape of my neck to suggest that I had merely been stretching a few crabbed vertebrae.

"Stupid to have research and no book," he continued. "I hadn't wanted to risk making a xerox. Now eight-year-old Andrew says he could've photographed and stored copies of the whole she-bang. Precocious brat." Sam rummaged in his rolltop desk and dragged out a folder. He went right to the page he wanted. "Here.

Wycliffe gave a line in *The Revelation of St. John* as 'The reynbowe was in the cumpas of the seete, lijk the siyt of smaragdyn.' Slightly screwed up—translated from the Latin, but the *Vulgate* had poorly rendered the line from Greek."

"An emerald rainbow around the throne of God," I said, guessing.

"Torsell says if a viper sees a smaragdine, her eyes melt: *her* eyes, mind you. Medievals thought birds put emeralds in nests as amulets. Listen to this: "beare the stone Smaragdus with the Griphon against Serpents." Great-uncle Samuel shrugged. "I've found a few screwball sources that refer to a smaragdine mirror. This fellow Bailey claims that it's the chief toy of angels."

I caught myself in a nod and jerked upright. "Do you remember the title meditation—the one about the knot?"

"I could tell you," he said. "If I felt like it. If, say, somebody fixed me a whiskey, nice and neat."

"You ought to drink beer, like the Puritans," I said.

"That was mostly funerals. They didn't mind the odd drunken tumble into a grave."

I fetched the whiskey, and when Great-uncle Samuel sloshed it back with a will, I poured him another and sat down to take notes. He was to show me a good deal of favor that afternoon, and, in doing so, allowed *The Smaragdine Knot* to overshadow my life in ways that I am only now beginning to penetrate.

The minister began his meditation late in the evening, after the children were in bed. It was cold, bitterly cold. He huddled on a stool by the hearth with a bed rug over his nightclothes. As he grew warmer, he attempted to look past the fire, though it was now well kindled and flickering with a lovely persimmon color.

Twig by twig, stone by stone, he built a scene in fancy until a garden spread before him, its sculpted boxwoods swooping into love-knots. He could see each leaf standing separately, burnished by the light. The walkways of slate were bedded on crushed limestone and crossed one another at right angles. Lovingly he traced the outline of the paths, touching the moss and the many clustered stems of a grove of filberts. Beyond the knot garden lay a regular apothecary's shop of blooming herbs, hedged in by pickets. Past the last fence lay fields with grain yielding to the wind.

He paused, caught by the gold sprouting from the leaden ground. It was an alchemical change, the puckered seed soaking up water and bursting its withered coat. Easy as ribbon unreeling through fingers, the allegory flashed through his mind: the philosopher's stone, distilling, transformation, the trying of ore, alloy and purification, the minting of angels—their gold faces radiant inside the stiff halo of the coin.

"Eden park," he said aloud, though he was not sure what or where his meditation had built. Was it the earthly paradise or a plat in heaven, or even the garden of his friend Richard Baxter? He had never met the Englishman except in letters always out of date. A greeting from such a sender might arrive from one already dead! Just such a garden of love-knots and herbs and pickets, with a farm of barley and millet beyond, Baxter had once described.

"Richard?" He felt hesitant; had he spoiled the meditation by beginning without a sufficient purpose in his mind?

A fragrant breeze lifted a tendril of hair from his cheek.

The pollarded willow at the center of a knot of shrubbery abruptly burst forth with new branches, and to the clergyman's surprise, sprang into blossom. In the midst of this froth of sun and hum of bees, a figure appeared. Glowing white, its beams began to fade as flowers dropped and stems started to bear fruit.

"What bough of wonders is this?" Tears moistened his eyes.

The angel—for so he appeared to be—stepped to the ground, and the radiance around the body resolved into wings. The willow also leafed out in feathers, its burgeoning foliage soft and wispy and utterly unlike the earthly trees Ned knew.

He, being of a poetical cast of mind, cried out, "Make me a golden trumpet on which to tootle thy praise!"

The light-minded angel laughed at these words, the trailing, willowlike branches of the wings trembling with enjoyment.

"You may keep your happy blasts to yourself, thank you kindly," he said.

"I didn't mean to summon—but here you are, a messenger of the Lord." Ned marveled at his own fortune. Never had he, in sweet meditation, seen an angel—though once his little son had spied one, when the sky was bright yet checkered by clouds.

The angel nodded in agreement. "A messenger. Just so."

Last petals from the tree twinkled to the moss, where they went on fluttering weakly as if they might gather themselves for a fresh flight.

Though the minister waited in anticipation, he received only a smile. "You have a message for me?"

The angel nodded again but offered nothing more than a cascade of merry laughter. Ned was surprised that no greeting of "Fear not!"—always the prelude to some fearful thing—appeared to be forthcoming. But surely it was enough to be in the presence of such a creature. A ring of the pale yellow butterflies called *sulphurs* fluttered around the floating hair before wobbling toward a patch of barley.

"And how shall I address you?"

"I shall call you Neddie," the angel said; "you may call me . . . Astariel. That is one of my names, suitable for human use."

"And a very pretty one." The minister did not like the name Neddie. He was also unaccustomed to the paying of compliments and did so awkwardly, with a small, stiff bow.

" 'My Lord Astariel' would be proper form."

"Ah," the minister said, growing uncomfortable.

"Perhaps you would like to worship me." The angel smiled, the barest hint of slyness serving as a veil to his sunny features.

"Worship? Would you test me? It's forbidden for mortals to worship powers such as thrones and principalities and archangels, cherubim, and seraphim."

Astariel appeared nettled by these words; or, at least, the flakes of stars that fell from his snowy wings and set the nearest boxwoods on fire might have seemed to suggest it. He made as though to return to his bower in the willow tree.

"Do not leave! I beg you not to—"

As the angel swept toward him, the great cloud of feathers swirled. The flow of warmth from the beating wings fanned the original flames, and now all the boxwoods were beginning to burn. Even the field of grain was tasseled in fire.

"You are nothing but a tiny pipkin to my Caesarian oil jar! What's an emmet to an emperor, or a mote to a monarch?" Astariel stamped a foot as white and heavy as that of a marble Roman.

Ned's gaze had been fixed with fascination on the opaline features and the mane of feathers that had bristled with the first sign of indignation. At last he noticed that the boxwoods were dying, their glossy leaves crumbling to the ground, every bit of stalk and twig flying away as glowing atoms.

"The world is being hacked so small," he cried out, frightened that what he had dreamed into place would dissolve and leave him who knows where. "It will be shredded and lost."

The nimbus of hair around the angel's head was now incandescent wire, and the vanes of feathers showed luminous against a growing darkness. He laughed once more, and the minister wondered at such changeable moods.

"You are not what you seemed—I thought that immortal sunshine had blinked into my mind, but now fear that I—"

Astariel finished the sentence. "Have been blinded by a hoodwink jerked over your eyes? Is that it, mortal man? I made this place, not you." As he gestured, the last of the scorched trunks of boxwoods crumbled, while what was left of the barley and millet dissolved into flecks and was blown into the sky, where it gyred like a dust devil.

"No angel ever created anything—you've thieved what's

mine, what I dreamed into a new pattern out of the treasure house of creation."

The words stilled the angel's feathers and the ash floating overhead. Emboldened, the minister struck out again.

"You're a fallen angel, one of the accursed: you've given up beauty and are a demon! You're like a gold-washed coin—inside you're only worthless brass!"

"Careful what you say, Neddie. Haven't I whisked by your windows and heard you at your prayers, crooked up tight in the chimney corner? I've heard you call yourself a lump of loathsomeness, a stall rich-hung with Satan's knicknacks, a shattered squitchen. And am I not to be called 'golden,' not 'beautiful'? You have the pertness to call me 'worthless brass'? I call that an almighty *cheek*."

The demon angel was taller than before, and his hair had lengthened and floated wildly about his head, echoing the turbulence of wings that now resembled a maelstrom of feathers. Ned looked about for assistance. The garden was crisped, the boxwoods were anthills of dust, and the whole landscape had gone strangely black, aside from a few pinpricks of stars.

"If only the true angels would hold up the blessed mirror of smaragdine that the devil fears—if only I had some weapon." He whirled about, finding no help, no splendor bursting from a surface of polished stone.

"Perhaps," Astariel mused, "you are looking for love-knots to pelt at me, or for that unfortunate shade of brilliant green that so annoyed me in the boxwoods. It's true that we demons are irritated by love-knots. Don't like love, for that matter. Nor the color you call smaragdine, and especially the gem. That's why I had to harvest the shrubbery, you see. It was a mistake, letting you think up that garden—I could've lured you into meditation on the third-best parlor of Hell, cozy and snug. I don't mind telling you, Neddie, because you like to study things, don't you? And this is almost the last you will learn. Because now I'm afraid that I will have to whisk you off to my nest, where I shall strip the living flesh from your bones and savor, sip by sip, the refined taste of your soul."

Wordless, the minister poet stared, his visions of the marvelous world to come dwindling fast. He felt light-headed, as though he might be about to dissolve into specks, as the love-knots of boxwood had done.

The demon stirred the ashes with his big toe. "I'm afraid there will be nothing at all left of you for Paradise."

Ned stepped backward. Sweat had soaked his skin, and his eyes stung from the smoke. He forgot how to pray.

"Scurry, my little man." The voice was pleasant and light. "You won't get far, but you can scuttle like a mouse until I snatch you by the neck."

And so Neddie ran, his legs churning across the burned-over ground. It was hard to see. At home, he never budged from his door once lamps were lit, not unless he was fetched by a man with a lantern to attend a deathbed. The village was plunged into a sack of darkness, and only the blaze of stars and an occasional glimmer at a window were to be seen. Fearsome creatures and painted men roamed the wilderness at night; they all knew it. He longed to be fast in bed, the shucks rustling as he turned to embrace his wife. She was pregnant again, her belly as round and firm as an unripe fruit. What would she do without him? He remembered his little son, tossing a ball painted green and blue in the garden and crying when the toy was lost—vanished, perhaps seized by the sky. The surface of the ground sucked at his feet, as though smeared with honey and molasses: a snare to trap him. His mind likewise slipped and couldn't hold a thought— he feared that the demon was exerting its powers, no doubt expecting him to conjure a picture of home.

Casting a rearward glance, he saw the fallen angel beginning to rouse. There was a fabulous, sleepy slowness and power about his thighs that struck Ned as utterly inhuman. Flashes of fire disclosed a nightjar reeling about his head. The wings seemed monstrous tangles of feathered serpents.

"Watch out, Neddie!" The warning might have been in the voice of a townsman, calling out as the minister stepped too close to the river by the water meadows.

"Ah!" He threw himself to the brink. For land had abruptly ended, plunging into the gulf of space. He closed his eyes against its relentless black, concentrating on green images—his mind roving from the mirror of the angels to love-knots and back again. But when he opened his eyes, no shining smaragdine glass or knot of ribbons had appeared. But there was something he hadn't seen before.

Far off, a blue and green ball hung like an earring against the cheek of night. It blurred, dissolved into his tears. Who would have thought that a simple meditation could have carried him so far from Earth? The demon had snatched his dream and set it here. He had been distant in other meditations—he had wandered through the shattered temple at Jerusalem, had seen bulls dragging a cart loaded with the horned creature called *rhinoceros* toward the even more monstrous hills of Rome, had hidden from lions in an artificial forest erected in the Coliseum—but never had he thought to soar to such an unearthly height as this. Again he recalled the boy with hands up and ball spinning against a backdrop of dark trees.

"My sweet child," he whispered.

He couldn't stop staring at the faraway planet, and his tears were mixed with a piercing recognition of the beauty of creation. The poet in him knelt before the altar of space and time, on which lay the round wafer of the world. A fuse of joy ignited and sparkled in his heart, as if to explode him to atoms.

The demon's feet shook the expanse of destroyed garden and scattered the ashes. The minister did not look but stared on and on at the precious sphere of Earth until he felt the warmth of breath at his nape.

Springing up, he flung out his arm.

"Behold the globe," he cried. "Behold the shining toy of angels! Behold the hand-mirror of sea and lake and flood—the footstool of God! Behold the smaragdine pebble brightening the nest of night!"

Astariel emitted a thunderclap of anger, his cumulus of feathers darkening and curling close to his body.

"Behold," the minister shouted, extending his palm so that the earth appeared to be a marble barely floating above his hand, "behold the philosopher's stone and alchemy of wonders that transforms all things of brass to gold! Behold the one true love-knot of the world, tied with ribbons of smaragdine!"

With a lightning cry of rage that made the jots of air quiver, the damned angel toppled from the edge and spiraled into the dark.

The unfortunate Ned was left perched on a plot of soil hijacked by a demon, and in only a few moments it began to crumble and sift into the sheer fall of space, so that soon he was pinwheeling downward, the little marble of a planet seeming to swell and move swiftly toward him—until with an immense thud, he landed on his backside on the hearthrug, now smoldering with sparks from a fire that was roaring up the chimney.

"And that's the gist of it," Great-uncle Samuel pronounced, once more quarrying in his pipe with Aunt Bideth's missing pickle fork. "I might've changed a bit, where I couldn't remember."

"That's—"

"Astonishing," Sam suggested.

"Ye-es, it certainly is that," I said.

"Neddie mourned that he had nothing but a titmouse's quill for a pen. I suppose he wanted an eagle or an angel's feather. But he didn't write too badly with it. Used the universe for his inkstand." My uncle jammed the stem between his teeth and began the interminable stagy business of an old man lighting a pipe.

"Want help with that match?"

He ignored me. "Old Neddie was a lively sort of fellow. Lots of flourish. Not to mention a formidable pack of offspring."

"Good thing for us," I said.

"He thought that souls were sin's bowling ground—seems about right." The ice cubes clinked as Sam held out his glass for more.

"You don't believe the rest of it, though."

"Maybe I do. What would we call his ramblings—astral projection, time travel? I've never had a whit of trouble believing in outlandish things. Maybe that's why I had a certain amount of difficulty believing in myself, once upon a time. I wasn't strange enough by half. Yet when I was a boy, I was asked to believe in marvels on an almost daily basis. As I've grown older, the world has dwindled and grown mundane. What the average child is asked to believe these days is far too dull and small." Great-uncle Sam inspected his pipe. "But in my extreme old age, I find that I'm growing quite, quite fabulous. I might as well be from another world. Soon I'll be as weird as a dodo, and after that I plan to go extinct. The rest of you descendants of Neddie will be left with Chauncy for your entertainment." The way he snorted indicated that this was a sorry lookout for us all.

It wasn't like Sam to talk about going extinct. He might have been a whiskery geezer of ninety-three, but he was a whiskery geezer with plenty of vim. I wondered if the loss of *The Smaragdine Knot* was a weightier blow than I had reckoned.

"I'm going to scour this house for the book and be the one to find it." I thumped the bottle down.

"Good for you," he said, "but you'll have to have dealings with that shriveled infant, Chauncy."

He tapped the stem of his pipe against his teeth.

"Tell you what. I'll make you the next G. H. K. of the *Knot* if you find it before anyone else. I was considering Saffin, but a younger person would be better, somebody with at least a good seventy years ahead. We're a long-lived bunch, and getting longer all the time."

I wasn't sure whether to be grateful or not. Seventy seemed a considerable swath of years. "Grand High Keeper is a big job," I said.

"Of course it is. Changes the keeper to suit itself. What else could appointment as steward of *The Smaragdine Knot* do? You hold the globe in the palm of your hand. The world in a nutshell bed, as Neddie would say. The mirror of angels, the love-knot of God."

I scrutinized him, but I couldn't tell—was he dead serious or pulling my leg? He puffed steadily on his pipe, obscuring the air between us.

"Thanks."

"No problem, young Simon. It'll be good for you to have the responsibility. Simon the Keeper-to-be. Nice ring to it, don't you think? So now, since you've got some serious questing about to do, why don't you just leave your ancient relic of an uncle to his dodo-bird meditations?"

"Yes, sir," I said. "I'll get started." But I just sat staring at him, wondering what he'd just done to me—and what exactly he'd meant by his "meditations." Nothing came to mind except the uninvited image of a boy tossing a green and blue ball in a snowy garden, against a background of dark trees.

When Sam cracked open an eyelid, I glimpsed an arc of pale green iris. "Simon, Grand High Keeper of *The Smaragdine Knot,*" he said slowly, as if savoring the syllables. "Be sure to start with that fool Chauncy."

A Portrait in Ivory

• • •

AN ELRIC STORY BY MICHAEL MOORCOCK

I

An Encounter with a Lady

ELRIC, WHO HAD SLEPT WELL and revived himself with fresh-brewed herbs, was in improved humour as he mixed honey and water into his cup of green breakfast wine. Typically, his night had been filled with distressing dreams, but any observer would see only a tall, insouciant "silverskin" with high cheekbones, slightly sloping eyes and tapering ears, revealing nothing of his inner thoughts.

He had found a quiet hostelry away from the noisy centre of Séred-Öma, this city of tall palms. Here, merchants from all over the Young Kingdoms gathered to trade their goods in return for the region's most valuable produce. This was not the dates or livestock on which Séred-Öma's original wealth had been founded, but the extraordinary creations of artists famed everywhere in the lands bordering the Sighing Desert. Their carvings, especially of animals and human portraits, were coveted by kings and princes. It was the reputation of these works of art which brought the crimson-eyed albino out of his way to see them for himself. Even in Melniboné, where barbarian art for the most part was regarded with distaste, the sculptors of Séred-Öma had been admired.

Though Elric had left the scabbarded runesword and black armour of his new calling in his chamber and wore the simple chequered clothing of a regional traveller, his fellow guests tended to keep a certain distance from him. Those who had heard little of Melniboné's fall had celebrated the Bright Empire's destruction with great glee until the implications of that sudden defeat were understood. Certainly, Melniboné no longer controlled the world's trade and could no longer demand ransom from the Young Kingdoms, but the world was these days in confusion as upstart nations vied to seize the power for themselves. And meanwhile, Melnibonéan mercenaries found employment in the armies of rival countries. Without being certain of his identity, they could tell at once that Elric was one of those misplaced unhuman warriors, infamous for their cold good manners and edgy pride.

Rather than find themselves in a quarrel with him, the customers of The Rolling Pig kept their distance. The haughty albino too seemed indisposed to open a conversation. Instead, he sat at his corner table staring into his morning wine, brooding on what could not be forgotten. His history was written on handsome features which would have been youthful were it not for his thoughts. He reflected on an unsettled past and an uneasy future. Even had someone dared approach him, however sympathetically, to ask what concerned him, he would have answered lightly and coldly, for, save in his nightmares, he refused to confront most of those concerns. Thus, he did not look up when a woman, wearing the conical russet hat and dark veil of her caste, approached him through the crowd of busy dealers.

"Sir?" Her voice was a dying melody. "Master Melnibonéan, could you tolerate my presence at your table?" Falling rose petals, sweet and brittle from the sun.

"Lady," said Elric, in the courteous tone his people reserved for their own highborn kin, "I am at my breakfast. But I will gladly order more wine . . ."

"Thank you, sir. I did not come here to share your hospitality. I came to ask a favour." Behind the veil her eyes were grey-green. Her skin had the golden bloom of the Na'äne, who had once ruled here and were said to be a race as ancient as Elric's own. "A favour you have every reason to refuse."

The albino was almost amused, perhaps because, as he looked into her eyes, he detected beauty behind the veil, an unexpected intelligence he had not encountered since he had left Immryr's burning ruins behind him. How he had longed to hear the swift wit of his own people, the eloquent argument, the careless insults. All that and more had been denied him for too long. To himself he had become sluggish, almost as dull as the conniving princelings and self-important merchants to whom he sold his sword. Now, there was something in the music of her speech, something in the lilt of irony colouring each phrase she uttered, that spoke to his own sleeping intellect. "You know me too well, lady. Clearly, my fate is in your hands, for you're able to anticipate my every attitude and response. I have good reason not to grant you a favour, yet you still come to ask one, so either you are prescient or I am already your servant."

"I would serve you, sir," she said gently. Her half-hidden lips curved in a narrow smile. She shrugged. "And, in so doing, serve myself."

"I thought my curiosity atrophied," he answered. "My imagination a petrified knot. Here you pick at threads to bring it back to life. This loosening is unlikely to be pleasant. Should I fear you?" He lifted a dented pewter cup to his lips and tasted the remains of his wine. "You are a witch, perhaps? Do you seek to revive the dead? I am not sure. . . ."

"I am not sure, either," she told him. "Will you trust me enough to come with me to my house?"

"I regret, madam, I am only lately bereaved—"

"I'm no sensation-seeker, sir, but an honest woman with an honest ambition. I do not tempt you with the pleasures of the flesh, but of the soul. Something which might engage you for a while, even ease your mind a little. I can more readily convince you of this if you come to my house. I live there alone, save for servants. You may bring your sword, if you wish. Indeed, if you have fellows, bring them also. Thus I offer you every advantage."

The albino rose slowly from his bench and placed the empty cup carefully on the well-worn wood. His own smile reflected hers. He bowed. "Lead on, madam." And he followed her through a crowd which parted like corn before the reaper, leaving a momentary silence behind him.

II
The Material

SHE HAD BROUGHT him to the depth of the city's oldest quarter, where artists of every skill, she told him, were licensed to work unhindered by landlord or—save in the gravest cases—the law. This ancient sanctuary was created by time-honoured tradition and the granting of certain guarantees by the clerics whose great university had once been the centre of the settlement. These guarantees had been strengthened during the reign of the great King Alo'ofd, an accomplished player of the nine-stringed *murmerlan,* who loved all the arts and struggled with a desire to throw off the burdens of his office and become a musician. King Alo'ofd's decrees had been law for the past millennium and his successors had never dared challenge them.

"Thus, this quarter harbours not only artists of great talent," she told him, "but many who have only the minimum of talent. Enough to allow them to live according to our ancient freedoms. Sadly, sir, there is as much forgery practised here, of every kind, as there is originality."

"Yours is not the only such quarter." He spoke absently, his eyes inspecting the colourful paintings, sculptures, and manuscripts displayed on every side. They were of varied quality, but only a few showed genuine inspiration and beauty. Yet the accomplishment was generally higher than Elric had usually observed in the Young Kingdoms. "Even in Melniboné we had these districts. Two of my cousins, for instance, were calligraphers. Another composed for the flute."

"I have heard of Melnibonéan arts," she said. "But we are too distant from your island home to have seen many examples. There are stories, of course." She smiled. "Some of them are decidedly sinister. . . ."

"Oh, they are doubtless true. We had no trouble if audiences, for instance, died for an artist's work. Many great composers would experiment, for instance, with the human voice." His eyes again clouded, remembering not a crime but his lost passion.

It seemed she misinterpreted him. "I feel for you, sir. I am not one of those who celebrated the fall of the Dreaming City."

"You could not know its influence, so far away," he murmured, picking up a remarkable little pot and studying its design. "But those who were our neighbours were glad to see us humiliated. I do not blame them. Our time was over." His expression was again one of cultivated insouciance. She turned her own gaze towards a house which leaned like an amiable drunkard on the buttressed walls of two neighbours, giving the impression that if it fell, then all would fall together. The house was of wood and sandy brick, of many floors, each at an angle to the rest, covered by a waved roof.

"This is the residence," she told him, "where my forefathers and myself have lived and worked. It is the House of the Th'ee and I am Rai-u Th'ee, last of my line. It is my ambition to leave a single great work of art behind, carved in a material which has been in our possession for centuries, yet until now always considered too valuable to use. It is a rare material, at least to us, and possessed of a number of qualities, some of which our ancestors only hinted at."

"My curiosity grows," said Elric, though now he found him-self wishing that he had accepted her offer and brought his sword. "What is this material?"

"It is a kind of ivory," she said, leading him into the ram-shackle house which, for all its age and decrepitude, had clearly once been rich. Even the wall hangings, now in rags, revealed traces of their former quality. There were paintings from floor to ceiling which, Elric knew, would have commanded magnificent prices at any market. The furniture was carved by genuine artists and showed the passing of a hundred fashions, from the plain, somewhat austere style of the city's secular period, to the ornate enrichments of her pagan age. Some were inset with jew-els, as were the many mirrors, framed with exquisite and elabo-rate ornament. Elric was surprised, given what she had told him of the quarter, that the House of Th'ee had never been robbed.

Apparently reading his thoughts, she said, "This place has been afforded certain protections down the years." She led him into a tall studio, lit by a single, unpapered window through which a great deal of light entered, illuminating the scrolls and boxed books lining the walls. Crowded on tables and shelves stood sculptures in every conceivable material. They were in bone and granite and hardwood and limestone. They were in clay and bronze, in iron and sea green basalt. Bright, glinting whites, deep, swirling blacks. Colours of every possible shade from dark-est blue to the lightest pinks and yellows. There was gold, silver, and delicate porphyry. There were heads and torsos and reclin-ing figures, beasts of every kind, some believed extinct. There were representations of the Lords and Ladies of Chaos and of Law, every supernatural aristocrat who had ever ruled in heaven, hell, or limbo. Elementals. Animal-bodied men, birds in flight, leaping deer, men and women at rest, historical subjects, group subjects, and half-finished subjects which hinted at something still to be discovered in the stone. They were the work of genius, decided the albino, and his respect for this bold woman grew.

"Yes." Again she anticipated a question, speaking with firm

pride. "They are all mine. I love to work. Many of these are taken from life."

He thought it impolitic to ask which.

"But you will note," she added, "that I have never had the pleasure of sculpting the head of a Melnibonéan. This could be my only opportunity."

"Ah," he began regretfully, but with great grace she silenced him, drawing him to a table on which sat a tall, shrouded object. She took away the cloth. "This is the material we have owned down the generations but for which we had never yet found an appropriate subject."

He recognised the material. He reached to run his hand over its warm smoothness. He had seen more than one of these in the old caves of the Ph'oorn, to whom his folk were related. He had seen them in living creatures who even now slept in Melniboné, wearied by their work of destruction, their old master made an exile, with no one to care for them save a few mad old men who knew how to do nothing else.

"Yes," she whispered, "it is what you know it is. It cost my forefathers a great fortune for, as you can imagine, your folk were not readily forthcoming with such things. It was smuggled from Melniboné and traded through many nations before it reached us, some two and a half centuries ago."

Elric found himself almost singing to the thing as he caressed it. He felt a mixture of nostalgia and deep sadness.

"It is dragon ivory, of course." Her hand joined his on the hard, brilliant surface of the great curved tusk. Few Ph'oorn had owned such fangs. Only the greatest of the patriarchs, legendary creatures of astonishing ferocity and wisdom, who had come from their old world to this, following their kin, the humanlike folk of Melniboné. The Ph'oorn, too, had not been native to this world, but had fled another. They, too, had always been alien and cruel, impossibly beautiful, impossibly strange. Elric felt kinship even now for this piece of bone. It was perhaps all that remained of the first generation to settle on this plane.

"It is a holy thing." His voice was growing cold again. Inexplicable pain forced him to withdraw from her. "It is my own kin. Blood for blood, the Ph'oorn and the folk of Melniboné are one. It was our power. It was our strength. It was our continuity. This is ancestral bone. Stolen bone. It would be sacrilege..."

"No, Prince Elric, in my hands it would be a unification. A resolution. A completion. You know why I have brought you here."

"Yes." His hand fell to his side. He swayed, as if faint. He felt a need for the herbs he carried with him. "But it is still sacrilege."

"Not if I am the one to give it life." Her veil was drawn back now and he saw how impossibly young she was, what beauty she had: a beauty mirrored in all the things she had carved and moulded. Her desire was, he was sure, an honest one. Two very different emotions warred within him. Part of him felt she was right, that she could unite the two kinsfolk in a single image and bring honour to all his ancestors, a kind of resolution to their mutual history. Part of him feared what she might create. In honouring his past, would she be destroying the future? Then some fundamental part of him made him gather himself up and turn to her. She gasped at what she saw burning in those terrible, ruby eyes.

"Life?"

"Yes," she said. "A new life honouring the old. Will you sit for me?" She, too, was caught up in his mood, for she, too, was endangering everything she valued, possibly her own soul, to make what might be her very last great work. "Will you allow me to create your memorial? Will you help me redeem that destruction whose burden is so heavy upon you? A symbol for everything that was Melniboné?"

He let go of his caution but felt no responsive glee. The fire dulled in his eyes. His mask returned. "I will need you to help me brew certain herbs, madam. They will sustain me while I sit for you."

Her step was light as she led him into a room where she had

lit a stove and on which water already boiled, but his own face still resembled the stone of her carvings. His gaze was turned inward; his eyes alternately flared and faded like a dying candle. His chest moved with deep, almost dying breaths as he gave himself up to her art.

III
The Sitting

HOW MANY HOURS did he sit, still and silent in the chair? At one point she remarked on the fact that he scarcely moved. He said that he had developed the habit over several hundred years, and when she voiced surprise, permitted himself a smile. "You have not heard of Melniboné's dream couches? They are doubtless destroyed with the rest. It is how we learn so much when young. The couches let us dream for a year, even centuries, while the time passing for those awake was but minutes. I appear to you as a relatively young man, lady. But actually I have lived for centuries. It took me that time to pursue my dream quests, which in turn taught me my craft and prepared me for . . ." And then he stopped speaking, his pale lids falling over his troubled, unlikely eyes.

She drew breath, as if to ask a further question, then thought better of it. She brewed him cup after cup of invigorating herbs and continued to work, her delicate chisels fashioning an extraordinary likeness. She had genius in her hands. Every line of the albino's head was rapidly reproduced. And Elric, almost dreaming again, stared into the middle distance. His thoughts were far away and in the past, where he had left the corpse of his beloved Cymoril to burn on the pyre he had made of his own ancient home, the great and beautiful Imrryr, the Dreaming City, the dreamer's city. Many had considered Imrryr indestructible, had believed it to be more conjuring than reality, created by the Melnibonéan sorcerer kings into a delicate reality, whose towers, so tall they disappeared amongst clouds, were actually the result of supernatural will rather than the creation of architects and masons.

Yet Elric had proven such theories false when Melniboné burned. Now all knew him for a traitor and none trusted him, even those whose ambition he had served. They said he was twice a traitor, once to his own folk, second to those he had led on the raid which had razed Imrryr and upon whom he had turned. But in his own mind he was thrice a traitor, for he had slain his beloved Cymoril, beautiful sister of cousin Yyrkoon, who had tricked Elric into killing her with that terrible black blade whose energy both sustained and drained him.

It was for Cymoril, more than Imrryr, that Elric mourned. But he showed none of this to the world and never spoke of it. Only in his dreams, those terrible, troubled dreams, did he see her again, which is why he almost always slept alone and presented a carefully cultivated air of insouciance to the world at large.

Had he agreed to the sculptress's request because she reminded him of his cousin?

Hour upon tireless hour she worked with her exquisitely made instruments until at last she had finished. She sighed and it seemed her breath was a gentle witch-wind, filling the head with vitality. She turned the sculpture for his inspection.

It was as if he stared into a mirror. For a moment he thought he saw movement in the bust, as if his own essence had been absorbed by it. Save for the blank eyes, the carving might have been himself. Even the hair had been carved to add to the portrait's lifelike qualities.

She looked to him for his approval and received the faintest of smiles. "You have made the likeness of a monster," he murmured. "I congratulate you. Now history will know the face of the man they call Elric Kinslayer."

"Ah," she said, "you curse yourself too much, my lord. Do you look into the face of one who bears a guilt-weighted conscience?"

And of course, he did. She had captured exactly that quality of melancholy and self-hatred behind the mask of insouciance which characterized the albino in repose.

"Whoever looks on this will not say you were careless of your crimes." Her voice was so soft it was almost a whisper now.

At this he rose suddenly, putting down his cup. "I need no sentimental forgiveness," he said coldly. "There is no forgiveness, no understanding, of that crime. History will be right to curse me for a coward, a traitor, a killer of women and of his own blood. You have done well, madam, to brew me those herbs, for I now feel strong enough to put all this and your city behind me!"

She watched him leave, walking a little unsteadily like a man carrying a heavy burden, through the busy night, back to the inn where he had left his sword and armour. She knew that by morning he would be gone, riding out of Séred-Öma, never to return. Her hands caressed the likeness she had made, the blind, staring eyes, the mouth which was set in a grimace of self-mocking carelessness.

And she knew he would always wonder, even as he put a thousand leagues between them, if he had not left at least a little of his yearning, desperate soul behind him.

The Cambist and Lord Iron: A Fairy Tale of Economics

● ● ●

DANIEL ABRAHAM

FOR AS MANY YEARS as anyone in the city could remember, Olaf Neddelsohn had been the cambist of the Magdalen Gate postal authority. Every morning, he could be seen making the trek from his rooms in the boardinghouse on State Street, down past the street vendors with their apples and cheese and into the bowels of the underground railway, only to emerge at the station across the wide boulevard from Magdalen Gate. Some mornings he would pause at the tobacconist's or the newsstand before entering the hallowed hall of the postal authority, but seven o'clock found him without fail at the ticker tape checking for the most recent exchange rates. At half past, he was invariably updating the slate board with a bit of chalk. And with the last chime of eight o'clock, he would nod his respect to his small portrait of His Majesty, King Walther IV, pull open the shutters, and greet whichever traveler had need of him.

From that moment until the lunch hour and again from one o'clock until six, Olaf lived and breathed the exchange of foreign currencies. Under his practiced hands, dollars became pounds sterling; rubles became marks; pesos, kroner; yen, francs. Whatever exotic combination was called for, Olaf arranged with a smile, a kind word, and a question about the countries which minted the currencies he passed under the barred window. Over years, he had built nations in his mind; continents. Every country that existed, he could name, along with its particular flavor of money, its great sights and monuments, its national cuisine.

At the deep brass call of the closing gong, he pulled the shutters closed again. From six until seven o'clock, he reconciled the books, filled out his reports, wiped his slate board clean with a wet rag, made certain he had chalk for the next day, paid his respects to the portrait of the king, and then went back to his boarding room. Some nights he made beans on the hotplate in his room. Others, he would join the other boarders for Mrs. Wells's somewhat dubious roasts. Afterward, he would take a short constitutional walk, read to himself from the men's adventure books that were his great vice, and put out the light. On Saturdays, he would visit the zoo or the fourth-rate gentleman's club that he could afford. On Sundays, he attended church.

He had a reputation as a man of few needs, tepid passions, and great kindness. The romantic fire that the exotic coins and bills awakened in him was something he would have been hard pressed to share, even had he anyone with whom to share it.

Which is to say there could not be a man in the whole of the city less like Lord Iron.

Born Edmund Scarasso, Lord Iron had taken his father's title and lands and ridden them first to war, then to power, and finally to a notorious fame. His family estate outside the city was reputed to rival the king's, but Lord Iron spent little time there. He had a house in the city with two hundred rooms arranged around a central courtyard garden in which trees bore fruits unfamiliar to the city and flowers bloomed with exotic and troubling scents. His servants were numberless as ants; his personal fortune greater than some smaller nations'. And never, it was said, had such wealth, power, and influence been squandered on such a debased soul.

No night passed without some new tale of Lord Iron. Ten thousand larks had been killed, their tongues harvested, and their bodies thrown aside in order that Lord Iron might have a novel hors d'oeuvre. Lord Biethan had been forced to repay his family's debt by sending his three daughters to perform as Lord Iron's creatures for a week; they had returned to their father with disturbing, languorous smiles and a rosewood cask filled with silver as "recompense for his Lordship's overuse." A fruit seller had the bad fortune not to recognize Lord Iron one dim, fogbound morning, and a flippant comment earned him a whipping that left him near dead.

There was no way for anyone besides Lord Iron himself to know which of the thousand stories and accusations that accreted around him were true. There was no doubt that Lord Iron was never seen wearing anything but the richest of velvets and silk. He was habitually in the company of beautiful women of negotiable virtue. He smoked the finest tobacco and other, more exotic weeds. Violence and sensuality and excess were the tissue of which his life was made. If his wealth and web of blackmail and extortion had not protected him, he would no doubt have been invited to the gallows dance years before. If he had been a hero in the war, so much the worse.

And so it was, perhaps, no surprise that when his lackey and drinking companion, Lord Caton, mentioned in passing an inconvenient curiosity of the code of exchange, Lord Iron's mind seized upon it. Among his many vices was a fondness for cruel pranks. And so it came to pass that Lord Iron and the handful of gaudy revelers who followed in his wake descended late one Tuesday morning upon the Magdalen Gate postal authority.

•   •   •

Olaf took the packet of bills, willing his hands not to tremble. Lord Iron's thin smile and river-stone eyes did nothing to calm him. The woman draping herself on Lord Iron's arm made a poor affectation of sincerity.

"Well," Olaf said, unfolding the papers. "Let me see."

These were unlike any currency he had ever seen; the sheets were just larger than a standard sheet of paper, the engraving a riot of colors—crimson, indigo, and a pale, delicate peach. The lordly face that stared out of the bill was Moorish. Ornate letters identified the bills as being valued at a thousand convertible guilders and issued by the Independent Protectorate of Analdi-Wat. Olaf wondered, as his fingers traced the lettering, how a protectorate could be independent.

"I'm very sorry, my lord," he said. "But this isn't a listed currency."

"And how is that *my* problem?" Lord Iron asked, stroking his beard. He had a rich voice, soft and masculine, that made Olaf blush.

"I only mean, my lord, that I couldn't give an exchange rate on these. I don't have them on my board, you see, and so I can't—"

"These are legal tender, issued by a sovereign state. I would like to change them into pounds sterling."

"I understand that, my lord, it's only that—"

"Are you familiar with the code of exchange?" Lord Iron asked. The dark-haired woman on his arm smiled at Olaf with all the pity a snake shows a rat.

"I . . . of course, my lord . . . that is . . ."

"Then you will recall the second provision of the Lord Chancellor's amendment of 1652?"

Olaf licked his lips. Confusion was like cotton ticking filling his head.

"The provision against speculation, my lord?"

"Very good," Lord Iron said. "It states that any cambist in the

employ of the crown must complete a requested transfer between legal tenders issued by sovereign states within twenty-
four hours or else face review of licensure."

"My...my lord, that isn't...I've been working here for
years, sir...."

"And of course," Lord Iron went on, his gaze implacable and
cool, "assigning arbitrary value to a currency also requires a review, doesn't it? And rest assured, my friend, that I am quite capable of determining the outcome of any such review."

Olaf swallowed to loosen the tightness in his throat. His
smile felt sickly.

"If I have done something to offend your lordship . . ."

"No," Lord Iron said with something oddly like compassion
in his eyes. "You were simply in the wrong place when I grew
bored. Destroying you seemed diverting. I will be back at this
time tomorrow. Good day, sir."

Lord Iron turned and walked away. His entourage followed.
When the last of them had stepped out the doors, the silence
that remained behind was profound as the grave. Olaf saw the
eyes of the postal clerks on him and managed a wan smile. The
great clock read twenty minutes past eleven. By noontime tomorrow, Olaf realized, it was quite possible he would no longer
be a licensed cambist.

He closed his shutters early with a note tacked to the front
that clients should knock on them if they were facing an emergency but otherwise return the next day. He pulled out the refer-
ences of his trade—gazetteer, logs of fiscal reports, conversion
tables. By midafternoon, he had discovered the location of the
Independent Protectorate of Analdi-Wat, but nothing that
would relate their system of convertible guilders to any known
currency. Apparently the last known conversion had been into a
system of cowrie shells, and the numbers involved were absent.

The day waned, the light pouring into the postal authority
warming and then fading to shadows. Olaf sent increasingly

desperate messages to his fellow cambists at other postal author-
ities, to the librarians at the city's central reference desk, to the
office of the Lord Exchequer. It became clear as the bells tolled
their increasing hours that no answer would come before morning. And indeed, no answer would come in time.

If Olaf delayed the exchange, his license could be suspended.
If he invented some random value for the guilders, his license
could be suspended. And there was no data from which to derive an appropriate equation.

Anger and despair warring in his belly, he closed his station,
returned his books to their places, cleaned his slate, logged the
few transactions he had made. His hand hovered for a moment
over his strongbox.

Here were the funds from which he drew each day to meet
the demands of his clientele. Pounds sterling, yen, rubles. He
wondered, if he were to fill his pockets with the box's present
contents, how far he would get before he was caught. The romance of flight bloomed in his mind and died all in the space of
a breath. He withdrew only the bright, venomous bills of the
Independent Protectorate of Analdi-Wat, replacing them with a
receipt. He locked the box with a steady hand, shrugged on his
coat, and left.

Lord Iron, he decided as he walked slowly down the marble
steps to the street, was evil. But he was also powerful, rich, and
well connected. There was little that a man like Olaf could do if
a man of that stature took it as his whim to destroy him. If it had
been the devil, he might at least have fallen back on prayer.

Olaf stopped at the newsstand, bought an evening paper and
a tin of lemon mints, and trudged to the station across the street.
Waiting on the platform, he listened to the underground trains
hiss and squeal. He read his newspaper with the numb disinter-
est of a man to whom the worst has already happened. A missing child had been found alive in Stonemarket; the diary of a
famous courtesan had sold at auction to an anonymous buyer

and for a record price; the police had begun a policy of restricting access to the river quays in hopes of reducing accidental death by drowning. The cheap ink left more of a mark on his fingers than on his mind.

At his boardinghouse, Olaf ate a perfunctory dinner at the common table, retired to his room, and tried in vain to lose himself in the pulp adventure tales. The presence of a killer among the members of the good Count Pendragon's safari proved less than captivating, even if the virtuous Hanna Gable was in danger. Near midnight, Olaf turned out his light, pulled his thin wool blanket up over his head, and wondered what he would do when his position at the postal authority was terminated.

Two hours later, he woke with a shout. Still in his nightclothes, he rushed out to the common room, digging through the pile of small kindling and newspaper that Mrs. Wells used to start her fires. When he found the evening newspaper, he read the article detailing the sale of the courtesan's diary again. There was nothing in it that pertained directly to his situation, and yet his startling, triumphant yawp woke the house.

He arrived at work the next day later than usual, with bags dark as bruises under his eyes but a spring in his step. He went through his morning ritual rather hurriedly to make up for the time he had lost, but was well prepared when the street doors opened at eleven o'clock and Lord Iron and his gang of rank nobility slouched in. Olaf held his spine straight and breathed deeply to ease the trip-hammer of his heart.

Lord Iron stepped up to the window like an executioner to the noose. The woman on his arm this morning was fair-haired, but otherwise might have been the twin of the previous day's woman. Olaf made a small, nervous bow to them both.

"Lord Iron," he said.

Lord Iron's expression was distant as the moon. Olaf wondered if perhaps his lordship had been drinking already this morning.

"Explain to me why you've failed."

"Well, my lord, I don't think I can do that. I have your money here. It comes to something less than ten pounds, I'm afraid. But that was all the market would bear."

With trembling hand, Olaf slid an envelope across the desk. Lord Iron didn't look down at it. Fury lit his eyes.

"The *market*? And pray what *market* is that?"

"The glassblower's shop in Harrington Square, my lord. I have quotes from three other establishments nearby, and theirs was the best. I doubt you would find better anywhere."

"What do they have to do with this?"

"Well, they were the ones who bought the guilders," Olaf said, his voice higher and faster than he liked. He also ran on longer than he had strictly speaking intended. "I believe that they intend to use them as wrapping paper. For the more delicate pieces. As a novelty."

Lord Iron's face darkened.

"You sold my bills?" he growled.

Olaf had anticipated many possible reactions. Violence, anger, amusement. He had imagined a hundred objections that Lord Iron might bring to his actions. Base ignorance had not been one of them. Olaf's surprise lent a steadiness to his voice.

"My lord, *you* sold them. To me. That's what exchange is, sir. Currency is something bought and sold, just as plums or gas fixtures are. It's what we do here."

"I came to get pounds sterling for guilders, not sell wrapping paper!"

Olaf saw in that moment that Lord Iron genuinely didn't understand. He pulled himself up, straightening his vest.

"Sir," he said. "When a client comes to me with a hundred dollars and I turn him back with seventy pounds, I haven't said some Latin phrase over them. There aren't suddenly seventy more pounds in the world and a hundred fewer dollars. I *buy* the dollars. You came to sell your guilders to me. Very well. I have bought them."

"As wrapping paper!"

"What does that matter?" Olaf snapped, surprising both Lord Iron and himself. "If I invest them in negotiable bonds in Analdi-Wat or burn them for kindling, it's no business of yours. Someone was willing to buy them. From that, I can now quote you with authority what people are willing to pay. There is your exchange rate. And there is your money. Thank you for your business, and good day."

"You made up the price," Lord Iron said. "To place an arbitrary worth on—"

"Good God, man," Olaf said. "Did you not hear me before? There's nothing *arbitrary* about it. I went to several prospective buyers and took the best offered price. What can you possibly mean by 'worth' if not what you can purchase with it? Five shillings is worth a loaf of bread, or a cup of wine, or a cheaply bound book of poetry because that is what it will buy. Your tens of thousands of negotiable guilders will buy you nine pounds and seven shillings because that is what someone will pay. And there it is, in that envelope."

Never before in his life had Olaf seen nobility agape at him. The coterie of Lord Iron stared at him as if he had belched fire and farted brimstone. The fair-haired woman stepped back, freeing his lordship's sword arm.

I have gone too far, Olaf thought. *He will kill me.*

Lord Iron was silent for a long moment while the world seemed to rotate around him. Then he chuckled.

"The measure of a thing's worth is what you can purchase with it," he said as if tasting the words, then turned to the woman. "I think he's talking about you, Marjorie."

The woman's cheeks flushed scarlet. Lord Iron leaned against the sill of Olaf's little, barred window and gestured Olaf closer. Against his best judgment, Olaf leaned in.

"You have a strange way of looking at things," Lord Iron said. There were fumes on his breath. Absinthe, Olaf guessed. "To hear you speak, the baker buys my five shillings with his bread."

"And how is that wrong, my lord?" the cambist asked.

"And then the wineseller buys the coins from him with a glass of wine. So why not buy the bread with the wine? If they're worth the same?"

"You could, my lord," Olaf said. "You can express anything in terms of anything else, my lord. How many lemon tarts is a horse worth? How many newspapers equate to a good dinner? It isn't harder to determine than some number of rubles for another number of yen, if you know the trick of it."

Lord Iron smiled again. The almost sleepy expression returned to his eyes. He nodded.

"Wrapping paper," he said. "You have amused me, little man, and I didn't think that could be done any longer. I accept your trade."

And with that, Lord Iron swept the envelope into his pocket, turned, and marched unsteadily out of the postal authority and into the noon light of Magdalen Gate. After the street doors were closed, there was a pause long as three breaths together and then one of the postal clerks began to clap.

A moment later, the staff of the postal authority had filled the vaults of their chambers with applause. Olaf, knees suddenly weak, bowed carefully, closed the shutters of his window, and made his way back to the men's privacy room where he emptied his breakfast into the toilet and then sat on the cool tile floor laughing until tears streamed from his eyes.

He had faced down Lord Iron and escaped with his career intact. It was, no doubt, the greatest adventure of his life. Nothing he had done before could match it, and he could imagine nothing in the future that would surpass it.

And nothing did, as it turned out, for almost six and a half months.

It was a cold, clear February, and the stars had come out long before Olaf had left the Magdalen Gate authority. All during the ride on the underground train, Olaf dreamed of a warm pot of tea, a small fire, and the conclusion of the latest novel. Atherton Crane was on the verge of exposing the plot of the vicious Junwang Ko, but didn't yet know that Kelly O'Callahan was in the villain's clutches. It promised to be a pleasant evening.

He knew as soon as he stepped into the boardinghouse that something was wrong. The other boarders, sitting around the common table, went silent as he shrugged out of his coat and plucked off his hat. They pointedly did not look at him as Mrs. Wells, her wide friendly face pale as uncooked dough, crossed the room to meet him.

"There's a message for you, Mr. Neddelsohn," she said. "A man came and left it for you. Very particular."

"Who was he?" Olaf asked, suspicion blooming in his heart more from her affect than from any guilt on his conscience.

"Don't know," Mrs. Wells said, wringing her hands in distress, "but he looked . . . well, here it is, Mr. Neddelsohn. This is the letter he left for you."

The envelope she thrust into his hand was the color of buttercream, smooth as linen, and thick. The coat of arms embossed upon it was Lord Iron's. Olaf started at the thing as if she'd handed him a viper.

Mrs. Wells simpered her apology as he broke the wax seal and drew out a single sheet of paper. It was written in an erratic but legible hand.

Mr. Neddelsohn—

I find I have need of you to settle a wager. You will bring yourself to the Club Baphomet immediately upon receipt of this note. I will, of course, recompense you for your troubles.

The note was not signed, but Olaf had no doubt of its authorship. Without a word, he pulled his coat back on, returned his hat to his head, and stepped out to hail a carriage. From the street, he could see the faces of Mrs. Wells and his fellow boarders at the window.

The Club Baphomet squatted in the uncertain territory between the tenements and beer halls of Stonemarket and the
mansions and ballrooms of Granite Hill. The glimmers behind
its windows did little to illuminate the street, perhaps by design.
From the tales Olaf had heard, there might well be members of
the club who would prefer not to be seen entering or leaving its
grounds. The service entrance was in a mud-paved alley stinking of piss and old food, but it opened quickly to his knock. He
was bundled inside and escorted to a private sitting room
where, it seemed, he was expected.

Of the five men who occupied the room, Olaf recognized
only Lord Iron. The months had not been kind; Lord Iron had
grown thinner, his eyes wilder, and a deep crimson cut was only
half healed on his cheek. The other four were dressed in fashion
similar to Lord Iron—well-razored hair, dark coats of the finest
wool, watch chains of gold. The eldest of them seemed vaguely
familiar.

Lord Iron rose and held his hand out toward Olaf, not as if to
greet him but rather to display him like a carnival barker pre-
senting a three-headed calf.

"Gentlemen," Lord Iron intoned. "This is the cambist I mentioned to you. I propose that he be my champion in this matter."

Olaf felt the rictus grin on his face, the idiot bobbing of his
head as he made small bows to the four assembled gentlemen.
He was humiliated, but could no more stop himself than a
puppy could keep from showing its belly to beg the mercy of
wolves.

One of the four—a younger man with gold hair and ice-blue
eyes—stepped forward with a smile. Olaf nodded to him for
what must have been the fifth time.

"I am Simon Cole," the gold-haired man said. "Lord Eichan,
to my enemies."

At this, Lord Iron raised a hand, as if to identify himself as
one such enemy. The other three men chuckled, and Lord
Eichan smiled as well before continuing.

"Our mutual acquaintance, Lord Iron, has made a suggestion I find somewhat unlikely, and we have made a wager of it. He is of the opinion that the value of anything can be expressed in terms of any other valuable thing. I think his example was the cost of a horse in lemon mints."

"Yes, my lord," Olaf said.

"Ah, you agree then," Lord Eichan said. "That's good. I was afraid our little Edmund had come up with his thesis in a drug-soaked haze."

"We've made the agreement," Lord Iron said pleasantly. "Simon, Satan's catamite that he is, will set the two things to be compared. I, meaning of course *you,* will have a week to determine their relative worth. These three bastards will judge the answer."

"I see," Olaf said.

"Excellent," Lord Iron said, slapping him on the back and leading him to a chair upholstered in rich leather. It wasn't until Olaf had descended into the chair's depths that he realized he had just agreed to this mad scheme. Lord Eichan had taken a seat opposite him and was thoughtfully lighting a pipe.

"I think I should say," Olaf began, casting his mind about wildly for some way to remove himself from the room without offending either party. "That is, I don't wish that . . . ah . . ."

Lord Eichan nodded as if Olaf had made some cogent point, then shaking his match until the flame died, turned to face Olaf directly.

"I would like to know the value of a day in the life of His Majesty, King Walther," Lord Eichan said. "And I would like that value described in days of life of an inmate in the crown's prison."

"A day in the life of the king expressed in days of a prisoner's life?"

"Certainly you must agree that life is valuable," Lord Eichan said. "You wouldn't lightly part with your own."

"Well, certainly—"

"And you can't suggest that the king is the same as a bread thief."

"No, I wouldn't—"

"Well, then," Lord Eichan said. "It's settled."

"Come along, my boy," Lord Iron said, clapping Olaf on the shoulder. "I'll see you out."

"One week!" Lord Eichan said as Olaf and Lord Iron stepped from the room and into the corridor. Lord Iron was smiling; Olaf was not.

"My lord," Olaf said. "This is . . . I'm not sure I know how to go about something like this."

"That's why I got you a week to do it in," Lord Iron said. "The rat-licker wanted to limit it to three days."

"I don't know for a certainty that I can accommodate you, my lord," Olaf said.

"Do your best," Lord Iron said. "If we lose, Simon, Lord Eichan is going to kill me. Well, and you for that."

Olaf stopped dead. Lord Iron took another few steps before pausing and looking back.

"He's what?"

"Going to kill us," Lord Iron said. "And take five hundred pounds I've set aside in earnest as well. If we win, I'll kill him and bed his sister."

Olaf, unthinking, murmured an obscenity. Lord Iron grinned and pulled him along the dim corridor toward the back of the club.

"Well, you needn't bed his sister if you don't care to. Just do your best, boy. And be back here in a week."

With that, Lord Iron stepped Olaf out the door and into the cold, bleak alley. It wasn't until the door had closed behind him that Olaf realized Lord Iron hadn't recompensed him for the carriage ride.

In the morning, the whole affair had the air of a bad dream. Olaf made his way to Magdalen Gate as he always did, checked the ticker tape, updated his slate. What was the value of life, he wondered. And how was one life best to be measured against another.

And, behind it all, the growing certainty that Lord Eichan would indeed kill him if he couldn't find an acceptable answer.

Twice before noon, Olaf found he had made errors in his accounting. After bolting down the snowy street after a woman who had left with ten pounds fewer than she deserved, Olaf gave up. He wrote a note claiming illness, pinned it to his shuttered window, and left. He paused at the tobacconist to buy a pouch and papers.

In his room at the boardinghouse, Olaf sketched out every tack he could think of to address the issue. The most obvious was to determine how much money the state spent to keep his majesty and how much to run the prisons. But objections to that arose almost immediately; was that a measure of the worth of life or of operational expenses appropriate to each career? He considered the relative costs of physician's care for king and prisoner, but this again was not a concern precisely of life, but health. Twenty years coughing and twenty years free from illness were still twenty years.

For three days, he ate little and slept less. He ventured out to the library to search among the stacks of books and periodicals for inspiration. He found nothing on which he would have been willing to stake his life. Lord Iron had done that for him.

On the morning of the fourth day he rolled the last pinch of tobacco into the last paper, wet it, rolled it, and sat on his bed unable to bring himself to the effort of lighting the thing. Despair had descended upon him. He saw the next three days stretching before him in a long, slow sleep.

It was how he imagined the prisoners felt who had so occupied his thoughts. But he, at least, could go out for more tobacco. And beer. And good, bloody beefsteak. If he was to live like a prisoner, he might at least eat like a king. It wasn't as if he'd give himself gout in three days' time, no matter how richly he ate or overmuch he drank.

Something stirred at the back of his mind, and he found himself grinning even before he knew why.

All that day and the two after it he spent in a whirl of activity, his despair forgotten. He visited physicians and the budget office, the office of the prison warden and the newspaperman who most reported on the activities of the king. The last day, he locked himself in his room with an abacus, a stub of pencil, and sheaves of paper.

When he came to the final accounting, his heart sank. He went through his figures again, certain that somewhere in the complexity of his argument, he had made an error. But the numbers tallied, and as little as he liked it, there was no more time. Putting on his best coat, he prepared the argument in his mind. Then, papers tucked under his arm, he went out past his silent fellow boarders and the ever-stricken countenance of Mrs. Wells, down to the wintry street, and hailed a carriage to carry him back to Club Baphomet.

The furniture of the sitting room had been rearranged. A single table now dominated the space, with five chairs all along one side like an examiner's panel. The three judges sat in the middle with Simon, Lord Eichan on the left and Lord Iron on the right. Lord Eichan looked somewhat amused, but there was a nervousness in his movement with which Olaf identified. Lord Iron looked as relaxed as a man stepping out of a sauna; the wound on his face was visibly more healed. Glasses of wine sat before each man, and cigars rested in onyx ashtrays when the gentlemen of the club weren't making better use of them.

A straight-backed wooden chair faced them, a small student desk at its side. Olaf sat and arranged his papers. The eldest of the judges leaned forward and with a smile more at home on the lips of a procurer spoke.

"You may proceed, sir."

Olaf nodded his thanks.

"I will need to do just a bit of groundwork before I present my analysis," he said. "I hope you would all agree that a man who decries embezzlement and also diverts money into his private accounts is not actually opposed to the theft?"

The judges looked at one another in amusement.

"Or, similarly," Olaf went on, "a woman who claims to embody chastity and yet beds all comers is not, in point of fact, chaste?"

"I think even Lord Eichan will have to allow those to stand," the eldest judge said. "Your point?"

"My point, sirs, is that we judge people not by what they claim, but what they do. Public declarations of sentiment are not a fit judge of true character."

"You are preaching," the youngest of the judges drawled, "to the choir. There is no group in the nation more adept at saying one thing and doing another."

Olaf smiled awkwardly.

"Just so," he said. "I will move forward. I have come to the determination, after careful consideration, that a day in the life of his majesty the king equates to nineteen and three quarter hours of a prisoner of the crown."

There was a moment's silence. Simon, Lord Eichan blinked and an incredulous smile began to work its way onto his countenance. Lord Iron sat forward, his expression unreadable. One of the judges who had not yet spoken took a meditative puff on his cigar.

"I was never particularly good at sums," the man said in an unsettlingly feminine voice, "but it seems to me that you've just said a prisoner's life is *more* valuable than that of the king?"

"Yes," Olaf said, his belly heavy as if he'd drunk a tankard of lead. The eldest judge glanced at Lord Iron with a pitying expression.

"Let me also make some few observations," Olaf said, fighting to keep the desperation from his voice. "I have met with several physicians in the last few days. I am sorry to report that overindulging in strong liquor is thought by the medical establishment to reduce life expectancy by as much as five years. A habit of eating rich foods may reduce a man's span on the earth by another three to four years. A sedentary lifestyle by as much as eight. Indulging in chocolate and coffee can unbalance the blood, and remove as many as three years of life."

"You have now ceased to preach to the choir," said Lord Eichan. And indeed, the judges had grown more somber. Olaf raised a hand, begging their patience.

"I have used these medical data as well as the reports of the warden of Chappell Hill Prison and the last two years of his majesty's reported activities in the newspapers. I beg you to consider. A prisoner of the crown is kept on a simple diet and subjected to a mandatory exercise period each day. No spirits of any kind are permitted him. No luxuries such as coffee or chocolate. By comparison . . ."

Olaf fumbled with the sheaves of papers, searching for the form he had created. The eldest judge cleared his throat.

"By comparison," Olaf continued, "in the last two years, his majesty has taken vigorous exercise only one day in seven. Has eaten at banquet daily, including the richest of dishes. He regularly drinks both coffee and chocolate, often together in the French style."

"This is ridiculous," Lord Eichan said. "His majesty has the finest physicians in the world at his command. His life is better safeguarded than any man's in the realm."

"No, sir," Olaf said, his voice taking on a certainty that he was beginning to genuinely feel. "We *say* that it is, much as the embezzler claims honesty and the wanton claims virtue. I present to you the actions, as we agreed. And I would point out that his majesty's excesses are subject only to his personal whim. If he wished, he could drink himself insensible each morning, eat nothing but butterfat and lard, and never move from his seat. He could drink half a tun of coffee and play games with raw gunpowder. Unlike a prisoner, there is no enforcement of behavior that could rein him in. I have, if anything, taken a conservative measure in reaching my conclusions."

A glimmer of amusement shone in Lord Iron's eyes, but his face remained otherwise frozen. Simon, Lord Eichan was fidgeting with his cigar. The eldest judge sucked his teeth audibly and shook his head.

"And yet prisoners do not, I think, have a greater lifespan than monarchs," he said.

"It is impossible to say," Olaf said. "For many criminals and poor men, the time spent in the care of the crown can be when they are safest, best overseen, best clothed, best fed. I would, however, point out that his majesty's father left us at the age of sixty-seven, and the oldest man in the care of the crown is ..."

Olaf paused, finding the name.

"The oldest man in the care of the crown is David Bennet, aged eighty. Incarcerated when he was sixteen for killing his brother."

He spread his hands.

"Your argument seems sound," the eldest judge said, "but your conclusion is ridiculous. I cannot believe that the king is of lesser value than a prisoner. I am afraid I remain unconvinced. What say you, gentlemen?"

But before the other two judges could answer Olaf rose to his feet.

"With all respect, sir, the question was not the value of the king or the prisoner, but of the days of their respective lives. I was not asked to judge their pleasures or their health insofar as their discomforts are less than mortal."

The effeminate judge lifted his chin. There was a livid scar across his neck where, Olaf imagined from his knowledge of men's adventure, a garrote might have cut. But it was Simon, Lord Eichan who spoke.

"How is it that a king can be more valuable than a prisoner, but his days be less? It makes no sense at all!"

"There are other things which his majesty has," Olaf said. He had warmed to his topic now, and the fact that his own life hung in the balance was all but forgotten. "A prisoner *must* take his exercise; a king has the power to refuse. A prisoner may wish dearly for a rich meal or a great glass of brandy, but since he cannot have them, he cannot exchange pleasure for . . . well, for some duration of life."

"This is a waste of—"

"Be quiet," the eldest judge said. "Let the man have his say."

"But—"

"Don't make me repeat myself, Simon."

Lord Eichan leaned back, sneering and gripping his wineglass until his knuckles were white.

"It's a choice every man in this room has made," Olaf went on, raising his arm like a priest delivering a homily. "You might all live as ascetics and survive years longer. But like the king, you choose to make a rational exchange of some span of your life for the pleasure of living as you please. A prisoner is barred from that exchange, and so I submit a greater value is placed on his life precisely to the degree that strictures are placed on his pleasure and his exercise of power.

"Gentlemen, ask yourselves this; if I had two sons and saw that one of them kept from drink and gluttony while letting the other run riot, which of them would you say I valued? The prodigal might have more pleasure. Certainly the king has more pleasure than an inmate. But pleasure and power are not *life*."

"Amen," said Lord Iron. It was the first time he had spoken since Olaf had entered. The silence that followed this declaration was broken only by the hissing of the fire in the grate and the rush of blood in Olaf's ears.

"Your reports were accurate, Lord Iron," the drawling judge said. "Your pet cambist is *quite* amusing."

"Perhaps it would be best if you gave us a moment to discuss your points," the eldest judge said. "If you would be so kind as to step out to the antechamber? Yes. Thank you."

With the blackwood door closed behind him, Olaf's fear returned. He was in the Club Baphomet with his survival linked to

Lord Iron's, and only an argument that seemed less and less tenable with each passing minute to protect him. But he had made his throw. His only other hope now was mad flight, and the door to the corridor was locked. He tried it.

What felt like hours passed, though the grandfather clock ticking away in the corner reported only a quarter hour. A pistol barked twice, and a moment later Lord Iron strode into the room. The door swung shut behind him before Olaf could make sense of the bloody scene. His gorge rose.

"Well done, boy," Lord Iron said, dropping something heavy into Olaf's lap. "I'll have you taken home in my personal carriage. I have Lord Eichan's sister to console this evening, and I won't be needing horses to do it. And I thought you should know; it wasn't unanimous. If his majesty hadn't taken your side, I think we might not have won the day."

"His majesty?"

Olaf's mind reeled. The face of the eldest judge resolved itself suddenly into the portrait he kept at his desk.

"You did well, boy," Lord Iron said. "Your country thanks you."

Without another word, Lord Iron unlocked the door, stepped out to the corridor, and was gone. Olaf looked down. A packet of bills squatted in his lap. Five hundred pounds at a guess, and blood smeared on the topmost bill.

He swore to himself in that moment that he would never answer another summons from Lord Iron, whatever the consequences. And, indeed, when the hour arrived, it was Lord Iron who came to him.

The weeks and months that followed were if anything richer in their tales of Lord Iron. While traveling in the Orient, he had forced a barkeep who had fallen into his debt to choose between cutting off one of his infant daughter's toes or three of his own fingers in lieu of payment. He had seduced six nuns in Rome, leaving two of them with child. He had ridden an ostrich down the streets of Cairo naked at midnight. Of the untimely death of Lord Eichan there was no word, but apart from removing the portrait of the king from his desk, Olaf took no action. The less he personally figured into the debaucheries of Lord Iron, the better pleased he was.

Instead, Olaf plunged more deeply than ever into his work, his routine, and the harmless escapism of his men's adventure novels. But for the first time in memory, the perils of the heroines seemed contrived and weak, and the masculine bravery of the heroes seemed overstated, like a boy who blusters and puffs out his chest when walking through the graveyard at dusk.

Clifford Knightly wrestled an alligator on the banks of the great Nile. Lord Morrow foiled the evil Chaplain Grut's plan to foul the waters of London. Emily Chastain fell gratefully into the mighty arms of the noble savage Maker-of-Justice. And Olaf found himself wondering what these great men would have done at Club Baphomet. Wrested the gun from Lord Iron? From Simon, Lord Eichan? Sternly spoken of God and truth and righteousness? Olaf doubted it would have had any great effect.

Winter passed into spring. Spring ripened to summer. Slowly, Olaf's discontent, like the nightmares from which he woke himself shouting, lessened. For weeks on end, he could forget what he had been part of. Many men who came to his window at the postal authority had traveled widely. Many had tales to tell of near misses: a runaway carriage that had come within a pace of running them down in the streets of Prague, a fever which had threatened to carry them away in Bombay, the hiss of an Afghan musket ball passing close to their head. These moments of real danger were more convincing than any novel Olaf had ever read. This was, in part, because he had tales of his own now, if he ever chose to share them.

And still, when autumn with its golden leaves and fog and chill rain also brought Lord Iron back into his life, Olaf was not surprised.

It was a Tuesday night in September. Olaf had spent his customary hours at the Magdalen Gate postal authority, come back to his boardinghouse, and eaten alone in his room. The evening air was cool but not biting, and he had propped his window open before sitting down to read. When he woke, he thought for a long, bleary moment that the cold night breeze had woken him. Then the knock at his door repeated itself.

His blanket wrapped around his shoulders, Olaf answered the door. Lord Iron stood in the hall. He looked powerfully out of place. His fine jacket and cravat, the polished boots, the well-groomed beard and moustache all belonged in a palace or club. And yet rather than making the boardinghouse hall seem shabby and below him, the hallway made Lord Iron, monster of the city, seem false as a boy playing dress-up. Olaf nodded as if he'd been expecting the man.

"I have need of you," Lord Iron said.

"Have I the option of refusal?"

Lord Iron smiled, and Olaf took it as the answer to his question. He stepped back and let the man come through. Lord Iron sat on the edge of the bed while Olaf closed his window, drew up his chair and sat. In the light from Olaf's reading lamp, Lord Iron's skin seemed waxen and pale. His voice, when he spoke, was as distant as a man shouting from across a square.

"There is a question plaguing me," Lord Iron said. "You are the only man I can think of who might answer it."

"Is there a life at stake?" Olaf asked.

"No," Lord Iron said. "Nothing so petty as that."

When Olaf failed to respond, Lord Iron, born Edmund Scarasso, looked up at him. There was a terrible weariness in his eyes.

"I would know the fair price for a man's soul," he said.

"Forgive me?" Olaf said.

"You heard me," Lord Iron said. "What would be fit trade for a soul? I . . . I can't tell any longer. And it is a question whose answer has . . . some relevance to my situation."

In an instant, Olaf's mind conjured the sitting room at the Club Baphomet. Lord Iron sitting in one deep leather chair, and the Prince of Lies across from him with a snifter of brandy in his black, clawed hands.

"I don't think that would be a wise course to follow," Olaf said, though in truth his mind was spinning out ways to avoid being party to this diabolism. He did not wish to make a case before that infernal judge. Lord Iron smiled and shook his head.

"There is no one in this besides yourself and me," he said. "You are an expert in the exchange of exotic currencies. I can think of none more curious than this. Come to my house on Mammon Street in a month's time. Tell me what conclusion you have reached."

"My Lord—"

"I will make good on the investment of your time," Lord Iron said, then rose and walked out, leaving the door open behind him.

Olaf gaped at the empty room. He was a cambist. Of theology, he knew only what he had heard in church. He had read more of satanic contracts in his adventure novels than in the Bible. He was, in fact, not wholly certain that the Bible had an example of a completed exchange. Satan had tempted Jesus. Perhaps there was something to be taken from the Gospel of Matthew. . . .

Olaf spent the remainder of the night poring over his Bible and considering what monetary value might be assigned to the ability to change stones to bread. But as the dawn broke and he turned to his morning ablutions, he found himself unsatisfied. The devil might have tempted Christ with all the kingdoms of the world, but it was obvious that such an offer wouldn't be open to everyone. He was approaching the problem from the wrong direction.

As he rode through the deep tunnels to Magdalen Gate, as he stopped at the newsstand for a morning paper, as he checked the ticker tape and updated his slate, his mind occupied itself by sifting through all the stories and folk wisdom he had ever heard. There had been a man who traded his soul to the devil for fame and wealth. Faust had done it for knowledge. Was there a way to represent the learning of Faust in terms of, say, semesters at the best universities of Europe? Then the rates of tuition might serve as a fingerhold.

It was nearly the day's end before the question occurred to him that put Lord Iron's commission in its proper light, and once that had happened, the answer was obvious. Olaf had to sit down, his mind afire with the answer and its implications. He didn't go home, but took himself to a small public house. Over a pint and a stale sandwich, he mentally tested his hypothesis. With the second pint, he celebrated. With the third, he steeled himself, then went out to the street and hailed a carriage to take him to the house of Lord Iron.

Revelers had infected the household like fleas on a dying rat. Masked men and women shrieked with laughter, not all of which bespoke mirth. No servant came to take his coat or ask his invitation, so Olaf made his own way through the great halls. He passed through the whole of the building before emerging from the back and finding Lord Iron himself sitting at a fountain in the gardens. His lordship's eyebrows rose to see Olaf, but he did not seem displeased.

"So soon, boy? It isn't a month," Lord Iron said as Olaf sat on the cool stone rail. The moon high above the city seemed also to dance in the water, lighting Lord Iron's face from below and above at once.

"There was no need," Olaf said. "I have your answer. But I will have to make something clear before I deliver it. If you will permit me?"

Lord Iron opened his hand in a motion of deference. Olaf cleared his throat.

"Wealth," he said, "is not a measure of money. It is a measure of well-being. Of happiness, if you will. Wealth is not traded, but rather is generated *by* trade. If you have a piece of art that I

wish to own and I have money that you would prefer to the art-
work, we trade. Each of us has something he prefers to the thing
he gave away; otherwise, we would not have agreed on the
trade. We are both better off. You see? Wealth is *generated*."

"I believe I can follow you so far," Lord Iron said. "Certainly I
can agree that a fat wallet is no guarantor of contentment."

"Very well. I considered your problem for the better part of
the day. I confess I came near to despairing; there is no good
data from which to work. But then I found my error. I assumed
that your soul, my lord, was valuable. Clearly it is not."

Lord Iron coughed out something akin to a laugh, shock in
his expression. Olaf raised a hand, palm out, asking that he not
interrupt.

"You are renowned for your practice of evil. This very
evening, walking through your house, I have seen things for
which I can imagine no proper penance. Why would Satan
bother to buy your soul? He has rights to it already."

"He does," Lord Iron said, staring into the middle distance.

"And so I saw," Olaf said, "you aren't seeking to sell a soul.
You are hoping to buy one."

Lord Iron sighed and looked at his hands. He seemed smaller
now. Not a supernatural being, but a man driven by human fears
and passions to acts that could only goad him on to worse and
worse actions. A man like any other, but with the wealth to mag-
nify his errors into the scale of legend.

"You are correct, boy," he said. "The angels wouldn't have my
soul if I drenched it in honey. I have . . . treated it poorly. It's left
me weary and sick. I am a waste of flesh. I know that. If there is
no way to become a better man than this, I suspect the best path
is to become a corpse."

"I understand, my lord. Here is the answer to your question:
the price of a soul is a life of humility and service."

"Ah, is that all," Lord Iron said, as if the cambist had suggested that he pull down the stars with his fingers.

"And as it happens," Olaf went on, "I have one such with which I would be willing to part."

Lord Iron met his gaze, began to laugh, and then went silent.

"Here," Olaf said, "is what I propose . . ."

Edmund, the new cambist of the Magdalen Gate postal authority, was by all accounts an adequate replacement for Olaf. Not as good, certainly. But his close-cropped hair and clean-shaven face lent him an eagerness that belonged on a younger man, and if he seemed sometimes more haughty than his position justified, it was a vice that lessened with every passing month. By Easter, he had even been asked to join in the Sunday picnic the girls in the accounting office sponsored. He seemed genuinely moved at the invitation.

The great scandal of the season was the disappearance of Lord Iron. The great beast of the city simply vanished one night. Rumor said that he had left his fortune and lands in trust. The identity of the trustee was a subject of tremendous speculation.

Olaf himself spent several months simply taking stock of his newfound position in the world. Once the financial situation was put in better order, he found himself with a substantial yearly allowance that still responsibly protected the initial capital.

He spent his monies traveling to India, Egypt, the sugar plantations of the Caribbean, the unworldly underground cities of Persia. He saw the sun set off the Gold Coast and rise from the waters east of Japan. He heard war songs in the jungles of the Congo and sang children's lullabies in a lonely tent made from yak skin in the dark of a Siberian winter.

And, when he paused to recover from the rigors and dangers of travel, he would retire to a cottage north of the city—the least of his holdings—and spend his time writing men's adventure novels set in the places he had been.

He named his protagonist Lord Iron.

Logorrhea

● ● ●

MICHELLE RICHMOND

HE HAD NOT BEEN born with the scales. Indeed, the origin of his condition was as enigmatic to the mother who bore him as it was to the scientists who studied him, for nowhere in his mother's family album or in the scientists' vast store of case histories was there another human being so gloriously squamulose.

He was three years old when the scales began to appear—on his upper legs, at first. Tiny, half-moon shaped bits, hard and thin, the rounded edges paper-sharp. One pediatrician diagnosed it as an allergic rash, another as a severe case of keratosis peritonitis, another as an indeterminable childhood abnormality that would surely right itself with age. But when the scales began to thicken and to stretch up his body—to his groin, his stomach, his arms, shoulders, neck, and eventually, his face—the doctors stopped trying to make a diagnosis. It was like nothing they had seen, it was miraculous, it was horrific.

One thing you should understand: the scales did not cover his skin, they *were* his skin. Unlike hair or fingernails, there was nothing extraneous about them. To rid him of the scales would have been to rid him of his very surface.

The doctors took pictures, they referred him to specialists, they did all of the things one does when an exceptional case is dropped, like a gift of manna, into one's hands. But they offered no answers, only a long series of lotions and pills and dermato-logical treatments of the abrasive and purative variety, all of which yielded nothing—nothing but a sobbing, put-upon boy.

"No one has ever loved me before," he said, by which he meant no one had ever fucked him—and to him, the two were one and the same.

All of these things he told me on our first night together. Our first! How could he hold it back, this dark history, when my skin bore the savage marks of his scales, when his flesh literally dug into mine?

It may surprise you to learn that the miracle of that night was not the cuts or his loquaciousness, was not even the fact of our having found each other on a deserted beach in Alabama. The miracle of that night was that I was moved to silence. I, who suf-fer so plainly from logorrhea, was so enthralled by his story that I dared not interrupt.

In earlier times, surely, a man like him would have been des-tined to be either a circus freak or a favored showpiece of some royal court. In this modern place and time, protected as he was from indigence by the blessing of disability pay, the effect of his condition had instead been to make him supremely lonely. Because he did not have to go out into the world to make a liv-ing, and because he could not be intimate with another human being without causing harm, he had chosen to live a life apart. Before we met, he had passed a decade of bachelorhood in a small house in Fairhope just steps from Mobile Bay, with the aid of a trusted assistant who did his shopping, ran his errands, and occasionally shared his meals.

And then he found me. Or, it should be said, I found him. On the Fairhope Pier, on a typically moonlit night. It is a minor miracle of that particular part of Alabama that the filthy bay is often bathed in a fine moonlight which makes it appear clean, inspiring foolhardy teenagers and tourists to go for midnight swims in the bleak mix of sewage and chemical waste. He appeared to me first as a statuesque figure at the end of the pier, dressed in a long-sleeved shirt and linen pants. I was having a difficult time of it, having recently lost, within the span of a few weeks, a decent job and a beloved pet, not to mention a boyfriend, when I saw him standing there, so still and silent that I first assumed a sculpture had been erected in that familiar spot. I stepped off the warm sand onto the pier, and when the boards creaked beneath me he turned, and that is when I understood that this splendid creature was alive.

For several moments I hesitated. Someone standing in such a way, at such a place, on such a night, surely does not want to be interrupted. Then the moonlight hit his face, and a flash of multicolored light shot off the tip of his elegant nose, and I found myself walking toward him as the old pier wobbled and groaned.

"Stop," he called out.

It was a slightly scratchy voice, halting, as if it was out of practice.

"Why?" I called back.

"Because," was his reply.

"It's a public pier," I said.

To this, he had no answer. He turned back toward the water and took a step forward. For a moment I thought he might jump. But he didn't. When I reached him, he said, with his back to me, "I came out here to be alone."

"Me too," I said. "I won't bother you." Then I moved to stand beside him, and he lifted a gloved hand to shield his face.

"Please," he said.

But by then, I had already seen.

We stood for a minute or two in silence before I said the only thing I could think of to say, which was, "You're beautiful."

"I'm ghastly," he replied.

"Not to me."

He produced a small paper bag, and when he opened it I could smell hot spice and salt and the sea. It was a strong, wonderful odor particular to the Gulf Coast, and immediately I was happy to be home again, after a long time away.

"Crawfish," he said.

"I know."

I reached into the bag, took one of the hard little shells, and twisted until the tail came clean from the head. I sucked the head, something I hadn't done in years, something that I had deemed in my new life up North to be somewhat barbaric. But the juice was delicious, even more so than I remembered, tangy and sweet in a way no other meat could replicate. The shimmering man followed suit, and it occurred to me that the boyfriend who had just kicked me out of his stylish apartment in the stylish city that had never really felt like home would never have done such a thing. Then I squeezed the tail end of the shell until the tender pink meat came out, popped it into my mouth, chewed luxuriously, licked my fingers, and only after I had swallowed did I have the good grace to thank him.

"No, thank *you*," he said, looking at me directly for the first time. "One should never eat crawfish alone. I've been doing it far too long." The combination of the words and the way he looked at me, as if we were complicit in some dream of love, seemed to cast forward into a future when we would do this together frequently, would, in fact, do many things together. It would not be an exaggeration to say that at that moment, I understood that the thing we were going to have together would be nothing short of a life.

We sat down on the end of the pier, removed our shoes, our feet dangling in the water, and ate. He produced a couple of warm beers, which seemed to materialize from thin air. We drank them in silence. When the crawfish and the beers were gone, he began to talk. Once he started, it was as if he couldn't stop. And I, who had driven away my last boyfriend and lost my last job because I couldn't shut up, sat and listened. For the first time in my life, I found listening to be effortless. Every now and then I'd feel a school of tiny fish moving past like a gentle wind, the mouths nibbling at my ankles.

When he was finished, I said, "I have something to tell you."

"What is it?"

"I have a problem."

He turned to look at me, and his blue eyes looked strangely dull, contrasted as they were against the glittering scales. "A problem?"

But when I opened my mouth to say it, the words would not come out. Why mar this perfect evening by confessing my worst character trait? I would be for him, that night, the ideal companion. I would let him think that I was the kind of woman a man might be lucky to have. *You'd be a real prize,* my ex had said, sliding his hands over my breasts, my hips, my thighs, *if you had your mouth surgically wired shut.*

"It's nothing," I said. "Never mind."

He shook the last bits of crawfish shell into the water, put the empty bottles into the paper bag, and said, "My house is just down the beach. Do you want to come home with me?"

"Yes."

Walking back with him along the quiet beach, I could not have imagined the physical pain that awaited me. In hindsight, I understand that when he removed his glove and took my hand in his, it was meant as a silent warning. He held my hand as gently as he could, and still I could feel the scales cutting into my palm and fingers. I wondered, but did not ask, whether the affliction covered his entire body. Later that night, pressing my face into a pillow to squelch my screams, I understood that it did.

That first time, I was covered with lacerations. Tiny red marks all over the front of my body, like thousands of paper cuts, and also on my back where his arms had embraced me. All through the night I kept waking in pain, the fresh wounds damp with blood, my body sticking to the soft flannel sheets as if held there by thousands of dots of glue. Beside me, he slept soundly, his scales wet-seeming in the moonlight, his face the picture of peace. I couldn't help but feel, somehow, that I had saved him, although it would occur to me later that it was the other way around. In any event, that first morning-after, when I woke to the sound of his scaled feet clicking softly against the tile floor, I knew that I would stay with him. That I would make a home there in that house by the bay. Maybe it was the disfiguring effect of our first attempt at love—after all, I had never been loved so dramatically. More likely, it was the fact of his having accomplished something no other man had ever been able to do: with him, I had fallen easily, happily, willingly into silence.

I can say without reservation that the weeks that followed were the best weeks of my life. Days, I went out looking for a new job while he concealed himself, as was his routine, in the house, making notes for a memoir he planned to write. He was very secretive about the book, would not let me see so much as a single page, kept the steadily growing manuscript locked away in a file cabinet, behind the locked door of his closet. It was a house of secrets to which I was not privy, but I had my secrets too. I did not mention to him the character flaw that had brought all my previous relationships, romantic and otherwise, to an abrupt and tearful end. I did not tell him that I had laid cruel waste to a long cadre of therapists, professionals who, though trained to listen, could not bear to listen to me. Or that my second-to-last boyfriend had been so put off by my incessant talking that, following our breakup, he'd taken up with a girl who was deaf and mute, a hot little Helen Keller who was fond of fishnets and funny hats. Or that my own mother would not take my calls.

He had fallen in love with a certain girl, the one he met that night at the end of the pier, the one who sat silently and listened to his stories. In order to keep him, I would remain that girl. It was easier than I could have imagined: he held my rapt attention, and I, miracle of miracles, held my fevered tongue.

Following that first night, we went an entire month without making love, during which time my body slowly healed. Mornings and evenings, he dressed the wounds with ointment. Of course, he had to wear gloves, but even so, I felt that I had never been touched so gently. Some nights, while he was sleeping, I stood in front of the bathroom mirror, peeled back the bandages, and examined my shorn skin. It was a source of fascination for me, this pain that made me feel, at the same time, horribly wounded and deeply desired.

Then, at the beginning of our second month together, I came home from work—by then I had landed a gig as a docent at the maritime museum—to find him dressed head to toe in a suit of clean white felt.

"Feel," he said, holding an arm out for me to touch. "It's impenetrable. I had it custom-made. The felt is the best one can buy, hand-beaten by Tuvan women in the village of Tsengal in Mongolia."

I stroked his moon-white arm. "So soft," I said. "It's beautiful."

But what I was thinking was that I missed his scales, the way they captured and reflected light, the way, when he moved across a room, he looked like a human chandelier.

Have I mentioned that his scales tinkled? Have I mentioned that, after bathing, while he stood in the middle of the tiled kitchen floor, dripping dry to avoid shredding the towels, he was like a fountain of light?

"There is a necessary flaw in the suit's design," he said, leading me to the bedroom.

"What's that?"

When we reached the bed, he turned to face me and unfastened two buttons on his groin. A flap of felt fell away to reveal that most beautiful part of him, of which I had been in awe from the beginning.

The cock is often described as an obvious and uninspired work of functionality, lacking in beauty. But his was different. It was average in size but exceptional in appearance, covered as it was with scales of many hues, ranging from the palest white to the deepest blue. Although it had been inside me only once, I had admired it often, amazed by the way, when in repose, it lay against his body like a cylindrical jewel. What cruelty, to be blessed with such a beautiful cock, but to be unable to share it with the world!

That night, separated from him by a layer of plush white felt, it was like making love to a pillow, or a human-shaped yurt. Except, of course, for the one part. Our way of making love was to be very, very still, to let the closeness of our two bodies be a substitute for motion; even so, I came away from the event cut and bleeding in the one place where I could feel it most. Afterward, it wasn't too bad as long as I was sitting or standing still. But walking around the maritime museum, instructing eager third-graders on the mating habits of stingrays and jumbo Gulf shrimp, proved excruciatingly painful. In a way it was terrible, but in another way it made me feel as though I had happened upon an exceptional love. He was like no man I'd ever been with. I could search for years, and never find anyone like him. It was satisfying to think of the women I knew at work—the secretary with her portentous hair, or the events planner with her eternally disappointed air of someone who has just missed out on a very good party—passing through the days with their ordinary loves, while in the little house by the bay, my own love waited, freakish and beautiful.

As it turned out, the suit was only an early prototype. Over the months and years it would be followed by many others, each one hand-sewn by a celebrated textile artist across the bay in

Mobile, each one an improvement upon the last. An improvement in that each new suit was less obvious, more natural-looking than the one before. The white felt gave way to something thinner and somewhat flesh-colored—also smooth, but with the faint hint of human hair. He gave the textile artist photos of himself as a very young child, before the scales began to appear, and gradually, the color of the suit came to resemble, more and more, the color his skin had been prior to the affliction. That's what he called it, in his more depressive moods, when the memoir was going badly—his *affliction*—and I didn't have the words to tell him that it was the affliction that drew me to him, more so than his personality, which, I came to realize, was rather ordinary, or his intelligence, which tended toward the esoteric, or his cooking, which, it turned out, was limited to boiled crawfish and oysters Rockefeller, the latter of which I'd never had the stomach for.

The suit's hair, too, became more supple and fine, placed discriminately in the appropriate places—thicker on the legs and upper arms, a lighter patch of it on the chest, and only a few stray hairs, for authenticity's sake, in the small of the back and on the wrists. By and by, the suit began to look alarmingly realistic, so one had to examine it closely to see that something was amiss, that he was wearing not his skin, but rather a suit of simulated skin, designed, ingeniously, to bruise upon impact and to emit faint odors reminiscent of the wearer's last meal and even, under the proper conditions, to sweat.

The suit was so realistic, in fact, that he gained a kind of confidence he'd never known before. Over time, as the suit improved to near perfection, he began to go out in public, to socialize with ordinary folk. Eventually he got a job. He kept his hair long and always wore a hat and scarf, even in the merciless humidity, in addition to a thick makeup that had been designed by the textile artist, who was branching out into clay work. With all of these precautions, he was able to keep his face pretty well concealed, and anyone who might catch a glimpse of scales was likely to think that he was sweating, or that he'd just undergone a very serious exfoliation.

But at night, when he came home from his job at the finance company—something he'd dreamed of his whole life, not least of all because it smacked of normalcy and unobtrusive prosperity—he allowed me to unzip the suit and peel it off of his shimmering skin in the pastel light cast through our windows by the sleeping Gulf, and to rinse the makeup from his face, and to do the one thing I desired most, the one thing that, unbeknownst to him, kept my love for him alive: to look at him, in all his scaled and glittering glory. When he was naked, stripped of the deceptions he had so meticulously acquired in order to pass in polite society, he was nothing short of beautiful.

When it came time to make love, I willingly zipped him into the suit again. With my job, it would have been difficult to endure the all-over scarring that would have occurred if we made love without the suit. Not to mention the fact that some genetic code was at play, some aging process peculiar to the squamulose was afoot, so that, while his suit grew softer and more pliant with each mutation, his scales grew sharper and more pointed.

During all this time, the suit's one supposed flaw remained: one key part of his body had to remain exposed during lovemaking. According to the textile artist, it had something to do with the chemical makeup of the fabric, which could not sustain exposure to certain types of bodily fluids. So it passed that, year after year, my feminine parts bore the brunt of our lovemaking, the result being that I felt, always, that I was somehow his, that I endured a sacrifice for him. This made our union seem to me somehow pure, for what is love if not sacrifice?

And then, one Friday afternoon nearly a decade after that night meeting at the pier, my husband—by then, we had walked down the aisle of a nondenominational church by the sea, and feasted on champagne and crawdads while a local zydeco band inspired the small group of wedding guests to flail about in the sand—came home to me and said, "It's been solved."

I was sitting at the kitchen table, reviewing the literature for a new live specimen the maritime museum had acquired, the *Tonicella lineata,* or lined chiton, a prehistoric-looking mollusk with a single large foot whose tongue, or *radula* to be precise, is covered with iron teeth. I suppose I didn't properly hear him, or didn't note the enthusiasm in his voice, because rather than asking him what exactly it was that had been solved, I was moved to share with him an interesting fact I'd just discovered in my reading. "It says here that the lined chiton can travel up to three feet on the ocean's surface to scrape algae off nearby rocks. Then it returns to its *home scar,* which is a depression in its own rock that is, get this, shaped just like the lined chiton." I shoved a potato chip into my mouth and kept talking. "I mean, the chiton has used his iron-coated teeth—they get that way, the teeth I mean, by a complicated chemical process called biomineralization—to shave away the rock until it fits his body just so. Like a glove! Like a lover!" I exclaimed, taking a swig of my beer, for by this point I had really made myself at home on the Gulf Coast, swigging beer and sucking crawfish heads with abandon, occasionally even attending a tent revival, forgetting that I'd ever lived in one of the strange cities of the North, or that in a past life, my beloved cat had, according to the veterinarian, actually committed suicide, "Most likely to avoid some trauma at home—is there something traumatic going on at home?" she had asked, looking at me accusingly, to which my boyfriend, the one with the stylish apartment, had replied, "Yeah, this one here won't shut the fuck up. Ever."

"Says here that chitons have flexible shells," I said, "composed of eight articulating valves, which are covered with thousands of tiny eyes called aesthetes. The largest chiton in the world is the *Cryptochiton stelleri,* or gumboot, which can reach thirteen inches and has valves shaped like butterflies. Butterflies, mind you! Never say there isn't poetry in the sea."

My husband, at this point, was staring at me in stunned silence.

And why shouldn't he? I'd never strung so many words together the entire time I'd known him. Something strange had happened that long-ago night on the pier; I had, without warning or effort, been cured. What I'd believed at the time to be a temporary reprieve from my own affliction had turned out to be permanent. Weeks turned into months, months into years, and I did not feel the need to talk. Quite the opposite, I felt compelled to silence, so that by the time I returned home each day from the museum, where it was my duty to speak at length about the wonders of the sea, I had little desire to say anything. Instead, I listened. It had always been this way with us.

"Didn't you hear me?" my husband said, taking a seat beside me at the table, and looking with some disgust at the oily stain the potato chips had made on my paper plate. "I said it has been solved." He was wearing Bermuda shorts, a T-shirt, and thongs—Fridays were mandatory casual day at the finance company—and his suit was so excruciatingly skinlike, so perfectly fitted to his body from neck to fingertips, that, had I not known better, I might think that he too had been cured. By this point we were making love infrequently, once every couple of months at most, and the intimacy we'd once shared had begun to melt away. He had taken to wearing his suit round-the-clock, even to bed, so that I rarely experienced the sweet thrill of disrobing him in the evening after work, peeling away his outer layer to reveal the man I loved.

At that moment, I felt that I was sitting across the table from someone no more familiar to me than the paperboy or the clerk at the 7-Eleven. Then, mercifully, he unwound the scarf that covered his chin, and took off his floppy hat, and brushed back his long hair, and I felt enormously grateful for this glimpse at his private self, this glimpse he allowed to no one but me.

"What's been solved?" I asked.

"This."

He stood and dropped his Bermuda shorts. And there before

me stood an entirely natural-looking man, adorned in curly pubic hair and dangling flaccidly in the heat, the scrotal sac appropriately wrinkled, the whole package dismally common.

"How did he do it?" I asked, reaching out to find the zipper.

At which point he began to swell at my touch, saying, "Baby, there's no zipper."

"Well then, how do we get this damn thing off?" I said, tugging at it in a completely utilitarian way, which he mistook for an erotic overture.

"There's no taking it off. I've been sealed into the suit. I can bathe in it, exercise in it, even make love in it."

By now I was using my teeth, trying to tear the wretched false skin away.

"It has to be removed once a year so that the skin can go through an aging process and any necessary alterations can be made," he panted, as if this thing I was doing with my teeth had something to do with sex, as if it were not a desperate attempt to reveal that most beautiful part of him, that most real and multi-colored thing, which was a specimen in its own right, deserving of its own field of scientific study, not to mention an entire school of experimental art and a movement in postmodern literature.

But I was no match for the suit, this soft and lifelike armor. I did not find what I was looking for.

That night, we made ordinary love. While he thrashed and thrusted above me, eventually filling me with a great rush of sperm which seemed to have cooled and coagulated on its journey through the suit, I faked an orgasm for the very first time. And when it was over I had nothing to say. My speech on the mighty chiton, that master of disguise who carved for itself a home in the rock and looked, to any possible predators, like nothing special, like a part of the rock itself—my speech had been a one-time thing. My logorrhea really was gone, relegated like the dead cat and the ex-boyfriends and the therapists and the big city to my distant past.

Before long, the textile artist came up with a way to disguise my husband's one remaining feature, his face. He fit in so well, even he seemed to forget that the skin he presented to the world was not his own. Eventually he got a promotion, and we moved across the bay to a restored antebellum home in downtown Mobile, keeping the little cottage by the bay for the sake, I suppose, of nostalgia. Mornings, I'd drive the Causeway to the maritime museum in Fairhope, watching the new sun blaze over the silver bay. Afternoons, on the return trip, I'd catch a glimpse of the old warship, the USS *Alabama,* sitting placidly in the water, a gigantic relic of some bygone glory, its dull grey cannons barely hinting at the violence they'd once wrought upon the world.

Nights, my husband and I would sit together in our well-appointed living room, reading: he read biographies of captains of industry, while I buried myself in colorful textbooks detailing the wondrous creatures who made their home in the sea: sharp-nosed puffer, ocellated frogfish, mushroom scorpion fish, flying gurnard, dragon wrasse, leafy seadragon. There were pictures of sea stars and urchins, mollusks of many varieties, crustaceans of indescribable beauty.

My husband had long since given up his dream of writing a memoir. After making several attempts to break the lock of the file cabinet in which the manuscript was concealed, I finally called in a locksmith. Upon opening the drawer I saw that the book had never really been started. It was little more than a list of potential titles and chapter headings, accompanied by a few photocopied documents from the medical files of his youth. These documents were characteristically clinical in nature, but among the dull listings of medications and false diagnoses, recommended treatments and such, a little light occasionally shone through. *Upon removal of a small sample of the scales,* one doctor had typed, *the subject bled profusely. Close examination of the scales under a microscope revealed a range of exceptional colors not found in nature.* And then, in nearly illegible handwriting in the margin was a note the doctor had apparently scribbled to himself, an afterthought. *Rare opportunity to witness a thing of wonder. Thanked his mother profusely for bringing him to me. No diagnosis possible. Very clearly one of a kind.*

I returned the files carefully to their places and had the locksmith conceal any sign that the lock had ever been compromised. I did, however, steal from the files the one piece of paper on which the doctor had allowed himself a moment of professional awe. I keep it hidden in a place so secret no one will ever find it. Every now and then, when the ease of our ordinary lives becomes overwhelming, when I think I cannot pass another day in the shadow of my husband's brilliant disguise, I take the paper from its hiding place and review the doctor's words, and I think of the treasure I found that night on the pier in the moonlight. It is almost close enough to touch, this treasure. Sometimes I dream of some point in the future when some ordinary disease or accident will take my husband's life, and I will lay him down in the good light of our little house by the bay, and I will go exploring. With my fingernails, my teeth, my eyes, I will search until I find his secret seam. Then I will open him up like some splendid fruit, like some creature from the depths of the mysterious sea, and behold, once again, his beauty.

po·co·cu·ran·te \ ˈpō-kō-k̡yu-ˈran-tē, ˈpō-kō-k̡u-ˈran-tē \
adjective

: indifferent, nonchalant

Pococurante

● ● ●

ANNA TAMBOUR

THE WHOLE TOWN sucked in such a big breath, a fly would of clutched its throat, gasping. Would Pococurante raise a sweat to stay alive? We waved flies away with more effort. Yet at a flick of his wrist, grown men ducked. Dad said a word he shouldn't of in mixed company, but nobody cared.

Astride the town's great river red gum on that blazing day in February, Pococurante didn't defy death. He humiliated it.

When finally he landed head up, feet exploding dust, I cheered like I never did before, nor since. Dad made strange sounds like rain hitting dry ground. He was *crying*! And he wasn't alone.

Smooth as a cold beer, Pococurante passed through the crowd and down the street, the gold letters on his shirt-back slithering.

The next morning I asked Dad, "What's Pococurante mean?"

He must of been thinking for breakfast, because he answered right off. "The god of thunder, I reckon."

That made sense to me. Before Pococurante, a bullock whip was just a bullock whip.

175

As for the circus, I forget its name, but it was a mangy thing. It didn't have a tent so it wasn't any more than a man who rode a horse with his head in the saddle and his feet in the air. We could do that before we were six. And a woman with a beard and hairy arms, and a clown who was only funny when he pulled the red nose off his face to sneeze, and a lion who wanted to sleep and a lion tamer who doubled as the fancy-talk introducer, and Pococurante.

As for the town, it was mangy, too. One of those unloved border towns that straddle two states, where the people on both sides think life on the other side is better but it isn't, and before you notice, everybody's slipped away including you, feeling guilty but bloody relieved, like how you leave a funeral.

As for Pococurante, I had a theory I carried around inside me till I saw my first action in war. I did think, you see, till I really shouldn't of, that this Pococurante *was* some sort of god. That my dad had nailed him good, but at the same time missed. My dad, you see, thought Pococurante had named himself in imitation of. But Mrs. Fletcher at school said there weren't any gods named Pococurante, and she reeled off all the ones there were. Plain God, who we knew. And to some, his son, so that took care of two. And Zeus and Mars and Pluto the dog-god and Neptune with his hayfork, and Tor the blond, and some more that I can't remember, but Pococurante? No.

Pococurante, I'd say each night. I knew he wouldn't like frilly stuff, so I talked to him straight. *Be a sport,* I'd say, all under my breath. *Toss me some of your bravery. You've got bags of it to spare. Make my face as still as yours. You can do it, but I can't on my own.* I certainly couldn't. *Make me look like I don't give a cuss what people think, like you. Tell me what you want from me and I'll do it. Anything.* He never answered directly, but he was the last god on earth I'd of expected to answer anyone like me.

Before Pococurante, if you'd have said that anyone in my town would ape a man with an embroidered shirt, well, you could spit your teeth good-bye. I imitated his walk, which is funny, looking back on it. But every boy did and many men, so it wasn't funny with everybody and his dog doing it. And even though two boys killed themselves trying to be Pococurante, no one wished otherwise any more than they wished that the good years didn't come because of the bad. But there was a limit. When Ridgy Bray was heard whistling "Nobody Cares for Me," he was given a friendly punch-up for putting on airs. I thought it was sacrilegious.

One day when a kick in the stockyard punched my kneecap so my leg folded front to back, I bit a hunk off my lower lip rather than scream. *Pococurante!* He gave me the strength to be a man, but he was as mysterious as weather.

And then I went to war and saw another Pococurante, and another. I saw four by the war's end. I felt shy around them. Lots of men did.

But when I saw Pococurante's face again on other men, and I saw that walk—all that I copied but knew was never me—I knew then the original wasn't a god, but what a man could be.

When the war ended, I asked one of the Pococurantes to be my business partner—the one who saved my life. I thought I'd have to beg him, but he said okay. Just "Okay."

I was so taken aback, I couldn't answer back, but he didn't seem to need that. I was honored that he thought me good enough.

He didn't have any plans so I made up plans for us both.

We opened a dry cleaning shop in Adelaide. I named the dry cleaners *Pococurante,* after he said he didn't care what it was called. It had a classy ring to it, the young girl at the business registry said.

"About time we had some tone here," she declared. "Adelaide's such a sleepy place."

I didn't know what she was talking about so I shut up. My partner leaned over the counter and looked at her, and I thought she'd die right there.

"Poco," she said. "Little! and cur-ahhn-tay."

She clicked her fingers and cocked her head. "Greased lightnin'! Pronto, current, see? I might work here but...say!" she said to my partner—I was a flyspeck on the wall—"You haven't by chance, seen the film at the Odeon?"

"Yar," he said, giving her a ghost of a smile.

So, *Pococurante* the window said, in swirly gold script, close but not quite the same as I remembered.

It wasn't as if my partner didn't work. He did. But the business didn't thrive. He was so attractive that the counter got mobbed, but he was hopeless with ticketing clothes. So, though we lost some love-struck women who'd been coming in bearing clean twin sets just to see him, I took over the counter and he worked in the back. But he didn't seem to get the knack of cleaning and pressing, either. Pleats came out cockeyed, buttons were torn off, and if I'd have wanted a wedding dress to look like the next morning after a night at the pub, I'd only have to give it to my partner, Po. Yes, I'd named him that in the war, and it stuck.

Faithful, many of our customers were. They tried so hard to stay with us. "Jiffy's open closer to my bus stop," one said to me. "But you're the only ones who treat us like intelligent beings." She was the girl from the business registry, our most fervent customer. And she had one helluva big mouth. Everybody thought of us as some classy Jiffy, though a dog could have slept on our jobs and done a better job than Po, and I couldn't do everything. I used to come in during the night and redo Po's work, so's he wouldn't know. He never caught on, though thinking back, he should have.

But Po never noticed. He pitched up every morning on the

dot, never took sickies, never loitered at the counter with his many admirers who came in to catch a glimpse of him. I'd say, "Just a tick, Miss Timble," and ring a bell. "Po!" I'd have to yell, to get my voice past the muffle of clothes, and through the racket of the tumble machines. "Look who's here." Po would push his head between the cello'd garments and give the customer his ghost-smile. "Yar," he'd say and disappear again. "Hard at work, poor boy," Miss Timble would say. "Just give him this," and she'd leave a little package of Lamington cake she'd made, and flee. Or Miss Crumb, or old Mrs. Methuine.

Even the old birds weren't immune to him, though he was immune to all.

I married during the first year, and my wife was a mystery as big as Po. I asked her early on why she wasn't stuck on him instead of me and she asked me back: "What's there to be stuck on?"

Sylvia helped in the shop the first few months, trying to teach Po how to press, but he never learned, and then she couldn't help because the Stoddard solvent made her sick, and she was sick enough anyway. And then Po, our first, came. And then of course she couldn't help anymore, except for bookkeeping, something that Po and I'd been hopeless at.

Syl liked Po, too, but—"He's a sadsack, isn't he?" she asked one night after I got home at midnight from my moonlight fixup job at my own place of business. "You're nuts," she said. She was peevish, Po being such a teether and her with a bun in the oven ready to come out.

"Sadsack!?" I regret I snarled. I opened the fridge and found only a chicken and a bottle of milk. Not one damn beer.

"And where's my bloody—"

"Pull your head out, Mal!" Syl wasn't a simperer. "You don't even listen to the radio in that place."

I didn't. It slowed me down and there was so much work.

But her voice did something to me now. I was never one for a fight, but she could knock me out with a word. "Sorry, Syl," I said.

"That's alright," she said. "Hey, let's not wake Po. But really, love, any man who doesn't know a beer strike's on is a man with a problem to solve."

"Beer?"

"Four days now," she said.

"Strewth!"

"Turn around," she said, and when I did, she stuck her big stomach into the small of my back and massaged my shoulders. "They're stiff as coat hangers. The books look better than you."

"Hmm," I said, knowing she was right and wanting her hands to stay doing that, and not wanting tomorrow to come. *Please don't say another word,* I silently implored her.

"He's not—" she said.

"I can't."

"No, you can't."

We couldn't, you see. We couldn't split the partnership. I couldn't imagine Po, Big Po, being on his own, out in the cold. Sure, there were a billion women who'd have liked to spirit Po away, but even if one succeeded, then what?

"I owe him," I said, and that was that, certainly since Little Po. For though Po wasn't god—"That's for sure," Sylvia laughed, and though it was irreverent to him, I had to laugh, thinking of how often I'd say *You bloody gorilla!* while I fixed his jobs at night—though he wasn't god in the dry cleaners, he was godly in the ways that count. Me being alive proved that. And certainly Po as a failed god would damn our newborn to something. . . .

"It's not like we're superstitious," Sylvia said. "But."

Sylvia always could put words in the right place.

So we had to do something, but what? We couldn't abandon

Po, but we couldn't keep the shop going like it was. "Is he good at anything?" she asked.

It was already two in the morning, so she ignored my "lotsa things" and went for the kill.

"What, precisely?"

Little Po woke for his twosies. I'd slept through them before, but this time I watched her feed him.

When she got him to sleep it was almost 3 A.M., and I had nothing to say except "nothing particular," thinking of something very particular.

"I suspected that." She sighed and shifted her stomach. "You're soft as a cream bun, Mal. He still living in that working-men's hotel?"

"Where else would he bunk, except with us?"

"Horrid places, those."

"No they aren't."

"You hated them."

"Yeah," I admitted, snuggling up to her. "But I like my comforts. I guess he doesn't care."

"Yar." She did him perfectly! I laughed till she hit me. "Wake Little Po at your peril!"

At that, it was impossible not to wake him, and we did, right and proper.

Syl had the idea of branching out instead of giving up. "There's a ton of new migrants we can choose from. Let's find us a nice little tailoress. We'll add dressmaking and fashion advisory to the window, and get little cards printed up."

So we did. Mrs. Kamensky even spoke a bit of English, and she certainly could sew. She had a very Parisian air to her, the customers thought. Unlike lots of Adelaide men who didn't talk about it, the women and girls had never been over there, so any Pole could of fooled them. Every Tuesday night was a free fashion advice evening, and it sure was attended.

I asked Po to come to the nights and sit in as security, but Syl had her own devious reasons and they worked a treat. When fashions were modelled before tea and cake was served, the natural thing was to look to the man in the room. When Mrs. Kamensky said "This is the way to do so-and-so," eyes would always turn to Po. He brought a great deal of *juh nuhsay quah,* as Gloria, the girl from the registry office (now Mrs. Braverman) said.

Shortly after the fashion nights began, a group of brickies' laborers came in one Friday lunch hour, their beery breath making me miss my bachelor days. "Where's this Po bloke?" said the guy in front, plonking a fist the size of a pumpkin on the counter.

"What you want him for?" I asked a bit too loud.

To my relief, Po suddenly appeared at my side.

"You Po?" the head bloke asked, looking a bit shaken.

"Yar," said Po.

"You got a ball and chain o' yur own?"

Po just looked at them.

"He's single, matey," I said, "but what's it to you? He pinch your sheilas?"

"Not likely!" said someone.

"What's your gripe then?" I demanded, Po lending me bluster I didn't own. I felt good defending him against whatever they wanted to accuse him of.

"He go to these ladies' nights?"

"Would you want to?" I asked.

The room exploded in laughter. Even Po smiled at that.

"What a man's gotta do for a quid," someone muttered.

"You're alright, mate," said the lead brickie, and they walked out.

The sessions brought us so much business that I could finally hire a girl to do the cleaning and pressing. She didn't speak much English, but she could put a knife pleat in a bowl of custard, that girl. She was so good that Po didn't need to do anything.

He took to doing only the ug-type work, lifting dirty loads and such, and otherwise sitting on a stool in the back, unless some customer wanted to say hello or ask his advice. His advice was always the same, it seemed to me. He gave them what they wanted, as far as confidence-building went, his smile letting them know that they knew best. But the women who liked him never noticed that. I won't say I understand women.

Then he'd go back to his stool. He wasn't a reader, so him sitting on that stool most of the time bothered me. He looked lost. I thought back to the war and remembered his spoons, so the next day I pinched two from home and gave them to him.

"Are these right?" I asked. "We could use some music."

He started out rusty, but it only took about a day for him to loosen up, and then those spoons clacked out all kinds of songs, and he played better than I remembered. It was okay, seeing him slouched over the stool, banging those spoons against his knee. The girl, Majka, liked his playing, though it was hard for me to hear with all the moaning and hissing and tumbling of the machines.

Those were good days. I slept so well that even the twosies of little Beatrice didn't get me up.

The Pococurante fashion evenings became so popular that we got a half page write-up in the *Adelaide Telegraph* as the place to be if you want to be in mode, with a big photo of the window:

POCOCURANTE CLEANERS
DRESSMAKING & FASHION ADVISORY SERVICE

The article was feisty: "A poke in the eye to all those who think of Adelaide as not able to hold its head up with the major cities as far as style is concerned."

I framed the page and hung it in the window.

*   *   *

The next week Jiffy Cleaners closed, and within days, I told Majka to bring in an offsider, we had so much business, so she brought in her younger sister. Now there were two girls working in the back of the shop, and Po mainly playing his spoons. It would of been odd if it were anyone but Po. And his songs were so full of life.

About a month later, I heard two screams and fought my way through a crush of cello'd suits to find Po holding up a red-bellied black snake with one hand and picking up a wedding veil with the other.

"It want kill me," Majka said, her hands on her heart. Her sister half hid behind her—their eyes big as oil stains.

Po dropped the snake into the middle of the wedding veil, pulled up the edges and knotted them. The snake squiggled but it couldn't get out. Po had bagged that snake so smooth, you'd of thought he bagged a snake a day before breakfast. I'd wondered before where Po came from. He never said.

He looked to me.

"Take it away!" begged Majka.

Her sister pointed. "No, that."

I agreed. I pulled a set of Alfred Hotel drapes from their laundry bag and handed Po the bag.

He dropped his improvised sack into the laundry bag, gave the girls one of his ghost-smiles, and left out the back door.

The front doorbell had tinkled several times and the counter bell was berserk, so I left the girls with a "You okay?" and their uncertain nods. As soon as I could, I joined them in the back and they told me the story. The red-belly had come out from a pile of musty woollens that looked like they hadn't been worn for years. "It want kill me!" Majka kept saying, and her sister acted like one of those jerk dolls where you pull the elastic to make its head nod. I didn't laugh. They wouldn't know that the snake just wanted to get away. I did say I'd never seen another snake in Adelaide, and then showed them from the style of clothes in that pile and their sheepy smell that the customer was a cockie, and since they didn't know that word either, I had to say *farmer,* but they didn't understand till I said *baaah!* And then they smiled.

Then I said so that they understood, regardless of whether they believed the rest of what I'd said: "You tell. No work." They both understood that. We couldn't have our lady customers thinking snakes were lurking in the Pococurante, eyeing their high heels.

Po didn't come back that day, but was security at the fashion night that night, reliable as ever.

The next morning when Majka and her sister arrived, they carried between them a huge old case made of something that looked like leather. They ducked to get it in the front door, and took it to the back. Po was already there, playing his spoons. The shop wasn't open yet, thank goodness, or I would of had to close, I was so curious.

Po stopped playing. We watched as Majka undid the buckles while her sister held the case upright. They opened the hinged lid together and Majka brought out what looked like a taxidermied snake from some Land of Giants, but instead of fangs, it had a little brass cup for a mouth. Majka's sister laid the case down and stood beside her in front of Po.

"You take," Majka said.

"From us Papa," said her sister.

"Wahzsh" or something like that, Majka said. "Snake." She pointed to the thing.

Po nodded to them, no smile at all. He got off the stool and took it from their hands like it was a baby. He inspected it as thoroughly as I've seen him check a gun. It proved to be some weird musical instrument. Black, thick as an anaconda, and in the shape of an S that then snaked down into another S. He found finger holes in the horizontal places of the snake, and put his mouth to the mouthpiece. He moved his lips around experimenting like you do with a new girl . . . and blew.

At first nothing happened, so he wet his lips again and stood up straighter.

He got a gurgle out of it like a toilet in an apartment house. His eyes crossed, looking at the mouthpiece. He shut his eyes and took a big breath and settled his lips again.

"Bwaaaah!"

I hadn't heard that since I left the place where I grew up. Take a six-month-old calf away from its mum, and if it doesn't make that bellow right off, give it time and it'll blast you to the next shire with that sound, and if it doesn't, you're deaf, guaranteed.

The Pococurante is a small place. I stumbled back, holding my ears, and would of fallen but for the press of hanging clothes.

The girls were prepared. They giggled but didn't take their hands from their ears.

Po grinned.

He took a breath and tried again, producing a more civilized sound. I looked at my watch. I had to open the shop. The girls tore their eyes from Po and the great snake, and turned their equipment on.

The day was punctuated with the call of the hungry calf. And it was funny, the reaction.

"You got a bull back there?" asked most.

I had a great time instructing city people on the particulars of bull calls compared to calf calls. "That's one hundred percent calf," I said. "You think a bull's got a great deep voice like that, don't you, Mrs. O'Brien? Mrs. James? Mrs. Braverman? No, a bull's got a soprano, beautiful and thin and high as a lady's. Like yours!"

"Get away with you," said Mrs. Braverman, waving her hand with its flashy wedding ring. "You're pulling my leg."

"Po," I yelled, but he couldn't hear so I had to step back and beckon him through. His eyes were closed so I had to get Majka to put her hand on his shoulder.

He didn't come immediately but when he did, "I was telling Mrs. Braverman here," I said, "that a bull's got a high voice, nothing like that calf call you're making, isn't that true?" Ever since that red-belly, I reckoned he must of come from a place like me.

"Yar," Po said. His lips were curiously red and swollen and he had a faraway look in his eyes.

A little pleat formed between Mrs. Braverman's eyes as she regarded Po.

"Let's see you play," she said.

I bowed to her and turned to Po.

He went back and returned, struggling through the clothes racks with the instrument in his arms. At the look of it, Gloria Braverman's pleat deepened but Po's eyes were closed by then, his lips pressed to the mouthpiece.

"*Bwaaaah!*" yelled the giant snake with the voice of a hungry calf.

Mrs. Braverman fled.

It was so funny, I laughed till I cried. But I didn't tell Syl.

From that day on, Po played only the snake instrument. All day. After a while, he could play like the wind in the grass, so soft that the equipment overpowered him, but the girls didn't like that. They liked him to make the calf sound. "Bwaah! Bwaah!" they'd urge, and "Bookat!" or something like that.

So he made up songs that sounded like they were yelled by a hungry calf. They loved them and they accomplished so much work that they were oftentimes standing around with their hands on their hips, waiting. By the end of a month, I think he could've made that snake whisper, but he didn't. It only yelled.

The first intimation that I had of anything wrong was when I noticed that women had stopped asking for Po.

Then one day when I opened the door, I found an envelope

that someone had shoved under the door. It was an article clipped from the *Melbourne Daily Courier*.

Adelaide Culture Taken to the Cleaners in a Word

In the mushroom culture that is Adelaide, your correspondent has come upon a delicious morsel of farce in the center of town: The Pococurante, where those with fashion at heart come every week, and the crème of Adelaide have their clothes created and cleaned to a T. This center of culture is run by two strange blokes, who must be laughing up their sleeves at the cognoscenti who don't know their Pococurante from their *frankly, Scarlett, I don't give a damn*. They serenade the beauties that flock here with Mozart. Not quite. Follow the sound of the angry bull, and you'll hit the bullseye.

All day I drove myself insane. What was the article on about? Some nasty anti-Adelaide bit of snideness? That's something that Melbourne and Sydney do, but I was trying all day to figure out what to do about Po, who really had to stop playing that snake thing, at least like that.

I'd never read the *Melbourne Daily Courier* before, and don't imagine that any of our customers did. But that article could of been slipped with the ink still damp under the pillow of every Adelaidian, such was the response we got. We hadn't been this slow since the old days, and the people who did come in, came in with silly questions, not things to clean. I could *feel* the city's anger.

In the back of the Pococurante, Po played his snake for the girls, who were getting through the work faster than it was coming in today. Po hadn't mentioned that I didn't call him to the front any more, but then Po never mentioned anything.

My one comfort that day was that Po didn't know about the newspaper article.

.   .   .

I didn't want Sylvia to find out about it either, but when I got home, she met me with "What's the bull? And what's this all about?" And she shoved an open book at me and pointed.

The dictionary. I didn't need her to point. On the left hand page, something was circled in angry red crayon.

I read it.

"Why didn't you just punch me in the eye?" I asked.

"Why didn't you look it up?"

"It was a name, not a word," I said. "He was *Pococurante*! I told you. Would you have looked up a name embroidered in gold on a bloke like that's shirt?"

"Huh!" she said and without taking her eyes off me, yelled, "Beatrice! Get your tea set off the hallway floor this second or—"

I heard a scuttle and a whimper, while I looked at the thing in my arms and wondered what to do with it.

"I don't know," she said to me. "But honestly . . . perhaps not."

Sylvia and I were just inside the front door. I walked past her and dropped into my chair. I couldn't decently strangle the dictionary, so it sat in my lap.

Syl walked over to me, picked it up and flung it against the wall. "There," she said. "You can put it in the bookcase later." She rested her hands on her hips.

"Now," she said, "I asked you about that bull."

"It's a calf," I said. Syl was born and bred in Adelaide.

"Get on with it."

"It's only an instrument that Po practices in slack times," I said. "Sometimes it sounds like a calf . . . only a calf."

After a while she said "Mmm," and then, "Must feed the kids."

She put them to bed as soon as they'd eaten. Then she fixed two tall, stiff drinks: brandy and water without the ice and without the water. She put the glasses on the table by my easy chair, shoved me into it, and sat on my lap.

"You can't change the name now," she said, "or everyone'll think they've got you. You must tough it out." Then she kissed me.

"I don't deserve that," I said.

"Too right you don't," she said, and kissed me again.

She talked, and we drank on empty stomachs, and I felt after another of her drinks that I could tough it out. But then there was Po.

"You must face Po," she said. "Buy him out."

"Yar," I said, but we didn't laugh.

I knew I couldn't do it.

The next day we might as well of been closed as far as customers giving us jobs went. The ones who picked up jobs were cold as a witch's tit, excuse my French. But in the late afternoon, a re-porter came in from the *Adelaide Telegraph*, just as Syl had told me to expect.

"They've picked a fight," she'd said. "And they'll get it."

So I was ready, I hoped.

I laughed at the Melburnians' *snideness* as Syl told me to call it, and shrugged my shoulders at *Pococurante,* saying that if Melbourne people think that Adelaide people don't know what it means, that just shows Melbourne's unworldliness.

"We can snap our fingers to what they're obsessed with," I said (something else memorized from Syl). "We've got *juh nuhsay quah,*" I added. That, I'd remembered from Gloria Braverman, who had said it a lot once, and Syl said that I should repeat that, too.

"I bet the reporter will ask you to say that twice," she said. And she was right.

"And about those sounds of an angry bull?" the reporter asked.

"You ever been to an opera?" I asked the reporter, and he laughed out loud as he wrote that down.

I laughed with him, but didn't feel any too good inside. Po hadn't come in, and didn't pitch up all day.

* * *

The article in the *Adelaide Telegraph* came out the next morning, and it was a triumph. Melburnians were *jealous sourpusses, as anyone would be with their weather. . . . According to Oxford professor W. K. Lister from the Royal Academy of Music, who is visiting his sister here in Adelaide, from descriptions of the instrument being played by Mr. Pococurante*—I distinctly told the reporter *Clarence Braithwaite,* so I don't know how this mistake occurred—*the instrument is a Schlangenrohr, otherwise known as a Serpent, invented hundreds of years ago to be played in churches as a choir enhancement. It is a credit to our city, and possibly of quite venerable age. It is extremely difficult to play. The professor said he would be honoured to meet . . .*

Customers came in all day waving the *Telegraph* like a flag. "Hooray for us!" they crowed. "Where's Po?"

Po didn't come in all day. And what's more, the snake-serpent-whateveryoucallit had disappeared. I'd been too preoccupied to pay any attention to Majka when she'd asked about both the day before. Po had always packed it in its case and left it in the shop before.

When I got home Sylvia was there to meet me at the door, a frothy glass in her hand and a smile as big as a house on her face.

I pasted a smile on my face, but couldn't face the drink.

The next day the girls were frantic. Still no Po. I served the crowd of customers at the counter and then told the girls I'd go find him, and to take the day off.

I closed the shop and walked the three blocks to the rooming house where we'd both lived till I got married. The manager went to his room at my request, but Po didn't answer the door. He was paid up to the end of the week so it was like pulling nails from ironwood to get the manager to open up his room, but finally he did when I said I'd leave and come back with the coppers.

Inside, a neat room greeted us, with nothing personal in it except what he'd left in the wastebasket: a magazine of physical culture—something of a surprise. A powder blue envelope with no writing on it, but it had once been sealed. A balled-up clipping from, you guessed it before I did: The *Melbourne Courier*. And a dried-up apple core.

I felt sick.

While I scouted around the room, I remembered what it was like living in the one next door. Alone in your room, you'd hear other men breathing, turning the pages of magazines, and the rest. The back of each door had a sign on it that said, *NO Women* topping a lot of other *No*s. The view from the window was a brick wall with a painted ad: *Bonds*.

I went home to Sylvia, not knowing what to do. We put the kids in the old Morris and drove all over Adelaide, even out to Snake Gully, looking, like lost farts in a haunted shithouse.

"He's gone," I said after two hours of this.

"Where would he go?"

"How should I know?"

We took the kids back. They were crying. I left her and them in the house, and went out again. I didn't know where, but I had to go out.

I walked till my feet were blistered. I hadn't walked this much for years. He could walk, I remembered. He never groused like the rest of us at the length of those tramps in mud.

When I felt so lost that my eyes were getting misty, I made my way back to my own house, and Sylvia.

Our stereo ran hot that evening—music took the place of talk. We didn't have too many records, so she had to play her Benny Goodman twice. That was fine by me. Any noise would do, because nothing would do.

We went to bed early and I looked at the ceiling for hours. I wanted to strangle whoever those people were—the nasty ones. He had protected me, and what had I done for him?

"You need your sleep, Mal," came Syl's voice through the darkness. She'd been pretending to sleep, too.

"I'll be all right," I said to Syl.

"Shh!" she said.

"I was," I said, miffed. It was Syl who had spoken, not me.

"Shut up, Mal. Listen!"

I heard it. A voice—high and thin as the night. One long note. It swelled . . . and then died away.

"How beautiful!" whispered Sylvia. "Shh!"

She didn't need to shush me. I felt my ears stretch, I was straining so hard to hear.

Again and again—that voice, and each time, farther away.

"There's no words," she whispered, "but then there aren't really in opera, are there?"

She wasn't wanting an answer, so I didn't give her one. She shut up again.

"If only I could sing like that," Sylvia finally sighed when the voice was too faint to catch anymore.

When dawn came, I heard her ladylike snores.

When I opened the door of the Pococurante only a few hours later, Majka and her sister came in as usual, but we each had our jobs to do, so we nodded to each other and got on with it.

A crowd of customers was already waiting, sounding like a flock of galahs: "Did you hear her too? My word! I wonder who . . ."

And they must of breakfasted on radio waves to come up with *Call of the Soprano, Phantom Lady of the Night, Dame Melba's Ghost, Heavenly Disturber of Our Peace* and such rot.

Well, Sylvia had been taken in completely, but I couldn't let it stand. All the customers got an earful of my correction, as I explained that the *lady* was a bull. After about an hour of this, an old guy who was quietly waiting, holding a hoary jacket, backed me up. "A bull's call is unmistakable," he said.

Finally, at that slack time just before noon, I was alone in the front, so I went to the back and told the girls that I was sorry they'd been too far away to hear that bull, living in their migrant camp, but they said that just around dawn the whole camp heard it, too.

"Papa say no bull," Maj said. And just then, a ghost tweaked three sets of lips.

A·U·T·O·C·H·T·H·O·N·O·U·S

au·toch·tho·nous \ o-'täk-thə-nəs \
adjective

1: indigenous, native
2: formed or originating in the place where found

From Around Here

• • •

TIM PRATT

I ARRIVED ON A FERRY made of gull cries and good ocean fog, and stepped from the liminal world into Jack London Square, down by Oakland's fine deep-water port. I walked, predawn, letting my form coalesce from local expectations, filtered through my own habits and preferences. I stopped at a plate glass window downtown by the 12th Street train station and took a look at myself: dreads and dark skin, tall but not epic tall, clothes a little too raggedy to make robbing me worth a mugger's time. I walked on, feeling the thrums and creaks of a city waking up or going to sleep or just keeping on around me. I strolled past the houses of sex offenders, one-time killers with high blood pressure, altruists, guilty activists, the good-hearted, the fearful, and all the rest of the usual human lot. I was looking for the reek of the deeply crazy, the kind of living crack in a city that can swallow whole neighborhoods and poison the well of human faith in a place utterly. The kind that could shatter lives on an afternoon spree or corrode them slowly over decades.

After awhile, I found a street like that, and then I went to get some breakfast.

It was the kind of diner where you sit at a counter and the menus are sticky with the last customer's pancake syrup and you hope for the best. There were no other customers—I was between morning rushes, which made me lonely—and when the waitress came to take my order she was frazzled, like nobody should look at five in the morning. I said, "I don't have any money, but maybe we can work something out." Either she was from around here, and I'd get some breakfast, or she wasn't, and I'd get thrown out.

She got that faraway look like they do, and said, "Let's work something out."

I nodded. "Where you from?"

"Grew up in Temecula."

"Ah. The Inland Empire. Pretty black walnut trees down that way."

She smiled, the way people do when you prod them into a nice memory.

People have different ideas about what "home" means. For her, home meant a good chunk of California, at least, since Temecula was down south a ways. I'd never been there, but I'd probably go eventually. For some people, home just means one town, and if they stray from there, they feel like foreigners in strange territory. For others, home is a neighborhood, or a block, or a street, or one room in one house where they grew up. And for some, home is *nowhere,* and me, I have a hard time talking to people like that.

"What can I offer you?" I said. My stomach rumbled. I'd never eaten before, at least not with these teeth, this tongue, this stomach. I couldn't even remember what food tasted like. Things of the body are the first things I forget.

She told me, and I knew it was true, because I wasn't talking to her conscious mind, the part that's capable of lies and self-deception. I was talking to the deepdown part of her, the part that stays awake at night, worrying, and making bargains with any gods she can imagine. She had a son, and he was in some shitty public school, and she was afraid he'd get hurt, beat up, hassled by the gangs, maybe even *join* a gang, though he was a good kid, really.

"Okay," I said. "Give me breakfast, and I'll make sure your son is safe."

She said yes, of course, and maybe that seems like a lopsided bargain, keeping a kid safe through years of school in exchange for a plate of eggs and sausage and toast and a glass of OJ, but if it's in my power to give, and doesn't cost more than I can afford, I don't worry much about parity.

The waitress snapped out of that deepdown state and took my order, knowing she'd pay for it, not sure why, but probably not fretting about it—and for the first time in however long, she wasn't worried about her boy getting stabbed in the school parking lot.

Breakfast was fine, too. Tasted as good as the first meal always does, I imagine.

The neighborhood I settled on wasn't in the worst part of Oakland, or the best—it was on the east side of Lake Merritt, maybe a mile from the water, in among a maze of residential streets that mingled million-dollar homes and old stucco apartment complexes. I walked there, over hills and curving streets with cul-de-sacs, through little roundabouts with towering redwoods in the middle, tiny triangular parks in places where three streets all ran into one another, and past terraced gardens and surprise staircases providing steep shortcuts down the hills. A good place, or it could have been, but there was a canker along one street, spiderwebbing out into the neighborhoods nearby, blood and crying and death somewhere in the near past, and lurking in the likely future.

First thing I needed was a place to stay. I picked a big house with a neat lawn but no flowers, out on the edge of the street that felt *bad*. I knocked, wondering what day it was, if I was likely to find anyone home at all. An old man opened the door and frowned. Was he suspicious because I was black, because I was smiling, because of bad things that had happened around here? "Yes?"

"I'm just looking for a room to rent for a few weeks," I said. "I can make it worth your while, if you've got the space."

"Nope," he said, and closed the door in my face.

Guess he wasn't from around here.

I went a little closer to the bad part, passing a church with a sign out front in Korean, and was surprised to see people sitting on their stoops drinking beers, kids yelling at one another in fence-hidden backyards, people washing their cars. Must be a Saturday or Sunday, and the weather was indeed springtime-fine, the air smelling of honeysuckle, but I'd expected a street with bars on the windows, people looking out through their curtains, the whole city-under-siege bit. This place *pulsed* with nastiness, the way an infected wound will radiate heat, and I knew other people couldn't feel the craziness the way I could, but shouldn't there have been some external sign? I wasn't sensing some hidden moral failings here—this was a place where violence had been done.

I looked for a likely house, and picked a small adobe place near a corner, where an elderly Chinese woman stood watering her plants. I greeted her in Cantonese, which delighted her, and it turned out she *was* from around here, so it only took a few minutes to work something out. She took me inside, showed me the tiny guest room, and gave me a spare key, zipping around the house in a sprightly way, since I'd gotten rid of her rheumatism and arthritis in exchange for bed and board. "We'll just tell everyone you're my nephew," she said. "By marriage. Ha ha ha!"

I laughed right along with her, kissed her cheek—she was good people—and went out onto the street.

I strolled down the sidewalk, smiling and nodding at everyone I met. The street was long and curving, cut off at either end by a couple of larger cross streets. There were some apartment houses near one end, with younger people, maybe grad students or starving artists, and some nice bigger houses where families lived. The residents were pure Oakland variety—Koreans, Chinese, whites, blacks, Latinos of various origins. Even the cars on the sidewalks were diverse, with motorcycles, beaters held together with primer and care, SUVs, even a couple of sports cars. I liked it. It felt neighborly. But it also felt *wrong,* and I couldn't pinpoint the badness. It was all around me. I was *in* it, too close to narrow it down further.

A pretty woman, probably half-Japanese, half-black—I'm good at guessing origins, and the look is a unique one—sat on the steps of a three-story apartment house with decorative castle crenellations on the roof, sipping an orange cream soda from a bottle and reading a slim book. There was something about her—ah, right, I got it. I was in a body again, and she was beautiful, and I was attracted.

"Afternoon," I said, walking up to the steps and nodding a greeting. "You know Miss Li?"

"Down on the corner?" she said. "Sure."

"I'm her nephew. I'll be staying with her for a while, maybe a few weeks, while I get settled."

"Nephew, huh?" She looked up at me speculatively. "By marriage, I'm guessing."

"You guessed right," I said, and extended my hand.

"I'm Sadie." She shook my hand. "Welcome to the neighborhood." There was no jolt of electricity, but she wasn't giving me go-away vibes, either, so I gave it a try.

"Are you from around here?"

"Me? No. I'm from Chicago, born and raised. Just came out here for school."

I grinned wider. I couldn't have a dalliance with someone from around here—it would be too easy to steer them, compel them, without even intending to, too easy to chat with their deepdown parts by accident. But she had a different home, so we could talk, like people. I was a person now, for the moment, more or less. "I could use someone to show me around the neighborhood, help get me oriented."

She shrugged. "What do you want to know?"

I sat down, not too close. "Oh, I don't know." How about *Why aren't you terrified? Don't you sense the presence of something monstrous in this place?* "Who's that guy?" I pointed at a young Latino man tinkering on a motorcycle in the garage across the street.

"Hmm. I think his name's Mike? I don't really know him. He goes on motorcycle rides most weekends."

"Okay. How about him?" This time I pointed at a big man in an unseasonable brown coat, walking up the hill dragging a wire grocery cart behind him. He was middle-aged, and had probably been a real bruiser in his prime.

"That's Ike Train," she said. "Nice guy, but kind of intense. He's a plumber, and he fixes stuff for people in the neighborhood for free sometimes, but he likes to hang around and talk for a while afterward, and he gets bad BO when he sweats, so not a lot of people take him up on it. He's got a deal with whoever owns my building, though, and he does all the plumbing stuff here."

"How about her?" I said. A woman in sunglasses, attractive in a blonde-and-brittle-and-gym-cultured way, was walking a little yipping dog.

"Martha." Sadie rolled her eyes. "Put your trash cans out on the curb a day early and you'll catch hell from her. I think she's in a hurry for this neighborhood to finish gentrifying. So why all the questions?"

"I just like talking to you," I said, which was the truth, but not the whole truth. "Asking about people passing by seemed like a good way to do that."

She laughed. "You never told me your name."

Why not? No one ever even remarked on the name—except to say it was weird—unless I was on a Pacific island, and even then, it meant so many things in so many different languages, no one ever guessed. "I'm Reva," I said.

"Interesting name. Where you from?"

"I was born on a little island in the Pacific," I said. "You wouldn't have heard of it. But I didn't stay there long. I've lived all over since then." I thought this was going well, but we were reaching the point where the conversation could founder on the rocks of nothing-in-common. "You said you're here for school? What do you—"

Someone shouted, "Sadie!" A short man with wispy hair, dressed like an IRS agent from the 1950s—black horn-rimmed glasses, white shirt, narrow black tie—bustled over from the house across the street, an ugly, boxy two-story with heavy drapes in the windows. He reached our side of the street and said "Vocabulary word: Obstruction."

"Oh, Christ," Sadie muttered.

"Something that gets in the *way*," he continued. "Another: Obstinate. Unreasonably stubborn; pigheaded."

"The back bumper of my car's only in front of your driveway by an *inch,* Oswald," she said. "The car in front of me is too far back, I'm sorry, it's not like it's actually in your *way*."

"In my way, and in the *red*," Oswald said, not even glancing at me, staring at Sadie with damp-looking eyes magnified behind thick lenses. "The police have been notified."

"Whatever," Sadie said. "Fine, I'll move it." She stood up, glared at him, looked at me apologetically, and walked over to a well-worn black compact that was, maybe, poking two inches into the little driveway that led to Oswald's garage. She got in and drove away.

I nodded at Oswald. "Beautiful day," I said.

He squinted at me, then turned and went back to his house, up the steps, and through the front door.

I glanced at the book Sadie had left on the steps. It was a monograph on contraceptive methods in the ancient world. I wondered what she was studying. A few moments later she came walking up the sidewalk and returned to her place on the steps. "Sorry," she said. "Oswald's a dick. He never even opens his garage. As far as I know he doesn't even have a car." She shook her head.

"Every neighborhood has a nasty, petty person or two."

"I guess. Most people here are pretty nice. I've only been here a year, but I know a lot of people well enough to say hello to, and Oswald's the only one I really can't stand. Him and his 'vo-cabulary words.' Somebody told me he's an English teacher, or used to be, or something. Can you imagine being stuck in a class with *him*?"

"I'd rather not think about it. So. Am I someone you'll say hello to in the future?"

"You haven't given me a reason not to yet," she said. "Look, it's nice meeting you, but I've got studying to do."

"What subject?"

"I'm getting my master's in human sexuality. Which, today, means reading about how ancient Egyptians used crocodile shit and sour milk as spermicide."

I wrinkled my nose. "Did it work?"

"Actually, yeah. But it can't have been very much fun." She rose, picked up her drink, and went into the apartment building.

I love a woman who can toss off a good exit line.

The next morning I ran into Sadie, and she invited me to brunch at a café down near the lake. We ate eggs and drank mimosas on the restaurant's patio, where bougainvillea vines hung all around us from pillars and trellises. She wanted to know things about me, and I was game, telling her a few stories from my travels. She was from Chicago, so I told her about the month I'd spent there, leaving out my battle in the trainyard with a golem made of hogmeat. I told her a bit about my months working on a riverboat casino on the Mississippi, though I didn't mention the immortal singer in the piano bar who'd once been a pirate and wanted to start plundering again, before I convinced him otherwise.

"So you're basically a drifter," she said, sipping her second mimosa.

"We prefer to be called 'people of no fixed address,' " I said.

"How long do you think you'll stay here?"

"Oh, I don't know," I said, leaning across the table, looking at her face, which seemed to fit some ideal of faces I'd never before imagined. "I'm like anybody else, I guess. Just looking for a place to call home."

She threw a napkin at me, and it bounced off my nose, and I thought I might be falling in love.

Sadie had to study, so I spent the rest of the lovely Sunday meeting people in the neighborhood. It's not hard, once you overcome their initial reluctance to talk to strangers, and hearing I was Miss Li's nephew made most folks open up, too—the lady was well liked. I visited the closest park, just a few blocks away, where some guys from the neighborhood were playing basketball. I got in on the game, and didn't play *too* well, and they liked me fine. I got invited to a barbecue for the next weekend. I helped an older guy wash his car, and then spent an hour with Mike, who was rebuilding the carburetor on his motorcycle—I didn't know much about machines, but I was able to hand him tools and talk about California scenic highways. I chatted with mothers pushing strollers, young kids riding scooters, surly teens, and old people on afternoon walks.

And every time I got someone alone, if they were from

around here, I talked to their deepdown parts, and I asked them what was wrong with this place.

I didn't find out anything unusual. Oh, there were crimes—this *was* a big city, after all, even if a residential neighborhood. There were occasional break-ins, and a mugging or two, though none right around here. A couple of car thefts. But nothing poisonously, unspeakably bad. Maybe my senses were out of whack, or I was picking up the irrelevant psychic residue of some long-ago atrocity. I have trouble adapting my mind to the shortness of human time scales, sometimes.

It was late afternoon when I went past Ike Train's place. He had a tidy little house, and a bigger yard than most. His porch was shadowed, but I could see the big man sitting on a creaking wooden swing, messing with something in his hands. I was going to hello the house, but Ike hailed me first. "You're new!" he shouted. "Come over!"

"Mr. Train," I said, delighted, because I do love meeting people, especially ones who love meeting me. "I've heard about you." I passed through the bushes, which overgrew his walk, and went up to his porch. He held a little man-shaped figure made of twisted wire and pipe cleaners. He set the thing aside and rose, reaching out to shake my hand. His grip was strong, but not a macho show-off strong, just the handshake of a man who wrestled with pipe wrenches on a regular basis.

"You're staying with Miss Li," he said, sitting down and gesturing for me to take a cane chair by his front door. "Her nephew?"

"I'm Reva. More of a grandnephew from the other side of the family, but yeah."

"What brings you to town?" He went back to twisting the wire, giving the little man an extra set of arms, like a Hindu deity.

"I've been traveling for a few years," I said. "Thought I might try settling here." Maybe I would, for a while, if I could find a way to get rid of the bad thing making the whole street's aura stink. Being in a body again was nice, and even on our short acquaintance there was something about Sadie I wanted to know better, like she was a flavor I'd been craving for ages.

"It's a nice enough place," Ike said.

"So tell me," I said, leaning forward. "Are you from around here?"

Ike's hands went still, the wire forgotten. "Oh, yeah," he said, and his voice was different now, slower and thicker. "This is my home. Nobody knows how hard I work to keep it clean, how filthy it gets. The whole fucking city is circling the drain. Dirty, nasty, rotten, wretched . . ."

I frowned. That was his deepdown self talking, but it didn't sound like him. "Ike, what do you—"

"We have to twist their heads all the way around," he said, his voice oddly placid, and turned the little wire man in his hands, twisting its round loop of a head tighter and tighter until it snapped and came off in his fingers. "Break them and sweep them up. Clean up the trash, keep things clean. Yeah. I'm from *around* here."

"Ike," I said, careful, because there were sinkholes in this man's mind, and I didn't know how deep they were, or what might be hidden inside them. "Maybe you and me can work something out."

"No," he said, and crushed the little man. "There's nothing to work out. Everything's already been worked out." He stared at me, through me, and his eyes were wet with tears. "There's nothing you can offer me."

I stood up and stepped back. He was from around here, I was talking to his deepdown self, but Ike wouldn't work something out with me. I didn't understand this refusal. It was like water refusing to freeze in winter, like leaves refusing to fall in autumn, a violation of everything I understood about natural law. "Don't worry about it, Ike. Let's just forget we had this talk, huh?"

Ike looked down at the broken wire thing in his hands. "Nice meeting you, uh, buddy," he said. "Say hi to Miss Li for me."

I headed back down the street toward Miss Li's, thinking maybe Ike was crazy. Maybe he had something to do with the badness here. Maybe he *was* the badness. I needed to know more. I asked Miss Li about him, over dinner that night, but she didn't know much about Ike. He'd lived on the street longer than anybody, and his parents had owned his house before him. He was seriously from around here. So why had talking to his deepdown self been so strange and disturbing?

"Hey, Reva," Sadie said when I answered the door. "You busy?"

It was Monday, and the street was quiet, most everybody off about their business. "Not for you," I said, leaning against the doorjamb.

"Could you come up to my place and help me with something?"

I grinned, and grinning felt good; I'd forgotten that about bodies, that genuinely smiling actually caused chemical changes and improved the mood. "I'm at your service." I pulled the door shut and followed Sadie down the steps and up the street. I didn't bother locking the door—nobody would rob the place while I was staying there.

"What do you know about spiders?" she said, leading me into the lobby of the apartment building. The floor was black tile with gold flecks, and there was a wall of old-fashioned brass and glass mailboxes. I liked it. The place had personality.

"Hmm. Eight legs. Mythologically complex—sometimes tricksters, sometimes creators, sometimes monsters, depending on who you ask."

She looked at me, half-smiling, as if she wasn't sure if I was joking. She opened a door, revealing an elevator with a sliding grate. We went inside, and she rattled the gate closed. Back in the old days there would have been a uniformed attendant to run the elevator. This must have been a classy place in its day. "Can you recognize poisonous spiders? I've heard there are some nasty ones out here, black widows and brown recluses, stuff like that. There's a spider in my tub and it's freaking me out a little."

"It's probably gone by now, right?" The elevator rattled and hummed as it ascended.

"I don't think it can get out. It keeps trying to climb the sides of the tub and sliding back down."

She was standing a little closer to me than she had to. I wondered if I should read anything into that. "So you want me to get rid of it?"

"If it was a snake or a rat or something, I'd do it myself. Most things like this don't bother me. But spiders . . ." She shuddered. "Especially when I don't know if they're poisonous or not. I heard the bite of a brown recluse can make your skin rot away. Bleah. Vicious little things."

I shrugged. "They're just trying to get by. Besides, there aren't any brown recluses in California."

She frowned. "But everybody says there are."

"It's a common misconception. Only a handful of brown recluses have ever been found here, and they all came with shipments from the south or midwest. They aren't native anywhere west of the Rockies. Hundreds of people go to their doctors in California every year saying they've been bitten by recluses, but the bites are always from some other bug, or they're just rashes or something." The fear of brown recluse spiders in California was an oddly persistent one. I'd once seen a billboard in San Francisco, with a several-million-times-life-size depiction of a fiddleback spider, and a strident warning in Spanish. People do tend toward the fearful, even without cause.

Sadie gave me a new, appraising look. "No shit? You're, like, a spider expert or something?"

I laughed. How could I explain that I just had a *really good sense* for where things came from? "Nah, just something I read about. Anyway, whatever kind of spider it is, I'll take care of it for you. There are lots of black widows out here. Not to mention scorpions."

"My hero," she said, and touched my arm. It was the first time I'd been touched in this body, other than a handshake and Miss Li's friendly embrace, and I had to stop myself from taking Sadie in my arms right then. Having a body again was wonderful. Why had I gone without for so long?

She let me into her apartment, which was furnished in student-poverty chic, mismatched furniture and beat-up bookcases overflowing with texts, prints of fine art hung alongside real art of the student-show variety. The apartment was big, though, for a single person in Oakland, with a nice-sized living room, a little kitchen separated by a counter, and a short hallway leading to other doors. "This is a nice place."

"I know!" she said, and I liked how sincere she sounded. "It's crazy cheap, too. I looked at a lot of apartments when I first moved here, and they were all way more than I could afford, but this one's half as much as other apartments this size. I've got a bedroom *and* an office. I guess the owner doesn't live around here, and doesn't realize how rents have gone up these past few years? I don't know, but it's my good luck."

"You don't know the landlord?" I disapprove of absentee landlords on principle.

"Nah, I just mail rent checks to a PO box. There's a tenant on the first floor who gets even cheaper rent than the rest of us for managing the place, making sure leases get signed, interviewing people, all that. If she ever moves out, I might try to get that gig. It can be a lot of work, though—there's a lot of turnover here. Because it's so cheap, we get plenty of people who are down on their luck, and some of them just take off without paying their last month's rent. I guess that's what deposits are for, though. Two or three girls have skipped out since I moved in, just leaving their stuff here. Not that they had much. They were all on drugs, I heard. Sometimes this place is like a halfway house."

"Huh," I said, thinking. "How are the pipes? You said Ike Train is the plumber here?"

"Yeah. I don't know if he's a lousy plumber or if the place just has shitty pipes, but it seems like he's over here all the time—somebody's always got a leak or a bad drain or something. But, hey, at these prices, we don't expect perfection. Anyway, speaking of bathrooms . . ." She led the way down the hallway, opening the door onto a nice big bathroom, with an old claw-footed tub.

I looked into the bathtub. "That," I said, "is a daddy long-legs." Specifically a Spermaphora, but why show off?

"Aren't they, like, the most poisonous spider in the world? But their fangs are too short to bite humans?"

"Another myth," I said. "They're pretty much harmless. They can bite, but it wouldn't do much to you." I reached down, picked up the spider by one of its comically long legs, and walked over to the open window. I set the spider on the sill, and it scurried off down the exterior wall. I looked back at Sadie, who stood by the door, looking at me.

I hadn't been in a body for long, but I knew that look. "You're not afraid of spiders at all, are you?"

"I needed *some* excuse to get you up here," she said, taking a step toward me. "I wasn't sure if you liked me, but the way you looked at me in the elevator . . ."

"I guess I'm not subtle." But I *was* lucky.

"That's okay. Games can be fun, but there's nothing wrong with the direct approach, either." She stepped in close and kissed me, putting the palm of her hand on my chest, over my heartbeat. I kissed back, my body responding in that wonderful way that bodies do.

"Mmm," I said after a moment. "So you're a student of human sexuality, huh?"

"Sure," she said. "But there are some things you can't get from a book."

•   •   •

Afterward, as she brewed tea in her kitchen and I sat, feeling loose-limbed and glorious, on a stool at the counter, she said, "Look, I don't want you to get the wrong idea..." She had her back turned to me, and that was too bad, because she wasn't saying anything she couldn't say to my face.

"Don't worry," I said. "It was what it was. And it was very nice. But I don't think it gives me a claim on you. Which doesn't mean I'd object if you wanted to do it *again*."

Now she turned, and she looked relieved. "Sometimes I just want to be with somebody. You seem nice, and *god* you're pretty, but I'm not looking for a boyfriend or anything right now. I'm so busy with school, you know?"

That gave me a little pang, I admit, because of course I wanted to be seen as irresistible boyfriend material, even though I *know* I'm no more constant than a bank of fog blowing through. But she was being honest with me, at least. A lot of bullshit in this world could be avoided if people just told the truth, however inconvenient it might be. And maybe, if I could get rid of the nastiness on this block, I could settle down here, and become more constant, and win Sadie over. I was pretty low maintenance. Hadn't I rambled around this world enough? Maybe it was time to pick a home and stick with it for a while.

I had an idea about the source of the badness here now, anyway. It's not like I'm a great detective or anything, but I can see how things fit together, when it's right in front of my face. I wondered why no one else had ever figured it out.

"Want to go out again sometime?" I asked. "I haven't taken in much of the local scene yet."

"Sure," she said, placing a cup of steaming tea on the counter before me. She looked me right in the eye. "We can do something this weekend. Or we could just stay in all weekend having sex. I've got toys in my bedroom I didn't even *show* you."

My heart went pitter-pat, and other parts of me did other things. Having a body was so wonderful, I wasn't sure what had ever possessed me to leave my last one.

*   *   *

Ike Train's backyard had a nine-foot wooden privacy fence, overgrown with vines that made it seem even higher. The lock on his gate was nothing special, though, so I popped it open pretty easily that night. He had a big garden back there, lots of tomato plants, the earth all churned up. I checked his back windows again—still dark, and he was probably deep asleep, like the rest of the block. I found a shovel and a likely mound of earth near the back fence, and started digging. I didn't worry about Ike waking up and noticing me. I wasn't going to get noticed unless I wanted to be. I was in a body, but that didn't mean I'd given up all my powers.

Ike had dug a good grave. I went about five feet down before I found the girl, wrapped in cloth sacks and sprinkled liberally with some kind of lye-based drain cleaner, though not enough to dissolve her body completely—that takes a *lot* of lye, even more than a plumber would have on hand. She was mostly just bones, at this point. I couldn't unwrap the burlap completely, because the lye could have burned my skin; that was one disadvantage to having a body. How many other girls were buried here? Lonely women with no families, women with drug problems who jumped at the cheap rents in the apartment house on the corner, who opened their doors to that nice plumber Ike Train and found out he wasn't so nice after all. I wondered if he lured them to his house, or somehow took their bodies out of the apartment building. I couldn't imagine how he'd gotten away with something like this—in a city, someone is *always* awake, and witnesses are a problem—but serial killers can be lucky motherfuckers.

Well, Ike didn't have good luck anymore. Now he had me instead.

"Here's my problem, Ike," I said, after he woke up and realized he couldn't free himself. He tried to yell at me, but he was gagged pretty good, and still woozy from the chemicals I'd knocked him out with, and it was just muffled noise. I leaned back in the chair I'd dragged over by the couch where he was bound. "I could just call the cops, and let them know about the bodies in the backyard. I can be really convincing, especially if the cops are from around here. You'd get arrested and put away for a long time. But that would be bad for the neighborhood. People here don't realize there's a monster like you in their midst. Everybody knows you. You've been in most of the *houses* on this street at one time or another. To find out you've been killing women and burying them in your back garden..." I shook my head. "Most of these people wouldn't trust anyone ever again. There'd be news reporters all over. Property values would plummet. People would move away. I'd hate to see that happen."

He made furious noises. I removed the gag. He tried to bite off my fingers. I couldn't blame him. "Make a fuss and I'll knock you out again," I said. "You've got lots of nice chemicals under your sink I can mix up."

His voice was low and intense. "You don't understand. This used to be a nice place, when I was a kid. Now all that trash lives on this street. Spics, chinks, whores, and junkies. Jabbering away in Spanish and Chinese, trying to cadge change off people so they can buy drugs, all that bullshit. This whole place is a toilet now. I wish I could flush them all."

I raised my eyebrow. "What about black folks? Want to flush us too?"

"I got nothing against black people," he said, wounded, as if I'd slandered him. "And there's decent Chinese people, like your aunt, and some Mexicans I don't mind, but the kind of garbage that rents rooms down at the castle apartments, they're just *worthless,* they—"

"So killing them has got nothing to do with your sexual gratification, then?"

"That's sick," Ike spat. "You're disgusting. I do what I do to keep this neighborhood *nice,* to keep it safe. A piece of shit like you couldn't possibly understand that."

"You're no prize yourself, Ike. You know it's all over now, right? You're finished."

"You can't mess with me," he said, his eyes shining, as they had when I'd spoken to his deepdown parts before. "This is *my* place."

"It's my place now. And you don't have a home here anymore." I put the rag of chemicals over his face again until he passed out.

I held a hammer in my hand with every intention of caving in Ike Train's skull, then disposing of his body out in the desert somewhere, but I couldn't do it. He was a *person*. I'd expected a monster, and yes, Ike was a monster too, but I couldn't see past his humanity. In my more natural state, without a body, I would have found executing Ike Train as simple as flicking an ant off a tablecloth. But for now I was wearing a human form, and Ike was one of my tribe, albeit a crazy, dangerous one. I couldn't smash his head in, not if I wanted to keep functioning in this body. Such an act would tear me apart. I put the hammer down.

Still, Ike had to die, and disappear, if I wanted to save this neighborhood from imploding. They could never know this monster had been in their midst—such a revelation would poison the wellspring of camaraderie and human kindness I'd found here. I had to do something fast, though. He was a big man, and he would wake up soon, and I couldn't bear talking to him again.

Sometimes, back in the old days, I'd watched people drown, disappearing beneath churning waves. Losing those people hurt me—diminished me—but it felt more natural, somehow, with the elements taking their lives, instead of a human hand.

I'm not stupid. I know killing is killing, even if some natural phenomenon is the murder weapon. If you cast someone into a churning sea and they die, you've murdered them, even if it's the water that ends their lives. But maybe you can sleep a little easier, since the blood isn't on your hands. Maybe.

Ike Train was a man who prepared for things. There were several gas cans in the garage, by his emergency generator. They sloshed full when I picked them up. Fortunately, Ike didn't wake, even when I piled pillows around the perimeter of the living room and doused them with fuel. The smoke would kill him before the fire touched him. A mercy, and more than he'd offered his victims. But I'm not about vengeance. I'm about finding bad homes and making them good again.

When I felt tears on my face, I tried to believe they were just stinging from the gas fumes.

House fires aren't exactly good for neighborhood morale, but they tend to make a community pull together. Everybody came out and watched Ike Train's house burn. The fire trucks got there pretty quickly, but not quickly enough. The roof collapsed while they were still hooking their hoses up, but Ike was surely gone by then.

Nobody paid any attention to me, not even Sadie, though she stood only a few yards away. Everyone was watching the flames. I needed to get cleaned up, and shower off the mud from Ike's backyard. Maybe I'd visit Sadie later, and see about making myself into boyfriend material. This could be a nice place now.

"Vocabulary word," said Oswald, walking over from his house down the block and joining the spectators. "Conflagration: a large fire. Also a conflict or war."

"Shut the fuck up, Oswald," someone said wearily. "We think Ike Train died in there."

"Another," Oswald said softly. "Cothurnus. A tragedy. Also the costume worn by an actor in a tragic play."

Then he looked at me, for a little too long, like he had something to say, but some people just have eyes like that, intense and too direct. I slipped away from the neighborhood crowd, though being among them was all I wanted. I knew the ugly burned-out lot in the middle of their street would be better than the ugliness that Ike Train had caused. I'd used fire to cauterize something much worse. But I still felt guilty. A shower would help, a little. You have to start getting clean somewhere.

I was on my way to visit Sadie the next Saturday, for our weekend of sex or tourism, when Oswald hailed me from his front yard, where he was brutalizing a patch of unkempt grass with a weed whacker. "Mr. Reva!" he said, turning off his buzzing yard tool.

"It's just Reva," I called back.

"I wonder if I might have a word with you," he said.

"What, vocabulary words?" I called back, trying to sound cheerful, because even a miserable little guy like this probably had some good in him somewhere. But I really just wanted to see Sadie.

"Very droll," he replied. "Please? Just a moment? I have something inside that might interest you."

Was this a come-on? Was Oswald so cranky because he was closeted and gay? I'd seen that sort of thing before. I wasn't interested in him, but maybe, if he was from around here, I could talk with his deepdown self and help him relax and be a better neighbor. "Sure," I said, and went up the steps, following him to his front door. He opened the door and gestured for me to enter. I did, and it was dark inside—*very* dark—so I paused just inside the door. "Maybe we should turn the lights on—" I began, and then he shoved me, hard, and I stumbled forward into empty air, falling on what felt like a mound of rubble and broken glass. "Fuck!" I shouted, and turned over, my eyes starting to adjust. There was no *house* inside his house—it was scooped out and hollow, just a few beams to support the roof and walls, otherwise an open pit of dirt and rocks.

I realized, then, that I'd seriously misinterpreted the situation on this street.

Oswald leapt down from the little scrap of flat floor just inside the door, landing in a crouch on the dirt before me. He moved more like a spider than a man, which made sense; he wasn't a spider, but he wasn't a man, either. I started to rise up, and he threw a rock at my head, hard enough that I don't remember the impact at all, just the coming of the darkness.

"Vocabulary word," Oswald said later, tying up my wrists with lengths of wire. I was naked, and the rocks in his house were cutting into my skin. "Chthonic. Dwelling under the earth. Gods of the underworld. *Me*."

"Oswald," I said, alarmed at the slur in my voice. How hard had that rock hit my head? Way too hard, judging by the pounding in my skull. "We can work something out."

"Another: Autarch. Absolute ruler. Tyrant. Me, here, in this place." He wired my legs together.

"You don't have to do this." I tried to twist, to kick, but he was agile, and I wasn't, and he didn't even stop talking while he dodged my flailing.

"Another: Autochthonous. Originating where it is found. Native. From *around here*. Me, me, *me*." He kicked me in the chest on the last word, and darker black dots swam into my vision against the darkness inside his housepit, and I gasped for breath.

"This is my place," Oswald said, "and Ike Train was my man. He made the proper sacrifices to me, kept me fed, kept me *happy*. And you spoiled that, stranger, outside agitator, you *ruined* it, and now I have to cultivate another man. But you'll die. Not a sacrifice to me. Just somebody who got in the way." He gnashed his teeth, and they clacked together like gemstones. "You didn't have to burn Ike. He wouldn't have killed that little bitch Sadie you like so much. She has too many friends. We only kill the ones no one will miss. Well, *usually*. Someone might miss you, but I don't care."

Oswald was the reason Ike Train's deepdown self had been so strange. I couldn't make a deal with Ike, because he'd *already* made a bargain with a creature like me. Well, *sort of* like me. Oswald and I had the same means, but different methods and motivations. That explained why nobody had ever discovered Ike Train's murders—Oswald had used his powers to protect him, and he probably did other things, too, like keeping the neighborhood safe from danger, but the price he demanded was just too high.

As far as Oswald knew, I was just a *guy,* somebody who came to town and discovered his lackey's secret. He didn't know what he was dealing with. Fortunately.

Oswald stood up, letting his human shape drop, revealing the shambling earthen thing underneath, the creature of the dark and deep who'd lived here, on this spot, for centuries. Oswald was a local spirit, tied to this place, but he was an ugly one, who chose to live off pain instead of prosperity. He reached out to me with arms of darkness, endless limbs that stank of minerals and stale air. "Vocabulary word," he hissed, in a voice that could never be mistaken for human. "Decapitate. To cut off a head. Another: Decedent. One who has died. *You.*"

Then he killed me.

While I was dying, I remembered the problem with having a body.

The problem is pain.

•　•　•

I wasn't able to return for a few days. My new body was Korean, older, shorter, dressed in a plaid shirt and khaki pants. I'd needed to pick up some supplies, and they were tricky to get, since I didn't have money, and had to rely on the kindness of locals. I traded a lucky gambling streak for the truck, and the miraculous regeneration of some missing fingers for the stun gun.

I knocked on Oswald's door, late that evening. He opened the door, scowled at me, and I hit him with the stun gun. He was fully in his body then, so he went down shuddering, and I bundled him up and got him in the back of the truck, one of those little moving vans you can rent, though this one belonged to me for as long as I wanted it. I drove fast, hitting the highway and racing, because if Oswald woke up too close to his neighborhood, he would shed that body like a baggy suit and come crashing right through the roof, and then we'd have the kind of epic fight that leads to waste and desolation and legends. Lucky for me Oswald didn't wake until we were miles and miles away from the place he called home, and he couldn't do anything but kick the wall behind the driver's seat with his very human feet.

I went north and east for miles and miles until I reached a good remote spot, down some dirt roads, out by a few old mines. It seemed appropriate for Oswald's end to come in a place with underground tunnels. I couldn't abide him to live, but I could respect his origins. I parked, cut the lights, and went around back to slide open the door. Oswald was on his side, still tied up. "Vocabulary word," he said, voice thick and a little slurry. "Fucked. What *you* are, once I get loose."

"You don't remember me, Oswald?" I said, climbing into the truck. "It's me, Reva. Last time you saw me, I had a different body, and you tore it to pieces and buried it in your lair. That wasn't very pleasant. I doubt this is going to be very pleasant for you."

He looked up at me from the floor. "Oh," he said, after a

moment, then frowned. "You're like me. But you shouldn't have been able to take me, not in my place, so far from *yours*."

"It's true," I said, kneeling beside him. "I'm a long way from the place I began. I've got a vocabulary word for you. Reva. It means habitation, or firmament, or water, or sky, or abyss, or god. Sometimes it's rewa or neva or other things, depending on where you are. It's a word from the islands, where I'm from. I used to be the spirit of an island, just a little patch of land in the sea, a long time ago. But you know what happened?"

I leaned in close to him. "The island *sank*. All the people who lived on it left, and I was alone for years. I could have just dissolved into the sea, but I made myself a body, and found myself a boat, and went with the currents."

"You abandoned your *place*," Oswald said, and tried to bite my face. "You're worthless."

"I didn't abandon it, it disappeared, so I had new options, Oswald. My people were travelers, and I became a traveler too. Anywhere I go is home, because I treat every place I go as home." I shook my head. "You're a monster. You poison the place you should protect."

"I *do* protect it. I keep it safe for the ones who belong there. I keep the trash out."

"You and I have different philosophies," I said, reaching over to open the toolbox I'd brought. There were lots of tools there, which I planned to use for purposes they weren't meant for. "My philosophy wins. Because you're so far away from home that you're just a man in a body now, and you don't have a choice."

He fought me, but he didn't know much about fighting without his usual powers, since he'd never left his street. I didn't try to cause him suffering, but I didn't go out of my way to prevent it, either.

By the time I was finished, he was altogether dead. Even if his spirit did manage to pull itself together again over the next decades, seeping out of the pieces of his corpse to reassemble, there was nothing around here but played-out mines, no people for him to make suffer, no sacrifices for him to draw strength from. I'd just made his neighborhood a better place for the people who lived there. They wouldn't have Oswald's protection anymore, it was true, but the price he demanded for that protection was too high. I didn't regret a thing.

I buried Oswald in about ten different places, left the truck where it was, and started walking the long way back to the neighborhood I now called home.

I didn't have any illusions about Sadie recognizing the real me in this new body, but I thought maybe I could be charming, and make her care about a middle-aged Korean guy. Stupid idea, but love—or even infatuation—lends itself to those. The thing was, once I knocked on her door, and she answered it, she didn't look the same. Or, well, she *did,* but the way she looked didn't do anything for me. My new body wasn't interested in her, not at all—this brain, this flesh, was attracted to a different kind of person, apparently. I always forgot how much "feelings" depend on the particular glands and muscles and nerve endings you happen to have at the moment. Having a body makes it hard to remember the limitations of being human.

"Can I help you?" she said.

"Ah," I said. "Reva asked me to give you a message. He said he had to leave town unexpectedly, and he's really sorry."

"Huh," she said. "Well, if you talk to him, tell him he doesn't have to be sorry. He doesn't owe me anything." I could tell from her face that she was hurt, and angry, and trying to hide it, and I *wished* she was from around here so I could talk to her deep-down parts, and make amends, give her something, apologize. But she wasn't, and I couldn't.

"Okay," I said. "I'll tell him."

She shut the door in my face.

I walked downstairs, and stood on the sidewalk, and looked

up the street. I felt as hollow as Oswald's house, as burned-out as the lot where Ike Train had lived. Why had I wanted to stay here? I wasn't needed anymore. I'd made things better. This wasn't my home, not really, no more than any other place.

Maybe I'd go south, down to the Inland Empire, to see those pretty black walnut trees. I could make myself at home there, for a while, at least.

V·I·G·N·E·T·T·E

vi·gnette \ vin-'yet, vēn-'yet \
noun

1: a running ornament (as of vine leaves, tendrils, and grapes) put on or just before a title page or at the beginning or end of a chapter; *also*: a small decorative design or picture so placed
2 a: a picture (as an engraving or photograph) that shades off gradually into the surrounding paper
2 b: the pictorial part of a postage stamp design as distinguished from the frame and lettering
3 a: a short descriptive literary sketch
3 b: a brief incident or scene (as in a play or movie)

verb transitive

1: to finish (as a photograph) like a vignette
2: to describe briefly

Vignette

• • •

ELIZABETH HAND

THE ROLLTOP DESK in this cabin belonged to your parents, you told me last night. Earlier in the evening you pointed to a top shelf in the lodge kitchen, three blown-glass bottles shaped like little birds, red, piss yellow, the deep brownish violet of kelp on the ledges outside.

"Those glass things were my grandmother's. They were always

in her house in Stony Brook. Now they're here. It's so weird, this stuff. All this stuff."

I would have said, *It follows you.* I was there; I am here now. One of the things that followed you.

This morning you interviewed me in your cabin, your computer set up on another desk, a big microphone on a stand. You sat in the chair before the computer and adjusted the mike, singing snatches of an old Bill Withers song, whispering, clicking your tongue, snapping your fingers.

"Don't look at this." You pointed at the monitor. Fizzy spikes rose and fell as you spoke. "It can be distracting. Seeing your voice."

You're interviewing all the visitors to the island. One by one all last week, today, after I leave. The Marriage Project. They go to your cabin and you ask them *Have you ever been married? What does love mean to you?* The sound bites are beautiful, spliced into swooping piano cadences, your guitar. Back on the mainland flames erupt, lines of people snake outside airports. Here on the island, there is music, wind in the trees, the persistent thump of the windmill that gives us power, rising from the island's highest point, a giant with one great eye. From your computer the sound of a woman laughing—we're all doomed— your brother's voice soft with alcohol. Your cigarette smoke in the cabin around me. Prayer flags strung from the ceiling, tiny red lights. A piano, every year the piano tuner stays on the island for a week in exchange for keeping it in tune. Your Gibson guitar. Bottles of your medication silhouetted against the window, sunlight glinting from the plastic vials like a tiny cityscape. A city I visit. You live there.

Neither of us lives here. Nothing can be sustained. Sex, drugs, art, electricity, even the trees. It's over.

Yesterday morning you showed me a letter, written to you by the poet who left the day before I arrived. Almost twenty years younger than me; you showed me her poems as well. Hard-edged, hard for me to read.

"This letter she wrote to me. It reminded me of your letters."

You handed it to me. The letter typed, an inky scrawl across the envelope. The boy in the tree. My name for you since we were seventeen. She has read all my books, she was explaining them to you, explaining what it means. The boy in the tree, a Dionysian figure, the consort of the goddess, a symbol of the eternal return.

Blah blah blah, I thought.

Then panic. My letters to you were written thirty-two years ago. She wasn't born yet.

Yesterday we walked along the ledges above the sea. Immense granite boulders split in two; we jumped between them, that horrifying jolt when I saw the long black mouth opening and knew how quickly it could happen.

"I feel like it's checking in on me regularly now," you said. Matter-of-fact, as always. You lit another cigarette. Your voice dropped. "Every month or so it taps me on the shoulder. 'Hey, Just checking. Just checking in.' Another month."

I felt sick, with nothing to steady myself against. If you. If we fell. Eventually they would find us, or the tide would. No radio here, no TV; one computer tied in to a router. Sometimes I hear a burst of static and words bleat from the radio on Billy's boat.

Everything is falling.

"We'll go up that way," you said, and pointed. A green spill of moss and lichen, cat firs. We clambered up the last long expanse of granite and into the woods, and returned to your cabin.

There are eleven people here. Writers, poets, painters. One performer: you. Your brother, who owns the island. A cook. The caretaker, Billy, who lives in Ellisport. Every year someone disappears; one person, maybe two. Usually they show up again in their hometowns, weeks or months later.

But sometimes people never come back. A few years ago, the body of one woman, a poet, was found in the woods near her home in Montana. Bones, hair, teeth; no clothing or jewelry. Her front teeth had been worn away to nubs. The first two joints of all her fingers were gone. There was no other sign of trauma. The official cause of death was exposure.

I arrived in Ellisport early in the morning. Billy came to get me in the boat.

"That all you got?" He looked at my one bag. "Some of these people, they bring everything. Cases of wine. One lady, she had two white Persian cats. She didn't last long."

"Cats?"

He nodded and peered at the boat's nav screen. Outlines of rocks, Ellisport's coastline. The island. "Traps, they don't show up," he said as the boat eased away from the dock. In the dark water, hundreds of bobbing lobster buoys, neon orange and green and blue and red. "That lady with the cats, she just showed up at the dock on the island yesterday morning, told me to bring her back. Never said anything, just left."

"Maybe the cats didn't like it."

Billy laughed. "The cats were gone. She was freaking crazy about it, too."

"Gone? Like they got lost?"

He shrugged. "Maybe. Well, no. Something got them."

"Like an animal?"

"Something. No animals on the island. I mean, birds. Sometimes a moose might swim over, that happened once." He squinted to where the sun shone through the morning fog. Jagged rocks and huge clumps of drifting kelp. Rising from the fog a grey-green cloud, your brother's island. "Nope. Something got 'em, though."

You were waiting at the dock when we arrived.

I could not stop trembling. We kissed in the clearing by the island sawmill. We had kissed the week before that at my house on the mainland, two bottles of wine, a joint. I hadn't been stoned in twenty years. A stash I'd saved for all that time, for when I might need it. Medicinal; now.

The full moon rose above the lake, yellow. Liquid, everything falling away into your mouth. Salt, smoke, your tongue sour with nicotine. Lying on your bed last night you said, "This is a great blowjob—this is the most beautiful blowjob. Much better than the other night."

"I was drunk then," I said.

I kissed you last week for the first time in twenty-six years. Your smell was the same. Your eyes, I always write of them as green, leaf green, sap green, beryl.

But they're not green. They're blue, turquoise, the most astonishing aquamarine. Liquid. Everything else about you is burning away. When I licked the blood from your cock I tasted ash. Your skin like the leaden bloom that covers the tiny fir seedlings in the forest; I touch it and it disappears, until I draw my hand before my face and smell you. Rotting wood. Rain and the sea. Blue not green. That glow from the mainland. Everything is burning away.

"I had an ominous voicemail from my dentist." You lit another cigarette. We were sitting by the picnic table outside your brother's house on the windward side of the island, the only place where a cell phone can pick up a signal. All day long people drift there and back again, walking in slow circles, talking to ghosts on the mainland. "He said, Angus, call me right away. We have to talk about your x-rays."

You laughed. I felt my heart skip. "Are you going to call?"

"Nah. When I go home. I don't want to hear any of that shit here. Work. Someone else quit this morning. Everyone's leaving."

You shook your head and laughed again. "What, do I have teeth cancer? I'm not afraid of dying."

I stared out at the water, at a lobster boat heading towards Ellisport. "Lots of people have fake teeth," you said. We walked back to your cabin.

After breakfast this morning I brought two of my books over to the lodge and left them on a table in the reading room. My other books are there, all the stories I wrote about you. We are on an island, surrounded by the reach and the open Atlantic. I am surrounded only by you.

What we took: cell phones, computers, paper, pens, paints, canvas, guitars, a harmonica, wine, scotch, beer, vodka, marijuana, amphetamines, cold medicine, sleeping pills, cigarettes, volumes of poetry, warm clothes, iPods, two white Persian cats. What we left: wives, husbands, children, cars, houses, air conditioning, TVs, radios, pets, houseplants, offices. Everyone keeps talking about those cats.

Everyone here is working on something, feverishly. You are doing The Marriage Project. You interviewed me and I spoke of my brief marriage. How inconsequential it is. All those interviews, all those people telling you about their first marriage. All those chopped-off voices. Yesterday I saw a letter on your desk dated months ago, when the mail still came on time. Little Buddhas

lined up on top of your computer. Taped to the wall above the
piano, pictures of your children. The two grown girls; the three
children by your second wife. I sat on the chair in front of the
mike and removed my glasses. Not for vanity, but because if I
saw you clearly I would not be able to speak. The air inside the
cabin was close, pine resin and cigarette smoke, marijuana,
Shambala incense. Your sweat. The tang the medication leaves
on your skin; bitter. You wore jeans, leather moccasins, a tie-
dyed T-shirt. I shivered uncontrollably and asked if I could wear
something of yours, so that my voice wouldn't break up for my
trembling. You gave me a brown zipped sweatshirt with yellow
stripes, a fake heraldic sigil. The kind of thing someone might
wear in high school. Did you wear something like this, a jacket,
a sweater? I can't remember.

There is a painter here named Annie. You're obsessed with her.

"Annie, she's a feral artist," you told me. We were in the lodge
kitchen. The cook was chopping parsley for dinner at the long
wooden countertop. Bottles of wine on the long mahogany table
Billy made, your iPod on the counter. The Beach Boys, Outkast,
"Hey Ya." Happy music. The cook was dancing. "She gets up
every day before the sun comes up and goes out to her rock and
just stays there all day, waiting."

"For what?"

"Who the fuck knows. The right moment. The final curtain.
She stays there all day, she only comes back here at dinnertime
to eat. She doesn't talk much. She paints, just this one spot. Her
rock. She's been coming here for three years now. I don't know
when she sleeps, she works all night and goes out again at
4 A.M."

Annie.

That night I met her at dinner. Tall, rawboned, long straight
straw-colored hair. Slightly rough skin, wide-set grey eyes. She
wore stained khakis, a blue sweater, ancient hip waders. Big

hands, the nails chewed down to nothing. She spoke very softly, her gaze flickering around the room the whole time.

"So you just go out there and work?" I asked. We were drinking red wine, moving slowly around the perimeter of the room. Annie kept her head down, her hair obscuring her face. Now and then she'd look aside, furtively, then gaze at me head-on for a moment before turning.

"Yes." Her voice soft, without affect yet musical. A swallow's voice. "On the far side of the island. By the rocks. Those trees there." She held her wineglass in one hand and kept the other hand in her pocket. "That tree. Yes."

"And you just . . . wait?"

She looked up. Her eyes flared. "Yes."

Her expression never changed; only those eyes. As though something moved inside her skull, cutting off the light. "Yes," she murmured again, and walked away.

"You know what I started to think about?"

You stared out at the edge of the woods, cat fir and moss-covered boulders, birch trees. Sea urchin shells broken on the rocks. "A woman having sex with a dog. Like a wolf or something. If she tries to get away, it rips her throat out."

I laughed. "I would never say something like that."

"Yeah. A really big dog."

Each cabin contains a single bed—a cot, really—so narrow it can barely hold one person, let alone two. At night I lie beside you as you sleep, your head turned from me, your arms curled up in front of your face, your fingers curled. Like one of those bodies at Pompeii. On the windowsills burn candles in small glasses. The smell of smoke on everything. My own skin; my mouth. Everything burns.

You asked me, "Have you noticed how you can smell things

here?" We sat on the cabin steps, sheltered beneath cat firs, and watched rain spatter the rocky beach below us. "Things you never notice back there, you can smell them here. I can, anyway. Like I can smell my brother when he's way down the path. And Annie—I went down to her place yesterday and I knew she wasn't there, because I couldn't smell her."

"Can you smell me?"

You stared out at the water greying beneath the storm. "No. You smell like me."

"The light," I said. "That's what's different for me. The light everywhere, it's so bright but I can look right at it. I can stare at the sun. Have you noticed that?"

"No. I mean, a little, maybe. I guess it's being on an island— the water everywhere, and the sky. It must all reflect off the rocks."

"I guess." I blinked and it hurt. Even with my glasses on, the dark lenses—my eyes ached. I turned and looked at you. "Hold still, there's something caught . . ."

You grimaced as I touched your tooth. "A piece of fluff," I said, and scraped it onto my finger. "There."

I stared at the tiny matted wad on my fingertip. At first I thought it was feathers, or a frayed bit of cloth. But when I held it up to the light I saw it was a minute clump of hair, silky, silvery-white.

"That's weird," I said, and flicked it into the rain.

That evening before dinner I stood on the porch at the lodge and stared out to sea. The wind so strong I wondered about the windmill, that sound like an airplane preparing for takeoff, steady thump and drone. When the wind dies, the windmill stops turning. Power fluctuates, the lights flicker and fail then shine once more. A vast black wedge of cloud loomed above the reach and sent spurs of lightning across the water. Each bolt seared my eyes, my nails left little half-moons in my arms but I didn't look away.

"You should be careful." Annie came up beside me, wrapped in a brown sweatshirt with yellow stripes. She pulled the hood up, her hands invisible inside the sleeves. "It will hurt you."

"Lightning? From way out there?" I laughed, but turned so she wouldn't see my face. Your shirt. "I think I'm okay here."

"Not lightning." She crouched beside me. The hood spilled over her forehead so that it was difficult to discern her features, anything but her eyes. "Oh, poor thing—"

She reached for a citronella candle in a large, netted glass holder. A brown leaf the size of my hand protruded from the opening. Annie tilted the glass towards her, wincing, then stroked the edge of the leaf.

"Polyphemus," she said.

It wasn't a leaf, but the remains of a moth, forewing and hindwing, each longer than my finger. The color of browned butter, edged with pale orange, with a small eyespot on the forewing and a larger eyespot on the hindwing. The spots were the same vivid sea blue as your eyes but ringed with black, as though the eye had been kohled. Within a sheath of yellow wax I could glimpse its body, like a furred thumb, its long feathered antennae and the other wing, charred, ragged.

"It's beautiful," I said. "That's so sad."

She lifted her finger, brown scales on the tip like soot. "The eyes, when it opens its wings suddenly they look like an owl's eyes."

She set down the candle and pressed her hands together, palm to palm, then spread them. "See? That's how it scares off whatever tries to eat it."

"What're you looking at?"

You came up the steps, stopped beside Annie and glanced down at the candle.

"It's a moth," I said.

"A Polyphemus moth," said Annie.

You stared at it then laughed. "What a way to go, huh?"

You lit another cigarette. I held out my hand and you gave me the lighter. I flicked it and stared at the flame, brought it so close to my face that I felt a hot pulse between my eyes, you and Annie blurred into lightning.

"Hey," you said. "Watch it."

"She keeps doing that," said Annie.

"Listen to this."

We were in your cabin. Another night, late. We'd left everyone else by the bonfire. A meteor shower was expected, someone said; maybe tonight, maybe tomorrow. No one could remember when. You sat in front of the computer and stared at your files, lines, and graphs, adjusted the volume then leaned back. "Listen."

Crickets. Outside faint laughter and voices from the fire, wind, but no insects. The crickets were inside with us.

"You're recording crickets?" I asked.

"No." Your brow furrowed. "I don't know what the fuck happened. These are the files—"

You tapped the monitor, columns of data with initials beneath them, words and numerals. "Those are my edits. But something got screwed up. I played them back this afternoon and this is all I get."

A steady line moved across the screen as crickets sang. You stood abruptly. "Come on, let's go look for Annie. I want to see if I can find her in the dark."

We walked into the woods. Behind us the sound of crickets faded into your cabin. The dull orange glow from the bonfire disappeared behind the trees. It was cool; autumn weather, not August. Wind brisk with salt and the scent of rugosa roses in bloom along the beach. Sky filled with stars, so many stars; a lake that holds a burning city.

Annie's rock was on the far side of the island and faced the open sea, a narrow spur of granite like a pointing finger. A fissure split its center, water pooled there and the pinpoint reflection of stars. You took my hand so I wouldn't fall. Twisted birches grew between the rocks, their leaves black with salt. Even in the dark I could see them.

But we couldn't see Annie. You called her name, quietly at first, then louder. At our feet waves lapped at the rocks; behind us, in the ferns, crickets. I heard bats ricochet and whine above our heads. You kissed me and we fucked on the rocks, my hands and knees soaked and bloodied. Your nails broke my skin, everything hurt so much that lights flashed behind my eyelids. I blinked and the lights were still there, streaking down the sky, a soundless eruption of green and crimson.

The voices by the distant bonfire softened into insect song.

The wind died, the windmill, the sound of a falling plane silenced. You held me and we were completely still. Neither of us came. In the trees above us the muted flutter of wings and two round eyes, green not blue; a soft flurry as it lifted from the branch and something soft fell and caught between my teeth.

"That was an owl," you whispered. "I think it was Annie."

You laughed. As we walked back to the beach we heard a low wailing from the other side of the island, one voice then another, and a third. Coyotes. Everyone was gone. The bonfire had burned to embers. You gave me your lighter and I started the fire again, fed it birch bark and twigs and red oak logs until the flames rose. In the sky above the sea things fell and burned. I watched as you walked along the beach, the red tip of your cigarette as you danced and swayed and sang. In the darkness something swooped above your head.

You should be careful, she whispered.

I held my hands in the flames until they glowed.

Plight of the Sycophant

• • •

ALAN DENIRO

THE BORDER BETWEEN the two worlds is hard to describe but easy to feel under the skin. Even a few miles away, you can sense its effect, in ways that you'll probably never understand. Much like when a person puts a gun in your mouth (though this has never happened to me). The bullet doesn't leave the gun—anticipation is its own weapon. And fear. One must never forget fear.

You can have this unsettling feeling on either side of the border, though you will likely prefer one side to the other. One world to the other. The sun will be bright, as it always is in this part of the world—except, perhaps, in September—and the giant angels will be patrolling the mist, as they always do. There will often be rainbows, on account of this bright sun and the mist. They grow boring.

The border is not actually a wall, but a waterfall. No one knows where the water comes from; there is never a cloud in the sky. But the water comes. The angels are rather mean and swear a lot. They wear bright yellow ponchos, with a red script in their language up and down the sleeves. There is only one checkpoint, one place to cross by foot (although it is not advised) or car. The cars have to be coated in a certain type of myrrh, or else the border patrol will not even consider letting you cross. And even then you have to have the right kinds of papers, the right bribes. And—the hardest part—the right attitude. Angels will detain a person trying to cross for months, sometimes years, trying to find out what attitude a border-crosser might have. What desires they have. Their prisons near the gate are little cottages and are actually kind of cute.

Sometimes the angels are satisfied by the answers and sometimes they are not. Some travelers end up leaving their cottages, and some do not.

This is all, of course, from my perspective, from my country. I have never been to the other country. I have not had appropriate business to take me there. And I'm afraid of the angels. They're not actual angels. That I'll grant you. They don't fly, or sing, or help people. But they are certainly tall—seven feet, maybe eight feet in height. They don't have wings, but their guns do. I've seen one of their guns fly, once. I was emptying the grease trap from the store—surely the nastiest job in the history of the world; believe me, there's a lot of competition—out in the garbage pit closer to the waterfall. One of the angels had to restrap his boot and the gun flapped furiously to stay aloft, like a hummingbird, and it did. The wings fluttered in a manner that my eye couldn't catch. I was watching it all with binoculars; the pit wasn't that close to the waterfall, and anyway, I didn't have a garbage permit, so I had to watch out for patrols. Fees and levies were designed to keep us safe—but if I actually paid them, then we'd be operating at a loss. Plus the scavengers around the pit liked the grease, and they were bold night and day—green bears and millipedes large as my arm. I was already risking an arm and a leg.

Anyway, the pawn shop where I work is in sight of the border. It's the last chance for a traveler to get rid of his or her belongings before going over to the other side—or maybe pick up something that might be useful farther down the road. We also sell fuel. By popular demand. And also hot dogs, frozen goods, pop, batteries, and the like. But we're not a convenience store. We sell a lot of beer and guns. Not the angels' guns, but regular guns. They're not allowed across the border, so people get what they can for them. There's always something going on in the shop—a lot of tourists come through, just to get a look at the waterfall, but you still get bored at the register. A pawn shop is a pawn shop.

No one comes back from the other side. In case you're wondering.

And just where does the water go, once it has fallen? You'd think that the ground would flood, but it doesn't. There might be grates leading into a sewer system, or something. There might be a vast, underground ocean under the surface of the earth, where mer-people live ordinary, screwed-up lives in screwed-up mer-civilizations, and no one can figure out where that waterfall comes from. I couldn't say one way or another, and there's no chance I'll find out.

There was only one time, years ago, when I came awfully close. Or at least, I thought I did; now I'm not so sure. I'm not sure what side I come down on. It was the time I was a sycophant, and it wasn't pretty. I was twenty or thereabouts, young and stupid, and I'd only been at the pawn shop for a year. I had wandered for a while before that, and since I couldn't find a way past the border, I stopped and looked for a job. No one liked to pump gas and pawn guns in sight of the angels, so the station was always hiring. Turnover is hell. But I kept my nose clean. I had a trailer that I was actually proud of. No one lived around me. I had no idea how lonely I was, especially after my double shifts.

It was at the tail end of one of those double shifts when a woman came in to tell me her car broke down, and could she get some help. It was Sunday, going on evening, and no one credible in town was going to jump-start her car, or fix her flat. Which was where I came in. She had her hair in a beehive bun, and wore a T-shirt that looked wooly and too warm. I figured she was driving from a ways off; she had a funny accent. I asked her where her car was. About three miles that way, she said. She pointed north, parallel to the border. My brother's still in the car. He's guarding it.

Like an angel? I said.

I . . . I guess, she said. It was even more obvious she wasn't from around here.

I smelled her, then—acrid, sour raspberries. It didn't smell like the stench of a long road trip, but neither did it smell like perfume. But I was bored all the time, like I said before, and so the intrigue won out against my better judgment. She was something different. I decided that I could be some use to her, and the blood in my head pounded.

Okay, I said. I'll help you in fifteen minutes. Can you wait fifteen minutes? That's when I get off.

She thanked me, and she seemed sincere, and she smiled. I became aroused. She was perfectly pretty, and I wasn't ashamed to notice this. It was a reaction—I knew that I wouldn't act on the reaction ever. It just wasn't how I operated, to make huge, unyielding assumptions about what a smile meant.

After my replacement came—I forget his name, after all of these years, like I've forgotten a lot of things—I took her to my car. A filthy Civic. It was embarrassing, but she didn't seem to mind the birdcages and miniature pinball games strewn on the floor of the shotgun seat. I also had a gun behind my shotgun seat—just a pistol, a nonangelic gun. The birdcages were from a man who pawned about a dozen parakeets on us. I'd bought them and set them free. I felt pretty bad for them, and no one was going to buy them.

Oh, just move that stuff out of the way, I said, starting the car. I was more ashamed about my vehicle than my erection. The erection was a private matter, while the car was definitely public space.

She smiled, not at me really, and rolled down the window. She was serene, undisturbed.

I love the breeze, she said, sticking her arm out as I pulled out. The mist, too.

The mist is pretty nice, I said. I hadn't gotten bored of the mist yet. It was fine and soft enough that you would realize, with the right wind, that your face was wet and cool. The mist made the heat bearable.

I drove closer to the waterfall. The land was a wasteland: no hills, no vegetation, all dust and sand and sandstone. After about a minute, she said, Turn down that road there.

I tried and tried but couldn't place her accent at all. I usually had an ear for those kinds of things. My father, right as I left his house to seek my fortune, had told me that I would always be wandering around the bottom of the world. Actually he shouted it as I was walking away. I think he had meant it as a curse, but I never saw him again anyway. I didn't want to ask her about the accent, where she came from.

But I wondered if I would find out anyway. I'd stupidly hoped that she'd abandon her brother and come with me back to my trailer for a few whiskey sours and she'd clench herself against me on my sofa, and I'd say, no, the sofa folds out, it's a hide-a-bed. Or something along those lines. This was breaking my vow of nonintervention that I made when I met her. I know that. But I didn't know what to expect. I figured there was a chance she wanted me, and that I could help her along the process of wanting me. I was, however, afraid of my own mouth, the bombshells that would pirouette from it.

Her arm hanging out the window did a little dance, a little hand puppetry, and she closed her eyes.

After she closed her eyes, I put away my seduction plan, folded it up like a map. It was a dumb plan anyway.

The road running parallel to the border was a kind of service alley at first, filled with speed bumps, behind fast-food restaurants and hotels you'd pay for by the hour. "Hotel" was probably too kind a word. But then the sprawl stopped and the road turned dirt. Soon we were in the bona fide desert, and the border was a half mile east of us. I heard the waterfall roar, and peering into the mist, saw the silhouette of angels—or at least their bright ponchos—here and there.

I hadn't known about this road at all. (It has since disappeared altogether. The main road fades into pure desert now. The beginning of the service alley that I remember is now an abandoned waterpark. Once a year I go looking for the road she took, but no luck.) It was bumpy, and the Civic's shocks were horrible. I apologized about the smoothness, or the lack of it, of the ride.

She must have been sleeping, or meditating, or something. She opened her eyes. What did you say?

The road is bumpy, I managed to say.

She shrugged. I told you I had a brother, right?

I think so, I said. A sudden spray turned the windshield to a fine mud and I turned on the wipers.

He has a birth defect, she said. I think I failed to mention this. Just to warn you, so you don't become alarmed or anything.

I nodded and smiled, as if to say, No problem. Whatever. I was secretly troubled. I wished that the brother wasn't in the picture at all, that I could take care of her car trouble with no familial witnesses. Perhaps, I reasoned, like I imagined a snake would reason, his birth defect meant that he was only a shell of a person, and could not interfere in any relationship that might develop between me and the stranded woman.

The sun was beginning to set. We hit a pothole and, startled, she grabbed my hand. Hers was warm but mine was warmer. She pulled away and didn't meet my gaze, even though I was offering it to her.

At last we reached her car, which was actually a Hummer. Maybe they were drug dealers, I thought, or smugglers, although that would have been impossible, on account of the waterfall border and the angels. I pulled up next to the Hummer and we got out.

Thank you so much, she said, sounding like she really meant it. She stretched her arms up.

No problem, I said. Happy to help. Let me look at the engine. Can you pop the hood?

I glanced at the interior of the car, looking for her brother. The windows of the Hummer didn't have tinting, and I could see her brother laying across one of the backseats. I forget which backseat, as there were three in the SUV. He seemed to be made out of water. He wore dark glasses that didn't seem to be made of water, but that was it. Water. I could see right through his body. He looked a few years younger than her. But for crying out loud—gauging such a thing was totally without value. Talk about a birth defect. I wasn't scared of him though.

She didn't pop the hood like I'd asked. She just kept stretching. At first her arms, and then her legs, as if she was getting ready to sprint. I almost wanted to cry. Instead I said, Is this some kind of joke? A prank? Is your car perfectly fine or is it not?

She then told me that I was to drive the Hummer into the waterfall.

But I'll die, I said. You'd die, too. If the angels don't kill you—and they will—well, you can't get through the waterfall. It can't be penetrated. It just can't.

She then explained to me how she wouldn't die, because she wouldn't be in the Hummer. She would just be watching, watching out for angels who might start to get ideas and try to stop them. And then she would stop them.

Even though she didn't threaten me, per se, I guess I should have been a little afraid of her threatlike statements.

But instead I laughed. I was getting angry, realizing now that she only wanted to use me. Not to fix a car, which was perfectly legitimate. But rather to drive, in suicidal fashion, in reach of the angels. I had worked myself into a lather over this? I wanted to please her, but not at such a ridiculous price.

Stop angels, I said. Huh.

Absolutely, she said. She stopped her stretching and walked towards me. Do you know what's on the other side? Do you know what's in the other country?

No, what? I said. I was ready, at that point, to drive away, good riddance.

People like me, she said.

She then revealed her true face, which I really don't want to talk about any more than I absolutely have to.

At any rate, after her revelation, I saw her point rather clearly, and I asked what I could do to help. Anything to help. I was desperate to, and there wasn't really any question about any previous, skeptical thought processes that I might have had regarding her and her needs.

She hid her true face again—one glance was enough for me to become her sycophant, no need to overdo it—and then explained the rest of her plan, which I considered extremely cunning.

My brother is the safecracker, she said, in her honeyed voice. He can turn off the waterfall, at least for a few instants. Your purpose—and it is a very noble purpose—is to collide into the waterfall and kill yourself. There's a good chance there'll be a spectacular explosion, which would be a nice touch. This will distract the angels just long enough for my brother and I to pass through.

Got it, I said. And so you'll be in the mist near the car, waiting for your brother to open up the waterfall.

Exactly! I knew you'd understand.

I was pleased by her words. I wanted to befriend her, now even more so, and this seemed to be the only way. I wished, naturally, that I wouldn't have to die to curry her favor. Barring mental disorder, or some kind of severe, unbearable depression, who wouldn't? But I searched the catacombs of my brain over and over, and came across only dead ends where any objections should have been. So that decided things.

Okay, I said, I'm ready! Let's do this.

She threw me the keys. The wind blew her wooly shirt up a little. I could see for a second some kind of armor above her knees. At this point my desire for her wasn't sexual at all. It was pure and altruistic. This point should be clear.

Okay, she said. Why don't you drive a little closer. Into the mist. I'll walk alongside the car, so drive slowly at first.

Great! I said. I'd never been happier. I opened the car door, stepped inside, and started the Hummer up. I began to buckle my seat belt, but that seemed absurd, considering that the point was to kill myself. Safety wasn't coming first. Her brother—although I wasn't sure whether it was her brother at all—was still laying behind me, totally still. He didn't say anything, but then I saw he had an orange handkerchief covering his mouth. It was almost like the handkerchief was gagging him.

Hey, I said behind me, taking the Hummer out of park and letting it crawl forward on Lydia's signal. I knew her name was Lydia all of a sudden. I didn't know the water-guy's name; otherwise I would have used it.

He still didn't say anything. I wondered briefly if the handkerchief in his mouth was impeding his speech. But I was preoccupied with the driving, really.

You'll be able to do your thing soon enough, I told him. And then you'll be home free. Scot free.

The man tried to say something, but it was muffled.

Did you say anything? Lydia asked me.

The man's eyes widened and he shook his head. I didn't know why it was important to him, but I called out to her, No, you must be hearing things.

I loved her! But the guy relaxed. He must have loved her, too, and wanted to please her; otherwise, he wouldn't be in this position.

I want to say, at this point, that in no way did I believe I was a sycophant. I was merely doing what I thought was in my best interest, which happened to be in her best interest. Others might consider alignment of desire some kind of flattery. But it's not the same. Even now, I'm not sure what to think about that time in the desert with Lydia and her brother. I had a customer come in about a week ago who was an angel. I didn't think this was at all strange. Why was that? He wanted chaw and ethanol for his truck, but he didn't seem to have a truck. He did, however, have a sword strapped to his belt. He wasn't wearing his poncho and seemed even taller up close. And there was no winged gun in sight. The sign on my door said BANS GUNNED ON PREMISES, but the antlered man seemed to be in the clear, since the sign didn't say anything about edged weapons. And what was a PREMISES, anyway? A group of more than one premise? Every word, in the presence of the angel, seemed to be utterly beautiful and yet completely inadequate as a means to communicate. He blinked at me, and he paid for the chaw, and I told him that we didn't have any ethanol-substitute fuel, we weren't really positioned in a progressive part of the country. He appeared mildly upset. It's for my truck, it's broken down just outside of town, he said. I pretended he wasn't there. Finally, he gave up on me. Have a good day! I called out to him as he left. Then I noticed that there was moss in the ice cream sandwiches case, and that I should probably clean it out after I close.

To call the moment dreamlike would have been inaccurate. My life was normal and real—and yet I did things for reasons I didn't understand, all the time. Especially when I was younger.

None of this was on my mind in the desert with Lydia, though.

After a minute she tapped my window and I stopped. The mist from the waterfall was really bad for driving, or good for hiding, depending on how you looked at it. I turned on the windshield wipers, because I wanted to see as clearly as possible when I slammed into the waterfall and killed myself.

Look there, she said, pointing to the eastern edge of the border, in the direction of the checkpoint.

I don't see anything, I said. I wished I had my binoculars— for no other reason than to give them to Lydia.

An angel is walking towards us, she said. Giving us a once-over. This is perfect. When you drive, maybe it's better if you aim for the angel.

It certainly seemed perfect, at that moment, and I didn't want to delve too deeply into the workings of her well-reasoned plan, so I nodded.

She opened the back door. Get out, she said to her brother. I went back and forth in my mind on whether the two of them had a blood relation. He held up his bound wrists, which I hadn't seen before.

Well, untie him, she told me. And remove the gag.

I got out of the car and went to untie him, as I was instructed. The water-man looked at me through his glasses, and I could tell he was trying to make a decision, size me up. I tried to be as inscrutable as possible, for Lydia's sake, as I loosened the handkerchief gagging him, and then the bands around his wrists. My hands sank into his wrists just a little bit. I recoiled. The man stood up, sliding out of the car. I stepped back. Lydia's brother seemed almost to blend into the mist around us, so that he had a kind of halo. I noticed the angel then, and I relished the thought of driving into him, even though he had noticed our little congress.

Ready? she asked.

Am I? I said. That was a joke, I wanted to add. She was silent, waiting for me to begin. I wanted, I guess, a little more gratitude from her, some recognition of my sacrifice. But then I figured I was just being selfish. I was about to step back into the Hummer when I saw Lydia and the water-man turn away and start walking west toward the wall. And then the water-man jumped on Lydia's back. It was stupid, I realized, to let his arms free. I should have known better, and felt horribly guilty. Even though Lydia gave the orders, I was to blame. I'm sure she felt utterly confident about her strength and his compliance.

But as he was trying to strangle her, I stood there beside the car in deep thought—just what was it about her that made me so attendant to her every whim? I thought about helping her right away, I really did. She was, however, handling him rather easily. She was, after all, Lydia.

When I was small and inchoate, a mere child, I wandered the annexed, grim factories of my youth, looking for work. I always kept my head down and sought out gross, thoughtless errands. Kind of like cleaning the grease trap. I worked in quite a few automobile factories, actually—delivering sandwiches and juices on catwalks twenty stories above the assembly lines for the snipers. Those grimy mercenaries joked about pushing me off— my bones being smelted into the workings of an Impala chassis— but I took their coins and continued on my way. In spite of the ruthless teasing, I didn't feel powerless.

Maybe I should have.

Then I snapped out of my state—Lydia was in trouble! Forget my lousy childhood! I stepped out of the car and pulled out my gun. Neither of them knew I had it. I'd forgotten that I had it, that I'd slipped it into my pocket as we were leaving my car. I really had forgotten. It was from my backseat, a snub-nosed pistol, but it could still kill. I didn't even give a warning. I aimed at the water-man's head and fired.

The bullet passed through him and into Lydia's head.

After she slumped to the ground, I realized that my life was a rabbit hole looking for a rabbit. The man made out of water looked at Lydia's body, looked at me, and then started walking.

Hey! I called out behind him, thinking there'd be some kind of camaraderie or bonding moment between us. I had, after all, freed him, albeit at her orders. But he kept walking.

I looked at Lydia's body, then the Hummer, then the man who I swore was sweating away and diminishing in the hot twilight. I didn't want to stare at Lydia too much, just in case I accidentally uncovered her true face again. But I did see, through her soaked shirt, that her armor was mangled and shrunken. She must not have anticipated its failure. Was it the heat? Or the water? Her brother might have been concocting a scheme to free himself through their entire journey. Or, who knew, maybe it was a desperate, blind chance that he took—to prove, once and for all, that he wasn't her sycophant, as I was.

He started sprinting toward the border. The angel moving towards us had drawn his gun, and the gun's wings unfurled.

I kept following the water-man. Soon the mist completely enveloped us. I lost his trail, but I assumed the angel and gun following us had as well. Unable to see far, I stumbled around for quite a while, directionless. I thought about Lydia's face— both of her faces actually—and wondered what I'd seen in them, what I'd hoped to accomplish by helping her out of a jam. I heard hissing gunshots here and there and I was afraid. The roar of the waterfall was deafening. I was afraid of getting caught in the waterfall, getting sucked down into whatever wet hell was below the earth's barren surface.

At some point when it was starting to get dark in earnest, I must have reached the border itself. Close enough to touch. I actually bumped into it, and quickly stepped back. I didn't die! The waterfall was cold and squishy and felt, I don't know, like I was touching an idea. I was pretty sure I was going to die there, that there was zero chance of home, or even my stupid pawn shop job.

Then I felt someone stroking my hair. No one was behind me that I could see. Then it stopped. For a second—a second—the waters parted in a sliver of a crevice. There was a humming sound. On the other side, I could see strange beings, with imprecise, blurry features, sitting on a hill, intently listening to music I could not hear on account of the humming, coming from instruments I couldn't see. The hills were shot with green so bright that my eyes were slain. But I couldn't stop looking. It was like looking into Lydia's actual face again, except it didn't bother me at all. There were tall grasses and thickets, and paradise's blackbirds soaring above them, between silver clouds—

Then the crevice closed. It was stupid not to jump through. But, you know, I'm not sure that I didn't. I mean, I walked back to my Civic. I did. The Civic was there. The angel and gun were poring over the Hummer, but paid me no mind. I was minuscule compared to the other entities at work. The watery man was nowhere to be found. I was soaked and also scared. I drove back to my trailer and drank for a few days, thinking that would fix things. No whiskey sours, though.

And then, I went back to work. Although things were different. And still are different. Mostly little things. Mops don't work particularly well inside the store; they're always soaked. Mist comes into the convenience store at odd times, making the guns unusable. We've stopped selling them. My boss doesn't mind since business is better than ever. Tons of cars. A lot of people on horseback have shown up recently, so we have opened a livery next to the gas pumps. My boss gave me a raise, on account of my "valuable, noble service." I moved out of the trailer on the edge of town and into an apartment complex.

I'm looking for a confidant, someone to follow, but no one has shown up at the store like that.

The angels and their guns are no longer fearsome to me. Several angels live in my apartment complex. They smoke a lot.

I often wonder about this—their dwelling amongst mere mortals—and I think I've finally figured it out. The angels are mere weapons—the sycophants, if you will—and the winged guns call the shots. The winged guns reproduce, follow or break customs of society, fall in love. They don't live in apartment complexes like the angels, but rather in burrows deep underneath the earth. The guns travel great distances through underground pneumatic tubes. I had always thought these were gopher holes in the desert, but obviously I was wrong.

And so, everything that happened with Lydia makes perfect sense to me now. If you're not a gun, then you're an angel. This includes me. Lydia was probably a gun. It doesn't matter if you're made of water or not, or flesh and blood, or . . . well, whatever angels are made of. Angels are meant to do things—guard borders, build cars, safecrack waterfalls, operate cash registers.

The guns, on the other hand, do what they love. They love the waterfall, and love to control it, to control who comes through.

Even now I'm not sure whose side I'm on. I only want to do the right thing, to live with what the world will give me. The question is, which world? Did I cross? That green hillside of music that I saw for just a few seconds—is it impossibly close or impossibly far away?

I want to know.

The Last Elegy

• • •

MATTHEW CHENEY

I RECEIVED A LETTER from Grete. I hadn't heard from her in at
least a decade, since before the war. After Andrea's death, I didn't
want to stay in contact with anyone who knew her, or anyone
who had known Anders, because I didn't know any other way to
escape my sadness than to erase all the memories of what had
happened, the memories of the cabarets and theaters, the cafés
and galleries, the late nights that became early mornings as we
talked about politics and poetry and philosophy, the hopes we
had. Hope has always been a source of sadness, because it makes
me vulnerable to fantasies and delusions, and it took me many

249

years to see that time with Anders and Grete as anything other than the most awful delusion of my life.

In her letter, Grete tells me she is ill, and she would like to see me again before she dies. She asks if I ever finished the elegy for Anders. She still lives in the apartment she shared with him, though it is different now, having been damaged in the war. She says she got married again, but her husband is no longer alive, and now she is alone, but she has wonderful friends. She still paints occasionally, though she says materials are sometimes hard to come by. She says she has missed me all these years.

I lie awake and stare at the rusted tin ceiling of my little bedroom. Perhaps I, too, am ill; perhaps I am dying. Perhaps the elegy I should write is for myself. Self-pity is my strongest talent. But I am not to blame for what happened. I may have been a fool, but I was a brave fool to risk so much, to feel so much, to lose so much. (I tell myself this, just as I have for many years now, even though after all this time, the sadness remains.)

Afterward, everything reminded me of him. For weeks, it seemed every item in my apartment, every object in the city had some memory attached to it. A pen he had given me sat on the desk. Above the desk I had hung a postcard he'd sent from Venice. I threw them both away. We'd talked about nearly every book I owned, and so I covered the bookcase with a sheet. One night, drunk and maudlin, tears streaming down my face, I carried all the books out to the street and threw them one by one into the river, saving his favorites, Baudelaire and Rimbaud, for last. (He read to me in French. I knew no French.) I had stuck a scrap of paper with the date of his birthday on it to the wall so I could not forget it. I took the paper in my hand and tore it into the tiniest shreds I could and threw them all out the window. I covered my ears when I heard familiar songs echoing through the streets at night. I avoided the parks where we had wandered so aimlessly so many times. There did not seem to be a café anywhere in the city that we had not been to at least once, and so I stopped going to cafés.

"Anders is dead," she told me. "Don't talk to me about Anders anymore."

This is the first time I have been on an airplane. It is noisier than I would have expected. For some reason, I thought once we got up off the ground, everything would be silent. When I first came to the city, I came by boat. Now, looking down at it all, it is not familiar. It could be any city in the world.

The plane descends.

It could be any city in the world.

I met Anders because of Grete. A newspaper had asked me to write about new artists, and not knowing of anything better to do with my time, I accepted and began going to gallery openings, even though I knew nothing about art. Grete's opening was the liveliest I'd ever attended, a hot and crowded room full of laughing people and abstract paintings in pastel colors, badly lit with small lamps set on tables every few feet throughout the room. Now and then someone jostled a table, a lamp fell, an explosion, laughter.

"This is my husband, Anders," Grete said, leading me to him by the arm. "He hates parties," she said. "He's an actor. You might have seen him in *Werther* at the State Theater. He's a genius," she said. "You'll love him."

I didn't like parties any more than he did, and so, after dutifully taking notes about a couple of paintings, I stepped outside with him. He gave me a cigarette and we walked down the street, stopping eventually at a café where a man on the balcony above played an oboe, its soft notes bobbing away on the breeze.

Anders spoke to me in clear, formal English. He said he had spent some years touring the British Isles, but had not yet had the chance to see the United States, a place that, in his mind, contained two types of territories: The West, a wild frontier enthralled and terrorized by the ghost of Jesse James, and New York City, which he talked of as if it were the size of Texas and filled with nothing but cigar-chomping capitalists and ladies bedecked in the furs of white leopards. I told him his impressions were entirely correct.

As Anders talked, I paid close attention to his face for the first time, his soft skin and eyes of such a light blue they seemed nearly translucent. His thin nose bent slightly to one side and his lips were narrow and somehow childlike. High, prominent cheekbones gave him a regal air, and he showed no trace at all of a beard. His dark blond hair was unfashionably long, and now and then he brushed strands back over his little ears. In the shadows and smoke of the café he had, I thought, the face of a nymph.

Grete meets me at the airport. The skin of her face is sallow and slack, her eyes sunken deep into shadows, her hair thin and grey. She was a tall woman once, but she is not now.

We ride to the apartment in a black taxi. "My English got better during the war," Grete says.

"Your English was never bad."

"Still, it got better. Anders made me read Shakespeare, thus I always sounded like Shakespeare. I don't sound like Shakespeare anymore." She laughs, and I force a smile.

The city is full of rubble. I don't want to look at Grete, so I stare out the window of the taxi. Shops with bright new signs stand beside shops with shattered windows. Women and men in expensive clothes climb into big American cars. An old man pushes a wooden cart filled with cabbages down the street.

"Do you still write poetry?" Grete asks.

"Not in a long time," I say.

The old man pushing the cart stops to rest. When he sets the end of the cart down, cabbages roll off onto the cobblestones. He leans over, picks them up, and puts them back in the cart, but for every cabbage he puts back, two or three more fall. We drive on.

As a young man, I quite inadvertently made a name for myself in certain parts of the world as an elegist. My first book was a slim volume of poems memorializing a lost love at a time when, because of war and illness, such a subject could find favor with a large audience. Intoxicated by the sudden attention, and even more so by the sudden wealth, I gave in to the pleas of my publisher for more and more poems, a seemingly endless series of elegies published in memory of every imaginable occasion, until newspaper cartoonists repeatedly turned me into a caricature (portraying such things as a man who writes verses for each grave in a graveyard stretching off to infinity), and my name appeared often in books and magazines, as well as some of the lesser motion pictures of the day. Each week I received hundreds of appeals for more elegies, poems to memorialize not only particular people, but also pets and objects and lost elections. Each week, I wrote fewer and fewer, as my poems felt even to me as if they had become parodies of their own parodies. Finally, unable to write a single word on a piece of paper without succumbing to utter nausea, I fled.

"Fame is so nice when you don't have it," Anders said to me once. We were sitting on a bench in a park at twilight.

"I'd rather have love than fame," I said, though I wasn't sure why.

"And what have you had for love?" He said it casually, not looking at me, watching people walk through the darkening shadows around us.

"That's how I started writing elegies," I said. "A lost love."

"Lost?" He turned to me. "How do you mean?"

"I wrote poem after poem to her. As if she had died."

"But she had not died?"

"No. We were great friends, and I had thought, I had hoped, that we might be something more than friends, eventually, but . . . no."

"I'm sorry," he said.

"And you? What have you had for love?"

"I love Grete," he said. "I have loved others. Three or four people, I think. When I was younger. But Grete was the first who could accept me for all that I am. And I realize how rare that is, how lucky."

Anders stood up, and a flock of birds that had gathered around our bench took flight, rising toward the grey sky, startling me, and for one tiny moment I thought he had shattered.

The apartment is not as I remember it, because most of the building has been rebuilt. The walls are clean and white, illuminated by light from many windows and from fixtures overhead. The air is fresh, and immediately I miss the old, comforting odor of cigarettes and incense and wine and people, the rich scent that used to relax me the moment I stepped inside. The furniture is much the same, the couch familiar in its hardness, but the doorknobs are all different, and as I wander through the apartment I find myself opening doors, feeling the knobs in my hand, each one smooth, and smoothly turning. I am fascinated by how new the doorknobs feel, free of any past or history, so typically American and out of place here. I laugh at myself, a previously intelligent and cultured man reduced to ruminating on doorknobs.

Grete makes me a cup of tea, and we sit across from each other in the little living room, me on the couch and her in a large chair with worn, red upholstery. I look around the apartment, noticing the framed posters from cabarets and galleries.

"I lost all my pictures in the war," she says. "I have no

photographs of anyone. The posters were sent to me by friends in Sweden. They found them in their attic. They forgot they'd put them there."

We sip our tea. She smiles and looks out the window. "There is so much to say. I don't have enough words."

I nod.

"You're the poet," she says. "Words are your business. I make pictures, that's all."

"I haven't written a poem in a very long time," I say.

"Why?"

"Because I couldn't finish the poem for Anders. It's the only one that feels worth writing, but I cannot write it."

I expect her to question me, to prod me, to praise my talent and remind me of something or other that Anders, or even Andrea, might have said on the subject. But she does not.

"It's funny," I say, my voice sounding strangely hollow in my ears. "I've spent every day since he asked me to write it feeling . . . well, feeling elegiacal. But I could not, I cannot, write . . ."

I am not a man who cries easily, except at chamber concerts and the conclusions of sentimental motion pictures, but suddenly, surprisingly, tears fill my eyes, and when Grete sits beside me, placing her hand gently on my back, I bow my head and weep.

During many evenings, before we would go out for dinner or to see a show, Anders and I spent an hour or two in my apartment, looking through books, reading poems and stories to each other. He had a lovely voice, high for a man, but his years on the stage had taught him fine articulation, and he had a perfect sense of cadence, so that his readings were the most emotionally affecting and most natural I have ever heard. Some of the purest moments of bliss I have experienced were those times when I listened to him and closed my eyes and let the sound of the words wash over me.

"What do you think makes a poem great?" he asked me one night. (We both had a weakness for grand questions.)

"Truth and feeling," I said.

"Doesn't one destroy the other?"

I told him I would need many more days to ponder the topic, and that really the only way to know a good poem was to read one, and so I read him the end of Spenser's "Daphnaida."

> So when I have with sorrow satisfide
> Th' importune fates, which vengeance on me seeke,
> And th' heavens with long languor pacifide,
> She, for pure pitie of my sufference meeke,
> Will send for me; for which I daylie long:
> And will till then my painful penance eeke.
> Weep, Shepheard! weep, to make my undersong!

I remember that moment well, because it was the only time Anders seemed truly moved, moved to the point of being unable to speak, by anything that I read to him. Finally, after a long silence, he said, "I think we should go out and have a terrible amount of fun."

"I always thought you were in love with Anders," Grete says to me. "Fond enough of Andrea, but in love with Anders. Why do you think that was?"

"I don't know," I say. "It's not something that can be understood with logic."

"No," Grete says, "I suppose not. Maybe poetry."

"I'm not sure any words help explain such things."

"Perhaps you should try painting," she says. "For me, the world makes more sense when I can shape it with colors."

"What color would you make me?"

"I'd begin with bright red, and then paint over that with a deep purple, and then cover it all with grey."

•   •   •

I first met Andrea at a dinner party at the apartment. She answered the door, handed me a glass of champagne, and led me inside. I noticed her eyes first, because they were as blue as Anders's eyes. "I'm Andrea," she said. She wore a light red dress, and amidst the curls of her blonde hair rested a lily.

"Are you a relative of Anders?" I asked.

"Oh yes," she said. "Very much so. But he will not be here tonight."

"Does he have a performance?"

"Of a certain type, yes."

Waiting at the table was Gilbert Barton, a British playwright I'd seen at various parties and gallery openings, a friend of Anders whom I found repulsive. Anders accused me of disliking Barton because he suffered the same disease as Oscar Wilde, but I assured him that I did not much care about that, unfortunate as it was, and that it was Barton's pathetic qualities, as well as his need to dominate a conversation, that made me dislike being in his presence. Grete felt sorry for him, though, because his plays were not popular and his life seemed to be perpetually crumbling into ruins, and Anders told me he liked Barton because he always felt sane and successful when the wretched man was around.

As I stepped into the room, I noticed that Barton's doughy face was red from, I assumed, already having had quite a few glasses of champagne, and he looked like some sort of waterlogged elf. He was regaling Grete with his latest tale of woe. "And then he tells me that because *he's* the director he can change any line he likes, and I tell him no no no *no,* that's not how it works, and he says he's just trying to make the play actually into a comedy, and I tell him that it was a comedy before he got his hands on it but now it is most certainly a tragedy, and a dull one at that—Oh, hello, Edward, what are you doing here?"

"I was invited," I said.

He chuckled. "Well, how nice."

We ate salad and steak and drank more champagne. Barton talked about actors and directors, how awful they all were. Andrea and Grete hardly spoke. I made little grunting noises of surprise and approval whenever it seemed necessary, but mostly I focused on drinking champagne. My gaze kept drifting to Andrea while Barton talked, because there was something familiar in the angle of her nose and in the shape of her lips hiding beneath the mask of lipstick, and in her eyes.

Later, sitting on the couch with Barton while Grete cleared the table and Andrea slipped off somewhere to get some bottles of wine, I learned the secret that had been kept from me, and that had I been more observant I would have easily discovered on my own.

Barton ran his hand up and down my leg, and when I pushed him away, he said, his voice a vicious whisper, "What do you want then? *Him?*"

I stood up without quite hearing what he had said. Andrea walked into the room then, a bottle of red wine in either hand.

"He's the one you want, isn't he?" Barton said. Andrea stopped. She set the bottles down on the coffee table in front of the couch.

"What are you talking about?" I said.

Andrea said, "Gilbert's being boorish. Just ignore him."

"Gilbert's always boorish," I said.

Barton stood up, unsteadily but successfully, and grabbed Andrea in an embrace. He thrust his hand beneath her dress. "It's still there," he said. Andrea pushed him away and he fell backward, tripping over the side of the couch and banging his head on the coffee table. He lay on the floor, blood from a gash in his forehead pouring over the wooden floor. Andrea ran to the bedroom and closed the door. Grete stood behind me. "I'm sorry," she said, and together we lifted Barton up onto the couch and covered his head with a towel.

"Just go," Grete said to me. "He'll be fine. We'll all be fine."

. . .

I didn't see Grete and Anders for another week. Nor did I see Andrea. I forced myself to go out during the days, even during early mornings, because the thought of walking the streets at night nauseated me, and often I went to sleep just as the sun slipped low enough in the sky to drench the city in shadows. The bustle of the market at morning comforted me, the noise of voices and the air filled with clashing, mingling scents of meat and fruit and flowers and people. I ate bread and cheese and apples, I drank beer, I avoided the cafés. I sat at a window in my apartment and watched people walking outside. I wrote notes about them on scraps of paper, imaginary portraits—a man with a tattered top hat became a secret agent seeking codes in long-forgotten books hidden in the dust of little shops; a woman with a child wrapped in a shawl in her arms became a mother widowed in the war and still in mourning; a man with a vague face and brown clothes became a movie star from another country. In the little stories I wrote about them, every person on the street was somehow lost and somehow lonely.

I was drinking one last bottle of beer when I heard a gentle knock on the door. I ignored it at first, but then there was another knock, gentle still but more insistent. I heard Anders's voice call my name. I finished the beer. He opened the door.

"Hello?" he said. "Haven't heard from you for a while."

I made some sort of meaningless movement, a nod or a shrug.

"I've wondered how you are," he said. "I'm sorry about what happened with Gilbert. I know you don't like him, and I'm sorry we invited him, but we thought, I don't know . . ."

"You thought it would be fun to play a joke on me."

"No," Anders said. "There was no joke at all."

"Gilbert getting drunk and insulting me was not a joke? Andrea was not a joke?"

"Andrea is not a joke."

"A little performance, then?"

"No," Anders said. "Not a performance. I wanted to talk to you about that, and I meant to tell you earlier, but it didn't feel right yet, and then . . . I don't know. I don't always have the best judgment."

"I don't understand anything that you're saying."

"Andrea is me, Edward. Andrea is more me than Anders is."

I am ashamed to admit it now, but I laughed. I was exhausted, a bit drunk, confused, and I laughed. Anders pursed his lips and looked away from me. After a moment of stillness and silence, he walked out of the room without closing the door.

Grete and I go to dinner at a basement restaurant where a year ago she helped the owner choose the colors of paint for the walls. Everything is bright: bright reds and yellows, bright green trim along the floor and ceiling and windows. The owner is a young man with a limp and a missing eye and blond hair cut so short he looks bald when he is not standing directly in front of us.

We eat a salad and drink water and white wine.

Before our dessert arrives, Grete says, "I am ill. I have cancer."

"Yes," I say.

"I'm told I have about a month to live, perhaps less. My husband died in the war. We had a daughter, but she was with him. I don't have any possessions to speak of, most of my paintings will be taken care of by the galleries, and the owner of the main gallery will serve as my estate agent. But I would like you to arrange my funeral. If you are willing."

I cannot speak. I want to say, *Yes, of course.* I want to say, *I will do whatever you need.* These are things I should have said to people in the past, and I know I will not get many chances to say them to anyone else during what's left of my life. But I cannot speak.

"I know it is a terrible thing to ask," Grete says. "I do not ask because I want you to write a poem. I do not want a poem. At the funeral, I want to be remembered not merely as myself, but as the woman who loved Anders. I want him to be remembered. And Andrea, too. By someone who can remember them both, and with joy."

My fingers slide across the edge of the table, feeling the sharp angle.

"Can you remember us all? With joy?"

I weave my hands together and hold them in my lap. I whisper my answer. "Yes."

"Wait—Anders!" I stood at the top of the stairs and called down to him. He stopped and turned. "I'm sorry," I said, as loudly as I could, the words like cinders in my mouth.

We sat in my room and drank gin. I turned on a small lamp, and in the shadows I could see both Anders and Andrea in his face.

"I am performing tomorrow night," he said after we had talked about Grete and Barton and the time when Andrea had first walked down the street in daylight, terrified of being laughed at, but instead gaining friendly smiles and responses from merchants and shopkeepers of, "Can I help you, miss?" and "Miss, would you like . . ." A slowly rising comfort with the self that had been so long hidden, so long hurt.

"Performing?"

"At a nightclub. I will be Andrea. Singing." He smiled sweetly, then covered his smile with his hand.

"Are you embarrassed?" I asked.

"No," he said. "Happy. Because you'll be there, won't you?"

"Yes," I said. "Of course I will."

He leaned forward and gave me a soft kiss.

Back at the apartment, Grete shows me some of her new paintings. They are small, because she still has trouble finding large

canvases that she can afford, but she says she has enjoyed painting in miniature, it suits her personality now. The paintings are
not much larger than postcards. They are more figurative than
the paintings of hers I knew from before, the paintings that
brought her some fame in certain circles. These are gentle paintings of women in long, flowing dresses, women with hats that
cover their eyes, women dancing in the rain.

It is a cold night in the city, a night with a sky of slate. Grete
lights candles throughout the apartment instead of turning on
the lights. We sit together on the couch.

"Who introduced him to Hirschfeld?" I ask.

"Barton, actually," Grete says. "Gilbert had been to the
Institute, had met Hirschfeld a few times. He always said there
was more to it, tried to play up their friendship, but the one time
I talked to them together, Hirschfeld barely seemed to know
him."

"I was not horrified when Anders told me."

"I know."

"He thought I was. He thought I was angry because of the
procedure. But that wasn't it."

"I know," Grete says, and rests her head on my shoulder.
Soon, she is asleep. The little flames of all the candles flicker and
the room shimmers with shadows.

In the nightclub, everything was either bright or dark, and most
of the brightness huddled near the stage, where Andrea stood in a
sparkling blue dress and sang soft songs in a breathy voice, popular tunes of the day, songs that began with innuendo and finished
with melancholy, their last notes trailing off as the little pianist
bent low and held the keys down until long after the melody
had drifted away and the light on Andrea had faded into smoke.

She performed there many times, and I went to every performance. Barton went to some, as did Grete, but both soon grew
tired of it, and Barton, thankfully, returned to England.

During the third or fourth week she had been performing, Andrea said to me after the show one night, "Wasn't the audience wonderful? I'm afraid I'll never get to sleep. Let's go for a drink!" And so we ended up at a little bar a few blocks away, a place where actors went after finishing their work, and we drank gin and laughed about the hunger in the eyes of the audience each night, and we tried to forget all that was going on around us.

"Let me take *you* home for once, Edward," she said as we found our way out of the bar.

"You shouldn't walk back alone," I said.

"I'll be fine. It's not far at all."

"I don't think—"

"Oh shush," she said, and we strolled toward my apartment.

"Won't you offer a lady a nightcap?" she said, and I ushered her inside and poured her a bit of whiskey, which was all that I had.

I had recently bought an old phonograph, a beastly large thing that amused me as much for its unwieldiness as for its music. Andrea put a record on and began to dance to it. She pulled me off of the chair where I was sitting and I danced with her. "Isn't this marvelous?" she said, and kissed me.

"Don't walk home alone tonight," I said as the song came to an end.

"What are you so afraid of?" she said.

"It's not safe at night now."

"It's not safe at all anymore." She sat on my bed and I sat beside her. "When you look at me, do you see a man pretending to be a woman, or do you see . . . something more?"

"Don't worry about what I see," I said. I tried to kiss her, but she stood up. She pulled hairpins out of her hair and let it fall down below her shoulders. She grabbed an old shirt of mine that was sitting on the floor by the bed and wiped her face with it as if she were trying to wipe off her skin as well as the rouge and mascara and eye shadow. She unzipped her dress and stepped out of it. She removed her underwear.

I sighed and stood up. I touched her arm and let a finger

wander up her chest to her neck, her chin, her cheek. "You have,"
I said, "the most beautiful eyes I've ever seen." She looked away.

I gave her some of my clothes, and she put them on. Anders
stood there with tears in his eyes. "Will I be safe now?" he said.

"You can stay here if you'd like."

"No," he said. "I'm sorry. I'm exhausted, I don't know what
I'm . . . I'm sorry." He picked up Andrea's clothes and walked out
into the night.

Grete asks me to call her doctor. She is not feeling well. She has
no strength or appetite. The doctor arrives and talks with her in
a light and cheery voice. He is a small man with a giant mustache. He takes me into the kitchen and tells me she should be
in the hospital. I tell him she does not want to be in the hospital,
that she wants to die here. He says she will die soon.

While Grete sleeps, I look through the papers she has given
me. Mostly they are contracts and old bills and various legal
documents, but among them is a letter from Anders, probably
the last he wrote:

> My dearest Grete,
>
> Never doubt that I loved you. A complicated love, yes,
> but the greatest love of my life. I owe you my life. The one re-
> gret I have is that I could not be the husband you deserved.
> The one good thing about being born into the wrong body
> was that you became my wife. We have a new world ahead of
> us, and as excited as I am by it, as much as I have wanted it
> for years and years and years, there is a tinge of sadness, too,
> because I know that, in some way or another, I am leaving
> you behind. Never forget me, as I will never forget you.
>
> Pleurant, je voyais de l'or—et ne plus boire—
>
> > All my love,
> > Anders

•   •   •

I stopped going to the performances, and I avoided Anders. He left a note under my door asking me to meet him in our favorite park at noon the next day.

I arrived late, but he was still waiting. He stood beneath a tall tree and smoked a cigarette.

"If this were a melodrama," he said, "I would ask you if you hate me."

"Why should I hate you?" I said.

"I don't know. But suddenly you disappeared. I thought you must be angry."

He offered me a cigarette, and I took it. He lit it with a silver lighter.

"Tell me about you and Grete," I said.

"What do you want to know?"

"Do you love her?"

"Yes. Very much."

"Do you have the regular relations of a husband and wife?"

"Sexual relations, you mean?"

"Yes."

"Sometimes," he said.

"What about Barton? Did you have relations with him?"

"No, of course not." He laughed contemptuously.

"Why of course not?"

"I'm not a homosexual," he said.

"Neither am I."

"Then why are you angry at me?"

I began to walk away, but he grabbed my arm. "Edward, I wanted to talk to you because I want to tell you about a doctor I have met, and what he has told me."

"A doctor?"

"Yes. Who can help me."

"How?"

"There is a procedure. It will give me the body that is natural to me. Andrea's body."

I pulled away from him. I ran away from him.

I stopped. I covered my face with my hands. People probably walked past, but I did not notice them. Eventually, I recovered myself. Anders remained where I had left him. He leaned back against the tree, his face covered with tears. I went to him and embraced him. "I don't want you to be Andrea," I said, even then horrified by how selfish I sounded, how much like a child.

Grete lies in her bed, swaddled in blankets, her eyes open, but foggy. She no longer speaks.

"Do you remember going to Venice with Anders?" I say to her. "He said it was to celebrate what was going to happen, to celebrate Andrea, but you also knew it was to say good-bye to him. I was angry when you went. I wanted to go with you, I wanted to share that moment, all those moments you got to have with him. I was so distraught that I didn't understand how awful I was being. I thought I could convince him to save himself. I didn't think about you at all, Grete. I didn't think about you as it was happening. I hurt so much. I wrote him letters. Long letters, sometimes more than one a day. All he sent back were a couple of postcards. You both seemed so happy when you returned, so refreshed and healthy. I hated you then. I thought if you didn't exist, perhaps something different would happen. I blamed you for what I thought he was doing to himself. Killing himself. During the whole time you were in Venice, I imagined one thing after another, fantasies of the life he and I could have together. I thought he would make me strong. I thought we could explore the world together, go hunting in deserts, sleep on the sidewalks of strange cities, without cares and without sorrow. I lived the life of a sleepwalker. I wandered the streets and talked to him, whole conversations I wanted to have with him, all the while everyone looking at me like I was a madman. I wanted to show him America. I wanted to bring him to New York and introduce him to all of my friends, the friends I had abandoned. I could get him work on Broadway and in the movies. I knew I could. I wanted to. I wanted nothing so much as to help him and to make him happy. I wanted him to look at me and smile and laugh, I wanted him to be grateful, because then I would know I had done something worthwhile in this life, I had helped someone, and they loved me, they could love me, and me alone. I was so desperate for someone to love me and only me that I couldn't see what effect this was having, I was blind to how much I wished for, how much I hoped for. I imagined moments when we could sit together, just the two of us, on beaches or in beautiful hotels, sharing moments no one else would know about. That's all I wanted, Grete. Moments only he and I would know about."

She closes her eyes. All the while I am talking, I think, *You mustn't talk, you mustn't remember, you must stop talking, stop remembering, you must stop. . . .*

After he returned from Venice, Anders came to see me. I asked him if he had gotten my letters, and he said he had.

"I'm worried about you, Edward."

"About me? How can you worry about me?"

"You have built up some idea of me that I don't understand," he said. "You have imagined me as something, someone . . . I don't know."

I took his hand. "Please," I said, "don't say anything."

"I don't want to hurt you, but I have to speak. You are trying to box me into being someone I'm not. You are pushing our friendship toward something unnatural, something beyond what it would be if you would relax and let things happen as they will happen. I begin the procedure next week, Edward, and that will change everything."

I let go of his hand. I turned away from him. "Please don't do it," I said.

"I have to do it. It is all I want in the world."

"Anders—"

"Anders is dead. Don't talk to me about Anders anymore."

My bones ached as I struggled to keep from screaming. I stood with my fists clenched and every muscle in my body taut. He put his hand on my shoulder, but I pulled away.

"I'm sorry," he said. "I never wanted to hurt you."

As he walked away, I whispered, "Please don't forget me."

We only met one more time. At a café, of course. I had ignored the notes he sent and I locked the door when he came to my apartment. It was not because I hated him, though I'm sure he thought that. It was to preserve myself. A thousand thoughts and ideas flashed through my mind in those days, all the shards of shattered fantasies that I barely understood. My intellect and my emotions had been severed from each other. Waves of sorrow filled me, raising questions in my mind: What had I wanted from him? Why had I behaved as I had? If I had gotten all that I wanted, what then? What was the all that I wanted?

I made plans to return to America. I contacted friends, I reserved a berth on a ship.

I don't know why I answered the door that day when I had not answered it any of the days before. Any of the other knocks could have been the last, but somehow I knew this one was.

He asked if we could talk. He said he had a request. He invited me to a café. I did not speak, but I followed him out.

He said he would begin the first surgery the next day. We ordered coffee and ate sugary pastries. He laughed as I got sugar all over my fingers and chin.

"Will you write me a poem?" he said.

I finished the pastry and did not look at him.

"A poem for Anders," he said. "An elegy."

I brushed the sugar off my fingers and stood up. I did not look at him. "Yes," I said.

As I walked into my apartment, my legs were shuddering so violently that I fell to the floor. I rolled onto my side and hugged my knees to my chest and squeezed my eyes closed as tightly as I could, trying to obliterate the world.

I did not return to America then. I cancelled the reservation on the ship, I told my friends I needed more time. In truth, I was embarrassed, and I did not want anyone who had known me before—who had known me as the famous poet and the delight of all the best parties—to see me as I was now, devastated and confused, ashamed of all that I had felt and thought. Also, I'm sure that somewhere within the snarled knot of my emotions was curiosity about and even concern for Anders and Andrea. I would not have admitted it to anyone, including myself, but I wanted to see the results of the doctor's magic procedure.

I received a letter:

Dear Edward,

It is Andrea who writes to you now. Forever Andrea. I wanted you to know that the first operation went well, and that though I am tired and in some pain, I am also excited and full of joy. I am sitting here right now wearing a silk nightdress and a pearl necklace (of all things!). They were both presents from Grete, who is here with me. I will soon be moved to the women's hospital for the major part of the procedure. I hope you are well. Please remember the poem that Anders asked you to write. I know you cared about him deeply, and that you care about me, and I do not have the words to tell you how much such a poem would mean to us, or how much you, my dear Edward, meant to Anders and mean to me. Please take care of yourself. I look forward to seeing you on my return.

Your Andrea

Six months later, Andrea returned to the city from the clinic where she had been convalescing. For a month, I avoided seeing her, making one excuse after another, despite phone calls and letters from her and from Grete. I wanted to be sure I would respond in only the best way, and that I would not foist my disappointments onto her, because there was nothing either of us could do about it now. Finally, I called Grete and asked her and Andrea to meet me at our favorite park.

She looked vaguely different from how she had looked before, like meeting a woman whom you've seen only in magazine pictures. We embraced and kissed and cried together for a moment and then laughed at ourselves. Grete stood on one side of me and Andrea on the other, and we all held hands as we walked through the park.

Andrea continued singing at the cabaret, and I went to see her whenever I could, but I had decided definitely to return to America, and there were people to say good-bye to and dinners to attend and arrangements to make, so I did not see her or Grete as often as I wished, and then one day we were all standing at the docks together, and I was walking up onto the ship and waving good-bye and watching the city drift away over the dark horizon.

Andrea rented a small room in the city, and Grete began to put a new life together for herself. They both sent me postcards and letters. Andrea did her best to keep her tone light and optimistic. She said she felt younger, that it seemed her entire brain had been changed as well as her body, that the last remnants of Anders had died and a new emotional life had arisen within her. But sometimes I perceived a sadness beneath her words. She hinted that many of Anders's friends spurned her, and she suggested that she was having trouble finding work other than singing at the cabaret, a job that no longer paid well. She said she worried about the political situation, but more for Grete than herself, because Grete was better known and might be targeted by the government. She said her health was not always good. She said she missed me and hoped I would be able to visit again soon. She did not mention the poem.

Grete told me the story of Anders's change had begun to circulate in the newspapers. So far, very few good photographs of Andrea had been taken, so she was able to walk down the streets without being recognized. The cabaret tried to publicize her, but she quit, saying she wanted to be known for her singing, nothing else. She had not found another job, but at least she was not hiding away in her little room every day. Thanks to Dr. Hirschfeld's advocacy, Andrea's legitimation papers had come through, and she was now officially allowed to use her name and sex on legal documents. Grete said that Andrea seemed to have a new group of friends, and even a man who paid some attention to her, a man who knew her history. Grete said that Andrea had talked to a doctor about what sort of operation might allow her to become a mother.

And then I received a short note from Andrea telling me that she was very sick, and that she was in a hospital. She said that she thought death was near, but that she did not have any regrets. She said she had dreamed of her mother, who had died long ago, and that in the dream her mother came to her and embraced her and told her that she loved her.

The next week, Grete sent a short note to let me know that Andrea had died of paralysis of the heart.

It is a gloriously bright and sunny day. We stand in the cemetery, Grete's few friends and I and the minister, and they wait for me to speak. We stand near where we believe Andrea's grave was;

we will never know for sure, because this area was destroyed during the war.

I had brought a stanza of Edmund Spenser to read in case I could not think of any words of my own, but I do not have the will to read it.

I step back, silent.

The coffin is lowered into the grave.

I look out over the city and hold in my hand the yellowed piece of hospital stationery on which Andrea, too weak to speak, had written her final words. I found the paper lying on the table beside the bed where Grete died. The handwriting is uneven and the ink is faded almost to nothing, but I can make out the words well enough, and as I stand here and read them again and again above a city of ruins saturated with the past, I know now what Anders and Andrea wanted from me, and why they thought it required a poem, because only a poem can begin to answer the question Andrea wrote on that paper, the question I know will haunt me until I am able to leave this horrible world: *What did I do to deserve so much love?*

Eudaemonic

● ● ●

JAY CASELBERG

"TOUCH ME BRIGHT with the demons of your soul," she'd said to him. Bright? Michael had sat back, tasted the word, wondering at her choice. She wanted his dark places to illuminate her, or so she'd said, and Michael had considered. Sometimes we go to strange locales in search of mutual understanding.

Around that time, Michael lived near the ocean, in a big wooden house, the sound of surf muttering and crashing him to sleep on those thick summer nights heavy with the heat, the faint salt breeze offering scant relief from the gleam of sweat across his chest. The semidark rooms full of the scent of brine and night jasmine. He lived alone then. After two failed marriages, he'd learned; it was better sometimes to have no one but yourself to blame. Bitterness is more than simply the taste of coffee in the morning. The house, a rambling, haphazard affair, came with its own memories, but Michael happily populated them with his own.

Claire filled it with something else entirely.

In summer, the beach thronged with tourists and holiday-makers. Even late at night, moon or no moon, there'd be couples strolling hand in hand along the water's edge. But in winter, it was a different matter, the broad, empty stretch of sand, the cold wind whipping tufts of beach grass back and forth, scattering grains in its wake, a few sun-bleached shells staring white like bones from between the hummocks in the crisp daylight. In those times, Michael would walk, alone with his thoughts and the grey ocean stirring and muttering beside him. Claire had been the last person he'd expected to meet there, along with the body that lay beside her.

Michael had seen them from afar, a woman crouched beside a male form lying there, unmoving in the sand. She was leaning over him, as if in conversation, and Michael would have given it not another thought, already changing his path to avoid them, except, just then, she half stood and waved him over. Michael had frowned, wondering what she could possibly want, here on this almost deserted beach in the late afternoon, but then it had struck him; the man was lying face down, and for some reason, that just didn't seem right. Still frowning, he changed his course and headed towards them. As he neared, he saw with more clarity; the scene was just wrong. The man was dressed casually, light brown trousers and a cream shirt, but there was discoloration mottling the trouser legs, and he was still, far too still. Claire had resumed her crouch, one hand gripped inside the other, looking down at the achingly immobile form. As Michael drew closer, she spoke.

"I don't know what to do," she said. "I think he's dead." She turned his head to the side.

Michael stood there, looking down at the man, taking in the details and not saying anything. The eyes were closed. Midlength blond hair clumped at the back of his head, but fell evenly across his forehead, as if it had been just combed. A fan of sand marked one cheek, the skin underneath simply the wrong colour. The trousers were stained up both legs in irregular patterns, rimed white at the edges, but darker towards the feet. The strangest thing was the look on the dead man's face; it was nothing more than simple joy. Standing there, Michael suddenly realized that he actually didn't know what to do either.

"Um," he said and crouched down beside the body opposite her, being careful not to touch it. "Do you know him?"

"Not really," she said.

He didn't think about the implication of her words then.

Finally managing to tear his gaze away from the man's face, he saw her properly for the first time. She was watching him intently with grey-green eyes. Reddish brown curls, the color of kelp, fell to her shoulders. She wore a simple dark top and black sweats. A dapple of pale freckles ran across the bridge of her nose, clearly visible against the paler skin beneath.

"Well?" she said, tired of waiting for him to say something else.

Michael looked down again at the body lying between them.

"Have you touched him?" he said.

"There's no pulse. I think he's dead."

Michael gestured back up the beach with a toss of his head. "I live just over there. I could go and call somebody. If you don't mind waiting here with him . . ."

"Okay," she said. "I don't mind. He's not going anywhere. Neither am I."

When he looked back up at her, her face was turned away, watching the water.

"You know," she said, her voice distracted. "They say the ocean is a great healer." And then she turned back to look at him. "Sometimes, I guess it's not."

He didn't know what to say to that either, and there was a pause as he waited for her to say something else.

"Okay, you wait here," he said finally. "I'll go call. I'll be back in a few minutes. My name's Michael by the way."

"Claire," she said. "Claire van Maren."

Michael left her staring out at the waves as she crouched beside the man who was no longer alive.

He walked as quickly as he could back up to the house, thinking about the strangeness of the situation and framing words he was going to say to the police. He thought the police were the right ones to call rather than an ambulance. They would sort out anyone else who needed to know. It wasn't up to him. Normally, he'd be reluctant to get involved, but this time, he hadn't even thought about it. He already *was* involved.

"What the hell are you doing, Michael?" he said to himself.

He didn't really have much choice in the matter. Not really.

The next time he saw her, she wore a simple peasant dress, green and patterned and a loose, pale blue blouse. He didn't recognize her at first. One weekend a month, the locals held a street market down by the park, stalls of bric-a-brac and oddments, things that people had cleared out of their garages and backyards, and of course the local home produce, jams, preserves, and the like. It served multiple purposes, bringing the community together, but also allowing them to exchange gossip and catch up with each other's lives. Michael rather drifted through it all, but he liked to go down and see what might turn up. Occasionally, there'd be a real find, an interesting curio, something that had been washed up on the beach that he could pay to take away and wonder about, to turn over and over in his fingers, making up secret histories that belonged to each little object.

There was one particular stallholder, a crusty old man who spent his retirement years combing the beach, collecting whatever he could find, and Michael always looked forward to discovering what his particular stall might hold. Now and again, Michael would see him wandering the beach with his lopsided gait, pausing to stare at apparently vacant spots on the sand. The old man wasn't the sort to use a metal detector, but wandered around using merely the keenness of his eye, or the instinct in his gut to find his little oddments, and from time to time, they would turn up on his stall. Sometimes, Michael would wonder if the old man kept them at home, inventing his own secret provenance before he tired of them and they eventually found their way to his table.

Michael had been meandering among the various stalls, keeping his favorite till last, not even looking in the direction of the old man's table. It was a little game he liked to play with himself, holding back the expectation until the last possible moment. When he finally did turn his eye in that direction, he was a little annoyed to see the view blocked by some woman leaning over the table, apparently in discussion with the old man about one of his oddments. Michael moved up behind her and waited impatiently for their conversation to end. Finally, he was rewarded, because she straightened and turned, moving to walk away, but instead, rounding almost into him. They were standing face-to-face, her eyes looking straight into his. There was a moment of confusion, and then she smiled.

"Why, hello," she said. "It's you. I remember you."

There was a warmth in her voice that spoke of familiarity and summer afternoons sitting together in a private garden. He blinked a couple of times before responding.

"Hi," he said. "It's Claire, isn't it?"

"Yes, from the beach."

"Uh-huh," he said, not really wanting to drag up the context, but forced into it anyway.

If anything, her smile grew broader and she lifted her hand and placed the tips of her fingers on his forearm.

"Fancy meeting you here," she said. "Listen, do you want to get a cup of coffee or something?"

Flustered by the directness, Michael could do little more than nod, and he acquiesced as she turned him around and led him up the street by his arm. They walked in silence, which he found strange, as if she was holding back all words until they had found an appropriate setting, away from the wave of voices and chatter of the marketplace. Once or twice, she glanced up at his face, smiling, and as they walked, he watched her, looking at the pretty peasant garb, the way the sun caught the red high-lights in her hair and her eyes that one moment looked green and the next were blue. He tried putting her in context with the woman he'd met on the beach, but she looked so different, or at least not exactly how he had remembered her. Her forthright-ness had put him a little on guard, and he wasn't quite certain that he should be doing this at all.

A small coffee shop lay at the end of the street, one of those places that did afternoon teas and pastries, with small tables covered in white chintz tablecloths and the smell of sweet cakes permeating the air. Michael didn't go there much—not his kind of place really—but in the current circumstance, it seemed as good a choice as any.

Claire ordered a spiced-apple tea and he a latte. When the mugs came steaming to the table, the scent of spiced apple wafted up from Claire's cup, surrounding them in an ethereal cloud that reminded Michael of the hippie shop down the street. She sat watching him for several moments, and then finally lifted her mug to her lips, still watching him over the rim.

"So," she said. "Michael, wasn't it?"

Michael nodded, returning her look, reaching for his own mug, but not lifting it, turning it slowly around and around on the table with his fingers.

"Imagine meeting up like this again," she said, slowly lower-ing her mug, and gave him a quick little smile.

He'd rather not consider the last time they'd met. It was the sort of thing he wanted to put completely from his mind.

"So, what's troubling you, Michael?" she said.

Michael frowned. "Um, I don't know that anything is particu-larly. Do I look troubled?" This time he reached for his coffee and took a tentative sip, watching her carefully.

She shook her head. "No, it's not that. It's just a . . . sense I get. As if you've forgotten how to be joyful."

Michael's frown deepened. Claire was attractive enough, perhaps a woman that he'd like to spend time with, but this was just weird. He wondered if maybe she was some sort of cultist and any minute she'd start talking about self-actualization or something equally absurd.

She'd apparently noticed his reticence, because she lowered her gaze and instead stared down into the depths of her cup.

"So what do you do, Claire?" he said. "And van Maren, right? What's that, Dutch?"

She looked up with a smile at the sound of his words. "Yes, way back, but not for a long time. And what is it I do? Good question. This and that. Always passing through. Sometimes I feel like a ghost."

This brought another frown from Michael. "I'm not sure I—"

She cut him off with a little shake of her head. "Doesn't matter," she said. "Ignore me. I'm just in one of my moods. Let's see if you can do something about that, Michael. So, what about you?"

"Well," he said. "I live in a house by the beach, but you know that. Apart from that, I'm a freelance artist. Commercial stuff, you know. Advertisements and the like. It means I do a lot of my work at home. It's not the real work though. It's just what I do to make enough to keep me doing what I really want to."

"And what's that?"

"I'm a painter. Oils."

She looked down at his hands and blinked. He followed her gaze and then looked back up at her and grinned. "What, you expect my hands to be covered in paint or something? Not all artists aspire to that image. I don't look that good in a beret and smock either."

She nodded and half-smiled in return.

"So what are you working on now?"

"Well . . . ," he said.

Again, he turned his mug on the table without lifting it and lightly bit his lower lip. When he looked up, she was watching him expectantly.

"Not really anything, at the moment," he said with a sigh. "I just can't seem to . . ."

She was leaning forward, her hands crossed on the table before her. "Tell me, Michael. Tell me what's stopping you."

He paused for a full three seconds before answering, watching her half-open lips, and then it was a nonanswer. "Um, I don't really know."

He really didn't know what it was, but he also didn't know what made her think she had the right to be probing his life like this; they'd barely met. Now he was on guard. And come to think of it, she'd told him virtually nothing about herself. It was all pretty one-sided.

The small café seemed awfully quiet just then. Claire stared down into her tea, and Michael sat watching her, thinking about cutting and running, making some sort of excuse to get out of the situation. It was not a very auspicious start. After a few moments, he cleared his throat, breaking through the awkwardness that lay palpable between them.

"Look," he said finally. "I've got a couple of things I need to do."

She looked up at him, the touch of disappointment barely discernible on her face, but there all the same. Awkwardly, he stood and fumbled for his wallet.

"Let me get this," he said, dragging his gaze away and heading for the counter. He paid quickly, self-consciously, aware of her eyes on his back.

"Good to see you," he said at the door.

She merely nodded.

The taste for browsing the old man's stall had gone, so instead he headed back to the house.

All the way, he was pondering what had just happened, wondering about what motivated this woman, this stranger.

* * *

He would have written the whole incident from his conscious-ness, but the thing was, Claire's face just wouldn't go away. He'd be making a cup of coffee, and he'd remember her, the mug of spicy tea held between her pale, long-fingered hands. He'd be looking out of the window at the sea, staring at the waves rolling in and crashing against the sand, and he'd remember her eyes, changeable as the ocean itself, and with the eyes would eventu-ally come her face and her hair. What had she said? That she'd felt like a ghost? Well maybe she was, because she was starting to haunt the spaces in his days.

A few days later, he was walking on the beach, discovering random patterns in the sand and the shapes hidden in the swirling waters, when she appeared again. He saw her from a distance, and this time, there was no mistaking who it was. The casual dark sports clothing were back, and she was standing by the waterline, watching him. It was funny, but Michael hadn't seen her walk down the beach. All of a sudden, she was just there.

Right then, he was in two minds. Should he ignore her? Should he acknowledge her presence? The last time had been such a disaster that he just didn't know. She took the decision away from him, striding purposefully across the sand in his di-rection. Michael shrugged to himself. The Fates seemed to be throwing this woman into his path at every turn, so he might as well go with the flow. It only took her about ten seconds to reach him and she stood before him, barefoot, looking up into his eyes.

"Michael," she said, reaching up with one hand to touch the side of his face, a fleeting contact, but one that initiated a spark of electricity through his nerves. "I was hoping I'd see you here. I've been thinking about you."

Had she been thinking about him in the same way that he'd been thinking about her?

He hadn't noticed it before, but on one side of her hair, there was a clear white streak running back from her left temple and intertwined with those red-brown locks. Funny that he hadn't seen it.

"How did you know I'd be here?" he said.

She reached for his hand. "Lucky guess."

For now, he wasn't questioning. He watched her face, studied her lips and her eyes and hair as she led him to a spot where the wet sand met the dry and sat him down, facing the incoming waves. She sat beside him, hugging her knees and staring out into the depths.

"Can you feel the power?" she said.

"There's a force there," he said in response.

"Hmmm." She nodded her head slowly. "Do you watch the waves often, Michael?"

"Yeah, I guess. You can see things deep inside the waves. Things moving, if you look hard enough. It's more than just the sand."

As each wave slid up the beach towards them and then sucked back into the darkness, Michael felt the apprehension drawn away from him. There was something comfortable about having her here, sitting beside him. He stole a glance at her face, but she was staring at the water. He turned his head to follow her gaze, wondering if she was seeing the same things he was.

"So, Michael, tell me about yourself," she said quietly. "I want to hear it all."

He was silent for several seconds before answering. The waves crashed in front of them, beating out the time.

"What do you want to know?"

"Everything, Michael. Everything."

He had to lean closer to hear her answer above the sound of the water; she'd said it so quietly. He straightened again, randomly brushed away some sand adhering to the leg of his trousers and cleared his throat.

"Okay," he said.

He lost track of how long he spoke for. Once he'd started, the words came easily and they kept coming—his frustrations, his disappointments, the darkness. The solitude he didn't mind. The aloneness, that was another thing. All of it came out and she listened, not saying anything, just staring out with those grey-green eyes into the ocean depths.

Eventually, the words ran dry, and left them sitting there together, both hugging their knees.

Claire pushed her feet into the wet sand and leaned back. "So, that's Michael," she said.

"Pretty much all of it," he answered, feeling slightly foolish and exposed.

"So, don't you think it's time for you to ask me back for a cup of tea?" She turned to him and smiled. "I like you, Michael," she said. "I think I could be very good for you."

Later, back at the house, she helped him out of his clothes and lay beside him, fingers tracing patterns on his skin, the half-finished mug of tea sitting forgotten on the bedside table.

Afterwards, she wandered around the house naked, picking up pieces and examining them, poking through bookshelves, peering at this and that, while he watched her appreciatively, propped up on one elbow, barely daring to question how they had come to this.

Over the next few weeks, Claire became almost a constant companion, spending more time at the house than away from it. Michael didn't mind at all. He still wasn't painting, but making love to Claire was more than enough to keep his mind off it. Somehow, she was filling the empty spaces inside him.

One day, he noticed that the white streak had disappeared from her hair. He wasn't quite sure when it had gone, but he dismissed it. She'd probably dyed it when she was away, though she didn't seem to be that self-conscious about her appearance. Not that she had any reason to be. White streak or no, Michael thought she was beautiful. He had ceased questioning how she had come into his life. The body on the beach seemed to drift out of their consciousness as if it had never been there at all. They could just as easily have met in a bar or in that first café, or at a party at somebody's house rather than across a corpse at the water's edge, for all the impact it had on their time together.

"Do you believe in the supernatural, Michael?" she asked him one day. The question had come completely out of the blue. She was sitting on the back steps looking down at the beach across the road. The air was full of the scent of summer grasses and the tang of seaweed. "Like demons, vampires . . . that sort of thing?"

"I don't know. Not really," he said, moving to sit beside her. "Why?"

"I just think it's an interesting idea," she said. "Taking from someone's life to sustain your own. Isn't that what people do to each other?"

He stared at her for a long time, but she didn't meet his gaze.

"Never mind," she said finally, pushing herself to her feet and disappearing through the back door into the comparative dimness of the back room. She had said something else as the door closed behind her that he didn't catch.

Later that day, he stood before a blank canvas for the first time in weeks. His studio felt unfamiliar, the brushes awkward in his hand. The first tentative stroke was wrong, the second worse. In the end, he put down the brushes, taking the time to clean them before putting them away. He stood for several minutes staring at the off-white surface, a couple of dark blotches of formlessness marring the clean surface. The smell of linseed was heavy in the air. Creativity was joy, and somewhere along the way, it was as if the joy had gone. Had they taken it with them, his failed relationships, the partnerships gone nowhere, the career leading to nothing? Thinking those thoughts, the emptiness filled him and settled in his chest. When he finally turned from the canvas, Claire was standing in the doorway watching him.

"Come on," she said, holding out one hand. "We need to go for a walk."

"What's the point?" said Michael.

"Oh, there's a point," she said, taking a step closer and reaching for his hand. "Come on."

Michael didn't really feel like it, but he let himself be led out of the house, across the road, and down to the beach. He could feel the squeak of sand beneath his feet, the breeze and the salt around his face, the stirring of the waves.

She led him right to the water's edge, without saying a word.

He looked down as the very edge of a wave splashed over his shoes, giving a slight frown.

Claire took his face in her hands and turned him to face her. "I told you once, a long time ago, that the ocean was a great healer."

He nodded. He remembered.

"And so it is," said Claire, looking deep into his eyes, her hands holding either side of his face. "Sometimes," she said, "the time just has to be right. Listen to the waves, Michael. Let them fill you."

Her hands were cool upon his cheeks. Cool and wet against the summer heat.

The sun was slipping down over the edge of the world, swallowed by a sea tinged with orange fire. The dying light was catching in her curls, and if he hadn't known better, he could have sworn that her hair was moving with the rhythm of the waves.

She kept hold of his face. "Listen to the water, Michael, just listen."

He felt the joy well up within him like the surge of the surf. And he knew that feeling was not his own, that it had come from her.

But that didn't really matter to him. All he felt was the joy.

He was barely aware of the damp sand coming up to meet his cheek. Somehow, it was comfortable. And as he closed off the world, finally, Michael was smiling.

The last thing he saw was the slight blur of Claire's fingers, as she moved to close his eyes.

M·A·C·E·R·A·T·E

mac·er·ate \ 'ma-sə-ˌrāt \

verb transitive

1: to cause to waste away by or as if by excessive fasting

2: to cause to become soft or separated into constituent elements by or as if by steeping in fluid

verb intransitive

: to soften and wear away esp. as a result of being wetted or steeped

Softer

• • •

PAOLO BACIGALUPI

JONATHAN LILLY SLUMPED in hot water up to his neck and studied his dead wife. She half-floated at the far end of the bath, soap bubbles wreathing her Nordic face. Blond hair clung to bloodless skin. Her half-lidded eyes stared at the ceiling. Jonathan rearranged his position, shoving Pia's tangling legs aside to make more room for himself, and wondered if this peaceful moment between crime and confession would make any difference in his sentencing.

He knew he should turn himself in. Let someone know that the day had gone wrong in Denver's Congress Park neighborhood. Maybe it wouldn't be that bad. He might not even be in prison for so very long. He'd read somewhere that pot growers

got more prison time than murderers, and he vaguely remembered that murder laws might provide leeway for unintended
deaths like this one. Was it manslaughter? Murder in the second
degree? He stirred soap suds, considering.

He'd have to Google it.

When he first jammed the pillow over Pia's face she hadn't
fought at all. She might have even laughed. Might have mum-
bled something from under the pillow's cotton swaddle: "Cut it
out," maybe, or, "Get off." Or perhaps she told him he wasn't
getting out of dish duty. That was what they'd been arguing
about: the dishes in the sink from the night before.

She rolled over and said, "You forgot to do the dishes last
night," and gave him a little nudge with her elbow. A little push
to get him moving. The words. The elbow. And then he jammed
the pillow over her face and her hands had come up and gently
pushed against him, coaxing him to let her go, and it was all a
joke.

Even he thought so.

He'd meant to lift the pillow and laugh and go start scrub-
bing dishes. And for one fragile crystal moment that had seemed
possible. Purple lilac scent had slipped in through the half-
opened windows and bees buzzed outside and lazy Sunday
morning sunshine streamed in between shade slats. They lived
lifetimes inside that moment. They laughed off the incident and
went out for eggs Benedict at Le Central; they got a divorce after
another fifteen years of marriage; they had four children and ar-
gued over whether Milo was a better baby name than Alistair;
Pia turned out to be gay, but they worked it out; he had an affair,
but they worked it out; she planted sunflowers and tomatoes
and zucchini in their backyard garden and he went to work on
Monday and got a promotion.

He meant to take the pillow off her face.

But then Pia started struggling and screaming and beating on
him with her fists and children and tomato plants and Le

Central and a hundred other futures blew away like dandelion seeds and Jonathan suddenly couldn't bear to let her up. He couldn't stand to see the hurt and horror in her grey eyes when he lifted the pillow, the rancid version of himself that he knew he'd find reflected there, so he threw all his weight onto her struggling body and jammed the pillow hard over her face and rode her down to Hell.

She twisted and flailed. Her nails slashed his cheek. Her body bucked. She almost squeezed out from under him, twisting like an eel, but he pinned her again and buried her screams in the pillow as her hands scrabbled at his eyes. He turned his face away and let her rip at his neck. She thrashed like a fish but she couldn't force him off and suddenly he wanted to laugh. He was winning. For once in his life he was really winning.

Her hands whipped from his face to the pillow and back, an animal's panicked, thoughtless movements. Gasping coughs filtered through the down. Her chest pumped convulsively, striving to suck air through the pillow. Her nails nicked his ear. She was losing coordination. She'd stopped bucking. Her body still writhed, but now it was easy to keep her trapped. It was only the muscle memories of struggle. He pressed harder with the pillow, putting his entire weight into killing her.

Her hands stopped scratching. They returned to the smothering pillow and touched it gently. A querying caress. As if they were a pair of creatures utterly separate from her, pale butterflies trying to discover the cause of their owner's distress. Two dumb insects trying to understand the nature of an airway obstruction.

Outside, a lawn mower buzzed to life, cutting back spring greenery. A meadowlark sang. Pia's body went slack and her hands fell away. Bright sunlight traced lazily across her blond hair where it tangled in the pillow and spread across the sheets. Slowly he became aware of wetness, the warmth of her releasing bladder.

Another lawnmower buzzed alive.

●   ●   ●

White soapsuds swirled, revealing one of Pia's pink nipples. Jonathan scooped up a blob of crackling bubbles and laid it gently over the breast, covering her again. He'd used half a bottle of moisturizing bath liquid, but still the bubbles kept fading, revealing her body and its increasing paleness as the blood settled deeper into her limbs. Her eyes stared away into the ceiling distance, at whatever things dead people saw.

Grey eyes. He'd thought they were creepy when he first met her. By the time he married her, he liked them. And now they were creepy again, half-lidded, staring at nothing. He wanted to lean over and close them, but hated the thought that rigor mortis might make them spring wide again. That he might find her staring at him, after he had pressed them closed. He shivered. He knew it was morbid to soak in the bathtub with his dead wife, but he didn't want to leave her. He still wanted to be close. He'd been washing her death-soiled body, and suddenly it had seemed so right, so appropriate, that he should climb in with her. That he should mutter an apology and climb into the overfilled tub and join her in a final soak. And so here he was in a cooling bath with a cooling corpse and all the consequences of his repressed angers settling heavy upon him.

He blamed spring sunshine.

If it had been a cloudy day, Pia would now be drawing up grocery lists instead of squeezed into the bath with her killer husband, her stiffening legs shoved to one side.

She'd never liked taking baths together. Didn't like having her space imposed on. It was her quiet time. A time to forget the irritations of a purchasing department that could never get its sourcing priorities in order. A time to close her eyes and relax completely. He'd respected that. Just like he respected her predilection for Amish quilts on their bed and her affection for wildlife photos on the walls and her pathological hatred of avocados. But now here they both were, sharing a tub that she'd never liked sharing, with her blood pooling into her ass and her face slipping underwater every so often so that he had to shove her upright again, shove her up out of the suds like a whale surfacing, and every time her face came out of the water he expected her to gasp for air and ask what the fuck he'd been thinking keeping her down so long.

Sunshine. After months of winter grey and drizzling spring it had suddenly turned warm. That was the cause. The elms had budded green and the lilacs had bloomed purple and after years of gritted teeth, dutiful attendance to work and marriage and home ownership and oil changes, he woke to a day permeated with electric possibility. He woke up smiling.

The last time he remembered feeling so alive he'd been in fifth grade with a beat-up blue BMX that he'd raced through subdivision streets—jumping curbs and stealing chromie caps all the way—to pour his entire allowance into Three Musketeers, Nerds, and Bubblicious at a 7-Eleven.

And then Pia had rolled over and poked him with her elbow and reminded him that he'd forgotten to do the dishes.

Jonathan stirred the bathwater. Their naked bodies rippled under the thinning suds: his pink, hers increasingly pale. He leaned out of the tub, jostling Pia's body and almost immersing her before he got hold of the bubble bath. He held the bottle high and let soap spill into the water, a viscous emerald tangle that trailed over her legs. He upended the bottle completely. *Green Tea Essence: Skin Revitalizing. Aloe, Cucumber and Green Tea Extracts. Soaks Away Tension, Softens and Moisturizes Skin, Revitalizes Spirit.* He tossed the empty bottle on the floor and turned on the water again. Scalding heat poured over his shoulders, filling the tub and gurgling down its overflow spout. He leaned back and closed his eyes.

He supposed this fit some pattern of domestic violence, some statistical map of human behavior. The FBI kept statistics: a murder every twenty minutes, a rape every fifteen, a shoplifting every thirty seconds. Someone had to kill their wife every so often to make the statistics work. It just turned out to be him. Statistical duty. In his job, he expected a certain amount of instability from the servers, from the hardware and software that hosted the applications he wrote. He planned for it. Just like the FBI did. Shit happens. While his friends were catching the last of Colorado spring skiing, or running to Home Depot for renovation projects, he was fulfilling statistical requirements.

From where he lay, he could just make out blue sky through the high bathroom window. The optimistic blue, infused with gaudy unrestrained sunshine. All he'd wanted was to do something nice with that sunshine. To go for a jog. Or a bike ride. Or go for brunch and read the paper. And then Pia said there were dishes to do and all he could think about was that: the scabby lasagna pan, the stained sauce pots, the filmy wineglasses, the breadboard crumbs and the dishwasher that he'd also forgotten to run so he'd have to do more dishes by hand. And dishes led to taxes, April 15 bearing down on him like a tank. He should have talked to his investment advisor about his 401(k) but now it was Sunday and there wasn't anything he could do, and he'd probably forget again on Monday. And that led to the electric and phone bills that he'd forgotten to mail and that he should have set up for direct deposit but he kept blowing it off and now there was probably going to be a service fee and then there was his laptop lying on the living room floor where he'd dumped it, a beartrap of billable hours just waiting to get its jaws latched onto his leg. The Astai Networks project kept refusing to compile and his demo was set for eleven on Monday and he had no idea why the program was suddenly so completely screwed.

Lately, he'd been looking at Starbucks barristas and wishing he had their jobs. Tall, grande, latte, cappuccino, skinny, whatever. Not much complexity there. And when you left work at the end of the day you didn't have to think about a fucking thing. Who cared if they made shit for money? At least they wouldn't have to pay much in tax.

Taxes. Did murderers even do taxes? What was the IRS going to do? Arrest him now?

Jonathan frowned at the thought of arrest. He should call the police. Or Pia's mother, at least. Maybe 911? But that was for emergencies. And while the murder had been an emergency, this slow, soaking aftermath wasn't. He stared at Pia's dead body. He should cry. He should feel bad for her. Or at least for himself. He put wet fists in his eyes and waited for tears, but they didn't come.

Why can't I cry?

She's dead. Dead as a doornail. You killed Pia. Everything about her is gone. She won't wear that blue and red peasant skirt you bought for her in San Francisco. She won't ask for a German shepherd puppy again. She won't call her mother and talk for three hours about whether to plant acorn squash or zucchini in the backyard.

He kept listing things that Pia wouldn't do again: no more lectures about flossing, no more holding hands after movies, no more Jelly Bellies and reading in bed . . . but it felt like a farce, just like the tears. A bit of playacting, in case God was watching.

He pulled his knuckles from his eyes and stared up at the ceiling. *It was an accident.* He closed his eyes and concentrated on God, whatever God was supposed to be like: a man with a white beard, some fat woman Gaia thing like in some of Pia's books, some round Buddha guy from when she'd been on her meditation kick.

I didn't mean to kill her. Really. You know that already, don't You? I didn't want to kill her. Forgive me, Father, for I have sinned . . .

He gave it up. He felt like he had when he'd been busted for stealing candy from the 7-Eleven after his allowance ran out. Faking the crying. Acting like he cared even though he couldn't summon sincerity. Mostly just wishing that they hadn't noticed the bandolier of Pez dangling from his pocket. He knew he should care. He did care, damn it. He didn't think Pia deserved to die with a pillow over her face and shit in her panties. He wanted to blame her nagging, but he was clearly the one in the wrong. But mostly he just felt . . . what?

Angry?

Frustrated?

Trapped?

Lost and without redemption?

He laughed to himself. That last one sounded trite.

Mostly he felt surprised. Stunned by his world's complete re-alignment: a life without a wife or taxes or a Monday morning deadline. *I'm a murderer.*

He tried the thought out again, saying it out loud. "I'm a murderer." Trying to make it mean something to him other than that he wasn't going to bother with the dinner dishes now.

A knock sounded at the front door.

Jonathan blinked, returning to the world around him: the dead wife rubbing against his hip, the cooling water. His hands were wrinkled with the bath. How long had he been soaking? The knocking came again. Louder. A thumping, insistent and authoritative. The police knocked like that.

Jonathan leaped out of the bath and ran dripping across the floorboards to peek out between the shades. He expected cruisers and red and blue strobing lights and the neighbors all standing out on their porches, watching the drama unfold right on their quiet tree-lined street. A murder in the Denver suburbs. Instead, all he saw was his neighbor, Gabrielle Roberts. Gabby. A hyperkinetic get-things-accomplished kind of girl he kept hoping would eventually be worn down by the disappointments of everyday life.

She spited him with summer mountain-biking expeditions, winter snowboarding jaunts, a continuous stream of home-improvement projects and apparent pleasure in a job that had to do with telecom customer relations, the kind of thing that seemed perfect for deadening the soul, and which she nonethe-less seemed to love.

She stood on the porch, black ponytail twitching, brows wrinkling as she leaned forward and beat on the door again. Bouncing from one foot to the other, moving to some internal techno beat that only she could hear. She had on shorts and a sweaty T-shirt that said *Marathoners Go Longer,* along with soiled leather gloves.

Jonathan grimaced. Another home-improvement project, then. He'd helped her move flagstones into her backyard one hot summer day a few years past, and she'd nearly broken him doing it. Pia had given him a back massage afterward and reminded him that he didn't have to do everything that people asked, but when Gabby had shown up at the door, he hadn't known how to refuse her. And now here she was again.

Couldn't she just stop and do nothing for a day? And why now, with Pia's body floating in the bath less than twenty feet away? How was he going to keep Gabby quiet? Would he have to kill her too? How would he do it? Not with a pillow, that was for sure. Gabby was fit. Hell, she was probably stronger than he was. A kitchen knife, maybe? If he could get her into the kitchen before she saw Pia in the bathtub, he could put a knife to her throat. She wouldn't be expecting that. . . .

He shook off the thought. He didn't want to kill Gabby. He didn't want a mountain of bodies and blood piling up around him. He wanted this all to be over. He'd just tell Gabby what happened, she'd run screaming and call the cops, and he could wait on the front porch for them to arrive. Problem solved. They'd find him sitting in his bathrobe and his wife macerating in the tub and he'd go to jail for murder one, two, three, or four or whatever it was and the neighbors would get their show.

They seemed like such a perfect couple.

But they were both so nice.

We had them take care of our cats when we went to Belize last year.

Fine. Bath time was over. Real life was starting up again.

Time to face the music. He went to find a bathrobe and came back just as Gabby hammered on the door again.

"Hey! Jon!" Gabby grinned as he opened the door. "Didn't mean to wake you. Lazy Sunday?"

"I just killed my wife."

"Could I borrow your shovel? Mine broke."

Jonathan goggled. Gabby bounced expectantly.

Had he confessed or not? He thought he had. But Gabby wasn't running and screaming for the cops. She was breaking the script completely. She was bouncing back and forth from the ball of one foot to the other and looking at him like a golden retriever. He replayed the exchange in his mind. Had she not heard? Or had he not said it?

Gabby said, "You look really hungover. Late night last night?"

Jonathan tried to confess again, but the words lodged in his throat. Maybe he hadn't said it the first time. Maybe he'd only thought it. He rubbed his eyes. "What did you say you wanted?"

"I broke my shovel. Can I borrow yours?"

"You broke it?"

"Not on purpose. I tried to pry a rock out of the backyard and the handle snapped."

I killed my wife. She's soaking in the tub right now. Could you call the cops for me? I can't decide whether I should call 911 or the police department's main line. Or if maybe I should just wait until Monday and call a lawyer first. What do you think? Finally he said, "Pia had a shovel in the back shed. You want me to get it?"

"That would be great. Where's Pia?"

"In the tub."

Gabby seemed to notice Jonathan's bathrobe for the first time. Her eyes widened. "Oh. Sorry. I didn't mean to—"

"It's not what you think."

Gabby waved her hand, embarrassed, and stepped back from the open door. "I shouldn't have barged over here. I should have called. I didn't mean to interrupt things. I can get the shovel myself if you tell me where it is."

"Umm. Okay. You can go around through the side gate. It's in the shed, hanging off the pegs by the door." Why didn't he come clean? He just kept playing the charade, pretending that he was still the man he'd been a few hours before.

"Thanks a ton. Sorry for barging in." Gabby turned and bounded down the steps, leaving Jonathan standing in the open doorway. He closed the door. Gabby's ponytail flashed briefly outside the living room window as she jogged past and slipped into the backyard. Jonathan wandered back into the bathroom and sat on the toilet's edge. Pia was floating.

"Nobody really cares, do they, honey?"

He studied her stiffened body and then turned the faucet to add more hot water. Steam rose. He shook his head, watching as it poured into the tub. "No one pays any attention at all."

People died all the time. And yet people still did their chores and went to the store for their groceries and dug rocks out of their backyards. Life went on. The sun was still bright outside and the lilac-scented air was still there and it was still a beautiful day, and he wasn't going to have to do his taxes ever again. He shut off the water. Electric energy tingled in his limbs, an antsy youthful hunger for sun and movement. It really was a wonderful day for a jog.

The nice thing about completely ruining your life, Jonathan decided, was that it was finally possible to enjoy it. As he ran past his neighbors and waved and called out to them, he thought about how little they truly understood about how glorious this warm spring day had become. It was a thousand times better than he'd even guessed when he woke up in the morning. The last day of freedom felt so much better than a million days of daily grind. Sunny days were wasted on the guilt-free. Warm spring air enfolded him as he ran. He stopped at every stop sign, jogging in place and luxuriating in a world that was exactly the same as it had always been, except for his place in it.

It almost felt as if he was jogging for the first time. He felt every sweet breeze, smelled every bright flower, and saw every warm person and they were all beautiful and he missed them all terribly. He observed them from an incredible distance, and yet with extraordinary clarity, as if he was viewing them with a powerful telescope from the surface of Mars.

He ran and ran and sweated and gasped and rested and ran again and he loved it all. He wondered if this was what it was to be Buddhist. If this was what Pia had sought in her meditations. This centered sense, this knowledge that all was transient, that everything was effervescent and lost so easily. Perhaps it would never have existed, except for this sudden nostalgic love spurred on because he was about to lose it all. God, it felt good to run. To simply work every muscle and feel the pavement hit his shoes, to see the trees with their newly greened neon leaves, and to feel for once that he was paying attention to it all.

He kept waiting for someone to notice his difference, to recognize the fact that he was now a murderer, but no one did. He stopped at a 7-Eleven and bought a bottle of Gatorade, grinning at the clerk as he got his change and thinking, *I'm a murderer. I smothered my wife this morning.* But the old man behind the counter didn't notice Jonathan's scarlet letter M.

In fact, as Jonathan chugged his green electrolytes, he suddenly felt that he was not at all different from this lovely man behind the counter with his orange vest and corporate convenience logo on his back. He had the feeling that he could invite the wrinkled guy home and they could pull a couple bottles of Fat Tire Ale out of the fridge, or if the old man preferred something lighter, PBRs perhaps, whatever the guy wanted, they'd open their cans of watery beer and they'd go into the backyard and lie on the grass and soak up sunshine, and at some point Jonathan would mention casually that his dead wife was soaking in the bathtub and the man would nod and say, "Oh yes, I did something similar with mine. Do you mind if I take a look?"

And they would both go back inside and stand in the bathroom's doorway, studying Jonathan's floating lily, and the clerk would nod his snowy head thoughtfully and suggest that she'd probably prefer to be buried in the backyard, in her garden.

After all, that was what his own wife had wanted, and she'd been a gardener, too.

On Monday, Jonathan emptied his bank accounts and IRAs and changed everything into cash: fifty- and hundred-dollar bills, fat wads of them that he stuffed into a messenger bag so that he walked out of the bank carrying $112,398. His life savings. The wages of sin. The profits of dutiful financial planning. The clerk had asked if he was getting a divorce, and he blushed and nodded and said it was something like that, but she didn't stop him from clearing out the account, and mostly seemed to think it was funny that he was beating his wife to the punch. He almost asked her on a date, before he remembered the reason she was counting all that cash onto the counter for him.

He came home and dropped his bag on the couch and carried the phone into the bathroom to sit with Pia while he bought himself some time. He called his job and told them his wife had family troubles and that he needed to take vacation and sick time early. Sorry about the Astai demo. Naeem could probably sort it out. He told a few of his and Pia's friends that Pia had a family emergency, and that she'd flown back to Illinois, to help. He notified Pia's work, saying that she'd be in touch when she knew more about what kind of emergency leave she might need. He chatted with Pia's parents and told them he was taking her on a surprise vacation for their anniversary and that phone service in Turkey would be unreliable. Every conversation closed doors of friendly inquiry. Every conversation lengthened the time between suspicion and discovery.

The steadiness of his voice surprised him. Somehow it was

hard to be nervous when the worst was already done. He bought a pair of plane tickets in his and Pia's name to Cambodia with a departure a month away. From Vancouver, just to confuse things a little more. And when he was done, he made himself a gin and tonic and sat and soaked with Pia one last time in her macerate. There was a smell about her now, the rot of her guts, the gasses of her belly. The ruin wreaked by hot water on dead flesh. But he soaked with her anyway and apologized as best he could for re-making his life via her dead body. Then he went over and re-claimed his shovel from Gabby.

By the light of a few alley streetlamps, he buried Pia in the backyard under a part of the garden. He left a note for the po-lice, describing generally what had happened—including an apology—for when he was finally caught and needed some face-less court to forgive him and let him out in less time than they would have demanded of a pot grower. He scattered sunflower and poppy and morning glory seeds on the mound and thought that the 7-Eleven clerk would approve.

That night, he drove across the mountains. He wondered if he had finally crossed the line between manslaughter and mur-der, or murder two and murder one, but didn't really care. A bit of travel just seemed in order. A long vacation before a longer prison sentence. Really, it wasn't much different from changing jobs. A bit of a break before the new job started up.

He sold his car in Las Vegas for another five thousand in cash, pretending to be a gambling junkie sure his luck would turn around. Then he struck off down the road, headed for the interstate and the wider world beyond.

On a desert on-ramp he stuck out his thumb. He wondered if his luck would keep holding and then he wondered how much he really cared. He marveled that he had ever worried about something as trivial as a 401(k) allocation. He was on the road to Mexico with its sun and sand and pleasant rhythms and . . . who knew? Perhaps he would be caught. Or perhaps he would simply disappear into his strange new life.

Jonathan had once read that Japanese samurai lived as if they had already died. But he doubted even they had any idea what that really felt like. Standing beside the hot Nevada interstate with gritty winds and big rigs blowing past him, he thought he might have an inkling.

By the time he'd pulled Pia from the bath and buried her, he'd feared she would fall apart from all her soaking. His mother used to say that if you stayed in a bath too long you'd shrivel up and disappear. But Pia had held together all right, even after a couple of days. She was gone, but still recognizable. He, on the other hand, was still around—and yet utterly changed.

A sporty RAV4 hit the on-ramp. It whipped past him in a flash of white, then slowed suddenly and pulled onto the margin. Jonathan jogged after it, his messenger bag of cash jouncing against his hip. He yanked open the little SUV's door. A kid with a crushed cowboy hat studied him through mirrored Ray-Bans.

"Where you headed?"

"San Diego?"

"You pay gas?"

Jonathan couldn't help grinning. "Yeah. I think I can help with that."

The kid motioned him in, gunned the little engine and accelerated onto the highway.

"What are you doing in San Diego?"

"I'm actually going to Mexico. Somewhere with beaches."

"I'm going to Cabo for spring break. Gonna get drunk, suck titties and go native."

"Sounds nice."

"Yeah, man. It's gonna be great."

The kid cranked up the stereo and whipped the RAV4 into the passing lane, zipping past eighteen-wheelers and late weekend traffic returning from Vegas to L.A.

Jonathan rolled down the window, reclined his seat and closed his eyes as the stereo throbbed and the kid yammered on about how he wanted to be in a skateboard video someday and how much he was going to get laid in Mexico and how you could buy phat weed down there for nothing.

The miles sped by. Jonathan let himself relax and think again about Pia. When he pulled her from the bath, he'd been amazed at how soft her skin had become.

The next time he got married, he hoped he'd be softer, too.

Crossing the Seven

• • •

JAY LAKE

WHEN HALCYONE WAS QUEEN in Cermalus the blackstar first came into the sky.

With the coming of the blackstar, tradesmen and civitors alike cried for protection from the throne. The working people of the city paid no more attention to the shouting on the hill than we did to the lights in the sky. The end of the world might be at hand, but there was still bread to be baked and dogs to be fed and gutters to be cleaned.

I myself was most concerned with the state of the tiles on the roof of the villa belonging to the first mistress of the civitor Tradelium. I was called Andrade, slave of the city.

The civitor was not an unkind man, in that he sometimes managed to remember his slaves and servants were human beings with needs and desires. It was more than most of that august class could keep in mind, who had been borne amid a cloud of attendants and would die there, either of old age or bloody assassination.

Kindness or no, his sweet mistress had experienced an in-pouring of water, ruining a set of silk sheets and some quite expensive leather intimates brought at significant cost from decadent Oppius. This had sent her into a rage of epic propor-tions. In turn, the civitor Tradelium experienced no little irrita-tion as the mistress had accosted his wife.

In accordance with the fundamental principle that feces flow downward, all became my responsibility for having failed to di-vine in advance of the need for repairing the roof. And thusly, while the second sons of the wealthy were rending their gar-ments in the streets for fear of the blackstar, I was up on the roof resetting glazed tiles across my carefully built grout-and-plaster. I had no intention of coming down from my perch for the sake of flood, fire, or barbarian invasion, not after the civitor's mix-ture of threats and promised bonuses.

I was standing on that roof with the long-bladed file in my hand, balanced on the slick curved tiles, when the high priestess of the Temple Regina rode astride her white ass down the cob-bled street below. She wore only the three veils of propriety and the seven beads of virtue. Her Worship being about ten stone and forty years to the far side of lissome, the three veils were as effective as a sneeze and a promise. It was a large ass. Both of them were, in fact—the one attached to her and the one beneath her. The high priestess's avoirdupois was of no moment as all good Cermalians knelt in prayer facing away from her line of procession. The bad Cermalians turned away too, out of a sense of good taste or possibly sheer self-preservation.

Even her temple guard marched with their eyes averted.

So it was that when the blackstar discharged its bolt of unholy violet lightning, mine were the only eyes hers chanced to meet.

Given that I stood a good fifty feet above her on the roofline, limned from behind by the blinding light—and I thank the stars themselves I was not looking into the bolt—what the high priestess saw was a purple angel descended from the heavens, harbinger of the blackstar.

What I saw was her great maw opening for a shriek. I figured it was me for a goner, on account of profaning the sacred form of the high priestess by casting my base eyes upon her. I'd have gladly given that vision of pulchritude right back to the pond from whence it flopped, if I had had the chance.

She yelled, a second bolt struck the long-bladed file, my hair caught fire, and I was blown off the roof.

After that, things got bad.

It might have gone better for me if I had not landed on the high priestess. She broke my fall, but together we broke the ass's back. I wound up with my face buried perilously close to her heavenly gates, which smelled of old shoe leather, while the poor, screaming animal had somehow collapsed upon my buttocks and thighs.

In very short order an impressive collection of ceremonial brass spear points pricked me, while an angry man with a face like a tamarind monkey was screeching for me to get on my feet immediately upon pain of sudden and excruciating death. I rolled my eyes at him above the quivering curve of her Worship's belly, contriving to indicate that I could neither move nor speak in my current situation, but he was clearly not a rational fellow.

"Raise up the heretic," he shouted.

The spear points fell away, the screaming ass was levered free, and several pairs of rough yet ungentle hands yanked me off the sacred person of the high priestess, who was promptly covered with a guard's sable cloak. Three cloaks, actually, it took to ensure the requirements of modesty were met.

I dangled in the air as someone finally put the poor beast out of its misery. The officer leaned close, his anger somewhat better under control. "Any confessions before your summary execution?"

"I didn't—" I began, but obviously I had. Dropped from the sky, interrupted the parade, seen her Worship in the forbidding flesh, harassed her Worship's person. There were doubtless a dozen more crimes of which I was guilty. Having neither wit nor patriotism to sustain me, I merely shook my head.

"Wait," bellowed the high priestess.

Half a dozen stabbing spears paused with a shiver. My gut was in such a pucker I almost wished they'd finished it.

She struggled to her feet, a titanic wave of loose sable and pale free-swinging flesh. "Somebody bring me my robe," she snapped to the world at large. Then, to the guard captain: "Don't you know who this is?"

His mouth worked, but he obviously made the same calculus so recently completed by my own panicked mind. "Madame," he said.

The response of cornered guard captains everywhere, I thought with sharp satisfaction. Though I had no idea what she meant either.

"He is our messenger from the blackstar!" she shouted.

An entire street full of people, rushing out of doors for the exciting prospect of an imminent execution, immediately cheered this news that one had come who could speak for, and presumably protect them from, the dreaded blackstar. While most of them cared no more than I did for the heavenly apparition, their masters or their masters' masters, or their masters' masters' masters certainly did.

There was a general riot of cheering. I quickly found myself lifted upon the shoulders and hands of a mob, and borne toward the Cermalic Palace. The high priestess bobbed somewhere behind me, moving at a slower pace, and if she was lucky, drinking heavily.

It was certainly what I wished in that moment—a stout drink, followed by a nice, safe execution.

So I came before Halcyone, borne by temple guards and a mob of plebes and proles and slaves who under normal circumstances would not have been allowed through the main gates of the palace. Somewhere in the course of the mad rush I discovered that all the hair on my head, and indeed even my eyebrows, had been burnt away by the violet bolt. Perhaps no one would know me.

Even as we muddled to a halt before the throne, a hasty delegation of civic dignitaries rushed in, led by none other than the civitor Tradelium.

Once more I found myself wishing for that drink.

The throne room of Halcyone is lined with two rows of pillars, each ten times the height of a man. Between them is a peaked clerestory, with colored glass that lights the floor far below in a pleasing array of shadows. I cannot tell you what is behind the pillars, for bright braziers set before them blinded my eyes to the deeper shadows. The floor is some complex mosaic which I never saw clearly.

Halcyone was a slim bird of a woman, sprawled sidewise within the Cermalic throne. The chair itself was gilded, in the shape of a giant lotus only partially opened, so that the queen resembled nothing so much as an overthin infant pushing its way out from betwixt its mother's womanly parts.

Though she might look the spoiled child, when confronted by an armed mob in her own throne room, Halcyone had the mind of a ruler. "What is your purpose?" she called out to me in a cool voice which should have been able to stop a battle.

It certainly stopped the mob.

"Majesty," said the guard captain, dropping to one knee as he swept off his helmet. Everyone else took this cue to kneel, which resulted in me being dumped on the floor. "Her Worship the high priestess of the Temple Regina has declared this man to be the messenger of the blackstar."

I stood, bowed, and tried to brush myself off. My tunic was singed by lightning, rent by spears, stained with blood, and covered with crisped strands of my hair. "Majesty."

She raised a hand to forestall further statements from me.

The queen slithered out of her throne and stood tall. She wore only a simple white chiton, pinned at the left shoulder, leaving her right shoulder and most of her right breast bare.

"It is known to us," she said slowly, "that the mighty of our city fear the coming of the blackstar. We are not an astrologer, nor are we a mathematician, but even a queen must give nod to a messenger from beyond the heavens. Here is the source and solution to our problems. Speak, and tell us what you will."

She gave me such a hard, calculating look that I knew I was being set up for a fall worse than the one I had just taken from the civitor's rooftop. I drew a great breath and said the only thing I could imagine which might save me. "I am come from the heavens to cross the Seven Cities. When I leave this greatest of cities, I will take your fears with me. Convey me now to Cispius."

Halcyone quirked a smile, and gave me a tiny nod. As I was swept up again by the mob I could hear the civitor Tradelium saying, "But that's the slave who maintains my rooftops."

When Sterope was queen in Cispius the messenger of the blackstar began his journey across the Seven Cities, the peregrination that in ancient times had been called the Transept.

The high priestess's guard officer, one Leutherion, was assigned to be my own guard captain, a duty he liked no more than I. The rest of my attendants were likewise selected at random from those in the throne room the day of my elevation—servants, plebes, and soldiers who were not pleased either. They considered my heavenly mission to the Seven Cities nothing more than a criminal deceit. The fact they were correct did nothing to ease my fears or my conscience. Instead I played haughty, as if I were a civitor and they no more than slaves.

We rode forth mounted on brown asses from the queen's stables, Leutherion bearing in my honor a black-on-black banner affixed to the haft of a spear. No noble destriers for us—her majesty was nothing if not practical. In our train we bore a great chest filled with slips of paper on which the great and plebian alike of Cermalus had written their greatest fears for the blackstar, to be carried forth by me, the messenger of heaven.

I was already mightily missing my rooftop duties.

Our journey passed with varying rounds of bickering and silence across a demon-haunted scrubland, in which old bones stood taller than my head and shadows gibbered, chuckled, and howled by night. I might have thought myself in the lands of the dead save for the blackstar which stood overhead day and night. In sunlight it was a hole in the sky. In darkness it crackled a baleful purple.

I could only be where I was thanks to its inimical agency.

After six days of infighting and shivering in the dark, we approached Cispius. Much like Cermalus, the city was situated upon a hill, proximate to open water and arable land. Unlike Cermalus, where wealth and power had migrated upward, the Cispians had built themselves a sort of circular palace, a circus of the mighty which ran the circumference of the base of the hill, leaving stables, huts, and slave camps for the upper slopes.

I later understood this had to do with the availability of water, and lack thereof, on the slopes of the hill. Cermalus is blessed with springs all the way up its heights and so I had in my naïveté assumed that all the Seven Cities were so arranged.

Flanked by two of his men, Ironpants and Pelletier, Leutherion stopped before the brass-bound great gate. The pair of doors were perhaps three man-heights tall, each a third as wide. Though a smaller wooden trade gate stood wide open nearby, out of which flowed a succession of carts and fieldhands bound for the farms, the formal entrance was closed to us until we stated our business and presented our credentials.

"The messenger of the blackstar is here," Leutherion called loudly. "Come to carry away the evil which descends from your skies."

Had we possessed a trumpet amongst our little caravan, I am certain he would have blown it.

An armored man leaned out of the shadows of the trade gate. "I knows a Cermalian accent when I hears one," he shouted. "Your embassy's done come and gone for the season. 'Less you got a caravan permit, be off with you."

Some of my attendants snickered as I glanced behind me at the days-long trail through the scrub, but my guard captain was made of sterner stuff. He and his outriders kicked their donkeys over to the trade gate. I did not deign to follow, but awaited negotiations. These appeared to be part bribery and part threat.

A few minutes later, we were waved through the lesser gate. Ignominious perhaps, but a better fate than being turned back into the wilderness. I suspected I would not long survive being turned out.

Once we were within the marble-floored street-halls of Cispius, our reception improved dramatically. Here I was not the villainous ex-slave that my attendants gossiped against by campfire. No, here I was an exotic dignitary from a distant city, come to save them from the blackstar.

The well-born and the wealthy were not the sort to throng their city in celebration. As we traveled toward the Palace Circumferential, the top level of this ring-city where Sterope dwelt, silent servants emerged from ornate doorways to offer presentation trays of flowers, fruits, and cunning folded paper dolls meant to resemble mythic figures. After a false start, I found we were not intended to take the trays or their contents— indeed, these were "eye-gifts," offerings of beauty which did not subtract from the mundane wealth of the giver, but only called for an investment of time.

I immediately conceived of a handy business packaging such offering trays in advance and storing them in chill chambers beneath the city, to be delivered at a premium when need called.

It was also passing strange that this city smelled of little but clean stone. I could only imagine the efforts at bringing up water and taking out waste which attended these people. On the other hand, it was in effect a single enormous house, and so less susceptible to litter and filth than any ordinary street in Cermalus.

We wound around the perimeter of the city three times in the ascension. The inner street was built as a gently graded ramp, rising one level per full transit of the circle, and lined with houses, shops, and ateliers. Where in my home city the wealthy showed their taste and resources with extravagant gardens, wild variations in architecture, and baroque rooflines, here all was invested in the front door and the facade which surrounded that portal.

For the wealthy, Cispius was a city of doors. One could live within this arrangement and easily never see the sky.

The Palace Circumferential was the rooftop of the ring-city. Even here there were many sheltered passages, overgrown bowers, and wide-eaved buildings. I was pleased to see some fine examples of the roofer's art.

Under a bower of grapevines, we dismounted as silent servants brought blue bowls of water for us to wash in. "Don't screw it up," growled Leutherion. His men snickered.

"Fear not. I value my life at least as much as you value yours."

We were soon enough brought before the court of Sterope, queen in Cispius. She sat on a glittering throne cut from one enormous crystal. Fires had been lit behind her throne so that the crystal gleamed along many facets and the queen was wrapped in a flickering glow. It was very hard to make out her face or form. Anyone could have sat upon that throne.

I bowed low, then rose to indicate the great chest which my attendants Pelletier and Finnric had brought up from our pack train.

"Majesty," I began, but someone immediately struck a huge gong. Brass thunder reverberated.

"Her Brilliance is to be addressed correctly," shouted a tiny man in pink silks. He was no taller than a small child, though there was stubble on his little chin. His face displayed a certain natural inclination toward violence, and he obviously relished his role in rectifying my errors.

"Uh . . . Brilliance." I was off my pacing now, carefully prepared words jumbled in my head. "Halcyone, queen in Cermalus—"

There was that damnable gong again. It would give me a headache quite soon.

"Her Brilliance is the sole queen upon earth, and sovereign of all beneath the sun!" The little bastard was grinning now. I could see his teeth were filed to points. Did he wrestle otters in his free hours? "Others rule elsewhere only at her sufferance!"

My thoughts were even more tangled, but I was determined to proceed.

"Brilliance," I said, rushing to get ahead of the next strike of the gong. "Halcyone, by your grace styled ruler in Cermalus, bade me come before you, being—"

The gong rang out once more. The little man drew breath to correct me again. "Silence," I screeched in frustration. "You mistreat the emissary of Heaven at your peril!"

There was a pause, punctuated only by the last dying echo of the gong. Then Sterope shifted on her throne. "We will hear the messenger in his own words. The court will be silent."

And silent they were, scarcely even breathing, with no more noise among them than a flock of paper birds.

Still I spoke too fast, spitting my introduction in one breath. "Brilliance, Halcyone in Cermalus bade me come being declared messenger of the blackstar and here to relieve the evil which has descended upon your people."

There. I hadn't quite taken personal responsibility for the claim of divine sending.

A long pause followed, the court still quiet as lice on a dead man's head, while the queen sat cloaked in light and—presumably—considered my words. Finally, she raised one arm upward. The hand which I could actually see above the glare of her throne was slim and pale and finely wrought as Halcyone's had been.

"The blackstar stands high in the heavens. Our servants on the hill have cried fear, and our priests burned great offerings on the rooftop temples. Here now is a messenger from the blackstar, graciously sent on to us by our daughter ruler in Cermalus. He will hold court in the Plaza of Punishment for a day and an hour. All will bring their dreads and fears to him. When that day and hour is done, we shall commend him to our daughter ruler in Fagutal. After that, we shall hear no more fear, for he shall carry away our evil."

The entire court turned to face me—servants, nobles, soldiers, priests all mixed together. Every one of them had a starveling look. Leutherion hooked an elbow into my ribs. "Nice work," he muttered.

"Our heads are not on pikes."

I never did sleep during my time in Cispius. With astonishing alacrity my entire train was brought to a plaza on the ground level of the ring-city. We had of course passed through this area on the way in, but I had not remarked the high posts topped with chains which surrounded the plaza, nor the barred doors of most of the establishments—prisons, oubliettes, and houses of pain.

Another great chest was procured, and a row of scribes was set out before me. The people great and small came. If they had their prayers already written, they were waved on to me by rough men in the uniform of the city. If not, the scribes took down their words. I received every one of those folded slips and silk-bound sheaves, while Leutherion and the others crammed them into the new chest.

This took the entire day and night, and into the next day. While I was kept well supplied with wine and delicacies, I was desperately exhausted. We were turned out of the city with remarkable efficiency at the appointed hour, there to be met by the tiny man and an enormous eunuch carrying that damnable gong.

"Her Brilliance has graced me with the honor of being your herald," the tiny man said with venom in his voice and face. "My gong accompanies me on its legs."

I leaned close. "If I hear that thing struck even once out here in the wilderness, I will have it fed to you. Do you understand?"

Leutherion beside me nodded. "And I will ensure the messenger's orders are carried out."

That was news to me.

When Celæno was queen in Fagutal the messenger of the blackstar made the third stop of his Transept.

We traveled now over a higher, broken country of purpled rocks stained with the empty glyphs written by lichen. There were myriad false paths that ended in blind walls or drop-offs, so Leutherion was forced to send outriders ahead to plot the way. Even so, we spent three days following a road that ended before a shattered temple with no way beyond.

The little man, whose name proved to be Osmio, had no idea of this country—he was born and raised in Cispius. His eunuch, who had no name at all save legs-of-the-gong, seemed bereft of ideas whatsoever.

The blackstar glowered and spat above us. It seemed to have come lower in the sky, as if following me. For the look of the thing, I made pretense at prayer, but no one was fooled.

Before we ran out of water we found a man standing at the edge of a high cliff. He was a squat fellow, wearing a high, square leather cap with matching armor. He carried a tall bow crafted from horn and hide. He appeared to be guarding rock and empty air.

"Make way," said Leutherion, "for the messenger of the blackstar, come by grace of Halcyone queen in Cermalus and Sterope queen in Cispius."

The gong rang loud, causing the armored stranger to flinch.

"Her Brilliance—" began Osmio, but was cut off with a squawk as Pelletier caught him in the ribs with a spear butt. There was a general muttered cheer. No one saw fit to discipline the eunuch. It seemed pointless, and besides which he could have broken any three of our heads.

Leutherion continued: "We seek admittance to the noble city of Fagutal there to present our words to the queen Celæno."

The guard stared at us all, no doubt taking in our numbers and the composition of our train. "None pass within the walls of Fagutal," he said, "save those who have paid the toll and sworn the tributary prayer." After a moment he added, "You must lay down your weapons as well."

Leutherion bristled at this, but I raised my hand to speak. "I am the messenger of Heaven, and have no care for weapons. But I will swear tribute to no one and pay no toll. Better that I pass on to another city and relieve them of their evil than that I bend to Celæno in Fagutal. I enter free, or not at all."

The sentry looked at all of us a moment, then came to a decision. "The messenger may go freely within, with one guard, and submit to the judgment of the queen. The rest of you must remain without."

"I accept your terms," I told him. "Leutherion, will you accompany me?"

There was some delay while Leutherion reorganized the train in our absence. I walked over to the guard's post, expecting some declivity in the rock beyond, but instead realized that we stood on the edge of a very high cliff. The ground below was quite far down, verdant with jungles and open prairies, and stretched miles away toward distant ridgelines. Silver-glinting rivers wound among the expanses.

I saw no city, only an endless horizon and a country broader than any I had ever thought existed.

Finally the guard led me and Leutherion to a hidden notch in the cliff face. Stairs descended toward the open air.

"Follow this down. You will not be challenged until you are within."

"What if we lose our way?" I asked.

The guard laughed. "There are only two ways to go. You may follow the trail, or you may try your wings in the empty air. In either case, you will know where you are going, though each journey is of a different length."

Down we went.

The less said of the descent, the better. Suffice to say that I did not have a fear of heights before, but I shall never work the rooftops again. Leutherion liked it no better than I, but his bearing as a soldier compelled him forward.

Fagutal is a city carved from the face of that vast purple cliff. I suppose that if one were to ride astride a dragon or air-demon one might see the whole thing in one sweep of the eye. It has the architectural detail familiar to any ordinary city dweller—columns and fascias and friezes and great facades—but every bit of that is carved from living rock high above the jungles below, and faces out toward the domain of birds.

Being a city of the cliff, these buildings are arranged in a haphazard manner. If one did have a flying view, one would see the building faces stacked as if by a child of the gods. The trail wound among these, never quite reaching an entrance or window through which we might escape inward to safety and a horizontal floor. At last it came to a landing where more square-helmeted soldiers lounged.

"Ah, messenger boy," one said. "We're to take you to the queen."

"Birds," whispered Leutherion. "A letter came a-wing before us."

The enclosure of the ring-city of Cispius was nothing to the carved caverns of Fagutal. All was lit by torches or lamps or a glowing fungus which clustered on the walls like pale green scabs. The architecture within was much like that without—elaborate imitations of an ordinary city. Like Cispius, Fagutal smelled clean, though there was an undertone of molder and earth. People moved quietly, cloaked against the stone chill, avoiding our little party.

We were led deeper and deeper within the cliff, ever further from the sun, until we came to a sort of leather tent. "Her Majesty's through here," said a grinning guard. The flaps were laced closed behind us, then we were whispered onward to pass a set of stone doors that pivoted at a touch and so into deepest shadow.

Queen Celæno's throne room was dark as the inside of a cow. There was nothing to be seen, not the faintest eye-gleam, and I was seized with the sudden thought that I had tumbled over an edge and was falling into a chasm. My head spun as if I were being tumbled by toughs. Leutherion laid his hand on my arm.

"Breathe deep and slow," he advised softly. "It might help to close your eyes, for then the dark will seem more sensible."

"Advance," said a voice which echoed from all around.

We shuffled like addled pensioners.

"Halt." It was a woman's voice, or perhaps a child's. "Who comes before us, untaxed and unsworn in violation of all our laws and customs?"

We both knelt. I nudged Leutherion with my elbow.

"The messenger of Heaven," he said. "He is here to bring surcease from the ills of the blackstar, sent by the grace of your sister queens in Cermalus and Cispius."

"What fear do we have of the blackstar, who live beneath a roof of living stone?"

"Majesty," I said. I waited a moment, lest another of those damnable gongs ring out, or some similar mischief. "Your Wisdom doubtless knows no fear, but there are those among your people who pass outward under the light of day and the gloom of night. To them I offer the opportunity to cast away the evil of their fears, that I might carry it with me back to Heaven. In return, I ask nothing of you or your city save a rest for my train, and possibly a few supplies."

Silence for a while, then the voice again, querulous. "And so those biddies have foisted you on us?"

That did not sound so good. "It was never our wish to burden you, majesty."

She laughed. Bitter, cold. "It is no matter to us. If our subjects wish to unburden themselves to sky dwellers, they may do so. We will direct the mayor of our palace to provide such provisions as he sees reasonable. There remains only the matter of the toll and the tributary prayer. As you did not pay on the way in, you shall forfeit the freedom of one of your traveling party. We are generous, we invite you to make your own choice."

Strong hands grasped both Leutherion and me to pull us away from the audience. "What do we do now?" I asked him when the guards had pushed us past the leather flap and into the light.

"You choose," Leutherion said, disgusted. "You have never bothered to learn the names of most who follow you, it should be easy enough."

Accepting prayers for the blackstar was easy in Fagutal. Leutherion and I sat upon a bench near a cave mouth, with a view of the jungle basin below. We kept a bucket between us. People came, singly or in small, furtive groups, and dropped tiny scrolls in. Most were soldiers, who would have of course seen the blackstar for themselves. None spoke, few smiled.

We waited on that bench two days, sleeping in a spare little house that seemed to have been set aside for guesting. The fare consisted mostly of mushrooms and cheeses. I did not inquire as to the source of the milk. There were no fruits nor fowl nor fish as might be hoped for from the vast jungle below.

On the third day, another high-helmeted soldier came with a small force at his back. "You have been invited to resume your journey," he said.

"What of our train?"

"They have been brought down the Second Trail to the lands below. Their provisions have been seen to. They await only your return, and your selection of the one who will stay here and serve our noble Queen Celæno."

It was on my lips to say Osmio, for the little man had done nothing to endear himself to me. But legs-of-the-gong would have been lost—I had marked how they slept curled together— and I conceived of a certain sympathy for the eunuch. Besides which, I might someday be called upon to return him to Queen Sterope.

"I will choose when we are a caravan assembled," I said, imagining that we might perhaps simply get underway. Perhaps the weakly Pincus would prosper here. He had been a palace servant in Cermalus. Or the adventurous Pelletier.

"Of course," the soldier replied blandly. "My men and I will accompany you to assist in your selection."

This time we walked down winding passages inside the cliff. There were occasional windows, or even natural cracks, that helped me gauge our progress. Otherwise we saw by the light of the torches we bore. The better part of half a mile passed before we reached the bottom.

One of the soldiers carried our bucket of messages. Leutherion would not speak to me. Angered, I suppose, by the penalty the queen Celæno had laid upon us.

We debouched from a gap in the rock to a high-walled corral made of close-set tree trunks. The jungle rose beyond. The caravan was assembled there, men mounted on our donkeys. I could not see a gate from the enclosure, which was more than passing strange. I realized there were more of Queen Celæno's men atop the walls. Therefore a rampart ran behind those logs.

"This is a trap," said Leutherion. "We are not a fighting force, nor do we carry war or disease in our packs."

"No." Our escort commander's voice was almost sympathetic.

"But no one who has stood before the queen is allowed to once more walk beneath the light. She is blind, you see, and jealous of the eyes of others. As almost all visitors refuse to be blinded, we find it easier to offer a quick, clean death." He stepped back from Leutherion and raised one hand to signal.

Bows appeared all around the wall top.

"Inside!" I screamed. The gong rang loud, the asses whinnied, and the air was full of the buzzing whir of arrows as I sprinted back toward the gap, Leutherion's labored breathing hard behind me.

I lay panting beneath a spreading bush with leaves the shape of a woman's hand. I still held the hacked stub of a torch with which I had fought. There were eight of us who had escaped. Finnric and Ironpants, and a third soldier whose name I was unsure of, as well as Pincus, myself, Leutherion, and somehow both Osmio and legs-of-the-gong. The Fagutalii soldiers had refused to pursue us into the jungle, so we had not been forced to run far, merely out of sight and range of the arrows.

There were eighteen more dead, including Pelletier and the rest of the guardsmen. We survivors were exhausted and bloody. The reek of smoke from the burning stockade stung my nose, mixed with the roast-pork smell of burned flesh. I could at least hope the prayers of three cities had burned and found their way to the blackstar.

It was an ill sign in the heavens indeed.

"I suppose it ends here," I said.

"Ends?" Leutherion dragged himself up on one elbow from where he had been lying. He was missing two fingers on his left hand, but hadn't seemed to notice yet. "No, it does not end." The guard captain leaned close. "I'm going to take you home and hang you for the murdering mountebank you are. And I cannot do that until we find our way out of here and onward to Oppius."

"Do you know where Oppius might lie from here?" I asked sweetly.

"I know," said Pincus.

"Lead on," I told him. "Lead on."

When Electra was queen in Oppius the messenger of the black-star came down the river on a greenwood raft, bearing a promise of hope from Heaven and the memory of the smell of smoke.

We tended our wounds and rested in the hottest parts of the day. Had the journey been upriver from the jungles at the foot of Fagutal, we might well have perished. But Pincus's knowledge of geography, gleaned from his work in the cartularium of Halcyone's palace, saved us.

Armed with two spears, three knives, and a broken sword, we made our way along the current of the great river through jungles infested with beetles the size of cats and snakes too large for any rational vision of the world. I had never understood how many colors of green there were, either. After the views of the open desert, and the stark world-edge of the cliff at Fagutal, it was almost a relief to travel amid the jungle's close confines.

Even here, the inimical blackstar was a close presence, unde-nied and undeniable. The violet rays of nighttime colored the sky even by day now, and in those moments when the world fell silent, I could swear it hummed.

Oppius, when we came to it some days into our passage downstream, was a city built upon the water. This jungle river was a wide, slow beast, languorous as the giant crocodiles which lazed upon its banks. We missed the first few houses standing stilt-legged like marsh birds as we passed them in the dawn, but when we came to a larger array of buildings, we took note.

The channel divided and subdivided to flow between rock foundations like stone prows. Other buildings sat, or floated, on great mattresses of logs, or rose on stilts as the little houses did.

Rope bridges danced between the islands and islets, and sometimes more substantial structures arched, so that the whole city was an accretion strung from one bank to the other by half a hundred ways and paths. Flocks of birds the color of bright jewels flittered between the building-islands, and green monkeys chattered from the high trees growing out of compounds and courtyards. Waterwheels creaked at all sides, while boys and girls fished from tiny flat-bottomed skiffs, grown men working in the faster shallows with throw-nets.

I fell in love in that moment.

Our raft had the crudest rudder, and responded like a mother-in-law on a wedding night, and so our arrival in Oppius was via a slow but destructive encounter with one of the stone-prowed islets.

Leutherion and legs-of-the-gong were able to pull the rest of us and our few remaining possessions to safety. We all clung to the top of the foundation on a narrow ledge before a whitewashed wall. Pincus stared about in awe, Osmio simply closed his eyes and rested, while Leutherion's three remaining men kept their weapons ready.

"We're not assaulting anything today," I said. "They're going to have to come fetch us out."

With some good-natured grumbling, the guards stood down. Children gathered in the river and along the roof of a low structure just across the channel, hooting at us and laughing. It was some time before a man dropped out of the air on a springy rope, a harness about his shoulders, to dangle before us and ask our business. He was nearly naked save for a sort of leather clout, and a matching mask which covered his entire face down to the neck, leaving openings only for his eyes and mouth.

"Take us to your Queen Electra," I said, tired of protocol and the strangenesses of rulers.

Then, by the stars, the eunuch rang his gong. Every bird in the city leapt screaming into the sky at the sound, a colored rain streaming toward the sun.

• • •

The court of Queen Electra was an open yard, surrounded by a three-story palace of bamboo—a wondrous wood thin as a pipe, not much heavier than grass, but seemingly strong as iron. Pools steamed, with that eggs-and-fart smell which indicated hot springs below.

Everything else was people. The queen had furnished her court with bodies. Some were entwined to form couches upon which others lay. Slaves crawled, mobile tables with food and drinks upon their backs. Men and women stood or were bound in positions of naked receptiveness, used for sexual release or casual amusement as the users continued their conversations with others who stood idly by. The pools were filled with slick, squealing flesh as sport was taken within and beneath the water.

And to think that in Cermalus we believed Oppius decadent for the intimate leather goods that came in trade. The greatest perverts of my home city would have been as bumpkins with goat manure in their hair compared to any of the sybarites writhing in this place.

Our man, spry as a cat but carrying himself with the authority of age, led us to the center pool. A woman lay in a patch of open water, though many thrashed and groaned nearby. She could have been sister to our Queen Halcyone, young and slim, save she was clothed only in water and sunlight. Her small breasts floated nicely in the water, pink nipples standing just at the surface. The thatch between her legs was the same glossy black as the long hair which spread around her in the pool.

The guide stopped before her and bowed low. "These men asked to see you, Elegance."

She looked from face to face before settling on me. I rubbed my chin stubble, then glanced up at the blackstar glowering dark in the daytime sky.

"Would you join us in our pool?"

My cock voted yes, but after my dealings with Queen Celæno

I was loathe to trust anything. It seemed quite possible to me that these men and women at their sport were condemned, or slaves, forced to stay there till they rotted or drowned or expired of expended lust.

"With profound thanks, your Elegance, I must decline. I am on a pilgrimage, bringing a message of hope from the heavens to all seven cities. I am making the Transept."

Osmio and the eunuch had the blessed good sense not to strike the gong, which somehow continued to survive the journey despite all our setbacks.

"No pilgrim has made the Transept in generations," she said, her interest obviously piqued. "We each have our diversions, and some small trade passes from city to city. From the look of you, we would presume you fared poorly in Fagutal."

"Indeed." I was reluctant to criticize Queen Celæno, for I did not know if these women were truly sisters. "Misunderstandings all around, I am afraid."

"Yes. She is ever jealous of those who live beneath the sun." Electra raised her arms and stretched, a pretty sight which nearly cost me all my dignity. "We further presume your message of hope from the heavens did not suit our sister queen's ears."

I tried to regain command of my words, and shift my stance so my ardor would not be so obvious. "That I cannot say, Maj— Elegance. Each must decide for Herself. I say only this: I have been named by Halcyone queen in Cermalus to be the messenger of the blackstar. I have come to bear away whatever evil or ill that may have befallen your people."

She considered that a moment. "Are you in fact such a messenger? Or only so named?"

Beside me, Leutherion stirred uneasily. I understood his fear. We had done far too poorly for ourselves and our train on this journey.

I tried my best. "I was an ordinary man, Elegance, until the blackstar struck me down. When I rose again, a high priestess named me messenger, and my queen sealed the epithet. I cannot tell you what to believe, only what I believe."

"Hmm. And how will you carry away our evils, assuming we have any?"

I looked around at falling whips, bodies in chains, children crying bloody-legged in quiet corners, and wondered how to answer that. Habit served. "It has been our custom thus far to take the fears and prayers of the people written on slips of paper, and carry them away with us. We lost our chests to fire at the foot of Fagutal's cliff."

Her voice was soft. "And what do you charge for this wondrous service?"

"We ask only safe passage, Elegance," blurted Leutherion. His voice was heavy, thick with lust.

"See them to rooms in the hyacinth wing," she said to our guide, who had remained crouched at the edge of our conversation. "Except for this brave soldier." She pointed at Leutherion. "I would have him stay and tell me more of his ideas of safety."

I bowed and took my leave, taking my party with me save for Leutherion. My last sight of them was the queen stroking her left nipple and my guard captain standing with his tongue between his lips like some wooden-headed beggar boy.

Our guide, still nameless, returned in the morning. He did not remark on our reduced numbers, but led those of us who remained down halls with sprung flooring, lined with billowing silk tapestries and strange pieces of riverdrift on little stands, until we were in the queen's court again.

Most of the people were gone. A line of several dozen men and women waited their turn at a frame where someone— Finnric, I realized—was strapped with legs spread wide. I tried not to hear his keening as one at the front thrust violently. I had a dreadful suspicion that the nude man floating facedown near the queen in her pool was Leutherion.

"Welcome," Queen Electra said.

I knelt again. "Indeed, your Elegance. My thanks for your hospitality."

"And our thanks to you for not abusing our hospitality."

I strained not to glance over at Finnric. "Indeed."

She smiled, sweet as an adder. "We have considered your message. Our people live beneath a canopy of leaves and fog. The blackstar to us is no more or less a cause of panic than the crocodiles in the river, or the illnesses that breed in the slow-flowing swamps. Some die, most live, life continues like the river itself. But we will package our evil safe and sound for you to carry away, as you have so kindly offered. As well we shall grant you a guide, and such supplies as a small expedition might require. Be ready to leave at dawn three days hence."

Bowing low, I thanked her profusely.

There were girls and boys awaiting us in our apartments, oiled and nude, in ages from scandalously young to maternally old, but I sent them away. We barred our little door, for all the good it would do with these puzzlebox bamboo walls, and set a watch. There was no choice but to eat the food the Oppians brought us. We were fully in their power, but there was little else we could do.

On the third day our guide led us along more bamboo corridors to a landing stage on the downstream side of the palace-island. A sleek, swift boat was tied there. A man sat in the prow wearing a mask much like our guide's, save there were no holes for eyes or mouth. His skin was pale and wrinkled, and he was too still, as if wired in place. There were two fingers missing from his left hand.

I did not need to ask where Queen Electra had set her evil to journey forth with us. There was not enough money under the sun for me to watch him take his mask off.

Panniers of food and gourds of water lined the boat. Unless

they meant to poison us, the Oppians had seen us well on our way.

We threw ourselves at the mercy of the current and departed gladly, each alone with his thoughts. As the boat bobbed through the city, the eunuch stroked his gong until it began to hum softly, muted by his knees, the faintest metal tears for what we had left behind.

When Maia was queen in Palatium the blackstar's messenger came toiling up the slopes from the feverlands, bearing his message of hope.

We spent six days shooting down the river, pulling into mid-current islands or snags at night to rest out the dark while the blackstar's violet light crackled in the sky. Pincus tried to calculate our position as he watched the cliffs march in from the east, at first just dark lines on the horizon just above the treetops, then closer and closer.

Our guide at the prow never ate, never slept, never spoke, never pissed. Never moved.

On the morning of the seventh day I had the tiller, while Ironpants tried to spear some fish for the sake of fresh meat—our supplies were in fact plentiful, but ran heavily to cured fruits and fowl. I looked forward to see the guide had lifted his arm and pointed at the east bank.

"Time to put in," I said softly. I steered the boat, while Ironpants and legs-of-the-gong put paddles in to help. Osmio was much too small to do that work, and Pincus had a tendency to dither when action was required. How the man had survived this far was past my understanding.

We cut across the current and found a landing hidden in an inlet, one we would have sped right by without noticing had our guide not pointed us in. I gave silent thanks to Leutherion's shade, which I hoped had found better rest than his body seemed to have done.

From there, the trail was clear enough. Obviously trade came this way with reasonable frequency. Someone had even invested time and effort in improvements to the path. It was two days of dreadful chest-tightening, leg-burning climbing to follow the path up the nose of the cliffs. There were little way stations every hour or two, wide spots to pause without clinging to a cliff face or dangling legs over a drop. Only the guide seemed to need no rest, following when we walked, standing immobile as stone when we tarried.

No one wanted to sleep in his presence, but we had no real choice. Still, we kept our night watch, more against him than against any imagined predators.

Eventually the slope gentled out, then I realized my legs hurt less. Ahead the trail came to a sort of wide flat spot, with a low wall in the middle. Anyone besides Osmio could have stepped over the wall, or walked around it easily enough, but I halted our little column and studied it.

The trail continued on the far side, but less worn. Whoever came up here stopped at this point, turned around and went back.

Why?

I looked ahead. There were crags in the distance, a sort of crown atop these cliffs that might have been a city. I turned and looked back. The trail meandered a bit, a stone ribbon on stone, before disappearing below the line of the slope. The jungle basin was visible far below. Wind whipped dry and chilly around me, making little complaints.

"Have people camped here?" I asked.

Ironpants and Pincus wandered about a bit. "Yes," called the guard. "There's a shitpit over here, not well filled in. There've been more."

I had to admire anyone who went to the trouble of hacking a latrine out of the barren rock.

Pincus came back with some broken iron spikes. "Tent stakes."

"So they come all the way up here, they stop at this little wall which wouldn't slow down a good-sized rat, and they wait . . . for what?"

"Brass," said Osmio.

The eunuch rang the gong.

An hour later Osmio spotted two men coming down the path from the other side. We stood on our side of the wall, even the guide. He was beginning to smell up here on the stone, like a raw fish left out too long.

When they arrived, the strangers were clad entirely in brass armor. They showed no skin, no eyes, nothing other than their mobility to mark themselves out from empty metal. The two stopped, paused for about half a minute, then turned and headed back up the path.

I stepped over the wall to follow. One by one my fellow travelers came with me, Osmio scrambling with the aid of legs-of-the-gong. Even the guide came, trailing the rest of us.

It was a strange silent journey toward the crown of crags. There was no huff of breath nor stink of sweat from our two escorts. They were like the guide, wrought in metal instead of leather and flesh. I wished mightily for Leutherion back, in his old self. He had not liked me one bit, but the old guard commander was both sensible and trustworthy. None of my current companions met those two criteria save possibly Ironpants, of whom I simply knew too little.

The crags resolved to walls, albeit crumbling. Palatium was a fortress, pure and simple, though I could not imagine what she had been built to defend. There were no fields around her, no town outside the walls. No roads led to or from.

This was by far the most desolate of the cities I had yet seen.

We passed from chilly sunlight to cold shadow through a shattered gate. The architecture was cyclopean. Great red-brown slabs laid together formed the walls. Other slabs stacked to make the inner halls of the fortress. There was no detail, just gaps for openings and incidental cracks which let a bit more light in. Everywhere was dust, with rubble on the floor save where little paths led from room to room.

The armor escorted us through a good mile of corridors, occasionally passing through narrow stone courtyards. It was a strange sort of maze. I was certain we crossed our own path several times, but eventually we were in the great hall. The place stank like a barn—the first smell of life which had hit my nose since abandoning the river for the heights.

A throne, made of the same huge, crude stones, stood in the middle of the hall. Light from overhead touched the foot of the thing, leaving the queen seated upon it in shadow.

"You come from the river." Her voice creaked and whistled, as if she didn't speak much.

"I come from much farther than the river, Majesty," I said.

The gong echoed again. I turned to snap at Osmio and legs-of-the-gong when I realized we were surrounded by the brass-armored men, all silent as the guide.

"Ah," I said, turning back.

"There is no law to protect you here." The queen's voice was sad.

"Are you not the law, Maia queen in Palatium?"

"No more. There is no law."

"I come . . ." I began, then stopped. I was tired of the charade, tired of the stupidity and deaths. I wished I was back in Cermalus fixing roofs and dodging beatings from old Tradelium's overseers. "I'm just trying to go home, Majesty, only I seem to be doomed to walk the Transept. Palatium is the fifth of seven cities, and I'd like to see Cermalus again before I die."

"That is an unfortunate wish."

That made me angry. After all I'd run from, fought, and lost, her hopelessness fired my anger. "Where is the law in Palatium, then? Did you burn the books and turn out the judges? Does no one care for custom, or for contract? What became of you that you should discard my life so easily?"

"Don't you speak so to me," the queen snapped.

"Why not?" I jumped into the light at the foot of her throne. "Who are you to tell me not to speak?"

She stood, and I saw how half her body trembled and shook. Her left eye drooped, and that side of her mouth trembled. "I am queen in Palatium, and I tell you not to speak."

I knelt. "If you are queen then you are the law, Majesty. The law and the judge of the law. As the judge, you are free to choose mercy."

The gong echoed again. I risked a look to one side. All the brass men were kneeling.

"They have not taken a knee since I was struck down," Queen Maia whispered.

"They heed the gong, Majesty," I said. "For it rings with a heart of brass. And the gong heeds you." I stood and turned, staring at the eunuch. "Legs-of-the-gong, would you stay here and serve the queen as the master of her brass?"

He stared back at me a while, then turned to Osmio with a puzzled expression. The little man shot me a venomous look before nodding at the eunuch.

"He is yours, Majesty. What says the law now?"

She smiled at me, and reached out with her trembling hand. "Go, before I forget myself once more. What is your name, sir?"

"I . . ." I stopped a moment. Andrade the slave fixed roofs in Cermalus. He did not revive queens in Palatium. "I am the messenger of the blackstar, and I have taken your evil from you."

We passed into an upland forest, so Pincus called it, populated by tall, narrow trees with needles on high, upswept branches. The tall, dry cliffs gave way to slopes running across our line of travel. Snow and ice gleamed on the heights. The blackstar cast purple shadows, so close none of us dared look skyward.

There was yet a trail here, though not quite so well-kept as the one from the river to Palatium. Still, we did not have to force our way through the underbrush and thistled meadows.

Sullen and bitter, Osmio walked with us. At the last moment he had elected not to stay with legs-of-the-gong. Pincus was happy as a child at festival time, exclaiming over rocks and trees and the most ordinary insects. Ironpants and I stayed close together but spoke little. The guide trailed behind, his function served, but still presumably carrying the evil of Oppius with him.

Was I to burn him, as the prayers were burned?

It was a matter of some days before our supplies gave out, but none of us had the least idea what could be eaten in this high country, save the squirrels and birds and woodchucks which we would need a bow to catch. No one thought that eating flowers and leaves would be wise, and the little flashing fish we could snatch out of the pools were so tiny as to mean nothing to our rumbling bellies.

Three days into the hunger, Pincus slipped and tumbled down a raw slope, slamming again and again into rocks until he fetched up against some trees some sixty yards below us.

His cries for help echoed up the mountainside.

Without the eunuch, the duty of a rescue seemed to fall to me or Ironpants. I looked at the soldier. "I'll go get him. You watch for . . . whatever."

We both knew I meant the guide.

"Bad idea, messenger," Ironpants said.

"I can't leave him!"

"Look at him. He's lying funny. Broken bones for sure. He's already done for. We got no food, the only water is from those streams, you got no way to fix him up even if you do pull him out of there without hurting yourself in the bargain."

I felt horribly sick. "He'll die."

Ironpants shrugged. "We'll die if we try to save him. How many of us have died already? He was a useless man, anyway."

In that moment I hated the soldier. But I hated myself, too, for I knew he was right. We didn't even have a rope. The chances I could climb down there and drag Pincus all the way back up without hurting myself, and him more, were small.

We didn't even have a bow to give him mercy.

There was nothing to be done. It was the ill luck of the blackstar, taking another of my people.

When Pincus saw us turn to walk on, he began calling, "Messenger, messenger."

My gut roiled hot with shame. My heart was hot iron in my chest. How would I feel in his place? But what could I do for him now?

As we walked, I realized the guide had stayed behind as well.

"Oh, holy hells," I whispered.

"With luck, he'll never catch us," said Ironpants.

Osmio made a sort of barking shriek. "What about me? I'm useless, too. You going to drop me down the next ravine?"

I looked him up and down, tried to think like Ironpants. "You don't eat much, you'll last."

The soldier snickered; I just felt shame.

When Merope was queen in Sucusa, the blackstar messenger came to her sore of foot and tired from his travels.

Two days later, my stomach hard and beginning to swell, we came to a grove of enormous trees in which a city was strung. Swaying walkways, platforms high and low, people climbing ropes. It was a bit like Oppius, except built within trees instead of along a river.

We came to what might have been a gate, in the sense that the path slipped between two great trunks growing quite close together some little ways inside the grove. Three lithe women met us there. They wore rough homespun tunics and carried small bows unslung. The one standing in the center set her hand toward me, palm up.

"You are the messenger," she said. There was an odd lilt to her voice.

"Yes."

"You come by the light of the blackstar, walking with the soldier and the fool. Where are the scholar and the dead man?"

There was a question I didn't want to answer. The taste of my choices was still quite bitter in my mouth. I glanced at my traveling companions. Ironpants just looked tired, Osmio had a bitter fire in his eyes. "The scholar fell, and had to be left behind. The dead man stayed to care for him."

"You have strange notions of care in your country," said one of the other women.

The first extended her hand sideways. "Queen Merope will see you."

I dipped my head. "Thank you."

The queen did not rule from a high bower, as I had expected. Nor did she have some seat of polished timbers amid the center of the grove. No, Merope queen in Sucusa was crouched among ferns spearing fish in the swift current of a stream when we were brought before her.

Behind her, really.

She stood and scrambled up the bank. Again, she could have been sister to the other queens. Young, lithe, though her skin was berry brown and her hair the color of walnuts.

"I see some of you are here." Her voice was bright bells.

"How did you know to mark our coming?" I asked.

"Your Transept has been the talk of wanderers for some time. Every trader, tracker, and footloose younger son we have seen here of late has mentioned you in some way or another. Did you know that you fly upon a cloud, messenger? And your fool travels in the arms of a giant."

"I did once, Majesty," muttered Osmio. "Messenger boy here gave my greatest friend away."

She cocked her head at the little man. "Was your friend the messenger's to give?" Then, to me: "I have no great brief for you, messenger, nor any against you. Our laws here are simple and just. You will only swear to do no harm while you stay within Sucusa, and you are free here as long as you wish."

That sounded simple enough. But I had seen too much already. "What do you define as harm, that I should avoid, Majesty?"

The queen laughed. "Well spoken, messenger. The obvious sorts of things."

"I will swear willingly not to lift my hand against anyone in your city. But beyond that . . . if I were to tell the children of your city the strange truths about Fagutal and Oppius, would that be harm? What if I described the hard choice I made when the scholar fell down the mountain? Is that harm? Is it harm to seek the bed of a woman, or a man, here? At what age or time of life may they give consent, and is their consent sufficient in the eyes of your law?"

"Enough, enough," she said. "You see the trap better than most. Though it is not meant for a trap. Rather, if we would not have books of the law binding us like chains, we must rely on the good sense of everyone who dwells here or passes through."

"Then I will swear to use good sense to the best of my ability, but only if you swear to respect and honor my good sense, Majesty."

"Enough swearing," she said. "Go find food, and rest, and when you are ready to speak to me of your purposes, ask after me. Almost anyone will be able tell you where I am. In our city, the queen serves all."

"Good day," I told her.

Rested and refreshed, I wandered a bit to learn more of this place. Eventually I came across a young man whittling arrows from birch twigs. I spent time watching him smooth them, testing their balance on his finger and rolling them to check the true.

After a time he looked up at me and smiled. His teeth were bright in a face as pale brown as the queen's. "Greetings, messenger. Does my work please you?"

"I find the mastery of craft in others to be fascinating," I said. Both polite and accurate.

"I am scarcely a master, but it is true; my arrows are said to fly well."

"It is no wonder."

He offered me a birch shaft. I tested it as I had seen him do, though the result meant little to me. "How are the winters here?"

He shrugged. "I would not know."

"Really? Why not?"

"We sleep, of course. Don't you?"

"All winter?" I blurted, then wished I hadn't.

"Ask for the heart trees. Someone can show you."

Soon enough, someone did. I found myself down beneath the soil, having passed through a narrow hole between two great roots. A giggling girl stood with me, her fingers brushing suggestively against my thigh. I wanted none of that just now, with a sick dread stealing upon me.

They had hollowed out wells, down amid the root systems of the forest giants. Each was perhaps fifteen feet deep, the walls combed like a beehive, but the cells were large enough for a man to climb into. Barrels of wax and pitch stood ready at the bottom of the wells to seal the sleepers in.

"We dream together," she said. "It is another life. A few stay out each season, to breach us in the spring, but the rest dream together." Her hand slipped inside my tunic, seeking my cock. "You have never known anything of the like."

Horror stained me. I wanted nothing to do with their soulless, inhuman dreaming. I fled up the ladders and out the hole, racing till I found Ironpants.

"We must go," I told him. I was panting, sweating from my run.

"Why?" His voice was mild.

"These people . . . are not like us."

"Of course not," said Merope, stepping into the little circle of sunlight where we spoke. "No people are like another. How did you find my sister's subjects in Oppius? Or the wall dwellers in Fagutal? If you want people like you, you must go home and hope they have not changed overmuch in your absence."

I bowed. "It is time for me to go, Majesty."

"Scouts tell me the dead man comes. He bears the scholar on his back." She smiled. I noticed for the first time that her teeth were too many and too small in her face. "Would you not abide for a reunion of your party?"

"They have their own concerns," I said roughly. "I have done no harm here, as we swore. I would find my way to Velia now and finish my Transept."

"And will you take your evil with you?" she asked me softly.

"Evil follows me wherever I go. I am the messenger of the blackstar."

"Then he goes," she said with a nod to Ironpants. Her voice was hard, a blade. "Three women he has bedded here, and in the heat of passion taken each of them in the manner of a boy without their permission or the good sense to use a little grease. They will all pass blood for days yet. And your fool, who asks disturbing questions and tries to incite murder against you. Take him as well. The dead man, too, is your evil. You have my permission to leave once he and the scholar have departed these woods."

She turned and stalked away. A number of her young women, with their little bows, remained close by. The strings were taut this time.

Ironpants shrugged. "We keep walking. It's been months, what's another walk?"

"You . . . bastard," I said, thinking of the women. "We swore an oath to do no harm."

"They weren't complaining when I shoved it into them. Besides, you don't seem to think they're human. What do you care?"

I lay close to a tree trunk and wept into the moss, wondering when I had become so vile.

When Taygete was queen in Velia, the messenger of the blackstar danced out of the night with the soldier, the fool, the scholar, and the dead man in his train, coming together to sing the blackstar down.

It was a long hike down and east from Sucusa, bending ever toward the north. Velia lay that way, and beyond it Cermalus should I ever choose to return to the city of my birth. The lower woods were warmer and leafier, with an abundance of game.

The Sucusans had patched my tunic and given me better boots. Osmio had traded the last of his silks for child's leathers. Ironpants still wore his old temple uniform, albeit patched and supplemented with bits gathered along the way. The guide remained naked save for the leather clout and his featureless sack. Pincus . . . breathed.

He rode now on the guide's back, clinging like a baby scorpion to its mother. His legs were twisted, his flesh slack and pale, and though nude he seemed as human as a spider's egg sac. Only the fact that he yet breathed kept me from grasping hold of Ironpants's spear during some night watch and plunging it into his quivering, leathered flanks. Pincus was worse than what had become of Leutherion. I could make a pretense about the guide, forget a few hours at a time who he had been. It was not my choice which had killed him.

But I had abandoned Pincus. Every shuddering breath accused me.

The cruelty of Queen Merope was exquisite.

My only solace was that the blackstar seemed to be finally diminishing. Perhaps it had followed the course of my Transept, giving truth to Queen Halcyone's lies.

We marched on.

This trail was well-traveled. From time to time we saw caravans, hunting parties, adventurers. Even a few foreigners, exotics from beyond the Seven Cities. These we knew by their skin color—blue-black in one party, fire red in another—and their strange beasts and stranger dress.

All had heard of us, to be sure. We were marked to be respected and avoided. If they saw us coming, they hid in the woods and left offerings of food, wine, and clothing. If they didn't see us coming, they pulled to one side of the trail and muttered prayers, sometimes tossing coins or flowers as we passed them.

Osmio cursed continuously. Ironpants said nothing that was not strictly necessary. I could not bear to look at the guide or Pincus, so I walked alone.

In time we crossed a gentle ridge. A valley spread wide and shallow, a series of little lakes strung along the small river that ran down it. Autumn was settling upon the trees there, underneath a sky that was almost wholesome once more. A city spread around the lakes, without walls or towers, more a town that went on for a mile or two. There were ruins rising from the middle of three of the lakes, ancient metal towers that gleamed with glass and rust and the afternoon sun.

This must be Velia, I thought. My Transept is done. All I need do is present myself to Taygete the queen, then I can go die of shame in some lowlife tavern. I stopped, turned to my companions. "You are released from any obligation to me. Go find your own interests among your own kind."

Osmio never stopped cursing, just kept walking without a backward glance.

Ironpants hefted his spear. "Figure I'll go see who's hiring. I'd never be able to explain him back home." He jerked his chin toward the guide. "Try not to get anyone else killed. Including yourself."

The soldier loped down the trail toward Velia, quickly passing Osmio.

I reached out and with trembling hands touched the guide's hood. The leather was wet, rotten, and the brush of my fingers raised a horrid stench. "I release you, too, old friend," I said softly. "Care for Pincus, and when he's done see that his death is decent. It's what I should have done. For both of you."

Slowly I set off downhill for Velia, taking care not to overtake Osmio.

There were no gates nor guards, so I wandered quiet streets awhile. Eventually I worked up the courage to ask a woman where I might find the palace of Queen Taygete. She looked at me as if I were foolish, then sent me to the next lake upstream.

I found the ruined metal in midlake was in fact the palace. The people on the waterfront gave me odd glances as well, but one man said, "You're that messenger, ain't you?"

"Yes."

He scratched at his bald scalp, then tugged a drooping moustache. "I can row you out there, I reckon. If you don't want to just swim."

The sun was sloping into the afternoon, and I really didn't wish to get wet. "Please, if you'll just drop me."

"Ain't nothing there no more," he said pleasantly. "But if you've got the hankering, why, you're the messenger."

As he rowed I looked up at the sky. The blackstar was gone, for the first time in many months. "Where did it go?"

"Figured you'd know," said the boatman. "You being the messenger and all. She was still up there this morning."

I climbed out of the boat on a metal landing, and realized I had nothing to tip the boatman with save the clothes on my back. Even the coins and oddments of the trail seemed to have been lost to me.

"I would offer you my blessing . . . ," I began.

"No." He smiled. "You just go on."

Inside the hallways were metal—floor, wall, and roof. Everything was wet, rotting, damp, with mold blossoming in a hundred colors muted by the deep shadows. I wandered awhile as the light failed, before finding myself on a balcony high up the wall in an open chamber with a great chair at the center.

Not open, I corrected myself. There was a glass roof.

The chair was on a dais made of seven six-sided figures linked together. Much like the cells in the ground at Sucusa, but laid sideways instead of vertically. I climbed down a rusted ladder and walked up to the throne. Each of the hexagons had a clear cover. There was a sort of cushion within, hoses, little buttons. A tiny cell of a different sort.

Queen Taygete lay curled on the big chair. She looked to have died very young, and had since become a sort of leathery corpse. I could see how her face resembled her sisters. I wondered if she had come out of a seventh cell beneath this throne.

Were they better off in Velia, ruled by a dead queen? No kindness, no cruelty, the law being whatever made sense to the people. I did not know.

"You freed him, you know."

Looking up, I saw Osmio on my balcony.

"I should not be so angry," the little man said. "Legs-of-the-gong is happy now." He turned and vanished.

I waited to see if anyone else would appear. Who, though? Ironpants was off drinking and whoring. As far as I knew, Pincus and the guide were in the woods finishing what they should have done long ago—becoming honestly, truly dead.

Would that I could speak to the high priestess back in Cermalus. I had taken her for a fat fool, but I now suspected she knew a lot more than I'd ever realized. Maybe this had all been my miracle, the blackstar and my journey of the Transept. Maybe it had been the queen's miracle. Maybe no one's at all.

I sat thinking awhile at Taygete's feet before I finally fell asleep.

In the morning someone had left three apples and some cheese near me. I put one apple on the throne for Taygete and ate the rest. As the day grew older in the glass roof above me, blessedly clear of the blackstar, the boatman came climbing down the balcony with two young men following him.

"They been fighting, messenger," he told me. "Won't stop. Over a girl. I told 'em you'd give a fair judging, being as how you don't know no one involved."

Hope, I thought. This man finds hope in me.

Maybe that's what the blackstar meant. Place your hope in what you don't know. I'd done the Transept after all, the first in generations. Maybe I'd found wisdom.

I could only hope.

"Tell me about the girl," I said.

Both young men began yelling at once.

```
. . . . . . . . . . . . . . . . . . . . . . . . . . . . . . . . . . . . . . . . . . . . . . . . .
:                                                                                           :
:        P · S · O · R · I · A · S · I · S                                                   :
:                                                                                           :
:        pso·ri·a·sis \ sə-ˈrī-ə-səs \                                                      :
:                                                                                           :
:                     noun                                                                  :
:                                                                                           :
:   : a chronic skin disease characterized by circumscribed red                             :
:   patches covered with white scales                                                       :
:                                                                                           :
. . . . . . . . . . . . . . . . . . . . . . . . . . . . . . . . . . . . . . . . . . . . . . . . .
```

Tsuris

• • •

LESLIE WHAT

WHEN I LOOK AT DENNY I can't see the man I married twenty-five years ago. I see what he has become: his malformed fingers, twisted and swollen at the joints; yellow discharge from his eyes; raised red skin patches that dry and die and transform into silvery scales that slough away, until the next cycle, with new eruptions of red. Psoriasis is no simple malady of the skin; it is the body attacking itself. The heat exacerbates the symptoms, and in the summer we keep the curtains drawn in protest. The weather is unnaturally muggy and our house is dark, especially in the bedroom. The room smells cave-dank. While Denny is outside, mowing the back field, I prepare to sweep up the death with a broom and dustpan. I shake out the top sheet, an act generating a breeze so abrupt it does nothing to cool the room. A flurry of white flakes rises and settles over the floorboards. It's a beautiful sight—like a dusting of snow on a dark road. But the moment is transient, and when it passes, I see skin cells dirtying the floor.

I sweep the faded oak planks, traversing a wide circle from the walls inward. The circle grows smaller with each broom pass, and a mound takes shape as I push detritus toward the center of the room. My dustpan fills with Denny's skin, and bits of dust and hair.

He woke up this morning with his joints burning, and got more salty than usual when I nagged him about the grass. He's been promising to mow it for days.

"This is why God made goats," Denny said, but he knew better than to argue theology with me—I majored in religious studies.

"This is why God made riding mowers," I said.

He scratched at his head and examined his nails for blood. He looked so uncomfortable I said, "Why don't you let me do it? Can't be all that hard to drive."

My offer just made things worse. He clomped outside and got to work, and now he's mowing like a martyr. His skin will crawl from so much sun, and he'll blame me, but won't say so.

I should have let him borrow the goat.

There's a funeral this afternoon—my friend Becky's only boy, killed by an IED in Baghdad. In another month, he would have been twenty-two. In another month, he would have come home from his tour of duty. He'd only just written to let Becky know he didn't plan to reenlist. I'm so sad for her I can't think about the irony.

Denny comes in and heads for the shower. The well's down so his shower will be shorter than he'd like. It hasn't rained in two months—no water for luxuries like keeping up the lawn. Certainly no water to wash your hair twice, my biggest sin— well, maybe not my biggest one. The fescue has deteriorated into a field of scrawny stick figures. It's a fire danger, and all it would take is one spark from the mower, or a partially crushed cigarette to set the world ablaze.

The phone rings.

Ned.

"What are you wearing?" he asks.

"Don't call me at home," I whisper, and he asks, "You'll stop by later?"

I think about hanging up. At first, I didn't care if anyone discovered my affair, but now that I've determined I don't love Ned, I want it to stay secret. I don't understand that about myself. "Sure," I say. "I'll try."

"See you then," Ned says.

It's too hot to bake, but I want to bring something for after the service. I look up a recipe for crab dip and crackers. A squeeze of lemon, chopped green onions, Worcestershire sauce, a dash of nutmeg, grated Parmesan, cream cheese, ground pepper and salt to taste. I doubt anyone else will appreciate the extravagance. I bought a can of crabmeat our last trip to Portland. It was very expensive, and too much meat for the two of us. We're five hours to the east of Portland, far enough so we only drive in three or four times a year. Blue Valley isn't that far as the crow flies. As the Dodge drives, you cross a mountain range and a cultural divide, and those kinds of crossing take their toll. We moved out here to get away from all the things we hated about the city life. In a way, it seems like cheating to return just to shop.

The pipes make noise like the sound of pebbles tumbling in the dryer. The faucets squeal and the flow of water closes to a trickle and stops. In a few minutes, Denny, a green towel wrapped around his hips, finds me in the kitchen and asks, "Will you do my back?" There are only a few spots he can't reach, but he likes when I do them all. When it first started, we made a game of it. I was younger then. I thought I loved him enough not to care. I scoop crab dip into Tupperware and burp it shut.

Our place is in the Blue Hills River Valley, on the twenty acres that's still left of Denny's family farm. We farm cantaloupes and onions and potatoes and keep a small henhouse and large garden. I trade the extra eggs for milk. I put up jars of zucchini like I'd learned how from my mother instead of from books, and once I won a ribbon for my deep-dish cherry cobbler. In winter, the creek fills and Denny hooks rainbows and the occasional steelhead that takes a wrong turn and ends up swimming through our property. What they didn't teach me in college was that when you married a farmer's son you married his acreage. Nor did I learn how hard I'd have to work to be accepted. Even if I die in the country I'll always be thought of as a city girl.

"My back?" Denny says. "I'll wait if you're busy."

I wash my hands, dry them on a linen towel that's older than I am. There's a black scar in the Formica, where the surface dips from when I set down a pan that had caught fire, and it slipped off the potholder. It looks like something that could be rubbed out, but it's there for the life of the counter. "It's okay," I say. His scalp reeks of coal tar, a pungent smell like something burnt.

Denny sits on a stool that's too short for him. Both knees are puffy and red. A blue jar sits out beside the canisters of salt and flour and sugar, and near the jar's the box of disposable gloves. I steady my nerves, open the jar, and smile, trying to make it look sincere.

"Go ahead," he says. "Might as well get this over with." He closes his eyes and waits for me to touch him. Silvery scales cover his back, whiten his chest. Across his shoulder is a tattooed skull whose flaming hair has mellowed into gray ringlets, just as his scaling skin has muted the once fiery ink. We met at the tattoo parlor. I was getting decorated, a rose on my ankle I thought would look sexy. He was adding to his collection of skulls—one for every buddy lost in Vietnam. Denny's tattooed skulls shine across both shoulders, his upper arms. There's a smaller skull on the back of one hand, and a treasure chest overflowing with snakelike jewels that squirm from five grinning skulls on his left forearm. His elbows are scratched raw and the hair under his arms grows in tufts. The skin looks like it should hurt, but the root of the pain is deeper, enflaming his joints and leaving him struggling to stand by the end of the day.

Back in college I wrote a paper on Miriam for my comparative religions class, and how the Bible says God caused her skin to whiten after she questioned the wisdom and prophecy of her brother, Moses. People assume God gave her leprosy, but that's inaccurate. The Hebrew word for her punishment was *tzara'as.* Say it out loud, a couple of times fast, and it sounds an awful lot like psoriasis. Scholars say tzara'as was more a disease of the soul than of the skin. Humans tend to conflate the two, but the Bible is all about explaining the differences. There's another word, this one Yiddish, *tsuris,* which means trouble, or the condition of being in trouble. Like Denny's skin disease, which is trouble you can see.

I dip my fingers into the gloves and dip the gloves into the jar and smear white over his skin. The cream won't cure anything; it just covers things up, keeps new scales from forming until his clothes wick up the moisture.

I feel the roughness through the gloves, grateful for the layer separating my skin from his. I smear cream in a circular motion, like polishing furniture. It's not so bad once the rhythm takes over. I'm soothing the small of Denny's back when he turns his body to face mine. He stills my hands and slides his arms around my waist. He pulls me toward him. I stumble into his lap and before I can think straight, he is kissing me.

"My blouse," I say, annoyed that he might stain more of my clothes, because the only thing that's worse than being a farm wife is looking like one.

"Screw the blouse. Take it off," he says. He claws the buttons.

"Let me do that," I say, but first I pull free from my gloves. I set them on the counter yet they fall to the floor, the call of gravity being stronger than the force of intent. The blouse soon follows.

He grabs beneath my waistband with sandpaper fingers.

My hands fall limp to my sides. I can't do this, I think, wanting it to end as quickly as it began.

The flame of his tongue licks at my ears. His hot breath blows against my neck. He lifts me to a stand, presses hard against me. His towel slides away. I withdraw from the probe of his tongue as his kisses intensify. He leads me to the bedroom, and I feel relieved to be back in that intimate darkness, where I can avoid looking at the part of him that's animal and raw, pulsing and decayed.

I close my eyes. He guides my hand toward him and I work to relax, to touch him with the love and longing I once felt. Then my fingers brush his scales and my hand falls limp. I cannot stifle my groan in time.

My husband is turning into a dragon.

Only now does he notice how my tongue lies dead against his. He recoils. "I'm still me," he says, and turns away.

The funeral starts at five, but we need to get there early because Denny's motorcycle group, the Patriot Guard Riders, were asked to be the honor guards. The Riders are a group of veterans who came together to do something to honor fallen soldiers. Some, like Denny, are against the war, but some are staunch believers in the president's policy. They set aside any differences to do what they think is right, go anywhere they're asked to go, cross the country if needed. Bikers or not, they're the good guys here. I'm proud that Denny's one of them.

We've been warned that some people from the Kansas Westboro Church have come out here to protest, as they've done at other soldiers' funerals over the last couple of years. The demonstrators are known to carry signs that say things like, "Thank God for Dead Soldiers," and "God Hates Fags." They insult the mourners, accuse the grieving parents of raising children who hate God. Their credo says that everything bad happens to show how God is punishing the United States for being an evil nation of "fags" and "fag enablers." These are terrible people and they don't belong here. Nobody understands why they do it. Losing someone you love is tragic enough. You shouldn't have to listen to taunts and jeers.

I iron a lightweight cotton blouse and pair of pants. I'd wear a dress if it wasn't too hot to wear pantyhose. My veins popped out last summer, tiny rivers meandering down my legs. I'm too embarrassed of my legs to go anywhere without stockings. Denny hauls his duffel bag out to his hog and straps it in place. "Sure you don't want to ride with me?" he asks, but it's too hot to think about wearing leather over my outfit just so I can look cool by showing up on the back of a Harley.

"I don't know," I say, like I'm thinking it over. "Hmm. Air conditioning, or a zillion degrees? Hmmm."

"Your hair flying in the wind or the scent of exhaust backing up into the cab?" Denny says.

"It's a draw, but I'll take the truck."

He salutes me and ties a bandana over his hair. He's wearing black jeans and leather chaps and a white T-shirt with an American flag on one side and an eagle holding a "Remember the POWs" banner on the other. He works himself into a black leather vest that's getting more and more snug. "See you there," he says. "Don't forget your crab dip."

Despite our problems, the man knows me. I've left the Tupperware in the fridge. "See you there," I say, and rush in to grab the crab dip and a couple of bottles of cold water. I find a serving tray and a box of Triscuits and climb into the cab to head toward church.

It's so hot that even with the air blasting me full force it can't disguise the furnace on the windshield's other side. It's not the dry heat that I'm used to, but the kind of steam heat we only get once or twice a year. I can feel my hair frizz and stand out with static electricity. The AC's on and cool air through the vents stirs up a whirlwind of white—scales that have crumbled into dust. I sneeze.

The farms are an uneven checkerboard of green fields and fallow patches. One red-winged blackbird chases another from the telephone wire. On the far side of the Blue Hills there's a flash of lightning. Even from this distance, its power is strong enough to ignite the resting juncos, who startle from a dead pine and scatter until the lead bird leads his flock in a spiral that disappears into the sky. The road before me looks like molten black glass and I slow down even though I know it's a mirage. But up ahead I see something—an old man walking on water—and because I've slowed, when I slam on the brakes, I stop a few yards short of hitting him.

Up close, the asphalt looks solid black; the shimmering light waves I thought were water have moved up the road. In my head I know this is an optical illusion, that this floating road is only the bending and distortion of light rays. But how close do you need to stand to discover the true nature of the world?

The old man's face is red and he's dripping in sweat. He's wearing wrinkled black wool pants and a white shirt made transparent by sweat. He's carrying his jacket, neatly folded over his arm. He points to a ten-year-old sky blue Buick with Kansas plates that's parked askew on the shoulder. The hood is open and the radiator steams. He looks like a grandfather who's wandered away from the family picnic and can't find his way home.

There's another lightning flash. I hope to God it's soon followed by rain, because the world out here looks ready to ignite. The old man comes around the side of the cab and I let down the window to talk.

"Miss," he says. His voice breaks and he makes a strangled sound like a tickle that's too dry to form a cough. Beneath the red burn, his face is sallow, wrinkled, dehydrated. His hands are thin, the fingers long, the skin transparent. "God bless you for stopping."

"Don't like to hit any folk before dinner," I say.

He doesn't laugh, doesn't even crack a smile.

There's something about him I don't trust, but he's old and it's still up near a hundred, and when I look for a Hannibal Lecter glint in his eyes, all I see is a grateful smile, and I realize it's his frailty I'm most afraid of.

"Can you give me a ride?" he asks.

"Where you headed?"

He straightens out his jacket and pulls a folded sheet of paper from the pocket. "Into town," he says. "To the Valley Church."

"You headed for the service?" I say, more an observation than a question. It explains the suit.

"In a matter of speaking," he says.

I'm puzzled. "Did you know Becky's boy, then?"

"No, I didn't."

I don't like this answer, but it's too hot to hold a thorough roadside inquisition, and I don't want to be late. "Get your stuff. I'll give you a ride in," I say.

"Much appreciate it," he says. "I just need to grab something from the car." He hobbles over and opens the back door. He pulls out a duffel bag and a rainbow sign on a wooden stake. He looks over at me to see if I'm watching and smiles and nods and calls, "Only be a second." He's about to cover up the sign with his jacket when I notice it says "TOO LATE TO PRAY," and then I see bumper stickers on his car that say "godhatesfags. com" and "America Will Burn in Hell." I get it then that he's one of them, one of those protestors, here to picket the funeral. An electrical storm builds inside me. Before me stands a man who brings tsuris to the world and doesn't care. He even expects me to chauffeur him to the funeral of my good friend's son.

My blood is a barometer and the pressure's rising. I experience hate in a way I don't understand. I don't know a thing about this man, why he believes what he does. I still want to hurt him. Kill him. Torture him first. A Rolodex flips open in my brain, listing every way I could accomplish the deed, starting with pinning him up against his Buick with my Ram. But then the lightning flashes on this side of the canyon, and for the first time that day, the thunder is close enough to hear. The racket blasts some much-needed clarity into my brain. I can't do it— help this man. For Becky's sake, I can't help him. He is trespassing on our lives and I cannot aid his passage. A storm is gathering and the rain will come, sooner or later. Just in case it's later, I take a bottle of cold water from my cooler, open the cab door, and roll it over his way. "If I were you, I wouldn't go to that funeral," I call, before closing my window and flattening my pedal to the floor.

I park and pretend to ignore the protestors as I pass through their ranks to cross the street. They number a dozen or so—men, women, and older teens. The younger ones wear athletic clothes and shoes; the older ones dresses or suits. Each holds a sign silk-screened with hate. Townspeople avert their eyes and walk past the demonstration and I watch as their expressions change from sorrow to anger. How long before that anger is expressed by hate?

I'm furious with these strangers. Why can't they let us give this young man the honor he deserves? Interrupting our grief is no business of theirs. I read in the paper that the leader of their church told a reporter he felt no sympathy for parents. "The family's in pain," he said, "because they haven't obeyed the Lord God."

Their hatred is as visceral as the electricity in the air. I see it on their faces, in their signs, in their presence. There's something very wrong with this picture. A young man dies so an old one can have his say. I'm tempted to gloat and confess to one of them that I've left the old man on the road. I come close to making that confession, until the most human of emotions washes over me. They don't belong here and any trouble that comes of this could have been prevented if they'd stayed away from our troubles. Let his own kind rescue him. The temperature feels cooler by a few degrees, but the air is so heavy it takes effort to walk through it. I'm ashamed. My heart feels as heavy as my step. I keep walking.

The Patriot Guard Riders seem to be the only ones wearing

black. The bikers stand between the sidewalk and the street to block the mourners' view of the protestors. Some of the Riders hoist oversized American flags. Denny's at one end of a line of reinforced blue tarps that stretches like a theater backdrop across the walkway.

"Thanks," I say to the first Rider I pass, a man I don't recognize. "Where you from?"

"Idaho Riders," he says. "Glad to be here."

He smells like cigarettes and wet leather. He's missing half his front teeth and his hair is wild and thin. His face is gaunt, so the skin hangs like a leather mask over his skull. In another situation, he'd be scary. He looks about the right age to have served with Denny in Vietnam. I don't ask because it doesn't matter. Their community is here and now, no matter where each man came from.

Becky's up ahead, walking with her husband. She's wearing a plain white dress and matching bolo jacket with a scalloped collar and eyelet embroidery on the sleeve caps. The pastor clasps her hands and holds them for a moment. She collapses enough that he slips his arm around her to help her walk the rest of the way down the sidewalk toward the chapel. Her husband's grief is strong enough to hold him upright.

Denny is sweating beneath his leathers and looks ill. His face is molting; his black vest sprayed with silver speckles. His once-blue eyes have specks of yellow. I both pity and resent him. I deserve more than this monster as my mate. I have cold water in the truck, but to get it means walking back, past the protestors. I can't do it now. Maybe I'll find strength after the service. "Are you okay?" I ask, and he nods and when he does, he sprinkles skin and sweat drops from his brow. I'm glad he has the Riders. Even when he's fully transformed, even when his skin has fallen away and he is fully armored by the scales of a dragon, he'll be welcome.

God punished Miriam for speaking against Moses, covering

her body with snow-white scales. Once her impurity was made visible, she was forced to leave the tent and live outside the community. This isolation was the punishment, more than the disease. And once she had atoned for her evil tongue, she was healed, allowed to return to the fold. Only then was she truly healed. The Bible story isn't about a skin ailment—it was about kinship.

There's shade at the top of the stairs. The assistant pastor's welcoming the mourners inside the foyer. The men's group stands near the entrance to the chapel and passes out one-page programs that have been folded in two. On one side of the program are black and white photos of a child with his cocker spaniel; a teenager in swim trunks, swinging from a rope swing over the pond; PFC Hinton in his dress blues. A caption says, "Say not in grief 'he is no more' but live in thankfulness that he was."

Prepubescent boys, cheeks blushed from heat and the excitement of wearing grown-up blue jackets with brass buttons, usher us to benches. The scents of lilies and roses mingle with baby-powder deodorants and cedar aftershave. Becky and her husband sit up front. Her parents flank her, leaning over in a way that hides her from me. It's just as well, for I can't bear to look directly at the face of grief.

We hear something then, like a pebble being thrown against the window. Then a rock, followed by more. There's the sound of horses galloping on the roof. At first I think it's the demonstrators, but someone announces, "Hail," and the thrum of it so overpowers the service that most of the congregants scoot from the pews and rush to the foyer doors, pressed against each other, to look outside. A lucky few crowd outside the entrance, where the Riders have taken shelter. The hail is round as quarters. Two boys go out and whoop and holler until one gets clipped on his lip by a hailstone the size of a charcoal briquette and cries for his mother. We stand and watch for several minutes, transfixed by the shower of hail that grows brittle and shatters when it touches down on earth.

"What about them?" someone says, with a glance toward the demonstrators, who cower, heads covered by placards.

"Invite them in," Becky says, humbling the rest of us with the charity of her grief. Our pastor nods, then steps through the crowd and motions for the trodden group to gather beneath the eaves.

A few of the children and a pregnant woman accept his offer. The others stand their ground and face their signs toward the church.

I look for the old man's face in the crowd, and when I don't find it, feel a wash of shame and pride and anger and worry. Whatever happens, I'm to blame.

The organist plays "Rock of Ages." The medley of coughing and sniffing and weeping and whispers transforms into a chorus of muted singing. The pastor invites us to stand and offer a prayer for forgiveness. Jesus is merciful. Jesus is just. Come unto me, all ye that labor and are heavy laden. And I will give you rest.

I recite the words without questioning them. I know what I believe and what the Westboro Church believes and what the Valley Church pastor believes. I know what Denny believes, even Becky. Instead of comforting me, this knowledge leaves me terrified. For all I've studied about religion, I don't have a clue what God believes, and it is this fearful ignorance—not the tsuris of our lives—that finally makes me break down and weep.

There's a meal of condolence in the community room. No one tries the crab dip except me, and Denny—who eats a few bites after prompting. I should have brought something more familiar. I stay late with a woman named Kath to clean up. Kath isn't from here, either. It takes an hour to wash dishes and clean up garbage and fold tables and chairs. How hard we try to fit in.

It feels late by the time we meet up with everyone at Ned's Place. Ned stands behind the bar, sees us, and lets his glance linger on mine long enough to show it means something. He can look at me longer than I can look at him without feeling shame.

He takes two chilled pint glasses from the cooler and leans them up against the PBR tap. Denny comes up behind me and gives me a kiss. His dry lips scratch my cheek. I imagine a strip of his skin stuck to mine and my hand goes to my cheek to wipe at nothing. Denny's already too drunk to notice. He pays, gets change for video poker and leaves a bigger tip than Ned deserves. Ned will defend him if anyone says something, but not because, as Denny thinks, he's given him hush money through his loyal consumption of Pabst. Ned will defend him out of kindness to me.

"Be there in a few," Denny tells me.

I sip off enough foam to carry the glass without wasting a lick of PBR.

Kath's boyfriend Joe is waiting at our usual table. Joe farms corn and pumpkins, saving out two acres for an autumn maze. He and Kath hooked up at a support group after both lost their spouses to cancer. "How're you folks?" Joe asks.

"Never better," I say. The wet heat's harder to take than a dry one, and I feel trampled, like the stick-figure grass. I slide into the booth and fit into my spot against the wall. I pick up the menu from habit, not because I plan to order anything I don't already know about.

Alice takes the order. She wears a pencil behind one ear and a cigarette behind the other. She reaches for the cigarette, holds it between her fingers for a second before replacing it and switching ears, for the pencil. She does it on purpose and sometimes gets a laugh. It's been so dry this summer the sheriff warned us all not to smoke outside, but that's made it hard for addicts like Alice, who don't like smoking in the break room because it makes her feel like she's being quarantined. "Your man gonna join us?"

My man. I don't know who that is. Denny's at his lucky poker machine, and since I hear neither cursing nor hollering, I let him be.

"Burger well done with salad, ranch dressing on the side, and he'll have a double cheeseburger, medium, with onion rings and macaroni salad. And a couple more pints."

"You got it," Alice says.

"What was that hail all about?" I say.

"God's way of telling us to listen," Joe says.

Kath is about to hush him, but I flash her a look because I like to hear what people believe.

"You think the hail is a sign?" I ask.

"Everything's a sign," Joe says. "We just don't get close enough to read, or else we ignore the instructions."

I remember helping Denny put together a toolshed. The instruction sheet was poorly translated Chinese and it took the two of us half a day to figure it out. "Maybe the instructions are written in another language," I say. "Like tzara'as."

"Czar who?"

"Tzara'as," I say. "It's a Hebrew word for a diseased soul."

"I don't know about that," Joe says. "I only know what the Good Book tells me."

But whose good book—Joe's, the old man's, or the Hebrews'? Or Bridget Jones's, for that matter. How does anyone know which book to follow?

Denny picks a good time to join us. "You order for me?" he asks.

"What do you think?"

He slides beside me in the booth. "That's my girl," he says, happy.

He doesn't see the things I see, doesn't know I've left him. I look past Denny to the bar and the man who stares back at me. I should feel shame, thinking about Ned even as I sit beside my husband and curse the vows we shared, vows I've renounced a thousand times when nobody was there to witness.

I don't know what I want, just that I don't want this. There's too much tsuris in my life, not enough joy. I signal Alice to hurry up with our refills. Denny rests a hand atop my thigh. With this much beer in him, he's brave enough to risk public rejection and slips an arm around my waist. His nails are thick, pitted, and yellow, scalloped by peeling cuticles. Another symptom of psoriasis. I suck in my breath and hold it inside. Alice takes our glasses, walks them back to the bar. Ned tilts the pints and hits the tap. I hold my breath until Alice returns, and then I gasp and take another. I feel faint. The heat. The beer. Everything. The glasses are sweating.

There's a thunderclap and a sudden hard, steady rain and the air thins and lightens and I find myself jumping to my feet. The bar turns inside out as everyone pushes outside to cool off in the rain. Denny swaggers past to lean over the rail. He tilts his chin to slurp up the new rain. There's a tang of wet mud mixed with alcohol. Cool breezes flit between the raindrops.

Ned sidles up behind me. "What you doing later?" he asks.

Electricity pulses through me, starting with a tingling heat in my crotch and bursting into hot sparks in my belly. I barely manage to stop myself from kissing him here and now. I don't care who sees, except for maybe Denny.

But Denny is drunk and happy and in another world.

This morning, so far away from this night, Denny watched me with a sorrowful expression that should have melted my resolve. Instead, it further hardened my heart. I looked at him as the monster he'd become and in my weakness, let him see my true feelings.

"I'm still me," Denny said.

I didn't believe him then.

Now, I see things as they are. Denny spoke the truth. Dragon or not, he is still the one I married. His transformation is only skin deep. It's my soul that's changed. I've become a monster. Here I stand, alone in a gathering of people who will always be strangers. Unlike Miriam, I cannot be forgiven and return.

Denny stumbles back to the table. He's going to need a ride home. I lean back and whisper into Ned's ear, "Wait for me. I'll be back to help you close up the bar."

Ned grins. He clicks his tongue and turns back. When the rain slows to a steady pour, the rest of us follow him inside. There we eat, gamble, drink, and find whatever merriment we can find before closing down the bar, driving home through fresh mud, and waiting for the sun to rise again and scorch the new day.

The Euonymist

• • •

NEIL WILLIAMSON

CALUM KNEW THERE WAS a word for it. This sick feeling that had been accreting stealthily in his gut since the transport burned down from the orbital and lit in over the North Atlantic; that had formed a discernible kernel over Arran and bubbled up to his chest when they landed. When he set foot on Scottish tarmac again, he felt it tickle his heart in a most unwelcome way. It was like anticipation of something you knew you should be looking forward to but suspected might not turn out the way you wanted at all. Anticipation, yes, and there was an element of leaden fatigue to it too. There was definitely a word. Calum pondered it as the government car shushed him southwards out of Prestwick on the rain-glittered expressway heading down the Ayrshire coast. If anyone should have been able to come up with the name of this feeling, it should have been him, but even with the implants off, his head was still mired in the Lexicon mindset. None of the words that came to him out of the residuals created in his flesh brain by the thousand-language database were quite right.

It was a human feeling. It needed a human word. He was sure it would come to him in time. Now that he was home.

Scotland in July. The lazy, wheeling polka of sun and rain, baking the earth to oven stillness before dousing it with steaming flash showers. Chasing the clouds down past Ayr, heading inland via Maybole, the car's windows were slapped with wet foliage so lush and luminous green that for a disorientating moment Calum could have been back in Ghessareen's island jungles. To stop from thinking about that he mouthed the names of the roadside plants to himself—the thick ferns, the wide-leafed sycamores and chestnuts, the tall, purple foxgloves springing erect, relieved of their burden of water by the car's passing. Calum enjoyed the foursquare precision of the Latin, the quirky, old folksiness of the English. On Ghessareen nothing had a name until he had given it one. Here, it had all been done centuries ago. *Foxglove,* he thought. Whoever it had been that came up with that, they had a sure gift for euonymy. The name fit perfectly. Of course it had originally been "folk's glove," but whoever had decided that the little bell-shaped blossoms might have been used as faerie mittens had created a lasting image. Calum sometimes wondered what it would have been like if the Unification Bloc had come here before humans had evolved language. What would a foxglove have been called then? If the influence of the Integrated Machine Intelligences had been ascendant at that point it would have been something horribly functional like, "flowering-plant-of-average-height: 0.7m-with-many-blossoms-of-hue: 400nm-wavelength." Thank Christ Earth had been overlooked for long enough for uniquely imaginative names like foxglove to rise up, get spread around, and achieve acceptance through established use and their own organic rightness.

"Foxglove." He said it aloud, and the unnamed feeling receded.

Calum looked into the baby's eyes once more, just to be sure. The infant gazed up, yawned in a way that suggested the serenity she had displayed for the last five minutes was about to slip into boredom. He took it as a warning sign. He'd had her long enough anyway.

When Calum opened the door the expectant sotto voce murmur stilled, and the faces of thirty or so extended family and close friends and neighbors all turned his way. En masse they leaned forward an inch or two. The youthful mother—his cousin Donna, who had barely started secondary school when Calum had left Earth—and her equally callow boyfriend beamed like idiots. This was almost as stressful as reporting a naming judgement to the Bloc.

"She looks to me," he said, "like an Ellen."

There was a pause before the predictable chorus of oohs came, followed by a smattering of applause. It had been just a hint of a pause, but it was a familiar one to Calum and it brought the feeling back with a vengeance. It was the pause that happened when no one wanted to react to a new name until they found out what the person it mattered most to thought. A grimace of consternation passed across the baby's features. It matched the look on her mother's face. Calum decided it was a good time to reunite them.

"There you go," he said. "Congratulations."

Donna offered a niggardly smile. "Thanks."

As if seeking to head off an onrushing display of petulant ingratitude, Calum's always harmonious Uncle Dan wedged himself into the picture.

"Well done, Calum, son." He pumped Calum's hand. "We're very grateful." His eyes widened. "Honored, even."

"There's no need really," Calum murmured. "For the family, it's a pleasure."

Through the resuming chatter, and the baby's precursory whimpers, Calum heard Donna whine peevishly to her mother. He matched Uncle Dan's fixed grin with one of his own.

"Honored," Dan repeated. "That a famous . . . er . . ."

"Euonymist," Calum supplied.

"Darling, you can always use it as a middle name." The whole room must have heard his Aunt Geraldine's whisper. The volume of conversation swelled with shared discomfort.

" . . . a famous unanimist . . ." Dan attempted gamely.

"Something classy, I agree . . ." Geraldine soothed.

" . . . should do us the honor of naming our wee Ellen."

"Shaz-nay!" bellowed Donna. "Her name's Shaznay!"

The feeling that Calum had been unable to name filled him completely. The heavy anticipation had blossomed into resigned embarrassment, and in its wake came that universal certainty of disappointment. And by the way that the rest of the onlookers were guzzling their drinks and inspecting the contents of their paper plates, he suspected they shared some of what he felt. He wondered if any of them knew what the feeling was called.

Calum looked around for a diversion but no one was helping him out on this one. Even his mum had vanished. Then an unlikely escape route appeared in the form of an old woman rearing up unsteadily off of one of the kitchen chairs that had been set out to provide extra seating. It was the dress Calum recognised. It was a violently puce floral affair that did nothing to disguise Auntie Bella's uncertain shape—a morphology of bone curvature and body fat redistribution peculiar to Scottish grand dames that Calum had long suspected was due to the accretion of density through years of accumulated nicotine, sarcasm, and fried potato scones. It hadn't happened yet, but with the increased longevity treatments coming out of Earth's trade with the Bloc it was surely only a matter of time before the first Scottish granny turned herself inside out and ended up as a kind of greasy black hole. All that would be left would be a set of false teeth, a pair of wrinkly tights, and a box of After Eight mints filled with empty wrappers.

"Whit's he cried the bairn then?" Auntie Bella's croaky caw had once engendered terror in all of Calum's cousins, seeing as it was usually followed by a smack on the legs or, worse, a flabby kiss. Now, however, it was more than welcome.

"She's called Shaznay." Donna's tone defied anyone to disagree.

Bella wobbled closer, peered at the increasingly fractious infant. "Shaznay?" she said. "Whit's that, Shaznay? Wha's cried Shaznay? Lookit thon face? Dis that resemmle a Shaznay to you?"

"Actually, the name was Ellen." Calum's mother had reappeared at the living room door. Better late than never. He made a mental note to thank her for her support later.

Bella regarded the baby again. "Aye, Ellen'd be fair eneuch, hen. Yer mither's got a second cuisin in Canada cawd Ellen."

"I have?" said a surprised Geraldine.

At that moment baby Shaznay/Ellen, or whatever she would eventually be known as when she was old enough to choose for herself, decided that enough was enough and began to scream.

"Aye, and she was a greeter an aw," finished Bella, turning her attention to a plate of hot sausage rolls.

Calum sat on the garden bench with his mother. Even at the end of the long-stretched summer evening, with the stars beginning to show in the deepening sky, it was still quite warm enough to sit out. If you didn't mind the midges. A cloud of them spun like a slow tornado around the nearby flowerbeds. There was another perfect euonym. The word just encapsulated the infuriating quality of the tiny insect; and it could be utilized as satisfying invective if the need arose.

"Midges." Calum smiled, then slapped his hand against his arm. "Wee bastards."

His mother smiled with him. "Thanks for doing that today," she said. "Pay no mind to Geraldine and Donna. They may not stick with the name you gave them, but they'll take the prestige that comes with it."

Calum shrugged. "I name planets for a living. What did they expect?"

The midge-cloud had gyrated above the roses, lingering there over the creamy, pinky, yellowy blossoms. Strange behavior. Usually they headed straight for him, but he'd only been pestered by a couple of stray ones so far. Something about the rosebeds was apparently more interesting than him tonight. He wondered if it was the perfume. Did midges have a sense of smell, or was that the insects on Yrrow he was thinking of?

"You were the model of diplomacy," his mother said.

Calum laughed. "I've played to tougher audiences."

"You always had a way with words, though. Ever since—"

"Ever since I was four years old, when I looked at myself in the mirror for a whole hour and then told you I wasn't to be called Brian anymore because my name should really be Calum. I remember."

"And when we told you not to be so silly, you screamed the place down."

The midges had moved on to the big rhododendron in the garden's back corner. His mother got up from the bench and approached the roses, slipping a pair of secateurs out of her cardigan pocket as she knelt by the bed. "I hope young Shaznay has a similar moment of self-determination when she . . . oh."

"What is it?" When his mother didn't answer, Calum went over to see.

"I don't know," she said. "I've never seen anything like this before." She leaned back to let him see.

At first Calum thought it was just a stray shoot. Some sort of weed, no more than three inches tall, dwarfed among the tall rose stems, but with spiky looking stiletto leaves to rival its neighbors' thorns. Then he saw the way it gleamed in the last of the sunlight, flaky amber on silver like rusted steel.

His insides lurched. He had a very bad feeling about this. Much worse than the unnamed one. This one was the cast-iron cannonball of dread.

• • •

When Calum came back into the house his mother had turned the kitchen into a research center. A stack of discarded gardening books surrounded her at the table where she had unrolled a screen and an interface to search the web for more exotic specimens. She tapped awkwardly at the flat keyboard. The lacerated gardening glove and blunted secateurs lay beside the screen. The end of her bandaged thumb was turning pink again.

"Nothing yet?" Calum asked, in hope rather than expectation. He wanted her to find it, but he was becoming increasingly certain that she would not. A viciously bladed bio-metallic organism like that. Not in all the botanical lists on this Earth. He sneaked a glance at the readout of his analyzer. Please wait, it read. It would take longer to consult the vast botanical databases of the Bloc, of course, and while discovering a known extro species in his mum's back garden carried with it a number of unpleasant implications, it would still be preferable to not finding anything at all. He hadn't turned on the Lexicon implants. That would come later, when all else had failed.

Calum looked out the window. It was too dark to see it now, but he could feel it out there, a problem growing with every minute that passed. It hadn't been there when his mother had been out that afternoon shortly before he arrived, she had assured him—and he believed her; gardeners had an eye for these things—which meant that it had grown four inches in a few hours. Which really wasn't a good thing at all.

Calum checked his analyzer before he went to bed. Please wait. He knew he didn't have to wait. He was pretty sure what the answer would be anyway, so he could act now—should act now—but given the option, he waited.

They started arriving not long after dawn. Calum woke to a gabble of voices, the kind of squabble that universally signified opposing vested interests. He checked his watch, his phone, the analyzer: 0512, seven missed calls, no species match. The unnamed feeling woke too. It shifted inside him like slipping sand.

Calum got up, pulled on some clothes, then, reluctantly, subvoxed a command that engaged the Lexicon implants.

The scene in the kitchen was chaotic. An auditory nightmare that his translator implants would have approached meltdown to make sense of. Fortunately, he had neglected to turn them on as well. Best just to leave it that way for now. That the majority of the yabbering occupants were human was something of a relief, but Calum immediately spotted representatives of at least three other Bloc races. A Peloquin pair were haranguing a black woman with a placatory attitude and a very expensive-looking suit. Earth-Bloc liaison, Calum decided. She could handle it. A breeze of movement and a purplish blur in the air in front of him told him there were Tage here too. He unfocused his gaze for a moment and saw it clearer, a vague indigo outline. A noise like a jar of wasps—a big jar. It was agitated about something. Calum shrugged, tapped his ear to show he didn't understand, and the Tage buzzed angrily and moved on. The third species he recognised was a tall, butter-skinned Uidean. That was encouraging. If this panned out as he feared, Earth was going to need all of their friends on their side. For now, though, the unfortunate sod had been cornered by Aunt Bella.

"Is sumbdy puttin the kettle on or no? I'm awfy drouthie, so I am," she told it.

The confused-looking extro was tapping the side of his head nervously, but Aunt Bella didn't seem to understand the signal. Calum thought about rescuing it, but the Uideans were seasoned diplomats. They'd surely faced worse—though perhaps not stranger—than Bella. Besides, there was activity in the garden that demanded his attendance.

There were maybe half a dozen people standing around—or in—the rosebed, which itself was now covered in heavy plastic sheeting. Calum's mother stood to one side in her dressing gown and slippers talking to a rumpled-looking man in a hairy suit. Calum would have recognized his boss from his posture alone.

"Good to see you, Clarence," he said. From the center of the group clustered around the roses came sounds of exertion and a metallic grating that made Calum think of sharpening knives.

Sneijder turned, and he didn't look happy, but then he rarely did. "You should have notified us."

"I followed procedure," Calum replied calmly. "Species discovered in prenomenclatured areas have to be cross-referenced with both local and Lexicon lists."

The Dutchman's lip curled. "Calum, you understand, don't you, the implications if this turns out to be a completely new species? You should have notified us straightaway. God, for containment and assessment, if nothing else."

Calum felt the feeling shift inside him again. He could almost hear the sighing of the slipping sand. One of the workers stepped to the side, revealing that the plant had already erupted into a dense bush as tall as his chest, sprouting fists of blade-leaves in all directions. One of the other workers did something that set the whole thing quivering with a noise like an emptying cutlery drawer. "Bloody . . . thing," the worker tailed off, at a loss for a suitable epithet. Then, examining his steel mail gloves for damage, he told someone to fetch the torch.

"All the more reason for following procedure," Calum told Sneijder. "Given the political ramifications, people will be examining every step of the process. We've got to be aboveboard all the way." This was true, but what was truer was that he'd suspected that he knew what was going on from the moment he saw the plant, and he'd wanted to postpone all of this as long as possible. If there was a contamination risk, the botanical one at least wasn't unmanageable. At least he'd got a decent night's sleep out of it.

"All right, what's done is done," Sneijder came closer. "But I need to ask you about Ghessareen."

Calum had thought he might. "What about it?"

"Well, specifically the quarantine procedures?" Sneijder said. "Is there any chance at all—"

"That I could have brought something back with me?" Calum sighed. "Well, let's see. They pulled us off Ghessareen with the job half done and no explanation, and replaced us with an inexperienced team of Bellussibellom. Then they quibbled about just about every item in our necessarily incomplete report, rendering any information about any of the catalogued species confused to the point of useless. And even though they made us go through the decontamination procedure three times before they let us leave the station, virtually everything on the Ghessareen orbital just happened to be glitching from a suspected virus that they never did track down. So, in short, yes, it's possible that I brought something back with me that wasn't killed dead like it should have been. It would certainly be one explanation for how this thing ended up in my mother's garden."

Sneijder's nose wrinkled in disgust. He might have known what the problem was with the Ghessareen survey, but he wasn't going to let on.

Calum wasn't going to let being kept in the dark about it upset him. "Look, there are plants not a million miles away from this in the northern archipelagos. Similar, but not the same. The plants that grow on Ghessareen wouldn't survive our alkaline soil, let alone flourish like this. This is totally new." He looked at Sneijder to see if he had caught the subtext.

The Dutchman arched a bushy brow, lowered his voice. "Mutation?"

"Almost certainly."

"Natural or engineered?"

"I'm not a botanist, Clarence, but given the source of the naming assignation that we used on Ghessareen . . ."

"I'm not going to like this, am I?"

"Peloquin."

"Fuck," Sneijder spat. "Fuck, fuck, fuck! I thought they were pretty quick to get out here."

"Exactly." This time Sneijder sighed with him.

"I'm going to have to get guidance from the diplomats on this," he said at length. "I shouldn't do this because of your involvement, but none of the others can get here sooner than a week, so I'm officially appointing you the case euonymist. But do me a favor. Don't go making any promises until you hear from me."

"No fear on that score," Calum said. "I'm going back to bed."

It turned out to be the best thing he could have done. Not only did it give him the chance to rest, but it also insulated him from having to actually interact with the various Bloc representatives who were still crowding the house. He didn't sleep, just lay there in the darkened room, staring at what had been his childhood bedroom walls. There beside the closet there had been an RSPB poster showing a montage of British garden birds, and he had memorized every one of them by the age of ten, spellbound by the names. Finches: chaffinch, bullfinch, goldfinch, greenfinch, crossbill, linnet, yellowhammer. . . . Yellowhammer. There was a euonym if ever there was one. Surrounded by names like those, it was little wonder that he'd found himself suited to a career in euonymy. If only there had turned out to be more naming and less strenuous diplomacy involved in the job, it would have been perfect.

Calum engaged his translator implant and listened in to the discussions still going on in the kitchen. Not surprisingly, the Peloquin pair were trying every trick in the book to get an audience with him, but the liaison Sneijder had left behind did a fine job of stonewalling. Eventually it was his mother who brought peace to the house by turfing them all out.

A quiet knock on the bedroom door.

"Can I come in?" It reminded him of when he was a teenager, made him smile.

"Of course," he said.

His mother sat on the end of the bed. "Is it always like this in your job?"

He nodded, shrugged. "Can be," he said. "Cultural imperialism is a big deal. There's a lot of prestige awarded when one race's languages are used for naming over another, and it can all get a bit heated. There have been wars fought over the naming of a new planet, civilizations wiped out. In fact, it's one of the reasons the Bloc exists. It was originally set up to ensure fairness, and encourage harmony and trade, but in lieu of conflict the various races have developed internecine one-upmanship to a fine art. My job is to ensure that all of the languages in the Lexicon are represented equally while at the same time apportioning a name that is apt."

"Sounds like a bit of a juggling act," his mother said.

"Mostly, it's close to impossible," he replied. "There's so much diplomatic bartering involved that your newly discovered planetary system ends up with a nomenclature comprising a hundred different languages. It's a mess."

"How do you decide which languages to use then?"

"We cross-reference terrain, flora, fauna, weather types—a whole bunch of criteria—and derive the names from the things that we already have names for. The Lexicon provides a ballpark and we go with that. The races whose languages are used gain a little extra cultural clout in the world in question." He sighed. "Which is why discovering a plant on Earth that resembles a species we have just named using a Peloquin language is a problem."

"Why?"

"If we use the same nomenclature, it gives them the first non-human cultural claim on Earth."

"That doesn't seem very fair. They don't let people name the plants that are grown in their own gardens?"

"Existing species are fine, they've already got names. And if contact had been yesterday, before we were adopted into the Bloc, we could have used any language we liked to name this thing. But on a Bloc world any newly discovered species has to be named using the Lexicon. And all of Earth's living languages—English, Mandarin, Spanish, German, all the way down to Gaelic and Swahili, everything that's taught in schools—are in the Lexicon. And they know this."

His mother looked shocked. "You think all of this is deliberate?" She whispered it as if she might be overheard.

"I'd bet on it," Calum muttered. "Of course we can't prove that I didn't bring back some germ with me from Ghessareen. That whole operation was such a mess that I'm not even certain of that myself. I'd be surprised if they don't conveniently provide a very clear trail of evidence to prove it. So I'm afraid they've succeeded. There's nothing we can do."

It was lunchtime when the call came through. Sneijder, who had smartened himself up in the intervening time, was back on the orbital. Calum recognized a canteen that had been turned into a makeshift hearing chamber. The Bloc representatives could be seen assembled in the background of the picture.

Calum had set his phone up to take in both his and his mother's deckchairs and the susurrating rust-silver tree that now overhung the corner of the garden.

"Calum, you've had time to consult the Lexicon. The representatives are eager to hear your judgement," Sneijder said. He fidgeted. "I should advise you that this call is being broadcast to the United Nations." He looked like he wanted to say more, but in the end didn't. The fact that Calum hadn't heard from Sneijder before this just meant that their hands were tied diplomatically as surely as they had been euonymically.

Calum straightened himself in his chair. "Yes, indeed," he said. He had spent the last few hours trawling all of the languages in the Lexicon for an alternative. Sneijder's silence confirmed what he already knew. That there were none. There was a clear path of semblance and antecedence. No matter what tack he took, the Lexicon always brought him round to using the Peloquin naming.

Calum looked squarely into the phone's little screen. The human contingent looked nervous, the Peloquin looked eager—but then they always did. He had delivered naming judgements to similar groups many times, and while some of those occasions had been fraught with complicated layers of vested interests, he had never felt so personally responsible before. In this moment he decided that he'd had enough. He'd perform this one last naming and later he'd call Sneijder and resign. The job had so little to do with an ability with names that there had been little or no satisfaction in it for him for years.

"Oh aye, that's it is it? Loonging aboot, ye docksie pair, when I'm after my twaloors. What's all this oancairy onywey?" Aunt Bella's timing could not have been better. Calum's mum sprang to her feet to turn the old woman around and fix her something to eat in the kitchen, but Bella had already covered the ground between them.

"Calum, who is that woman?" It was Sneijder's voice, but the phone's screen was blocked by Bella's stout frame. "I can't make out a word she is saying."

"Aye, well?" Bella said, either ignoring or not hearing Sneijder. "Brian, son, you look awfy peelie-wallie. You maun be scunnered with all the palaiver that's been ongaun the day."

Calum looked at Bella with wonder. That was the word. Scunnered.

"Calum?"

That was the euonym for the feeling he had been trying to name since Ghessareen. Scunnered. In fact, pure scunnered. He'd not heard that word in years. Like most Scots words, it was essentially dead in linguistic terms. The old language, a historical victim of wave after wave of cultural erosion, had been steadily supplanted over generations with Anglicisms, Americanisms, Euroisms and most recently the backwash of intergalactic contact. Only the eldest in the rural areas still used it, spoke it, thought in it. Calum had been steeped in the Lexicon so long he had almost forgotten it existed. A few of the words had been absorbed into English, but never having been ratified as an official language in its own right, the Scots tongue had never made it into the Lexicon.

"Calum, if you can sort out the domestic business as soon as possible." Sneijder didn't try to hide the sarcasm. "The representatives are waiting."

Calum reached around Bella, spoke to the screen. "I'll call you right back." Then he took his elderly relative by the hand and led her gently to the knife tree.

"Bella, how long have you lived around here?" he asked.

"All my puff," she replied, looked at him sidelong. "How?"

Calum grinned. "I think you just might be about to save the planet," he said. "See this here? We're having a lot of trouble with it." He indicated the tree. "What would you call it?" In your native language, that's not in the Lexicon.

She peered at the plant, slowly from its impenetrable roots right up to its branches and the deadly hanging blades of its leaves, twanged a steely twig with her finger. "Aye it's a scunner for sure," she declared at length. "You should howk it out and chuck it on the midden."

"A scunner, is it?" he asked, seeking confirmation.

"Aye, a scunner right enough." That said, Bella turned to Calum's mother. "Now, Magret, I'm hauf stairved, here."

"A scunner it is then," Calum said to himself, and picked up the phone. They weren't going to be happy about the use of a local language not in the Lexicon. In fact they'd be arguing about the legality of it for years. And by the time they sorted it out it'd be someone else's problem.

Now he'd made the decision he knew it was the right one. And now the feeling was gone, he was aware that it'd been with him for a lot longer than he'd realized. Before coming home, before Ghessareen even. A long time . . .

Scunnered.

He knew there had been a word for it.

Singing of Mount Abora

● ● ●

THEODORA GOSS

A HUNDRED YEARS AGO, the blind instrument-maker known as Alem Das, or Alem the Master, made a dulcimer whose sound was sweeter, more passionate, and more filled with longing than any instrument that had ever been made. It was carved entirely from the wood of an almond tree that had grown in the garden of Al Meseret, that palace with a thousand rooms where the Empress Nasren had chosen to spend her widowhood. The doors of the palace were shaped like moons, its windows like stars. It was a palace of night, and every night the Empress walked through its thousand rooms, wearing the veil she had worn for her wedding to the Great Khan. If the cooks, who sometimes saw her wandering through the kitchen, had not known who she was, they would have mistaken her for a ghost. The dulcimer was strung with the whiskers of the Cloud Dragon, who wreaths his body around the slopes of Mount Abora. He can always be found there in the early morning, and that is when Alem Das approached him, walking up the path on the arm of his niece Kamora.

"What do you want?" asked the dragon.

"Your whiskers, luminous one," said Alem Das.

"My whiskers! You must be that instrument-maker. I've heard of you. You're the reason my cousin, the River Dragon, no longer has spines along his back, and why my other cousin, the Phoenix, no longer has tail feathers. Why should I give you my whiskers?"

"Because when I have made my dulcimer, my niece Kamora will come and play for you, and sing to you the secrets of your soul," said Alem Das.

"We dragons have no souls," said the Cloud Dragon, wreathing himself around and around, like a cat.

"You dragons are souls," said Alem Das, and he asked his niece to sing one of the songs that she sang at night, to soothe the Empress Nasren. Kamora sang, and the Cloud Dragon stopped wreathing himself around and around. Instead, he lay at her feet, which disappeared into mist. When she was done, he said, "All right, instrument-maker. You may have my whiskers, but on one condition. First, your niece Kamora must marry me. And when you have made your dulcimer, she must sing to me every night the secrets of my soul."

Kamora knew how the Cloud Dragon looked at night, when he took the form of a man, so she said, "I will marry you, if my Empress allows it." And that is my first song.

You can't imagine how cold Boston is in winter, not for someone from a considerably warmer climate. In my apartment, I sat as close as I could to the radiator, sometimes with my back against it. The library at the university was warmer, but the chairs were wooden and hard, so it was a compromise: the comforts of my apartment, where I had to wrap my fingers around incessant cups of chamomile tea to warm them, or the warmth and discomfort of the library. I had been born in Abyssinia, which is now Ethiopia, and had been brought up in so many places that they seemed no place at all, Italy and France and Spain. Finally, I had come to cold, shining North America, where the universities, I told my mother, were the best in the world. And the best of the best universities were in Boston.

My mother was beautiful. I should say rather that she was a beauty, for to her, beauty was not a quality but a state of being. Beauty was her art, her profession. I don't mean that she was anything as vulgar as a model, or even an actress. No, she was simply beautiful, and so life gave her what it gives the beautiful: apartments in Italy, France, and Spain, and an airplane to travel between them, and a diamond called the Robin's Egg, because it was as big as a robin's egg, and as blue.

"Oh, Sabra," she would say to me, "what will we do about you? You look exactly like your father." And it was true. In old photographs, I saw my nose, the bones of my cheeks and jaws, on a man who had not needed to be handsome, because he was rich. But his riches had not saved his life. Although he could have bought his way out of the revolution, he had remained loyal to the Emperor. He had died when his airplane was shot down, with the Emperor in it, just before crossing the border. This was after the Generals had taken power and the border had been closed. My mother and I were already on our way to Italy, with the Robin's Egg in her brassiere. "Loyalty is nothing," my mother would say. "If your father had been more sensible, he would still be with us. Loyalty is a breath. It is not worth the ring on my finger."

"But he had courage," I said. "Did he not have courage?"

"Courage, of course. He was, after all, my husband. But it is better to have diamonds."

Her beauty gave her ruthless practicality an indescribable charm.

"You are like him, Sabra. Always with your head in the clouds. When are you going to get married? When are you going to live properly?" She thought it was foolish that I insisted on living on my stipend, but she approved of my studying literature, which was a decorative discipline. "That Samuel Coleridge whose poem you read to me," she would say, "I am convinced he must have been a handsome man."

I insisted on providing for myself, and living in a city that was too cold for her, because it kept me from feeling the enchantment that she threw over everything around her. She was an enchantress without intention, as a spider gathers flies by instinct. One longed to be in her web. In her presence, one could not help loving her, without judgement. And I was proud of my independence, if of nothing else.

Let me sing about the marriage of Kamora and the Cloud Dragon. Among all the maidens of the Empress Nasren, there was none so clever as Kamora. She knew every song that had ever been sung, since the world was made. When she sang, she could draw the nightingales into the Empress's garden, where they would sit on the branches of the almond trees and sing accompaniment. Each night she followed the Empress through the thousand rooms of the palace, singing her songs. Only Kamora could soothe the Empress when Nasren sank down on the courtyard stones and wept into her hands with the wild abandon of a storm.

On the night after Alem Das had visited the Cloud Dragon, Kamora said to the Empress, "Lady, whose face is as bright as the moon, there is nothing more wonderful in the world than serving you, except for marrying the one I love. And you know this is true, because you have known the delights of such a marriage."

The Empress, who sat in a chair that Alem Das had carved for her from the horns of Leviathan, stood suddenly, so that the chair fell back, and a figure of Noah broke off from one corner. "Kamora, would you too leave me, as the Great Khan left me to wander among the stars? Some night, it may be this night, he will come back to me. But until that night, you must not leave me!" And she stared at Kamora with eyes that were apprehensive, and a little mad.

"Lady, whose eyes are as dark as the night," said Kamora, in her most soothing voice, "you know that the Great Khan lies in his tomb on Mount Abora. You built it yourself of white marble, stone on stone, and before you placed the last stone, you kissed his lips. Do you think that your husband would leave the bed you made for him? You would not keep me from marrying the one I love."

The Empress turned and walked, out of that room and into another, and another, and through all the thousand rooms of the palace. Kamora followed her, not singing tonight, but silent. When the Empress had reached the last room of the palace, a pantry in which the head cook kept her rose-petal jam, she said, "Very well. You may marry your Cloud Dragon. Do not look surprised that I know whom you love. I am not so insensible as all that. But first, you must complete one task for me. When you have completed it, then you may marry whom you please."

"What is that task?" asked Kamora.

"You must find me someone who amuses me more than you do."

It was Michael who introduced me to Coleridge. "Listen to this," he said.

> "In Xanadu did Kubla Khan
> A stately pleasure-dome decree:
> Where Alph, the sacred river, ran
> Through caverns measureless to man
> Down to a sunless sea."

"I can't believe you've never read it before. I mean, I learned that in high school."

"Who is this Michael Cavuto you keep talking about?" asked my mother over the telephone. "Where does he come from?"

"Ohio," I said.

She was as silent as though I had said, "The surface of the moon."

We were teaching assistants together, for a class on the Romantics. We read sentences to each other from our students' papers. "A nightingale is a bird that comes out at night to which Keats has written an ode." "William and his wife Dorothy lived together for many years until she died and left him lamenting." "Coleridge smoked a lot of opium, which explains a lot." We laughed, and marked our papers together, and one day, when we were both sitting in the library, making up essay questions for the final exam, we started talking about our families.

"Yours is much more interesting than mine," he told me. "I'd like to meet your mother."

You never will, I told myself. I liked him, with his spiky hair that stood up although he was always trying to gel it down, the angular bones that made him look graceless, as though his joints were not quite knit together, and his humor. I did not want him, too, to fall hopelessly in love. For goodness' sake, the woman was fifty-four. She was in Italy again, with a British rock star. He was twenty-seven. They had been together for two years. I could tell that she was already beginning to get bored.

"There's no one like Coleridge," Michael had said. "You'll see."

I have told you that Kamora was clever. Listen to how clever she was. She said to the Empress, "I will bring you what you ask for,

but you must give me a month to find it, and a knapsack filled
with bread and cheese and dried apricots, and a jar of honey."

"Very well," said the Empress. "You shall have all these
things, although I will miss you, Kamora. But at the end of that
month you will return to me, won't you?"

"If at the end of that month I have not found someone who
amuses you more than I do, then I will return to you, and remain with you as long as you wish," said Kamora.

The Empress said, "Now I can sleep, because I know you will
remain with me forever."

The next day, Kamora put her knapsack on her back. "I wish
you luck, I do," said the head cook. "It can't be easy, spending
every night with Her Craziness upstairs. Though why you
would want to marry a dragon is beyond me."

Kamora smiled but did not answer. Then she turned and
walked through the palace gates, chewing a dried apricot.

First, Kamora went to the house of her uncle Alem Das,
which was built against the wall that surrounded the palace. She
found him sitting on the stone floor, carving a bird for the
youngest daughter of the River Dragon. When you wound it
with a key, it could sing by itself. "Uncle," she said, "they call me
clever, but I know that you are more clever than I am. You talked
the horns off Leviathan, and once Bilkis, the sun herself, gave
you three of her shining hairs. Who can amuse the Empress
more than I can?"

Alem Das sat and thought. Kamora was his favorite niece,
and he did not want to disappoint her. "You might bring her the
Laughing Hound, who dances on his hind legs, and rides a don-
key, and tells jokes all day long, or the Tree of Tales, whose
leaves whisper all the secrets that men do not wish to reveal. But
she would eventually tire of these. You, my dear, can sing all the
songs that were ever sung. If she tires of a song, you can sing her
another. If she is sad, you can comb her hair with the comb I
carved for you, and cover her with a blanket, and sit by her

until she has fallen asleep. It will be difficult to find anyone as amusing as you are."

Kamora sighed. "I hoped that you could help me. Oh, Uncle," and for the first time she did not sound perfectly confident, "I do love him, you know."

"I'm not clever enough to help you," said Alem Das, "but I know who is. Kamora, I will tell you a secret. If you climb to the top of Mount Abora, even higher than the Cloud Dragon, you will find the Stone Woman. She is the oldest of all things, and I think she will be able to help you. But you must tell no one where she lives, and allow no one to follow you, because she values her privacy. If it grows dark, take out the tail feather of the Phoenix, which I gave you for your fourteenth birthday. It will light your way up the mountain."

Kamora said, "But uncle, why should the Stone Woman help me?"

"Take this drum," said Alem Das. "I made it from the skin that the Sea Serpent sheds once a year. The Stone Woman is old, and the old always like a present."

"Thank you, Uncle," said Kamora, kissing him on both cheeks. "There truly is no one in the world as clever as you."

Kamora walked through the village, chewing a dried apricot. She walked over the hills, to the foot of Mount Abora. At the foot of the mountain, where the climb begins in earnest, she picked a handful of lilies, which grow by the streams that flow down the mountain to become the Alph. She left them at the tomb of the Great Khan, who had given her sugared almonds when she was a girl. Then she began to climb the path up the mountain. Halfway up, Kamora ate her lunch, bread and cheese and dried apricots. She washed her hands in one of the streams, put her knapsack on her back, and continued to climb. Near the top, she stopped to see the Cloud Dragon and tell him the Empress's condition.

"Well, good luck to you," he said. "If you were anyone else, I would be certain that you would fail, but I've been told that you're almost as clever as your uncle."

"I will not fail," said Kamora, and she gave him a look that made him break into puffs that flew every which way over the mountain. *And this is the woman I'm going to marry?* he thought. *What have I gotten myself into?*

In his house by the palace wall, Alem Das thought about his niece and smiled. He said to himself, "Sometimes she is too clever, that girl. First she asked for one of the Phoenix's tail feathers, then for a comb carved from the shell of the Great Turtle. And now I've given her my drum. Does she really think she's tricked me? Oh, Kamora! It's certainly time you got married."

I'm not sure when we started dating. There was a gradual progression between friend and boyfriend. We were comfortable together, we seemed to fit together like two pieces of a puzzle. But a puzzle that showed what picture? I did not know.

It was a Friday. I remember because we had just turned back a set of graded papers. I was still taking classes, and for my own class on the Romantics, taught by the same professor for whom I was TAing, I had decided to write a final paper on Coleridge. *This will be easy,* I thought. *Michael and I have talked about him so often.*

I was in my apartment. It was cold. It felt like a cave of ice.

And suddenly, I was there.

The Kubla Khan of Coleridge's poem is not the historical Kubla Khan, founder of the Yuan Dynasty, and Xanadu is not Shangdu. Both are dreams or hallucinations. Indeed, if we examine Coleridge's description of the palace itself, we notice that it does not make sense. Here, the river Alph, fed by the streams that flow down Mount Abora, does something strange: it disappears into a series of fissures in the ground, flowing through them until it comes to an underground lake. Coleridge's identification of this lake as a "sunless sea" or "lifeless ocean" is certainly poetic exaggeration, as my experience will show.

The palace itself is situated where the river disappears, so that seen from one side, it seems to sit on the river itself. Seen from the other, it is surrounded by an extensive garden, where the Khan has collected specimens from all the fantastical countries, plants from lost Atlantis and Hyperborea and Thule. The palace is built of stone, and rises out of the stone beneath it, so that an outcropping will suddenly turn into a wall. Although Coleridge describes "caves of ice," this is again a poetic exaggeration. He means that since the palace is built of stone, even in summer the rooms are cold, so cold. I was always cold in that palace, as long as I was there.

It was empty. There were silk cushions on the floor, embroidered with dragons and orange trees, but no one to sit on them. There were tables inlaid with tulips and gazelles and chessboards, but no one to play. The curtains that hung in the doorways, filtering the sunlight, rose and fell with the breath of the river. But there was no other breath, and no noise other than a ceaseless rushing as the river swept through the caves below. As I walked, my steps sounded hollow, and I knew that the floors hung over rushing water and empty space. As an architectural feat, the Khan's palace is impossible.

There was water everywhere, in pools where ornamental fish swam, dappled white and orange and black, and basins in which the inhabitants, if there were any, would have washed their hands. The air had the clean, curiously empty smell of sunlight and water.

"I have looked. There is no one but ourselves."

He was dressed as you might expect, in breeches and a waistcoat over a linen shirt which seemed too large for him. He had thick brown hair, and a thin, inquisitive face, and his hands moved nervously. The young poet, already an addict.

I was not sure how to respond. "Have you been here long?"

"Several hours, and I confess that I'm beginning to feel hungry. Surely there is a kitchen? Shall we attempt to find it?"

The kitchen was empty as well, but the pantry was full. We ate sugared almonds, and a sweet cheese studded with raisins, and dried fish that was better than it looked. We drank a wine that tasted like honey.

"Sabra is a pretty name," he said. "Mine is Samuel, not so pretty, you see, but then I'm not as pretty as you." He wiped the corner of his mouth with a handkerchief. "Here we are, Samuel and Sabra, in the palace of the Khan. Where is the Khan, I wonder? Is he out hunting, or in another of his palaces? Perhaps when he returns he will execute us for being here. Have you thought of that, Sabra? We are, after all, trespassers."

"I don't know," I said. "I don't feel like a trespasser. And anyway, he isn't here now."

"That is true," he said. "Would you like the last of the almonds? I've never much cared for almonds." He leaned back against a cushion, his hair spread out over an apricot tree in bloom, with a phoenix in its boughs. "Will you sing to me, Sabra? I am tired, and I feel that I have been speaking inanities. There is an instrument, on that table. Can you play it, do you think?"

"Yes," I said, and picked up the instrument: a dulcimer. While my friends in school were at soccer practice, I was learning to play the dulcimer. It was another of my mother's charming impracticalities.

"Then sing me something, won't you, pretty Sabra? I'm so tired, and my head aches, I don't know why."

So I put away the last of the sugared almonds, picked up the dulcimer, and began to sing.

Kamora could feel blisters forming where her sandals rubbed against her feet, but she climbed steadily. It was late afternoon, and the sun was already sinking into the west, when she reached the summit. The Stone Woman was waiting for her. She was wrapped in a grey shawl and hunched over with age, so that she looked like a part of the mountain itself.

"Back again, are you? And did you ever find your own true love, the one whose face you saw in my mirror?"

"I found him, lady who is wiser than the stars," said Kamora. "But now I have to win him."

"None of your flattery for me, girl," said the Stone Woman. "I know exactly how wise I am. What are you going to give me for my help?"

Kamora took the drum out of her knapsack.

The Stone Woman looked at it appreciatively. "Ah, this is better than that other stuff you gave me. Although the tail feather of the Phoenix, which you gave me for teaching you all the songs that have ever been sung, burns all night long, so I can weave my tapestries. And every morning I use the comb made from the shell of the Great Turtle, which you gave me for showing you the Cloud Dragon in my mirror, and my hair never tangles." She ran one hand over her braid of grey hair, which was so long that it touched the ground. "But this!" She tapped the drum once with her finger, and Kamora heard a reverberation, not only from the drum itself, but from the stones around her, the scrubby cedars, bent by the wind, and even the air. It seemed to echo over the forested slopes of the mountain, and the hills below, on which she could see the tomb of the Great Khan, as white as the rising moon, and the plains stretching away into the distance.

"What is it?" asked Kamora.

"Your uncle didn't tell you? That sound is the beat of the world, which governs everything, even the beating of your heart, and on this drum I can play it slower or faster, more sadly or more joyfully. No one can make an instrument like your uncle Alem, but I think this is his masterpiece. No wonder he wanted you to bring it to me. I'm the only one in whose hands it is perfectly safe. Think, girl, what would a man do who could alter the beat of the world? And by getting you to carry it, he saved himself a trip up the mountain! He is a clever man, your uncle. Now, it's dinnertime, and I'm hungry. Have you brought me any food?"

Kamora took out the honey, of which she knew the Stone Woman was inordinately fond.

"Good girl. Well, come inside, then, and tell me what you want this time."

The walls of the Stone Woman's cave were covered with tapestries. On one you could see the creation of the world by Lilit, and her marriage to the Sea Serpent, in which she wore a veil of stars. On another you could see the flood that resulted from their thrashing when they lay together, so that many of the first creatures she had created, the great dragons with horns like Leviathan's and eyes like rubies and emeralds, and the great turtles that carried mountains and even small lakes on their backs, were drowned. The whole history of the world was there, and on a panel that Kamora had not seen before, she saw Mount Abora, and the marriage of the Empress Nasren, the oldest daughter of the River Dragon, to the Great Khan, with the apricot trees on the mountain blooming around them.

The Stone Woman sat on a cushion and opened the honeypot. She dipped a wooden spoon into it, tasted the honey, and licked her lips. "Very good, very good. Well, what do you want this time?"

Kamora knew that it was time to be, not clever, but direct. "The Empress, whose hands move like doves, will not let me marry until I have brought her someone who amuses her more than I do."

"So that's how it is," said the Stone Woman. "You can't marry your Cloud Dragon until she lets you, and she won't let you until she has found a substitute. You have been too clever, Kamora. When you asked me to teach you all the songs that have ever been sung, so the Empress would choose you as one of her maidens, to serve her and live in the palace, did you consider that she might want to keep you forever? Getting what you wish for isn't always a good thing, you know."

"If I had not learned all the songs that have ever been sung," said Kamora, "the Cloud Dragon would not have wanted to marry me. And I love him, I can't help loving him, since I saw how he looks at night, when he is a man. Perhaps I should not have looked in your mirror and asked to see my own true love, but when I saw how happy the Empress was with the Great Khan . . ." A tear slid down her cheek, and she wiped it away with her hand.

"Ah, clever Kamora! So you wanted to love and be loved. You have a heart after all," said the Stone Woman. "Just remember that cleverness is not enough to keep a husband, not even the Cloud Dragon, who is less clever than you are. You must show him your heart as well. I warned him about choosing such a clever wife! But how do you expect me to help you?"

Kamora said, "I thought about that, when I walked through the thousand rooms of the palace at night with the Empress. What is more amusing than a person who knows all the songs that have ever been sung? Only a person who can create new songs. Only a poet."

"If you know the answer yourself," said the Stone Woman, "why do you need me?"

"Because I need you to make me a poet. Not one of those poets who sit in the marketplace, selling rhymes so that soldiers, and anyone with a silver coin, can sing them to the Empress's maidens—out of tune! I need a true poet, who can write what has never been sung before."

"A poet?" asked the Stone Woman. "And how do you expect me to make you a poet?"

"In the same way you made the world, Lilit."

Kamora and the Stone Woman stared at each other. Finally the Stone Woman said, "You are as clever as your uncle. How did you know who I was?"

Kamora smiled. "Who else would know all the songs that

have ever been sung? Who else would keep the Mirror of Truth in a cave on Mount Abora? And when the Great Khan was laid in his tomb, the Empress put honey on his lips so you would kiss them when he entered the land of the dead. Even songs from the making of the world mention how fond you are of honey. You have created the Sea Serpent, the Lion of the Sun who carries Bilkis on his back, and whose walk across the sky warms the earth, the Silver Stag who summons men to the land of the dead—only you can make a poet."

"Very well," said the Stone Woman. "I will make you a poet, Kamora. But only because I like you. And this is my wedding gift, and the last thing I will do for you. You have had three gifts from me already, and that is enough for anyone." She stood and considered. "But I haven't made a poet for a long time. I wonder if I remember how?"

Have you seen the stone caves beneath the palace of Kubla Khan, called the Lesser Khan because for all his palaces, he could not match the conquests of his grandfather, the Great Khan? Where the stone is thin, it is translucent, so that the caves are filled with a strange, ghostly light. In the dark waters, which are still and no longer rushing, since the river has mingled into the underground lake, there are luminescent fish. When they swim to the surface, they shine like moving stars.

Samuel took off his breeches and swam in the dark water, in just his shirt. I sat on the bank, strumming the dulcimer, thinking of songs that he might like. He floated on his back, his hair spreading around his face like seaweed.

"There seems to be no time here," he said. "At home, I was expecting a person from Porlock. But here, I feel that no person from Porlock will ever come. Time has stopped, and nothing will ever happen. Except that you will keep singing, Sabra. You will keep singing, won't you? Sing to me about how the Stone Woman made a poet."

But I did not finish my song, then.

Later, we walked in the garden that surrounded the palace.

"They go on for ten miles," I said.

"How do you know that?" he asked, but I did not answer. It was hot, even in the shade of the almond trees, and the roses, which had been transported at great expense from Nineveh, were releasing their fragrance into the evening. "I think I could stay here forever," he said. "Forget my damned debts. Forget my . . . marriage. Never write again, never write anything else. I'm no good at it anyway. I never finish anything."

"That's not what Lilit said, when she made you."

"What do you mean?"

"Lilit created the poet out of clay. Kamora watched her mold the figure, the height and shape of a man. It was late now. Outside, the moon had risen, and it shone in through the opening of the cave, its pale light meeting the light of the Phoenix's tail feather. Kamora sat on the floor and watched, but she was so tired that her eyes kept closing, and somehow, between one blink of her eyes and another, the man was complete. He was tall, well-formed, and grey, the color of the clay at the bottom of the river Alph. His mouth was open, as though already speaking a poem.

" 'Now we must awaken him,' said Lilit. 'I will walk around him three times one way, and you must walk around him three times the other. Then I will spread honey on his lips, and you must put honey into his mouth, so that his words will be both nourishing and sweet.'

"Kamora rose. She was so tired that she stumbled as she walked, but three times she stumbled around the poet, and when she had done so, she took the jar from Lilit and put honey into the poet's open mouth.

" 'There,' said Lilit. 'And I really think that this time I have outdone myself. He will be the greatest poet that ever lived, and every night he will write a poem that has never been heard before for the Empress Nasren. He will be like the river Alph, endlessly replenished by the streams that flow down Mount Abora.' The poet was no longer the color of clay. Now he had brown hair hanging down to his shoulders, and his skin was as white as milk and covered, irregularly, with brown hair. Lilit took off her gray shawl and wrapped it around his hipbones. 'Speak, poet. Give us the gift of your first poem.'

"The poet turned to her and said,

> *'A damsel with a dulcimer*
> *In a vision once I saw:*
> *It was an Abyssinian maid,*
> *And on her dulcimer she played,*
> *Singing of Mount Abora.'*

" 'That's enough for now,' said Lilit. 'You see, Kamora, your poet works. Now take him to your Empress, and marry your Cloud Dragon. But don't visit me again, because the next time you come I won't be here.' "

"And was he the greatest poet that ever lived?" asked Samuel. We were sitting on the riverbank, where the Alph begins to disappear into the fissures below, surrounded by the scent of roses. The sun was setting, and the walls of the palace had changed from white to gold, and then to indigo. I could not see his face, but his voice sounded sad.

"He was, in the palace of the Empress Nasren," I said. "He wrote a different poem for her every night, and she gathered scribes around her to make copies so they could be taken to every village. They were set to music, as poems were in those days, and sung at every village fair. And when her ambassadors traveled to other countries, they carried the volumes of his poems, fourteen of them, the number of the constellations, on the back of a white elephant, so they could be presented to foreign sultans and caliphs and tzars."

"But elsewhere, in the country of daffodils and mutton and rain? Because I think, Sabra, that you come from outside this dream, as I do."

"In that country, he was a poet who could not finish his poems, and who, for many years, did not write poems at all. How could he, when every night in the palace of the Empress, he wrote a new poem entirely for her? What was left over, after that?"

"Perhaps. Yes, perhaps that is true."

We heard it then: lightning, crashing over the palace, turning the walls again from indigo to white. Once, twice, three times.

"He has come," said Samuel. "He has come, the person from Porlock." And then suddenly, he was gone.

I was staring at my computer screen, on which I had written, "The Kubla Khan of Coleridge's poem is not the historical Kubla Khan, founder of the Yuan Dynasty, and Xanadu is not Shangdu."

Again, I heard three knocks on the apartment door. "Sabra, are you there? It's Michael."

I rose, and went to open the door. "You people!" I said, as Michael walked in, carrying two bags of groceries.

"What do you mean?" he asked, startled.

"You people from Porlock, always interrupting."

He kissed me and put the bags he had been carrying on the table. "I was thinking of making a curry, but—you've had better curry than I can make. Are you going to laugh at my curry?"

"I would never laugh at your curry."

He began unpacking the grocery bags. "So, what were you thinking about so hard that you didn't hear me knock?"

"Coleridge. About how he never finished anything. And about how I'm not sure I want to finish this PhD. Michael, what would you think if I became a writer?"

"Fine by me, as long as you become famous—and rich, so you can keep me in a style to which I am not accustomed."

Later, after dinner, which was not as disastrous as I had expected, I called my mother. "Nasren Makeda, please."

"Just a moment. Madame Makeda, it's your daughter."

"Sabra! How good it is to hear your voice. I'm in Vienna with Ronnie. Darling, I'm so bored. Won't you come visit your poor mother? You can't imagine these rock and roll people. They have no culture whatsoever. One can't talk to them about anything."

"Mom, I'd like you to come to Boston and meet Michael."

"The one from Ohio? Oh, Sabra. Well, I suppose we can't control whom we fall in love with. It was like that with your father. He was the only man I ever loved, and yet he was shorter than I am by three inches, and that nose—such a pity you inherited it, although you have my ears, thank goodness. But I tell you the truth, I would have married him even if he had not been rich. He was that sort of man. So, I will come and meet your Michael. I can fly over in Ronnie's plane. Is there a month when Boston is warm? I can come then."

Perhaps he would fall in love with her. But sometimes one has to take chances.

For Kamora's marriage to the Cloud Dragon, the Empress's poet Samuel wrote a new poem, one that no one had heard before. It began,

> *Do you ask what the birds say? The sparrow, the dove,*
> *The linnet and thrush say, "I love and I love."*

Alem Das himself sang it, playing a dulcimer strung with the whiskers of the Cloud Dragon, whose sound was sweeter, more passionate, and more filled with longing than any instrument that had ever been made. When he was finished, the Empress

Nasren clapped, and Kamora, in the Empress's wedding veil, turned to her husband and blushed.

Later that night, in the cave of the Cloud Dragon, he said to her, "It may be that you are too clever to be my wife."

She stroked his silver hair and looked with wonder at his pale shoulders, shy for once before his human form. "And perhaps you are too beautiful to be my husband."

"Then we are well-matched," he said, "for together there is none in the world more clever or more beautiful than we. And now, my clever wife, are you going to kiss your husband?"

That night, the top of Mount Abora was wreathed in clouds. The Empress Nasren saw it as she walked in the garden of her palace, and she told blind Alem Das, who was walking with her. "Did you know, my friend, that it would end like this?" she asked.

Alem Das laughed in the darkness. "I suspected, from the moment Kamora insisted that my dulcimer should be strung with the whiskers of the Cloud Dragon. She always was a clever girl, although not as clever, I like to think, as her uncle."

"So, your niece is happy," said the Empress. "It is good that she is happy, although we who are old, Alem, know that happiness is fleeting." And she sighed her soft, mad sigh.

"Yes, lady," said Alem Das. "But tonight your roses are blooming, and I can hear the splashing of fountains. Somewhere inside the palace, your poet is reciting to the wedding guests, who are drunk on honey wine. And we who are old can remember what it was like to be young and foolish and happy, and be content." And they walked on in the moonlight, the instrument-maker and the Empress.

Appoggiatura

• • •

JEFF VANDERMEER

Autochthonous

AT THE UNIVERSITY TODAY, I cracked an egg yolk into my coworker Farid's coffee while he was off photocopying something. The yolk looked like the sun disappearing into a deep well. The smell made me think of the chickens on my parents' farm and then it wasn't long before I was thinking about my father and his temper. It made me almost regret doing it. But when Farid came back he didn't even notice the taste. He was too busy researching the architecture of some American city for one of the professors. My yolk and his research were a good fit as far as I was concerned, especially since that was supposed to be my project. But he was always pushing and he was an artist, whereas I was just getting a history and religion degree. I wouldn't have anything to show for that until much later.

After he left and the building was empty, I set a fire in the wastebasket on the fourth floor, being careful to use a bit of string as a fuse so it wouldn't start to blaze until after I'd gotten on the bus down the street.

On the way home to my apartment, through the usual road-blocks and searches, I embedded a personal command into the minds of the other people on the bus using the image of the saintly Hermes Trismegistus. He said to them, "Tomorrow, you will do something extraordinary for the Green."

When I got to the complex, I stopped at each landing and used a piece of chalk to draw a random symbol. If there was a newspaper in front of someone's door, I would write on it or rip it or whatever came to mind.

I walked into my box of an apartment, grey walls grey rooms, and took off my clothes. I painted myself green and leapt at the walls until the green mixed with the red of my blood and the grey was gone. Then I turned on the family TV that my mother had made me take when I came to the city and at the same moment I drove a paperweight through the screen. My fingers and arm vibrated from the shock.

But nothing else happened. There was no revelation. No sign.

I crumpled to the floor and began to cry.

When will the Green move through me? What will it take?

Cambist

AT THE ANADOLUBANK in Istanbul, Hazine Tarosian has handled them all. Crinkled and smooth, crisp and softly old. To her, new bills smell like ink and presses moving at high speed. There's a hint of friction in the paper, of burning smoke, that gives motion to the images, living contrast to inert cold coins. A burst of sunflower, bee in orbit around pollen, for the Netherlands. Ireland's beefy headshot of James Joyce, with *Ulysses* on the other side. The sibilance of Egypt's Arabic letters against a backdrop of Caliph-era battlements, in the distance a verdigris dome, last link to fabled Smaragdine. The careful detail of Thai King Bhumanibol calm upon his throne, sword across his lap, a flaming mandala at his back. Or even Portugal's massed galleons listing, sails taut against the whorled wind, sun a complex compass.

Hazine has begun to believe that the value of such wonders should be based on something more lasting than the rate of exchange. The verdigris dome in particular has so enthralled her that she even bought a book about Smaragdine called *The Myths of the Green Tablet* and a few old coins that she keeps in a display at her bank office.

For months now the image of the dome has come to her at night. She is floating over it and it is floating up toward her, until she's falling down through the dome and she can see, distant but ever closer: a green tablet, a ruined tower, an entire ancient city.

This dream is so vivid that Hazine always wakes gasping, the solution to some great mystery already receding into the darkness. Friends tell her the dream is about her job, and yet it informs her waking life in unexpected ways, imbues certain people and things with vibrant light and color. She keeps the Egyptian bill in her wallet. The suggestion, the hint, of Smaragdine, is so potent, as if a place must be hidden to become real.

Is this, then, the power of money? Hazine thinks, bringing tea and the newspaper back to bed with her in the mornings, her lover asleep and dreamless beside her.

Chiaroscuro

I WAS STILL SEARCHING for the missing daughter of a wealthy industrialist from Cyprus when the locals brought me in on another case. They'd heard I was staying at the Hilton—an American and a detective, in a city where neither passed through with any regularity. The police deputy, a weathered old man with a scar through his left eyesocket, made it clear that it would be best if I got into his beat-up Ford Fiesta with the lonely siren on top, and ventured out into the sun-beaten city to help him.

It was a crap ride, through a welter of tan buildings with no hint anymore of the green that had made the place famous since antiquity. The river had become a stream. The lake that it fed into was entombed in salt. The cotton they turned to as a crop just made it all worse. They'd survived a dictator, too, who had starved and disappeared people while building a monstrous palace. Becoming modern is a bitch for some people.

The dead guy, a painter the deputy told me, turned out to have lived on the seventh floor of what looked like a Soviet-era housing project made from those metal shelves you see at hardware stores. The smell of piss and cigarettes in the stairwell almost made me want to take up cigs again and find a bar. Most of the complex was deserted.

The painter's place had an unwashed, turpentine-and-glue smell. Several large canvases had been leaned against the wall, under cloth. Through a huge window the light entered with a ferocious velocity. Somewhere out in that glare lay the ruins of the old city center.

In the middle of the floor, a young man lay in the usual pool of blood. I could see a large, tissue-filled hole in his back. Behind him, one canvas remained uncovered on an easel.

Against a soft dark-green background so intense it hit me like the taste of mouthwash, a girl sat on a stone bench in an explosion of light. Pale skin. A simple black dress. No shoes. No nail polish. A sash around her waist that almost hid a pack of cigs shoved in at the left side. Her head was tilted, chin out, as if looking up at someone. A thin smile that could have been caution or control. She held something even greener than the background, but someone—the murderer I guessed—had scratched it out with a knife. It could have been a book; at least, she held it like a book, although there was something too fleshy about the hints of it still left on the canvas.

For a moment, I thought I'd found the missing girl. For a moment, I thought I'd found something even more important.

I looked around the apartment a bit, but my gaze kept coming back to the painting. It was signed in the corner with the initials "F.S."

I kept thinking, *Why did they defile the painting?*

After awhile, the police deputy asked me in his imperfect English, "You know what happen? Who?"

Somewhere in this rat's warren of apartments there was probably a man whose wife or daughter the artist had been screwing. Or someone he owed a lot of money to. Or just a psychopath. You get used to the options after awhile. They aren't complicated.

I breathed in the smoky air. They weren't ever going to find the guy who had done this. Not in this country. It was still reinventing itself. Deaths like these were part of the price you paid. The police deputy probably didn't expect it to be solved. He probably didn't really care, so long as he could say he'd tried.

"I have no fucking idea," I said. "But how much to let me take that painting?"

Dulcimer

From the *Book of Smaragdine*, 212th Edition:

The dulcimer has many esoteric uses in the spiritual and medical worlds. Playing the dulcimer while attaching a wresting thread to a person with a sprain will hasten the winding of the thread and the healing of the sprain. A man who plays the dulcimer over the grave of his dead wife will ensure that she stays dead and does not pay unexpected visits. A woman who plays the dulcimer holding it backwards will reverse her bad luck and bring home a wayward lover. A child who stands on one leg and attempts the dulcimer with chin and left hand while the right arm is tied behind the back will inevitably fall. If making a doppelganger using the priests' emerald powder, the dulcimer should be played during the mixing; otherwise, your monster may coalesce with a vestigial tale or tail. It is also known that playing the dulcimer after dinner increases the chance of pleasant conversation, if accompanied by wine and a nice dessert.

Eczema

ANYONE WHO HAS SEEN Eczema's act for the Babilim Traveling Circus knows it is only enhanced by the equal and opposite reaction created by Psoriasis. Touring erratically throughout Central Asia and the Far East (where not banned by law), the circus has only rarely been captured on film or in still photographs.

Although myths about Eczema's act abound, most eyewitnesses agree on the basics: Eczema, so nicknamed by her late father, a doctor, for the predominant condition of her formative years, enters the ring accompanied by helpers who carry several small boxes under their arms. Eczema is heavily made up in whiteface and wears a man's costume more fitting for a sultan, including curved shoes. A fake mustache completes the illusion. In the background a local band plays something approximating circus music.

Eczema's assistants, dressed all in black, fan out around her. Some of them place shiny green models of buildings upon the floor while others arrange a variety of insects in amongst the buildings, including scarab beetles, praying mantises, and grasshoppers. Some are green or have been painted green, while others are red or have been painted red. A few flies, large moths, and butterflies weakly buzz or flutter above on long, glittering strands of hair plucked from the heads of Tibetan holy men, the leads held by specially trained insect handlers.

Eczema stands in the background as an announcer or ring-master comes forward and says, "The King of Smaragdine now recreates for you, using his minions, the Great Battle between the Smaragdineans of the Green Tablet and the Turks."

Reports differ on the battle's historical accuracy. Certainly, the Turks ruled the area around Smaragdine for some three hundred years, but records from the time are often incomplete.

As for the act itself, some describe it as "insects wandering around a badly made scale model of an ancient city, after which the crowd rioted to show their displeasure." Others describe "the incredible sight of beetles, ants, and other insects recreating miniature set pieces of ancient battles amongst the spires and fortifications of a realistic and highly detailed cityscape. One of the most marvelous things ever seen."

During this spectacle, Eczema stands to the side, gesturing like an orchestra conductor and blowing on a whistle that makes no sound.

Most accounts agree that the act comes to an abrupt end when the insects that have not escaped are swept up by the helpers. A few eyewitnesses, however, tell tales of an ending in which "huge bass-like mudskippers hop on their fins through the cityscape, gobbling up the insects."

Eczema then comes forward and says, in a grave tone, "What is below is like that which is above, and what is above is like that which is below for performing the miracle of one thing. And as all things were produced from one by the Meditation of one, so all things are produced from this one thing by adaptation."

After this short speech, the audience usually leaves in confusion.

Psoriasis does not join Eczema until the end of the act. That Eczema and Psoriasis are Siamese twins only becomes evident when they stand together and bow, and the declivity between them—that outline, that echo—tells the story of another act altogether.

Elegiacal

BROWN DUST ACROSS a grey sky, with mountains in the distance. A metallic smell and taste. A burning.

Abdul Ahad and his sister Parveen were searching for a coin she'd lost. They stood by a wall of what was otherwise a rubble of stone and wood. A frayed length of red carpet wound its way through the debris.

"It has to be here somewhere," Parveen said. It had been a present from her uncle, a merchant who was the only one in their family to travel outside the country.

Her uncle had pressed it into her hand when she was eight and said, "This is an old coin from Smaragdine. There, everything is green."

The coin was heavy. On the front was a man in a helmet and on the back letters in a strange language, like something from another world. For weeks, she had held it, smooth and cool, in her right hand—to school, during lunch, back at their house, during dinner. She loved the color of it; there was no green like that here. Everything was brown or grey or yellow or black, except for the rugs, which were red. But this green—she didn't even need a photograph. She could see Smaragdine in her mind just from the texture and color of the coin.

"I don't see it," Abdul Ahad said, his voice flat and strange.

"We should keep looking."

"I think we should stop." Abdul Ahad had a sharp gash across his forehead. Parveen's clothes had ash on them. Her elbows and the back of her arms were lacerated from where she had tried to protect herself from the bomb blasts.

"We should keep looking," Parveen said. She had to keep swallowing; her throat hurt badly. She heard her brother's words through a sighing roar.

Now the muddled sound of sirens.

A harsh wind roiled down the brown street, carrying sand and specks of dirt.

Abdul Ahad sat down heavily on the broken rock.

Now Parveen could hear the screams and wails of people farther down the block. Flickers of flame three houses down, redorange through the shadows of stones.

Their father had been dead for a year. Now their mother lay under the rubble. They'd seen a leg, bloodied and twisted. Had pulled away rocks, revealing an unseeing gaze, a face coated with dust.

Her brother had checked her pulse.

Now they were searching for the coin. Or Parveen was. She knew why her brother didn't want to. Because he thought it wouldn't make a difference. But Parveen felt that, somehow, if she found it, if she held it again, everything would be normal again. She had only survived the air strike because she was holding the coin at the time, she was sure of it, and Abdul Ahad had only survived because he had been standing next to her.

"You don't have to look, Ahad," she said, giving him a hug. "You should sit there for a while, and I'll find it."

He nodded, gaze lost on the mountains in the distance.

Parveen walked away from him, kneeled in the dirt. She stuck her arm into a gap between jagged blocks of stone, grasping through dust and gravel, looking for something smooth and cool and far away. In a moment, she knew she'd have it.

Eudaemonic

From the *Book of Smaragdine,* 1st Edition:

People from far-off places ask why we worship the Green. They think of us as fools or outcasts. Yet even an ape can understand that human beings are born, live, and die. Even a beggar knows the alchemy in this basic transformation. To achieve true understanding, then, and thus true happiness, it is important to understand that transformation. Otherwise, our stay here is a ceaseless wandering, whether we roam or not.

Would you like to hear a riddle?

What power is strong with all power and will defeat every subtle thing and penetrate every solid thing?

In giving yourself to the Green you will know what it means to search for answers to questions such as these. You will become secure in your happiness.

People say that we do not know what happened to the Tablet, that it has been hidden from us for a reason. But this matters not. If we fail in the finding or the reaching, should ever our own city fall and be forgotten, then still we shall be eudaemonic in the failure.

Euonym

THAT FIRST NIGHT on the train, we were so free there was nothing to do but yell out the window at the darkness, into the cool breeze laced with honeysuckle and coal smoke.

Our father always thought he knew the value of a good and true name. He named us Eczema and Psoriasis much as he would name a medical procedure. It was an odd choice by a sometimes secretive man. Yes, my sister and I had had disfiguring skin conditions as children, but this was so minor compared to our other problems. We were conjoined twins. Before our first birthday, our father performed three surgeries to separate us. (In a sense, he not only named us twice, he created us twice.) Psoriasis looked as if someone had attached the male part of a puzzle piece to her side. I looked like a shark had taken a bite out of me.

My real name was Kamilah and my sister's real name was Anbar, but our father used Eczema and Psoriasis so much that around the house in Tashkent we learned to give up those names.

We had come to Tashkent because of our father's skill as a surgeon; despite the repressive regime, the medical facilities there were "second to none," as he liked to say. And it was at a dinner party our parents hosted for colleagues from the medical school that someone called me "Kamilah," and for the first time, I did not respond. Who was "Kamilah"? I was Eczema. I did not realize then that I might have a third name, one I could choose myself. I was ten.

After everyone had left the house that night, our mother berated our father for his cruelty. She was a beautiful, intelligent, tough woman who loved us too much.

"How can you continue to call them that?" she asked him as he sat drinking scotch in the living room. "Haven't they been through enough?"

At the time, we were having terrible trouble in school. We didn't fit in. We would never fit in.

Our father replied, "When I was growing up, I gave myself horrible nicknames. That way nothing the other boys said could be worse."

It was true that our father never treated anyone worse than he treated himself. A childhood disease had crippled his left arm: it was smaller and paler than his right arm. Because of it, our father was a kind of genius when he held the scalpel.

He never told us the names he'd given himself in school. Instead, he would tell us that he had used his skills and a green powder given to him by a Smaragdinean priest to reanimate a dead woman's arm, which he then used to replace his own, "the better to perform surgery."

Another time—we must have been seventeen—we were sitting at the kitchen table, drinking coffee with our mother, when he walked out of his study in his bathrobe.

He smiled at us and said, "The real reason I call you what I do is that neither of you is comfortable. You never have been. Your brains are itchy—restless and curious—and there is no cure for that other than death. Never forget that."

Then he retreated into his study, padding along in the silly mouse slippers that he'd worn for as long as I could remember.

I would like to think that he already knew our plans and had forgiven us.

A month later, we ran away on the train, desperate to change the reality that had been imposed on us by the world.

A year later we found the Green in the form of the ringmaster who called himself Hermes Trismegistus and talked like a silk ribbon tied slowly around the wrist.

Two years and we came up with our first act for the Babilim Traveling Circus.

Four years and we began to have a sense of what our third, our self-chosen names might be, and how we might best serve the Green and thus ourselves.

Five years later our father died without either of us ever having had a chance to tell him any of this.

Insouciant

—BOOTS SMASHING through brambles to the soft pine-needle floor, left hand lacerated by branches from reaching out for support at the wrong moment, heartbeat rapid, blood on the grip of his Glock, sharp pain in the shoulders as he whipped around long enough to get a few rounds off at an enemy that shattered in his vision because of the recoil, Lake Baikal behind him and more forest ahead and no hope in hell now of staking out the cabin where he suspected the girl was being held by the Russian toughs that had flushed him out, although he wondered as a bullet flecked a pine tree to his left and the bark exploded against his arm was the girl really there how could he be sure and why the hell did his watch itch so badly against his sweating wrist and all the time trying not to fall, when he heard a bellowing behind him and the sound of his pursuers brought up short, followed by a cry of surprise, and he just kept running because he'd caught a hint of something green that reminded him of a painting he'd bought but didn't connect to his idea of reality, or anybody's idea of reality, and it wasn't until that moment that he realized all through the chase, until the sight of the smudge of green, that he'd been as carefree as he could ever hope to be in his line of work and how strange that was and yet so true, then tripped over something large and fleshy, fell on his side against some tree roots and, dazed, gasping for air, raised his head to find the smudge of green resolved into something so improbable that he lay there staring at it for far too long, knowing instinctively that this was part of some great mystery, a mystery he might pursue for years and never solve and yet must pursue anyway, and realizing too that because of it he would rarely know any kind of peace for the rest of his life—

Logorrhea

(Excerpted from "Yetis, Loch Ness, and Talking Fish?" in the English magazine *Strange Phenomenon, April 1935.)

"There is really no sight that stirs the blood more than witnessing a giant Logorrheic Coelacanth plowing its way across the floor of old-growth Siberian forest, bellowing for all it's worth."
— DR. G. MERRILL SMITH

The freshwater walking fish called by some the "Logorrheic Coelacanth" has again been sighted in and around Siberia's Lake Baikal, as it has at regular intervals for hundreds of years. Most sightings occur miles from any water source, the fish reported to crawl awkwardly on its thick pectoral fins. Speculation leads this reporter to the conclusion that the Logorrheic Coelacanth must have a remarkable capacity to store water in pouches concealed by its gills. Thirdhand accounts tell of hunters encountering the voice of this fish before ever sighting it. (This reporter believes that the force of cycling water through the gills creates the sibilant yet throaty noise.)

In August 1934, the Logorrheic Coelacanth's gill mutterings came under rigorous observation by Dr. G. Merrill Smith's zoological expedition to track and tag Lake Baikal's freshwater seals. Dr. Smith told this reporter that he saw "what looked like a squadron of raucous walking fish ugly as bulldogs at the edge of a clearing. Imagine my surprise when I realized they were speaking in an ancient shamanistic language associated with a lost race once close kin to the Smaragdineans." Independent analysis of the field recordings made by Dr. Smith confirms the resemblance to certain rare languages. Some scientists have postulated a kind of inadvertent mimicry to explain the phenomenon. (Dr. Smith has stated, "I think it might be as coincidental as a cat coughing up a hairball sounding like speech.") Others have proposed more outré theories, such as symbiosis between Neanderthals and the fish. Although no serious scientist accepts this theory, no one can explain the fish's wanderings, the long intervals between sightings, nor give any reason for the fish to have developed this "adaptation."

Lyceum

From the *Book of Smaragdine,* 543rd Edition:

The Lyceum at Smaragdine began as a convalescence retreat for the children of the wealthy, often prescribed by court physicians. It also served as a center for teaching about medicine and philosophy, but during the Rule Without Kings, the Lyceum fell into disrepair. When finally refurbished by the insane Reformer King Jankamora, the Lyceum took on ever more mystical undertones. King Jankamora had secret doors and tunnels added to the interior and made of the exterior a complex illusion. A facade created by skilled painters made it

appear that it was always dusk inside. A certain organic quality began to permeate the architecture. Water features began
to dominate the exterior gardens. Inside, King Jankamora
had trees planted and knocked holes in the ceiling to accommodate them. Wherever possible, he lengthened the corridors and made them more difficult. Soon, it was nearly
impossible to find the way from one room to another. The
King also created what he called a "circus that is not a circus"
and had it train and perform solely inside of the Lyceum, often to an audience of dead insects he had collected in his
travels. Members of the court began to complain that the
Lyceum had become "a hideaway for the uncanny and the
unseemly." When King Jankamora disappeared, it was ru-
mored that he had become lost in the Lyceum. Sadly, when
Smaragdine was taken during World War I by the British, the
Lyceum was lost. Some claimed it had spontaneously sucked
itself into the earth. Others, that King Jankamora reappeared
and, with the help of his secret followers, disassembled the
Lyceum and reassembled it in the mountains. Claims that
the Lyceum and all of its elements had been created by
Jankamora to somehow assist in the search for the Green
Tablet cannot be substantiated. Regardless, ever since that
time there have been only hints of the Lyceum in the form of
the brilliant green shards and wooden beams today found in
the museums of other countries.

Macerate

To: The President of Emerald Delta River Cruises

Dear Sir or Madam:

I am writing to complain in no uncertain terms.

My wife and I are not rich people, nor extravagant. I, for example, work part-time at a grocery store since my retirement.

But this past summer, we decided to treat ourselves to a river cruise. We chose your service because it had come highly recommended by one of our cousins and because the rates were reasonable. Five days on a river cruise! Nothing could have delighted us more, and my poor Macha, who works twelve-hour days in a factory, deserved it. Besides, the name of the boat seemed rather romantic: *The Light of the Moon.*

We departed in late August with the river calm and swallows skimming over the water. Our cabin seemed nice if cramped, and the people on board were pleasant. It was a surprise to find that a number of pigs had been brought on board by another traveler, but they were kept below deck and made surprisingly little sound. We looked forward to a relaxing experience.

All was well until the second night, when, as you know, river pirates tried to board *The Light of the Moon,* under, well I must say it, the light of the moon. We were horrified, of course, but stayed in our cabin as the crew commanded. We heard all kinds of terrible noises and what sounded like shots fired, as well as a great uproar among the pigs. But this settled down and we were reassured by some new crew members in the morning that the pirates had been repelled and would no longer be a problem. Being a war veteran, I had remained calm and my poor Macha had been calm, too, although I made her take a sleeping tablet after.

Pirates simply made an adventure for us, this late in our lives. Nor did we mind the next day when two fellow travelers playing cards shot at one another before being subdued by members of the crew. Besides, Macha missed all of it, having overslept.

Shortly thereafter, however, the menu began to change and this is where I believe the nature of our complaint will become clear. It will also explain why we began to lose weight on this so-called "idyllic cruise downriver, ending at the site of ancient Smaragdine." Perhaps typing up a description from the menu will be enough to convince you of our claim:

> Thrice-Shoved Frogs, Whole—Two whole emerald frogs, flayed alive and then lightly braised and macerated, after which the whole skin of one is pulled back over the other and vice versa. The frogs are then impaled, still fresh, on a two-headed skewer and cooked over an open flame. Both frogs are then put inside a hollowed-out river iguana, which is then stuffed into a large river fish and placed inside a box full of coals that is heated and tossed out behind the boat for further maceration. The resulting taste of the then panfried Thrice-Shoved Frogs is indescribable.

For three days, your crew and the two women serving as cooks prepared a series of dishes that included macerating anything and everything, usually "shoving" or "stuffing" it inside of some other animal. I have never seen such senseless violence done to anything or anyone as to these creatures with their bulging eyes and gutted rears. When we complained, we were told by both women that we should be happy to receive such delicacies.

Many other strange things went on aboard that ship, sir or madam. Some of them I do not feel comfortable relating to you, even now, two months after our ordeal. The crew did not seem to sleep and once, when I peeked out from the door of our cabin after midnight, I saw two of them painted green from head to foot, stark naked, engaged in a dance involving scarab beetles. During the day, they would say odd things designed, I believe, to make us react in some specific way.

After a time, we did not know if perhaps the crew had gone mad or if they just practiced insolence as a wall against boredom.

When we arrived at our destination, the crew disappeared, leaving us there by the dock. We had to take a train back to our little apartment the very next day—a trip of some thirty hours, and very hard on my poor Macha.

We do not need or want apologies. We would like a refund of our money and vouchers for free meals from our favorite restaurant. It is only symbolic, of course, to have these vouchers separate from a general refund. But there is the principle involved, isn't there? We cannot get those "Thrice-Shoved Frogs" on *The Light of the Moon* out of our heads.

> Thank you for your kind attention,
> Saladin Davidos, Esq.

Pococurante

From the *Book of Smaragdine,* 212th Edition:

A careless person has no cure, unlike a careless thought or animal. Calling a careless person a 'pococurante' or other fancy name will not, by the precision of the term, suddenly make the careless careful. Once, a careless farmer living outside of Smaragdine lost his own name and had to take the name of his ox, Baff, much to the delight of the villagers (one of whom found the farmer's name and used it as his own). A woman once lost her vagina and by the time she found it she had twelve children. Losing one's shadow is perhaps the most common affliction of the careless, which explains why, on a hot afternoon day, you will find so many little dribbles of shadow in every lonesome crack and crevice. A lost shadow has no wish to be found, because, inevitably, it will just be lost again.

But the truly careless—the person who has descended into a place that not many can understand—will lose much more than that. These truly cursed people can lose even a love so strong that it radiates like heat. The kind of love that creates laughter around even the simplest act. When enough love is lost to this kind of indifference or carelessness, wars begin—sometimes in lands far distant from the occurrence, but always these wars come home. Such effects are magnified depending on the status of the individual. Thus, when statesmen, when queens, when caliphs, become careless, they lose whole armies and people die on vast scales in foreign lands. The innocent taste sand in their mouths, not the green spring air of their native country. Their bones line the roads of places so far away and exotic that not even the wind through their skulls can say the names. A careless commoner often loses hate as well, even though such hate will replace itself indefinitely and the person therefore never realizes their own carelessness. But for this reason, many careful kings and queens find the hate of others and use it as if it were their own.

Alas, a careless person has no cure, unlike a careless thought or animal. It is just the way of the world.

Psoriasis

ANYONE WHO HAS SEEN Psoriasis's act for the Babilim Traveling Circus knows it is only matched by the equal and opposite reaction created by Eczema.

Myths about Psoriasis's act abound, but this is what eyewitnesses report: Psoriasis, so nicknamed by her late doctor father for the predominant condition of her formative years, dressed as a man with a fake mustache, in clothes similar to whatever the locals favor, sits in the stands with the audience while below Eczema enters the ring in her sultan disguise accompanied by helpers who carry several small boxes. Eczema begins her act, which consists of an insect re-creation of a mythical Smaragdine battle.

At the same time, Psoriasis begins to complain about the act from the stands, in oddly modulated tones. The loudness and quality of this disturbance varies from city to city. Woven in with the complaints are phrases such as "The father of it is the sun," "The wind carried it in its belly," and "So the world was created," all delivered in a peculiar singsong intonation. These phrases come from the fabled Emerald Tablet, attributed to the ancient alchemist Hermes Trismegistus.

After a time, the people listening to Psoriasis experience a heightened sense of happiness, followed by a profound drowsiness. One boy of thirteen recounts that "I know I must have fallen asleep, because my next memory is of feeling something smooth in my left hand and finding a strange green coin there."

That Psoriasis attempts to aid in the audience's enjoyment of her sister's insect battle seems apparent. Whether this is by simple hypnosis or some deeper technique is unknown. What, if anything, the audience does while under this possible hypnosis is also unknown. However, in the weeks and months after seeing the performance, many people report intense shifts of emotion, visions, and a desire for the color green.

Psoriasis does not join Eczema until the end of the act. That Eczema and Psoriasis are Siamese twins only becomes evident when they stand together and bow, and the declivity between them—that outline, that echo—tells the story of another act altogether.

Semaphore

WHEN TRUEWILL MASHBURN turned eighteen, he left the U.S. with forged documents and passed himself off as a thirty-something ESE teacher at a Costa Rican university. He'd always looked older than his age and at six-four with sandy blond hair and a Viking's eyes and chin, people usually believed what he said. By the time he left Latin America at the age of twenty-two and headed for Europe, he'd hitchhiked through twelve countries, been a missionary, a doctor's aide, and a bank teller.

Now twenty-five, Mashburn found himself living in an abandoned semaphore tower on the banks of a Central Asian river that eventually wound its way down to the ruins of old Smaragdine and the tired modern city that surrounded it.

He'd read about the semaphore towers while hanging out in a Tashkent library. They'd once been vital in Smaragdine's epic battles against the dreaded Turk. Now they were just free apartments ripe for the taking, in Mashburn's eyes.

Mashburn took the book—*The Myth of the Green Tablet*—and headed south. By the time he found the towers, he was ready to settle down awhile anyway, having been hassled at half a dozen borders. He could fish in the river, exchange some of his limited cash for food in the nearby village, read the book he'd stolen, or just hang out with the locals smoking dope. A few times a week, the village women walked past, giggling and talking about him. He couldn't understand them, but he knew what they were saying.

It should have been perfect, but an odd sense of responsibility began to grow inside him with each day he lived there. He felt it in his chest every time he walked up the three stories of crumbling stone steps to stare at the tower a half-mile downriver that doubled his own.

The book was to blame, even though the author seemed contemptuous of the subject. On some level, the more Mashburn read about the fascinating history of Smaragdine, the more he couldn't help but feel an obligation to continue its ancient fight against the Turk. It didn't make sense, and yet it did.

Mashburn decided to become the true keeper of the tower. He removed the weeds inside and along the circular fringe. He did his best with his limited knowledge of drywall to repair the worst areas. He began to wear his tattered army surplus jacket all the time. He bought a pair of old binoculars from a villager. He even assigned himself guard duty, more often at dusk than during the day.

At night, the tower looked less ruined and it was easier to

imagine he was back in Time and that he might need to use the tower's windmill-like semaphore spokes to warn of some danger.

Then, too, Mashburn saw many strange things the longer he stood watch at night. Fish that bellowed at him from the water. Debris and bodies from some battle that had taken place many countries upriver. A man in a motorboat who looked vaguely American in a leather jacket and dark shades, a gun holster on his exposed ankle. Something was happening, Mashburn was certain. He just didn't know what.

One moonlit night just before dawn, he saw the most curious thing of all: a river cruise ship with several smaller boats pursuing it. When they caught up, what looked like a band of circus performers jumped on board: a couple of women dressed like caliphs, a snake charmer, a mime, and a fire-eater, among others. The battle raged as Mashburn looked on with mouth open.

By the time the conflict had subsided, far to the south of his position, he couldn't tell who had won, only that the boats remained empty and most of the river cruise crew was walking around on deck again.

Sometimes Mashburn felt prematurely old from all of his travels, but in that moment, he felt both dumbfounded and oddly blessed.

By midmorning, he had the semaphore spokes turning for the first time in two centuries and he was sending his message out across the water. He didn't care if the next station was manned or not. That wasn't the point.

Smaragdine

"IN THE VAST CITY of Smaragdine on the edge of a dying sea-lake, from which come palm trees and a wasting disease, the color green is much prized. It matters not where it is found, nor the exact shade. The cloth-makers produce nothing but clothing in green, so that the people of the city are always swathed in it. The buildings are painted in emerald, in verdigris, edged in a bronze that quickly turns. Even the white domesticated parrots that the denizens have such affection for—these birds they dye green. Year by year the lake becomes smaller and the river that feeds into it more of a stream. Year by year, the palm trees become yellower and fewer. Yet the people hold vast and expensive festivals in celebration of the arcane and the uncanny. There is a constant state of celebration. Yet also it is a point of pride for buildings to fall into disrepair, if at the limits of their disillusion there creeps into the corners of rooms, across the ceilings, some hint of green. Someday, Smaragdine will be as a ruin and the lake will be gone and the river with it. But, in the end, it will not matter, for even when the last water is gone, this city will still be rich and fertile in color. This is all the inhabitants ask. It is all they can hope for. I know, for I lived in Smaragdine for a time. I knew the calm beauty of its streets, the dyed-green water of its many fountains, filled with green carp. I knew the slogans of the leaders in their green cloaks. I knew, too, the feel of the hot sun and was blinded by the mirage of sand eclipsed by the shimmer of the ever-more-distant lake. One day, I will return and know once again the richness of that place by its devotion to its color. One day I will walk through those empty streets and know the very definition of madness."

—*Told to one of Marco Polo's men by a merchant selling green cloth in a Mumbai marketplace*

Sycophant

THE YOUNG MAN who sat down beside the writer Baryut Aquelus in a Tashkent coffeehouse wore a black blazer over a green T-shirt and blue jeans. He had sallow skin, an open, round face, and thick eyebrows. His mouth was fleshy, as if he'd suffered a split lip.

The writer thought he recognized the type. The first words confirmed it.

"Are you—? Are you really—?" The rasp of a mouthbreather, along with the stain and smell of betel nut.

"Yes."

He no longer bothered to smile or straighten his jacket when people came up to him. It had been a few years since he'd removed himself from the great, the smoldering, eye of fame, but he remembered its heat.

"I've read all of your work, sir. Even *Myths of the Green Tablet*. A very brave book."

"You speak like a native Smaragdinean," the writer said.

The man looked away, actually blushed. The writer found this charming.

"Thank you. I came there as a child. I know English. And French, too. A little. I read you in French, at first."

How long ago? He'd been out of print in France for at least half a decade.

"That's very good, um . . . ?"

"Oh—Farid. You can call me Farid Sabouri."

"Nice to meet you, Farid."

The notebook in front of him now seemed inert, useless. The thoughts welling up behind the pen receded into some middle distance, waiting for him to call them forth again.

"Tell me, if I'm not bothering you," Farid said, "how you came to write *Myths of the Green Tablet*."

"You mean you don't know?" He'd meant it as self-deprecating but it came out vainglorious. "I guess I've told it so many times I expect anyone who wanted to know would know."

It had gotten him in trouble. Vague death threats from a bunch of doddering priests. A shorter stint at the university in Smaragdine than he would have liked. *The Green Tablet not the gospel, not even vaguely true?* He hadn't realized the effect it would have when he was writing it—he just wrote it.

"I know, but it's different reading it in the paper."

"Well, if you insist." *Do I really mind that much?* "I wrote it because I think that Smaragdine has suffered from its fetish for the color green. It keeps us looking at the past. I feel that, for the average Smaragdinean, the future is behind him. I mean, it's practically fantastical. Medieval. Alchemy? Airy-fairy about earth-air-water-fire? No offense," he added, noting the intent look on Farid's face.

Farid smiled, revealing yellowing teeth, and said, "I am fascinated by the bravery in the act. To become a . . . a lightning rod for many difficulties."

"Yes, well . . ."

Above them the fans swirled slowly and out on the street a steady procession of outdated vehicles used the worn street. The waiter came with two coffees.

"My gift for our meeting," Farid said. "Please, enjoy it."

"Thank you," the writer said. And he was, actually, surprised. Usually the people who came up to him wanted something but offered nothing, no matter how trivial, in return.

"So what brings you to Tashkent?" the writer asked.

Farid did not look away this time. "I came to see you. I studied your work at university. I've studied your life, too."

Oh no, the writer thought, *here it comes.* Sometimes he felt his personal life had become the size of a postage stamp.

"And did I measure up?"

"Oh, you are very brave," Farid said. "Although I don't know if you understand that."

"It's kind of you to say," the writer said, although Farid's syntax seemed odd.

Farid almost said something, stopped, bit his lip, leaned forward. "No, it's the truth. It makes me weep a little, thinking about it. If you don't mind me saying it. You've used your talent for things that don't always make sense to me."

The writer tried to shrug it off with a chuckle.

Is this where the conversation turns obsessional?

"And here I took you for a bit of a sycophant, Farid. A bit of a hanger-on, as the Brits here like to say."

"Not in the least—you believe too little but know too much,"

Farid said, and pulled out a gun and shot the writer in the stomach.

Baryut had the odd sensation of Farid walking over him and past while he lay there staring up at the ceiling fan and people were running around screaming. There was no pain. Nothing so fast could really be painful, could it?

Possessed of a sudden and terrible clarity, Baryut thought: *What can I write in the next few minutes?*

Transept

WHY CHURCH BROKE? That question all ask when get Barahkad? Though no many tourist now—just detective last week, bad circus week before. But I tell you—even drunk sitting end of bar give answer if you want answer—he say we run out money when no water. That man, head on table, see? He tell you merchants. Merchants of Barakhad break church because priests too big, too big. Or I, sir, I tell you Devil visit Barakhad when church of Smaragdineans building and break it.

Or it could be that the architect's plans were too complicated and they planned not one but three transepts, with gold leaf that wouldn't flake off for the archways and brushes made from the tongues of hummingbirds to paint the column detail.

What? Oh, don't be mad. Just a little joke I like to play on tourists. So many of you think that our command of English is crumbling along with our infrastructure. But I went to university, even spent a summer at the University of San Diego on an exchange program, a long time ago. You're lucky you bumped into me, my friend. That young man over there, for example— he doesn't want to speak English anymore. His whole family died last year. Mother, father, daughter.

But do you really want to know why the church isn't "finished"? Why not get a drink and sit down. It won't take long, but you might need the drink. Don't worry, I'll keep it simple. I know the names around here confuse foreigners.

So: The real reason the church looks unfinished is that until recently we had a civil war in this country. Hadn't heard of it? Well, we're not in an area with anything of any value, really. Not anymore.

First one side held Barahkad. They starved us and killed some of us and took some of us away. Then the other side took over. They starved us and killed some of us and took some of us away. Then the peacekeepers came to our country, although we never saw one in Barakhad, not once, and a coalition of countries so far away that none of us here in Barahkad had ever visited any of them began to use planes to bomb us. I believe your country participated in that effort.

We already had little food, no electricity. Now when people walked down to the market, they might become splintered bones and shredded flesh and a stain of red on the roadside in a blink of the eye. We lost maybe half of the people in Barakhad during those months.

Now that the bombs have stopped, we are doing our best. The priests who might have helped are gone. There has been no time to rebuild the church, my friend. We haven't had time to rebuild many things, as you may have seen when you came into town.

So at the moment the church is crumbling and overgrown with weeds. It's green enough to make even a Smaragdinean happy. The north side of the transept remains one wall and a promise of a roof. No one likes a church where the wind can catch you up like the breath of God. No one likes a church with the rain on the inside. Except me, since that's where I'm forced to live for now.

Am I talking to you? Are we speaking? Are you hearing me?

Vignette

ONCE, A VERY LONG TIME AGO, an adventurer became a problem for the King of Smaragdine. Something to do with the king's daughter. Something to do with the king's daughter and wine and a dance hall. So the king decreed that this adventurer should be sent "on a long quest for the good of the Green." The quest? To find the lost Tablet and bring it back to Smaragdine. The Tablet was in Siberia or Palestine or somewhere in South America or even possibly on the Moon, depending on one's interpretation of the writings. Regardless, this fit the very definition of "a long quest." Unfortunately for the adventurer, he had earned the nickname of "Vignette" because his adventures, although intense and satisfying in the retelling, were always short and occurred in and around the city.

Vignette wasn't very happy about the king's decision, but a long quest was better than immediate death, so off he went. Through Samarkand and East Asia he traveled; up into Siberia and around Lake Baikal; down to Mongolia; across China to Japan; by sailing ship to India; a brief stop in North Africa; up into the Mediterranean; over to Greenland; doubling back to England; braving the trip to the New World for several storm-tossed months; finding nothing there and sailing briefly down to South America.

He talked to everyone he could find—Arabs, Jews, Christians, Bantus, Moslems. Holy men and beggars. Merchants and royalty. Over time, his body grew lean and weathered but strong. His eyes narrowed against the sun and yet he saw more clearly. Fighting brigands in the steppes. Running from Indians with blow darts in the Amazon.

If only they could see "Vignette" now, he thought as he pulled an arrow from his shoulder and prepared a charge with Sudanese warriors against the fortifications of some other tribe. Climbing a mountain in the Himalayas, eyelashes clotted with frost, an avalanche crushed over them in a blink and as he dug himself out, he thought, *I'll show you the good of the Green.*

After a time, though, it really didn't matter to him if he ever found the Tablet—in fact, he no longer believed in its existence. He was homesick for Smaragdine and his friends there. So one day he began to head back, slowly. Some months later, he was close enough that all he had to do was cross the river by ferry and the walls shimmering in the distance would be real once more.

But he wasn't a fool. He'd brought three miraculous things with him, in a chest banded with gold: an ancient book from Siberia made of broad, thick leaves, written in a secret language none alive knew; a healing tincture from the Yucatan that smelled like honeysuckle and chocolate; and a shiny green stone that tribesmen in the Amazon had told him was a god's eyeball that had fallen from the sky one night. At least he wasn't returning empty-handed. With any luck the king would reward his efforts, or at least forgive his trespasses.

Word must have spread about his return, for a royal pavilion awaited him on the far side of the river.

But it was not the king who greeted him there. Instead, it was a woman and her retinue. At first he did not recognize her. Then he realized it was the King's daughter, five years older. She had wrinkles at the corners of her eyes. She had let her hair grow long. It hung free to her shoulders, framing a face that seemed too wistful, too sad, for one still so young.

"Where is the king?" he asked.

"He died a year ago," she said, and he could feel her gaze upon him, lingering over every scar and bruise on his stubbled face. "I rule Smaragdine now."

"I didn't find the Tablet, but I brought back a chest of treasures," he said. It was somewhere behind him, but he couldn't stop looking at her.

"I don't give a damn about any of that," she said, and leaned up and kissed him on the lips.

Vivisepulture

AND THE TURK came down upon Smaragdine like a storm of plagues and breached the city gates and slew the defenders on the walls with arrows and their horsemen, led by their captain Baryut Aquelus, outstripped their infantry and so came unto the great Lyceum where the priests had hidden the Green Tablet, and Baryut took the heart of Smaragdine from that place, leaving the priests dead upon the steps as they rode out again.

And in the streets beyond they came upon the din of fierce battle, for the Smaragdineans had recovered from their surprise and now fought like demons for their city and men fell in great numbers on both sides as the city began to burn.

Raising his sword, Baryut led the way for the Turk, cutting down any who opposed them.

But when he rode under the shadow of the city gates and looked back, Baryut saw that the Smaragdinean prince Farid, upon a black charger, had come up behind and slain his riders and would soon overtake him.

Safety lay at the semaphore tower by the river, but Farid outstripped the Turk and forced him up into the hills and ravines and the coffeehouse beyond.

Farid was only a few paces behind him, driven by righteous conviction.

The Tablet became heavier and heavier in the Turk's hands and the prince shouted at him now, sword slicing the sky into jagged pieces.

"Bring it back or I'll feed you to my dogs!" Farid shouted. "You are very brave, although I don't know if you understand that!"

"And here I took you for a bit of a sycophant, Farid," Baryut shouted back. "A bit of a hanger-on."

"Not in the least. You believe too little and know too much."

Soon Baryut was trapped at the edge of a ravine. In a coffeehouse. A ravine. The prince would kill him now and the Tablet would go back to Smaragdine and he would never write another book. Or perhaps even another sentence.

Baryut wheeled around and drew his sword to make his stand at the edge of the ravine.

"Sacrilege!" Farid screamed, galloping forward. Their horses came together and they were now so close that Baryut could smell the betel nut on Farid's breath, could see the design on the green T-shirt he wore under the blazer.

The force of their swords clashing shuddered up and down his arm and the ground beneath their horses' hooves caved away and they fell headlong into the ravine, still in their stirrups.

The horses were dead by the time they reached the bottom, necks snapped. The tablet had cracked into a hundred pieces.

Baryut and Farid were buried alive under the pebbles and rocks and boulders dislodged by their descent. Their mouths filled with dirt. Their bones broke.

Then, because Farid could not reach his sword, he shot Baryut in the stomach.

Baryut looked up at the ceiling fan and could hear a slow pounding that he knew was his blood abandoning his body.

As Baryut died, he had the satisfaction of knowing Farid would die, too, soon enough.

Within a month, the flesh decayed from the bodies of the two men, leaving only bones. In four months, the shifting of earth confused the collapsed skeletons of the horses and the men until there was no difference between the two.

That spring, the rains came and water trickled through the ravine, loosening the stones, picking through the bones and the pieces of the Green Tablet. Every year, the water dislodged more and more fragments until over time the Tablet became not a hundred pieces but two hundred and then a thousand, until no one piece was any larger than a Smaragdine coin.

Beyond the ravine, more wars were fought. Some the Turk won, some the Smaragdineans won. Men died searching for the Tablet. Smaragdine became a backwater held together by the weight of dead ritual and then, eventually, broken by a mad dictator who fancied himself an architect on a grand scale.

Pieces of the Tablet were carried away by the rainwater and entered the river. Fish ate them and became strange with the knowledge, uttering sentences in a language no one understood. Herons ate the fish and fishermen noticed how mournful and heavy their eyes became.

In a hundred ways, the Green Tablet reentered the world, but like the men, it had been buried alive and its knowledge with it. Reborn, it became a hidden thing, seen in glimpses from the corner of the eye. Sometimes things happened because of the Tablet that no one could understand because no one knew what the Tablet said anymore. Perhaps they never had.

And still people searched for it, never realizing it was all around them and in them, and that they could search their whole lives, die because of it, and yet it was there all the time, in front of them, even in the pattern of green mold across a dirty floor in a Tashkent coffeehouse or somewhere in the blood leaking from my body or in the patient whir of the ceiling fan overhead or in anything in the world that received love or hate or some lingering attention or . . . *anything* always forever.

LOGORRHEA BIOGRAPHICAL NOTES

DANIEL ABRAHAM (cambist) has been published in the *Vanishing Acts, Bones of the World,* and *The Dark* anthologies, and been included in Gardner Dozois's *Year's Best Science Fiction* anthology. *A Shadow in Summer* is his first novel. He is currently working on the *Long Price Quartet,* the second volume of which, *A Betrayal in Winter,* will be published in 2007. He lives in New Mexico with his wife.

PAOLO BACIGALUPI's (macerate) writing has appeared in *High Country News,* Salon.com, the *Magazine of Fantasy and Science Fiction,* and *Asimov's Science Fiction Magazine.* It has been anthologized in various "Year's Best" collections of short science fiction and fantasy, nominated for the Nebula and Hugo awards; his story "The Calorie Man" won the Theodore Sturgeon Memorial Award for best science fiction short story of the year in 2006. Paolo lives in Colorado.

JAY CASELBERG (eudaemonic) has published short fiction in such markets as *Interzone, Electric Velocipede,* and *Amazon Shorts,* and is the author of the Jack Stein book series which includes *Wyrmhole, Metal Sky, The Star Tablet,* and *Wall of Mirrors.* He currently resides in Germany.

MATTHEW CHENEY's (elegiacal) work has appeared in a wide variety of venues, including *English Journal, One Story, Locus, SF Site,*

Failbetter.com, and *Ideomancer.* He writes regularly about SF and literature at his blog, *The Mumpsimus.* He currently lives in New Hampshire.

ALAN DENIRO (sycophant) is the author of the short-story collection *Skinny Dipping in the Lake of the Dead* from Small Beer Press. He lives in Minneapolis.

CLARE DUDMAN (eczema) is the author of the novels *Edge of Danger, One Day the Ice Will Reveal All Its Dead,* and *98 Reasons for Being* (all published by Penguin). She has won three awards for her writing and has worked as a scientist and teacher.

HAL DUNCAN (chiaroscuro) is the author of the *Book of All Hours,* which is comprised of the novel *Vellum* and its follow-up, *Ink.* He lives in Glasgow.

THEODORA GOSS (dulcimer) has published stories in places such as *Realms of Fantasy, Fantasy Magazine, Alchemy,* and *Polyphony.* Prime Books recently published her short-story collection *In the Forest of Forgetting.* She currently lives in Massachusetts.

ELIZABETH HAND (vignette) is the author of eight novels, including *Generation Loss,* and three collections of short fiction, the most recent of which is *Saffron & Brimstone.* She lives on the coast of Maine.

ALEX IRVINE (sacrilege, semaphore) is the author of several novels including *A Scattering of Jades* and *The Narrows.* His short fiction has been collected into *Unintended Consequences* and *Pictures from an Expedition.* He currently lives in Maine.

JAY LAKE (transept) lives and works in Portland, Oregon, within sight of an 11,000 foot volcano. He is the author of over two hundred short stories, four collections, and a chapbook, along with novels from Tor Books, Night Shade Books, and Fairwood Press. Jay is also the coeditor with Deborah Layne of the critically acclaimed Polyphony anthology series from Wheatland Press. His next few projects include

The River Knows Its Own from Wheatland Press, *The Trial of Flowers* from Night Shade Books, and *Stemwinder* and *Mainspring* from Tor Books. In 2004, Jay won the John W. Campbell Award for Best New Writer. He has also been a Hugo nominee for his short fiction and a three-time World Fantasy Award nominee for his editing. Jay can be reached at www.jlake.com or by email at jlake@jlake.com.

MICHAEL MOORCOCK (insouciant) is the author of more than ninety novels. Moorcock's most popular works by far have been the Elric novels. His writing has won the Nebula Award, the World Fantasy Award, and the British Fantasy Award, among others. His novel *Mother London* was shortlisted for the Whitbread Prize and the Cornelius quartet won the Guardian Fiction Prize. He currently splits his time between Texas and France.

TIM PRATT (autochthonous) lives in Oakland, California, with his wife, Heather Shaw. His fiction and poetry have appeared in *The Best American Short Stories: 2005, The Year's Best Fantasy and Horror, Strange Horizons, Realms of Fantasy, Asimov's, Lady Churchill's Rosebud Wristlet,* and *Year's Best Fantasy,* among others.

DAVID PRILL (vivisepulture) is the author of the cult novels *The Unnatural, Serial Killer Days,* and *Second Coming Attractions,* and the collection *Dating Secrets of the Dead.* His short fiction has appeared in *Salon Fantastique,* the *Magazine of Fantasy and Science Fiction, Subterranean, SCI FICTION,* and *Cemetery Dance.* He lives in a small town in the Minnesota north woods.

MICHELLE RICHMOND's (logorrhea) new novel, *The Year of Fog,* will be published in March by Delacorte Press. Richmond's previous books are the story collection *The Girl in the Fall-Away Dress,* which won the Associated Writing Programs Award, and the novel *Dream of the Blue Room,* a finalist for the Northern California Book Award. Her stories and essays have appeared in or are forthcoming from *Glimmer Train, Playboy,* the *Kenyon Review, Oxford American,* the *Believer, Salon,* and elsewhere. She is the recipient of the 2006 Mississippi Review Fiction Prize.

ANNA TAMBOUR (pococurante) lives in the Australian bush with a large family of other species, including one man. Her collection *Monterra's Deliciosa & Other Tales &* . . . and her first novel, *Spotted Lily*, were both Locus Recommended Reading List selections.

JEFF VANDERMEER (appoggiatura) is a two-time winner of the World Fantasy Award, as well as a past finalist for the Hugo, Philip K. Dick, International Horror Guild, British Fantasy, Bram Stoker, and Theodore Sturgeon Memorial awards. Jeff is the author of several books, most recently *Shriek: An Afterword*. VanderMeer's books, including *City of Saints and Madmen*, have made the year's best lists of *Publishers Weekly*, the *San Francisco Chronicle*, the *Los Angeles Weekly*, *Publishers' News*, and Amazon.com. Jeff's editorial work includes the *Leviathan* anthology series and the *Thackery T. Lambshead Pocket Guide to Eccentric & Discredited Diseases*. He currently lives in Tallahassee, Florida, with his wife, Ann.

LESLIE WHAT (psoriasis) attended the Clarion Writers' Workshop in 1976 but stopped writing to do other things, like maskmaking and puppetry, tap-dancing and stage performance, babies, and community work. She published her first story in *Asimov's* in 1992 and has since added over one hundred publication credits in a variety of forms: plays, nonfiction, fiction, poetry, and documentary scripts. She won the Nebula Award for her short story "The Cost of Doing Business" and received her MFA in writing from Pacific University in 2006. She teaches fiction writing through the UCLA Extension Writers' Program.

LIZ WILLIAMS (lyceum) did a variety of part-time jobs, including a now-infamous stint on Brighton Pier as a tarot reader, before full-time work as administrator for an education program in Kazakhstan. This was not entirely successful and resulted in a partial collapse of the Kazakhstani cabinet. She is the author of ten novels, most recently the Inspector Chen novels *Snake Agent* and *The Demon and the City*. She currently resides in England.

NEIL WILLIAMSON (euonym) coedited the all Scottish anthology *Nova Scotia* with Andrew J. Wilson. He is a member of the Glasgow

SF Writers' Circle. His stories have been published in magazines like the *Third Alternative, Interzone,* and *Lady Churchill's Rosebud Wristlet,* and are collected in book form in *The Ephemera,* published by Elastic Press. He lives in Glasgow.

MARLY YOUMANS (smaragdine) is the author of six books, including two young-adult fantasies, *The Curse of the Raven Mocker* and *Ingledove.* Her awards include The 2001 Michael Shaara Award for *The Wolf Pit,* and her short fiction has appeared in places like *SciFiction, Fantasy Magazine,* and *Salon Fantastique.* She lives in upstate New York, a place that is a bit like the Snow Queen's palace: too cold for mortals and too far from the Carolinas, though still on the Appalachian spine.

ABOUT THE EDITOR

John Klima has previously worked at *Asimov's, Analog,* and Tor Books before returning to school to earn his Master's in Library and Information Science. He now works full time as a librarian. When he is not conquering the world of indexing, John edits and publishes the acclaimed genre zine *Electric Velocipede,* through which he has published authors such as: Jeffrey Ford, Catherynne M. Valente, Hal Duncan, Liz Williams, Jeff VanderMeer, and many others. John and his family recently escaped the hustle and bustle of the East Coast by moving to the Midwest.